Aether BEYOND THE BINARY

A DUCK PRINTS PRESS
ANTHOLOGY

Duck Prints Press, LLC
Schenectady, NY

The stories in this anthology are works of fiction. The characters and events portrayed are a product of the authors' imaginations. Businesses, places, and incidents pulled from the real world or history are used in a fictional manner. Any resemblance to real people or events is coincidental.

Aether Beyond the Binary © 2024, Duck Prints Press, LLC

"City of Light" © 2024, Ellen Faye
"N(ae)ghbours" © 2024, Scarlett Gale
"To Hold the World Close" © 2024, Catherine E. Green
"Epiphanies of Friendship, and Other White Whales" © 2024, Elior Haley
"Flower and Rot" © 2024, Zel Howland
"chameleon trick" © 2024, ilgaksu
"Finding Resonance" © 2024, Bettina Juszak
"How Your Garden Grows" © 2024, Nicola Kapron
"True" © 2024, Kelas Lloyd
"We Might Contain Multitudes" © 2024, Lyonel Loy
"Mixed Dough" © 2024, Mikki Madison
"Un Charco, Un Lago" © 2024, Sebastian Marie
"You're Gonna Get Older" © 2024, Alec J. Marsh
"The Light Organ" © 2024, Flore Picard
"Razzmatazz" © 2024, S. J. Ralston
"Cadillac's Bus" © 2024, Em Rowntree
"Ancient Hearts Unearthed" © 2024, Terra P. Waters

Wrap-around Cover Art © 2024, Mar Spragge (www.marspragge.com)

Edited by Kit Alexander, boneturtle, E. Conway, Rhosyn Goodfellow, Catherine E. Green, Aeryn Jemariel Knox, Alec J. Marsh, Nina Waters, and Rachael L. Young. Significant contributions also made by Aceriee, A. L. Heard, E. V. Dean, Lacey Hays, Annabeth Lynch, Pallas Perilous, Rhosyn Goodfellow, and Alessa Riel.
Print manuscript formatting by Hermit Writes.
E-book formatting by Nina Waters.

Published by Duck Prints Press, LLC
Schenectady, New York
duckprintspress.com

ISBN (ePub): 978-1-962488-03-7
ISBN (PDF): 978-1-962488-04-4
ISBN (Softcover Trade Paperback): 978-1-962488-05-1
ISBN (Hard Cover): 978-1-962488-06-8

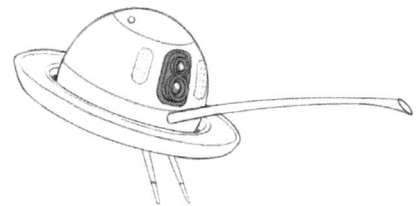

Table of Contents

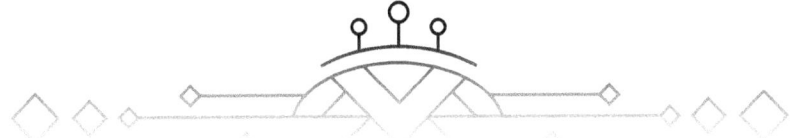

Alec J. Marsh

You're Gonna Get Older

arranged marriage, christian, coming of age, coming out, cults, fraught family dynamics, friends, in the closet, lesbian, midwest, misgendering, non-binary, north dakota, past tense, post-apocalyptic, relationship of convenience, religion, teenager, third person limited point of view, transphobia, united states of america

The hole in the heavens opened, and the stars rained down. Blessed were those who were welcomed into the Kingdom of Heaven when the end came. Doubly blessed were those who remained, for they were tasked with creating a heaven on Earth. They were purified, and they rebuilt with the glorious bounty of the skies. There were few of them left, and they lived simple lives, away from outside influence, but God saw fit to provide, and they were fruitful.

They named their children for their blessings, and they taught them always to keep the heavenly aether safe from those who might steal it. And so it was that, on the cusp of manhood, the child who was not a boy made a discovery of the temptations outside the safety of Eden, North Dakota.

Stardancer slid their bike to a stop in the ghost town of Delmont as the low summer sun painted the plains gold and pink. It had been most of a day's journey, and sweat trickled between their shoulder blades and down the creases of their thighs. They paced the cramps out of their legs,

1

reveling in the quiet. Only the faintest breeze rustled the grass, and there was no one around for miles.

Eden was filled with people stacked on top of each other, gossiping and watching for more things to gossip about. Stardancer was young and strong, supporting their family by riding their bike for miles and foraging for supplies. While they were alone under the expanse of the sky and spread across the freedom of prairie grass, they were only Stardancer, not a brother or a son or a fiancé.

Stardancer walked their bike and wagon the last few blocks to the center of town. They hadn't been allowed to drive the one truck that ran on aether, not when it was more useful for farm work, so this expedition would take them several days.

Delmont hadn't been picked over yet, and they would have a full day looking for wood and bricks to build new structures with. They had been selected to receive a new house now that they were engaged, but they had to build it first, and they had come far to Delmont. Eden was blessed with prosperity, so prosperous on the remnants of the meteor that it was expanding faster than supplies could be found. They traveled widely in their search and thanked God for granting them the time alone and more time before their wedding, which lurked on the horizon like a shadow just past the curve of the earth.

Nevaeh was their best friend and had all the qualities of a good wife. If Stardancer was the right kind of man, they would have been elated and honored. As it was, they would be entering their marriage with only the relief that it was not as bad as it could have been, which was a selfish way to feel about marrying a good woman.

The last time they had escaped to Delmont, they had built their camp inside the sheriff station. It was safe from passing thieves or drifters, with thick concrete walls and shuttered windows that left it cool and dark inside. It had been looted long ago, in the days when it had seemed like the world was ending and people killed each other for resources. But then life had settled, as it always did. The meteors were mined for energy, and the rifles were used for hunting deer, and the SUVs ran out of gas.

Stardancer slipped inside. The 20th century fluorescents had long since burned out, and the halls echoed and amplified the whisper of Stardancer's slippers against linoleum. They toed the shoes off and took a running start into a flying leap, then slid the rest of the way down the hall. For a moment, they were weightless, whizzing effortlessly through the cool cement-scented air. They slammed into the far wall, laughing, and flung themselves around to slide again, until they were dizzy and breathless.

Their stash of bedding and canned food was in a nest under the big desk in the dispatch office, which still had carpeting on the floor. This was the only place where they had the luxury of sleeping alone, and they both ached for it and feared it. They weren't ready to lose their solitude to sleep.

There was a radio in the room, an old two-way they had found on their last visit and hidden in an empty supply closet. It was still there. They slid open the battery pack and snapped in a fresh battery from their aether lantern. Chips of the meteor had been encased in metal tubing to mimic the lithium batteries of the Before, but they were precious and had to be used sparingly. Stardancer knew better than to use precious energy on something this frivolous.

They popped the battery cover in place and pressed the power button. It crackled to life.

Their heart jolted, and their knuckles tightened on the radio. They'd been sure it would need to be adapted to aether batteries, bit by bit, in the moments they'd snatch at the maker's space. They had feared they would never know if it was properly broken, only that they couldn't make it work. But here it was in their hands, power light blinking, softly humming with static.

They cradled it like it was made from glass. The dials made a *tak-tak-tak* noise as Stardancer scrolled through channels. Music came through softly. It faded in and out, cut through with static, but it was music, and not the kind made on an acoustic guitar. They adjusted the antenna and turned up the volume.

It was like nothing they had heard before, fast paced with a heavy beat. Even over the fuzzy AM connection, it was invigorating. They wanted to dance. They wanted to sing along with words they had never heard before. The singer screamed their triumph, and Stardancer felt invincible.

The song faded. They sat perfectly still, but every cell vibrated with coiled excitement and tension, ready to leap into action. They loved the worship music at church, but it didn't make them feel like this.

A voice came over the radio. "This is River from Sioux Falls. My pronouns are he/him, and I'm operating at 189 MHz. The song you just heard was 'Changes' by David Bowie. Up next, we have a request from Luna, also of Sioux Falls—"

There was a *thump* and a burst of static, and Stardancer nearly dropped the radio. They hadn't done anything but hold it, but it was an old machine and easily could have shorted out. But one heart-stopping moment later, the voice was back. "The request is from Luna, a HAM radio aficionado who is definitely not sitting in my bedroom right now. Please enjoy 'Montero' by Lil Nas X."

Stardancer squeezed their eyes shut and let the music crash over them and fill them up. Four more songs played as the room grew darker around them, until the only light was the tiny red power button on the radio. They should conserve their power in case they needed the lantern, and if the battery ran out, they would need to explain to their mother why they needed another. They took a sharp breath and steeled themselves to click off the radio as the strains of "Heart-Shaped Box" by Nirvana came to a close.

The crackle came back, and a new voice came over the line. "This is Alpha-niner-niner calling in."

"Alpha!" River's voice was distinct enough that Stardancer already recognized it, a mid-range tenor with a fuzzy thickness that made him sound like a young teenager. "What can I do for you?"

"I turned in my last essay of the season," Alpha answered. "Can you play me something to celebrate?"

"Hell yeah I can," River answered, and their voice cracked. "I'm proud of you, Champ."

Luna said something that was lost in the static of distance.

"Say that again on the record?" River asked.

Luna spoke so close to the mic that her breath crackled. "I said you're corny, old man."

"That's okay—old men have the best taste in music. I'll play you something from my granddad's time, okay, Alpha? This is Queen's 'Don't Stop Me Now.'"

Stardancer traced their fingers over the dials and buttons they could read in the dark. Alpha had called in from somewhere. Could Stardancer call, too? Did they want to?

They curled up in their nest under the desk and listened to the music for as long as they could bear, and then they turned the radio off and fell asleep with it tucked against their chest.

They spent their day stacking bricks from a collapsed building while the sun beat down. The music was a jumble in their mind, cascading hints of chords that tumbled over each other. They hummed snatches of tunes while they worked. The small black radio was a magnet, pulling them back to their backpack. Everywhere they went, they oriented themselves to it, their heart a compass guiding them toward Lady Gaga's "Poker Face."

As they ate lunch, they studied the radio. There was a button on the side labeled "Talk," and they rubbed their thumb over the button, wondering if it was that easy. They turned on the radio and heard only silence at 189 MHz.

When evening fell and their cart was full, they bathed and prayed and returned to their nest. They would set out early in the morning, just as dawn broke, so they could make most of their slow and laborious progress before the sun got too hot. They had one night of privacy left.

They turned on the radio.

A song was ending, and it faded out to be replaced with the voice that Stardancer was yearning for. "This is River, coming to you with the soothing sounds of Prince," they crooned. "It's a few minutes after 9 p.m., and it was a hot one today—"

"We know that," Luna cut in. "Play the music."

"I can't be a DJ if you don't let me DJ!" River protested, but he was laughing. "I want to do a call-in," he said, voice back to the announcer timbre. "I know you're listening on your radios, so tell me what you're looking forward to this summer."

Stardancer lurched with excitement and fear. Who was River talking to? When Pastor Blythe spoke to his congregation, he truly wanted everyone to testify. Maybe River did too. A DJ could be a pastor of a kind, shepherding Stardancer to a revelation. They shook, as they always did before they testified that they could feel the Holy Spirit moving through them. They could speak of the feeling of the wind in the grass and the blue bowl of the sky that reminded them that life was precious and beautiful and to be lived to its fullest. They could speak of the way David Bowie had quickened their heart and filled them with profound joy, the way they suddenly felt that they had the strength to carry on.

Someone had already cut into the radio waves. A low baritone voice said, "Hi, this is Emma."

"Hel*lo* Emma!" River crowed. "Have we met before?"

Emma laughed nervously. "No. I—I've never got the guts to call before. But I finally came out to my family, and I'm so happy that I had to share it with someone. This is the first summer I'll get to be Emma."

There was a beat of silence, and a deep, wordless fear clawed at Stardancer's throat. But River answered in a voice that was low and sincere, "That's wonderful, Emma. Welcome to the family. Let me play you some Ezra Furman to celebrate the good news."

Stardancer clutched the radio to their chest as other people called in to congratulate Emma or to share their own stories. Their eyes burned with unshed tears. The family. The family.

There were so many people out there like them. If there were four who called into River's radio show, how many more existed? They tried to picture a family of people like them, people who got to be who they were instead of who they needed to be for the good of the church. They stood on the edge of a vast precipice. They were ready to fly, when before all they had wanted was to free themselves in the fall, heedless of the rocks below.

They knew they didn't fit Eden's idea of masculinity. If they had had anyone to talk to, they might have said they weren't a man at all. But they didn't know how to articulate any of those feelings, and they didn't know what the consequences might be if they tried, so they hadn't bothered to speak their doubts aloud. Even Nevaeh, who always had a kind shoulder for them to lean on, wouldn't have understood.

They could press the "Call" button and tell River what they were feeling. They could testify to the feelings that churned in their heart. They could be welcomed.

They weren't ready yet.

Stardancer unloaded their scavenged bricks at the site of their new home. The community had made progress in the three days they had been gone, and the foundation clearly marked out the three rooms. Soon they would be a husband, a homemaker. They would have a wife to support, and children, if God saw fit to bless them.

The sense of yawning horror creeping over the horizon was back.

Nevaeh approached across the dirt patch that would one day be their lawn. She was a good girl, a proud member of the church. Stardancer was pretty sure she was beautiful. She had a round face and a winning smile and soft brown curls. Today she wore a modest dress covered in pink flowers that fluttered around her long legs in the hot summer sun. Stardancer untucked their T-shirt from where it was pasted to their back by sweat. Their belt dug into their hips and left them feeling strangled and unwell. A floral dress in light cotton would be better.

Nevaeh's hair danced in the breeze, and something strange and yearning settled in Stardancer's chest. It wasn't desire for her. She reached out to take Stardancer's hand, but then she hesitated and let it fall to her side, empty and awkward.

Stardancer cleared their throat. Once, they had been as close to Nevaeh as a boy could be to a girl, singing harmonies in the church choir and catching fireflies at night and sharing books under their school desks. They had their own secret castle, a car with a rusted floor that kept them dry in winter and gave them a place to hide their paltry treasures away from grabbing siblings' hands. They argued about which girls were prettiest, and later, how to decide which boys were pretty at all. Everyone knew they would get married. Stardancer's mother had called their friendship "courting" for years.

"I'm glad you're back," she said softly.

"Me too," Stardancer lied. Before their engagement, they would have eagerly shared their radio with Nevaeh. She loved music. She would remember the melodies that Stardancer struggled with. She wished for more, too.

But soon, everything that belonged to Stardancer would belong to Nevaeh and they needed a few more weeks of being one person before they were cleaved to a wife.

The meteor glowed, a second sunset watching over Eden. Stardancer slipped out of the room they shared with three brothers and walked toward it. They huddled under their favorite tree and listened to the entirety of *Dirty Computer*, radio clutched to their chest.

Summer got hotter and angrier, and the thick air held everyone in place.

The walls of their house went up, and Stardancer stood in their shade and feared the day a door would be hung to lock them inside.

The radio grew fainter and fuzzier, and finally died before Stardancer ever called to talk to River. Instead, they imagined what they might say, the way River would whistle in sympathy, the way his voice would crack as he told Stardancer he believed in them. Maybe he would play a song for Stardancer. They still didn't know what they would request, something with enough anger and energy to shake them from their trance.

The sky turned gray, then green, then split open as the long-awaited rain came, rolling across the plains with winds stronger than God's wrath. Cool water washed over Stardancer's skin, thunder crashed, and once again there was more in their life than heat, and fear, and waiting.

The meteor had come from the heavens and now, too, did their baptism.

The glow seeped between the slats of the fence meant to keep out roaming thieves and foolish children. Stardancer was forced to be a man now, so if they chose to use the aether, that was their right. They ran their thumb along their mother's key and thought, a bit wildly, that if they unlocked this door then everyone would know, and there would be no going back.

To touch the aether was to take the mana of God, to accept His blessing.

Stardancer couldn't say if it was the Lord who had blessed them, or if it was simply the stars for which they were named, set in motion long ago. If God had given them Eden, as they had been told, then God had also given them an apple to eat.

If God had given them Eden, He had given them hymns of worship, and He had given them music that promised changes were possible.

They opened the gate, and it was only a gate. Inside sat the meteor, larger than a church, twisted black iron veined with amber and gold. It smelled of pine and oranges. Stardancer shut the door behind them and stood, bathed in heat and incense.

They had meant to take only a sliver off the ground, just enough to charge their radio without asking for a new battery from Pastor Blythe or their mother. They had been told many times that the meteor was a limited blessing, that they could not be greedy lest their children be left without electricity. The people of Eden had no music in their homes, no heat in the winter, no motors in their cars. Those were precious resources, reserved for the old and the holy.

The meteor was large in a way Stardancer couldn't wrap their mind around. It towered above them, a monolith of magic, stretching into the distance on the left and right, only the glitter of the aether limning its edges. They could have been warm and comfortable their whole life, and the meteor would never have shown traces of their need.

They reached toward the meteor, and it reached back to them, sticky electricity jumping between warm flesh and warmer stone. It was here for them to use. It was here for everyone.

They took a chunk as large as their head and hid it under their tree.

Aether wanted to be used and to be useful. It was meant to bring salvation to the righteous, which is why Eden had survived the meteor crash.

Stardancer had been told this many times. They had also been told not to be greedy, that good sons went without to take care of the community, that covetousness was a sin. So when they had been told they couldn't have something, they had thought it was a blessing to be allowed to experience deprivation.

The problem now was that River sounded so joyful as he reveled in his music and his radio and his community, and listening to him filled Stardancer with so much secondhand joy that they may as well have been sinning themselves.

The problem now was that this sin didn't hurt anyone, so why should Stardancer go without?

The problem now was that Stardancer had tasted hunger, and they couldn't stop from slaking themselves with everything within their grasp. They spent their days hiding in tall grass like they were a child again, fists full of aether, building batteries on a picnic blanket. Their back ached, their neck burned pink and then peeled, and their batteries got bigger. The aether grew warm under the sun and sticky in their hands, filled with power. It wanted to be used; it flowed into their radio, and they chiseled and wrapped it in copper wires and felt life and freedom pulse against their fingertips.

Nevaeh found them a week before their wedding. Her shadow reached Stardancer far before she did, long and smelling of freshly laundered cotton. She was only a silhouette, but her shoulders were tight.

"Is this where you've been all summer?"

"Yes."

"And what about our house?"

"Build it yourself." It came out like a dismissal, but it was more than that. Stardancer didn't want a house. Nevaeh did.

She sat in the grass and folded her arms. "You know I can't."

"You're as capable as I am."

She rolled her eyes. "Do you know what it would look like, to build a house without my husband there beside me?" She reached out and picked up one of the bits of wire. "What are you building?"

Stardancer barely heard the question. That panic and tightness was back, the urge to run into the grassy plains or start digging until they were hidden like a prairie dog.

"I don't want to marry you," they said.

They didn't realize they had said it out loud until pain passed across Nevaeh's face. The wire fell from her hands; her lips were parted, frozen in shock. Only her hair waved in the eternal prairie wind.

"I'm sorry," they said, and wished they could take it back.

"What did I do wrong?"

"Nothing! Anyone would be lucky to have you. I should be blessed—you're my best friend. I love you so much. But I can't be a husband."

There was another silence, probably only the space of two breaths, but Stardancer felt like they were dying. And then Nevaeh's face cleared, and she smiled. "Is this because you would rather be a wife?"

Of course she understood. They knew each other. They should have known everything about each other. "I don't know," they said. "Wife" sounded just as wrong. "But you know Pastor Blythe would never allow it, even if I asked."

Her eyes blazed. "Pastor Blythe can't decide who you are."

It wasn't that simple. Whoever Stardancer knew they were, if everyone insisted on seeing them as something else, some part of them would always be missing. "Father Blythe won't let me tell him who I am," they answered.

Nevaeh plucked a blade of grass and spun it between her fingers. It was broad-leafed prairie grass, sharp and thick-leaved, and she twisted and shredded it into tassels before she spoke.

"I thought you understood," she said finally.

"Understood what?"

Her chin trembled, and the grass strings buckled under her twisting. "You know I—you're my best friend too. But I don't love you either. And that's okay."

"You deserve someone who adores you," they argued fiercely. Mere weeks before, they might have agreed with Nevaeh. That was before they had listened to River and Luna tease each other effortlessly, before listeners had called in to talk about their beloveds, before Stardancer realized that a wife was more than half a household.

"There's—" Her voice broke, and she continued at a whisper, "There's no one in Eden who will ever love me like that."

Stardancer couldn't believe that, but they waited as Nevaeh clenched her jaw, inhaled sharply. Finally, they said, "Because you don't want a man to love you."

Her lips formed the word "yes."

"I'm sorry I made you tell me."

"I should have told you sooner."

"No," they said. "No. You shouldn't have had to say it at all." They swallowed. "You're right. I'll protect you. I'll be who you need."

Pastor Blythe would care if Nevaeh succumbed to sinful urges. He would care if she didn't provide for the future of Eden. And Stardancer would protect her because they loved her, even if it wasn't the right kind of love. For her, they could be brave.

"I can't ask," she said. "I know how it feels. We'll tell Pastor Blythe—I don't know."

"Don't tell him anything yet." They picked up the battery they were building. There were many kinds of bravery. They could find another way.

⊷═⊳⊗⊲═⊶

That night, as the hot silence of September pressed down like a smothering shroud, Stardancer finally pressed the talk button.

"Hi," they said into the silence.

"Welcome to the show," River said, jovial as always with the patter of a youth pastor. "Where do you hail from, fair listener?"

Stardancer began to speak, then stopped, struck with the fear that they would expose too much.

"Speak up, comrade," River said. "I can't quite hear you."

"I—" They swallowed and forced themselves to be brave. "My name is Stardancer. I live in a—in a really small town that's basically one church congregation, and I—I'd like to use 'they' pronouns. If that's okay."

"Of course it's okay," River said. "Thanks for introducing yourself. What did you want to talk about tonight?"

Stardancer had to answer or they would waste everyone's time. They wanted to answer. "I don't know," they said, because they couldn't ask what they wanted to ask—how could they leave what they knew?

"Stardancer is a great name," River said, smoothly covering for their hesitance. "How'd you pick it?"

"I didn't," they said, startled. "My parents named me after the meteors. They said there were shooting stars the night I was born." They choked down tears. Their mother had loved them, did love them. Even if she didn't know them. "She said she wanted me to be as free as the stars."

A crackle, a silence. They'd said too much.

River whistled. "That's beautiful," he said. "And are you free?"

Oh. *Oh.*

They squeezed their eyes shut, and hot tears rolled down their cheeks. "I want to be," they said, "but I'll have to leave the church."

"You'll do what's right for you," River said with confidence. "You'll be brave, I know it. Telling my family I was a man was the scariest thing I ever did, but it was the best thing, too. And loving myself made me a better man."

Stardancer felt that love. River's support flowed through the radio, as strong as the scent of sticky orange that flowed from the meteor. They might be glowing. They were star born, star named, star blessed.

"I've got a song for you," River said. "It might be on the nose, but it's one of my favorites. And if you ever make it out to Sioux Falls, you look us up, you hear? We're always looking for more friends. We have to look out for each other."

"Thank you," Stardancer choked out. "Thank you. Thank—"

"I got you, beloved," River said earnestly. "This is David Bowie's 'Starman.'"

They listened to the song, and they sobbed, and they rose lighter for having handed their burdens to River.

Nevaeh was good at everything she put her mind to, and she could sew and build and plan in a way Stardancer never could. With her clarity, with her need, their trousseau grew.

Stardancer took apart the engine of the car, stripped out the oil and spark plugs, and rigged up a battery.

Nevaeh took wood from the construction site and fixed the rusted hole in the floor. She cut out the parts of the cushions that had grown over with moss and patched the driver's seat with one of the curtains she had sewn for their windows.

Stardancer spent every moment with their hands sticky with aether, molding the miraculous substance until it flowed through every tube in the car. They had no way to know how far they could get. Aether wasn't a science; it worked when it wanted to work, and it couldn't do everything the gasoline of old could. They worried, and fiddled, and idled the car over and over as if it would eventually speak to them and tell them it was ready. They couldn't ask anyone who worked with aether without revealing their plan, but if they drove no farther than the boundary of town and broke down, they would be dragged back to be cleansed of their sins.

Stardancer wanted to call River, to hear his reassurances and his bravado. They could hear River already saying that he believed in them. Saying that they were brave. River would play them a song, something that gave them strength. They closed their eyes and summoned their own inspiration, and they started the car one last time, just to be sure.

Finally, they had one day until their wedding and no more time to plan. Nevaeh and her mother cooked the summer harvest into salads and cakes and casseroles. Stardancer spent the day with their family, finishing the house and checking their clothes and trying not to panic. They were wasting time that could be spent working on the car. They could have left days ago, but they hadn't been ready. They needed more aether. They needed a better map. They needed to know how long they would need to drive.

They took their mother's keys and slipped away as she fussed about table settings. The meteor was waiting for them, thrumming in the daylight.

They scooped fistfuls of sun-warmed aether into their backpack until it strained under the weight. Gone was any thought about rationing or leaving some for later generations. They would take everything they could hold, let their car feed on it forever. They had tasted freedom, and now they wanted to run, run, run.

Their mother waited for them at the gate, Pastor Blythe at her shoulder.

They stared at each other for a tense moment, and then she sighed the sigh of a condemnation.

"Star, what are you doing?"

They couldn't think of any explanation that would suffice. "I wanted to look at it," they said. As if wanting anything was enough to justify stealing. As if their mother would understand in the slightest.

"You know I would have taken you, had you asked." This voice wasn't his mother's, but Pastor Blythe's. Stardancer cringed from the gentle reprimand, dripping with disappointment.

"I didn't want to bother anyone," Stardancer answered, voice trailing off into nothing.

"Is this where you've been all summer?" their mother hissed. She grabbed at Stardancer's backpack, the splitting seams revealing their crimes. "I've been taking care of you, covering up for your flightiness, and you've been stealing from us? You are no son of mine!"

"I am not the son you thought," Stardancer answered.

There was nothing to be done for it. Their backpack was taken and they were marched back to the church in shame. There was nowhere to go except out into the prairie, and they wouldn't have gotten far on their own two feet. Stardancer was a day away from adulthood and should have behaved accordingly. Pastor Blythe made his disappointment clear.

They were brought into mediation, left in a small room with gray carpet and a bible and little else. Pastor Blythe preached and lectured, and the longer Stardancer sat, the more they realized that Pastor Blythe didn't care why they had taken the aether. It hadn't even occurred to him that there might have been a reason. There was only sin and those weak enough to answer its song. So they sat, and held the bible like the paper and leather and glue might do them some good, and let Pastor Blythe talk.

They wanted to be loved, desperately. They wanted to be looked out for, as River had said. Pastor Blythe had claimed to tend his flock, and even now he spoke of forgiveness. They could have it. They could be enfolded, one of the lambs, and all they had to do was exactly what they were told. It would be so much easier if they were the man they had been raised to be.

River had seen Stardancer better and affirmed them more in one conversation than Pastor Blythe had managed in nineteen years. A long-dead pop star had reached into Stardancer's heart and showed it to them with more accuracy than a lifetime of Sunday sermons. They were not a son of Eden anymore. Their heart was in the air, in the sky.

The stars were out tonight, and Stardancer would be free.

Nevaeh came to intervene, eyes bright and jaw tight. She reached out, clasped their hand, and struggled to speak. Pastor Blythe watched them like a cat, perfectly still and waiting for some hint that Stardancer was dragging a good woman down with them.

She put her ring in Stardancer's palm and closed their fingers around it one by one.

"I see you, and I forgive you," she said, in her soft, clear voice. They didn't need to ask for it. They didn't need to stand before a crowd and speak their sins. They only had to hold her hand.

"I still want a life with you," she said, and what Stardancer heard was,

"I will go with you."

They had to look out for each other.

They couldn't call River. Their radio was still in the car that their mother still didn't know about. They lay on the thin, ragged carpet that had been in the church since before the stars crashed to earth, and they closed their eyes. If they called him, he would welcome them to Sioux Falls.

He would call them brave.

He would call them comrade.

He would give them a song that meant more than anything.

They didn't know River, not really, not yet. But they wanted to. They could. They would be welcome, and they wouldn't have to change a single thing about themselves.

They could go to Pastor Blythe; they could get on their knees and lie, and they could return to their home. But they had been taught not to lie, and to lie about who they were seemed a sin they could not forgive themselves for.

Stardancer was a day away from adulthood and it was time for them to act accordingly. That meant no more sneaking or planning escapes. It meant no more begging for love from those who didn't want to give it. It meant turning and facing the world, growing up and growing out of Eden.

They knew what they were looking for.

It was the darkest part of the night when Stardancer walked out of the church. It was that easy, and it was that hard. They would disappoint their mother, and they would be free. They walked out of the gates of Eden, back to the car that they had rebuilt themselves. And then they drove back into Eden, where Nevaeh was waiting for them on her front porch, hair wild in the breeze, skirts billowing like she was a war bride on a dock, clutching a duffel bag of all she owned in the world.

She climbed into the passenger seat, and it didn't matter that everyone they had ever known thought they were children who didn't know their minds. They drove into the heat and the sun and the freedom, and they faced the strange of what their lives could be.

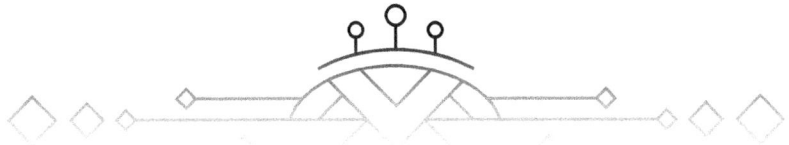

Flore Picard

The Light Organ

capitalism is the real villain, coming out, emotional hurt/comfort, family, fraught family dynamics, has a disability, illusion powers, in the closet, magic use, mechanic, musician, non-binary, parenthood, present tense, science fiction with magic, teenager, third person limited point of view, transphobia (mentions of) (past)

"*N*o, no, no—the organ, the light ring—it's all about the imagination, not the mechanics," Kas exclaims, gesturing widely to encompass the aether pool behind the glass.

The pool glows softly in the receding light of the evening, still and silent. It's encircled by a wide ring of vertical glass tubes, each wide enough to fit a man inside. The tallest of them, across from the console room, shoots up toward the sky. Above the shorter tubes, the stands are filling with people, but the noise only barely reaches them backstage.

"I'm just here for the tubes," the tech—Gilbert—says flatly.

His face betrays no emotions, not even annoyance. Kas almost wishes he would yell or be rude, if only so it'll feel like they're having an actual conversation, but Gilbert has always been polite. He just never seems to *care*.

"Fine," Kas gives up. "We've got glitches. They started about a week ago. It could be a leaking tube."

"What kind of glitches?"

"It's as if…as if the story stops responding to me. I know how that sounds, but I swear that's what happens. It doesn't last more than a few seconds, but it's getting worse. Earlier, I powered everything up to tune it and it kept flickering."

"Flickering," Gilbert repeats, mumbling into his neatly trimmed beard.

Kas grabs a cane in each hand and makes their way to the organ's seat. "I can show you."

The console sits in a gap between the tubes, facing the ring but separated from it by thick glass. It's set slightly below the level of the pool so the organist can see the entirety of the stage over the six stacked keyboards. Above, a maze of wires runs toward the tubes, all around the ring. Kas adjusts themself into the cushioned seat in front of the console, turning to set their canes in their holder at the back, when a movement catches their attention.

There's a teenager standing on the doorstep, bent over the small square of a lightscreen. Their face is mostly hidden by a curtain of straight, dark hair.

"Who are you?" Kas calls out. "This room is off-limits to the audience."

"This is my daughter, Rae," Gilbert says. "She's staying right here."

Kas tilts their head at her. "You're interested in how the organ works?"

Rae barely looks up from the lightscreen, but she pulls back her hair, revealing a rounded face and dark almond eyes. "No." Kas can see little resemblance between her and her red-headed, pale-skinned father aside from their sulky demeanor. She looks about sixteen, short and thin, clad in an oversize band T-shirt and black leggings.

"She's grounded," Gilbert explains with a warning look to his daughter. "I'm not leaving her home alone until she earns my trust back."

Rae glowers at him as Kas shrugs. "All right. Don't get in the way."

"Mom's messaging me again," Rae says to her father, holding up her lightscreen. "She wants to know where I am."

"Why? She hasn't even been around for months."

"I don't know. Do I really have to be *here*? I could go sit—"

"You're staying where I can see you."

Kas tunes out their arguing and powers up the organ. The connection with the aether is always the trickiest part, and it requires all of their attention, especially now with the glitches.

The console takes up two vertical boards on each side of the organ's keyboards. Rows upon rows of brass switches are set into the lacquered wood, each handling a section of the tubes.

The first row of switches goes fine. The glow of the pool grows softly as, one by one, the tubes around the ring fill with quintessence.

Second row. The liquid aether starts twirling in the middle of the pool.

Third row. The hint of a shape emerges. Kas closes their eyes, left hand on the lowest keyboard as their right pulls the switch. Upstairs, the crowd has fallen silent. Gilbert and Rae finally stop sniping at each other, and Kas feels more than hears Gilbert come up to stand behind them.

"There," they say. "Look."

They move to the next switch, and the shape in the pool, almost human now, falters. It turns to liquid again, then to gas, then solid, dripping light from its aethereal body. Kas presses a key, then another. The shape rises.

The connection has been made.

Another switch. A flicker. The quintessence collapses in a wave; occluding light briefly obscures the glass wall. It leaves streaks of luminescent liquid behind, snaking their way to the pool as it starts to swirl once more.

"Stop!" Gilbert shouts. "Turn it off!"

Kas freezes without letting go of the switch. "I have to keep going, now. The aether won't rest until I've finished this row."

"Then we have to evacuate the stands. This is too dangerous."

Kas carefully keeps their hands still on the console. "That means losing an evening. We'll have to reimburse all the tickets."

They can scarcely afford it. The light ring is underfunded as it is, barely able to keep afloat most years. It's always a toss whether they'll break even—and that's without having to interrupt performances for repairs.

In the middle of the pool, the shape reforms. Flickers again. A smaller wave hits the glass.

"We don't have a choice," Gilbert growls. He reaches over Kas's shoulder to push the comm's button. "The show's canceled. Evacuate the stands. Make sure no one's left in the ring outside of this room."

"Roger that," comes the voice of the security agent.

"Dad?" Rae calls in a small voice, stepping closer to them. Mirrored in the glass wall, Kas can see her fidgeting nervously with her lightscreen.

"It's okay," Gilbert says. "It's just a precaution. The glass is aether-proof."

"I can't hold it like this until everyone's gone," Kas warns. Their fingers are already shaking on the switch. "I have to keep going until it's stable."

The rest of the sequence is thankfully short, and the pool only falters once more. Kas's muscles uncoil as the warmth of the connection fills their body. Their hands fly on the keyboards, and their consciousness blends into the swirling light of the pool. For an instant, they forget about the people in the room, the audience moving out of the stands, everything but the liquid aether flowing through the tubes and into the pool.

Then the glitch happens again. They feel it in their teeth. It jerks them back to their body, to the ever-present ache in their back and legs.

Their fingers slip, once, twice, their focus shot. Their skin feels too tight, stretched out, as the aether pulls from them without giving back. They breathe out slowly and rub the bump stickers on the keys, left there long ago by a blind organist.

The familiar texture settles the feeling of wrongness. They set their shoulders, suppressing a pained wince, and start to play an old, simple sequence—one of the first they learned. The warmth trickles back in and they again plunge into the trance. With their mind supplementing their body, the connection eases back into a flow.

"There." Gilbert speaks up suddenly. Kas starts at hearing his voice so close to their ear—he's right behind them. He leans over Kas's shoulder to point at the other side of the ring. "The sixth tube on the left from the middle. There's something in there."

Kas squints at the tubes, but they don't see anything. The sixth tube looks exactly like the others. It's one of the longer tubes, across from the console where the ring's height starts its gentle downward slope and the stands emerge behind their glass protection window.

"Are you sure?"

"This is my job," Gilbert points out. "It's almost at the mouth. I won't be able to pull it out from above. I need to go inside the ring."

Kas blinks. "That's too dangerous." It would be mildly risky with the aether at rest in the pool and the tubes empty, but now? There's no telling what the aether might do to a human body that comes so close.

"This is my job," Gilbert repeats, his tone flat.

Kas wants to point out that it's really not, that no one should ask a tech to risk their life, but it's not as if they have another option, do they? Powering down the organ was tricky earlier when it was only glitching occasionally. Trying to empty the tubes now might be catastrophic.

"Shouldn't we…call for backup or something?"

How long can Kas hold the aether still? Not long enough for someone to come from the maintenance company's headquarters. Unless they have another tech already in town—unlikely, out here in the boonies—they won't arrive in time.

"They can't do what I can do," Gilbert answers, pulling a nauseatingly orange protective suit out of his locker, tucked away in the corner closest to the door. "Unless you want to shut down your ring for the next three to five weeks, I'm your best bet."

Kas exhales slowly. "Right."

They watch Gilbert zip up the suit out of the corner of their eye and pull a personal aetherboard from the locker. It hums a low tune as it hovers above the floor.

"Your PAB won't work in there," Kas adds, gently pressing a series of keys to soothe the aether rising from the pool.

"It will. I modified it."

The aetherboard, left alone, drifts to Rae, who looks up from her lightscreen long enough to push it back and glance at her father. "Don't forget the gloves," she says.

Gilbert opens the panel for the comms and starts fiddling with the wires. "There—I've plugged in my comm," he tells Kas. "You'll hear me and I'll hear you. I need you to keep playing."

"I can't play while you're in there! If you get splattered—"

"The suit will protect me. If you don't play, I can't fix the leak."

Kas twists around to look at him properly, careful to keep their hands on the keys. "But…"

"Look, I might not care about your stories, but you're good at this. You know how to control the quintessence. I trust you to keep it away from me."

Kas sucks in a breath and tilts their head in acknowledgment. "I'll do my best."

"Rae, you stay here with him."

"Them," Kas corrects him.

"What?"

"I use 'they' and 'them' as pronouns. Not 'him.'"

"Oh," Gilbert blinks. "Right. Okay."

He dons his gas mask and unlocks the door. Turning back to the console, Kas catches Rae watching them intently, her lightscreen forgotten. She drops her gaze as soon as they look at her.

Silence stretches uncomfortably as they watch Gilbert carefully hover around the pool. Kas scrambles for a conversation topic—Rae hasn't said more than a single word to them since walking in.

"So. What did you do to get grounded?" they ask finally, more awkwardly than they'd like, but half their attention is focused on the swirling aether in the middle of the pool.

"Snuck away to an aether-funk concert," Rae says. She comes to stand closer to the glass to watch her father's progress.

"You like music?"

"Why do you care?"

Kas shrugs. "I'm a musician first. I played the piano and the guitar before I started on the light organ."

"I hate the light ring," Rae mutters.

"Why?"

She doesn't answer for a moment, just fiddles with the black case of her lightscreen. "None of it is real, you know? When you're a kid, you get pulled into the story; it's happening right in front of you. And then it ends, and...it's all fake. I hate it. I hate stories."

"They're real in my mind," Kas says. "The ring shows are only as good as their performer. You have to believe in them."

"So, what, you actually believe in elves and magic and stuff?"

"That's not what I—" Kas is interrupted by the click of the comm.

"Start playing now," Gilbert says, his voice distorted.

Kas hums in response and hits a few keys, a classic opening to let the quintessence warm up.

"What story would you like to see?" they ask Rae.

She shrugs moodily. "Whatever."

"Really? Nothing?"

She eyes Kas for a moment. "Something true," she decides. "Not one of your stupid fairy tales."

Kas considers that. "How old are you?"

"Sixteen. How old are *you*?" she repeats in a bored teenager drawl.

"Twenty-eight," Kas answers absently, their mind already spinning the threads of an idea. "Sixteen. That's how old I was when I discovered the light organ."

They reach out to flip two switches from the bottom row. When the twirl in the quintessence turns into a small whirlpool, pulling on their consciousness, Kas sees movement in the stands out of the corner of their eye. A shadow, there and gone again. There shouldn't be anyone there. Kas almost drops the connection.

No, there's nothing. An illusion, a trick of the light. Gilbert is counting on them.

They breathe out and settle in for a long night. Improvising on the organ is exhausting.

A shape arises from the pool. A teenager, too short for their age, awkwardly running on uneven ground, arms flailing. Kas doesn't look at the kid's face.

The others are faceless, formless, more liquid than children, darting around the ring. One of them briefly stands out, takes a human visage. "Come on, Kasim!" Kas breathes into their microphone. "Why are you always so slow?"

The voice is pulled straight from their memory, and it grates at them even now. They're good at doing the voices, but this is different.

"Please slow down," teenage-Kas and adult-Kas plead in a single voice. Their eyes burn.

There is no music. The bottom keyboard is a regular piano, amplified to sound out throughout the stands, but playing it while improvising and keeping the aether away from Gilbert is too difficult. Larger light rings have organs that can accommodate several organists, plus musicians and voice actors to offer complete shows, but here Kas performs every task themself.

"We lived right beside a light ring, but we never had the money to see a show," they say, letting the habit of narration settle their voice.

Rae's eyes flicker between them and teenage-Kas in the ring. She's lost her affected disinterest, and she's standing straighter already.

"I always wanted to see one, or even just to see the pool. One night, I got some friends to come with me. We stayed outside until closing time and picked the lock."

"They were your friends?" Rae asks, giving the glowing silhouettes in the ring a suspicious glance.

"I thought they were. They were in it for the thrill of breaking in, I think. I just wanted to see quintessence. I didn't even care about the shows that much. Stories, I could write in my head. But people said that quintessence was like nothing else."

Aether-Kas stumbles and almost falls to the ground, splashing in the pool. The shape flickers, and Kas hurriedly works in another theme before it dissolves entirely. Gilbert is crouching on his board at the other end of the ring, his back to the swirling aether. The splatters barely miss him.

Flowing shadows of stands emerge, swirling around the silhouetted teenager, and a console solidifies before them, similar to the wood and brass one before flesh-and-bone-Kas. Aether-Kas looks up, awestruck.

Kas remembers that moment like it was yesterday. They'd always imagined that quintessence would look like the way the aether sometimes shimmers in the twilight, just before the sun disappears over the horizon. The reality of it was so much brighter, so much more beautiful than their wildest dreams.

As aether-Kas reaches a hand toward the glass window, Kas almost does the same, lost in their memory. Their fingers aren't even an inch off the keyboard before the scene glitches again.

"No!" they yell as Rae presses her hands to the glass for a completely different reason, alarmed.

Gilbert has turned around, and the half-shaped body of quintessence is exploding straight toward him.

Kas regains control just in time. As unbothered by the laws of physics as always, the drops freeze in the air and reshape obediently under their demand, their hands dancing across the keyboards.

"You okay?" they ask into the microphone.

"All good," Gilbert says, though he sounds a little breathless. "Keep playing."

Kas breathes out carefully, wondering how long they can keep going at this pace. Their fingertips are numb already.

"What happened in the ring?" Rae asks softly. "Back then?"

The console slowly reforms above the pool, showing aether-Kas with their hand still poised close to the glass. They gingerly sit down on the edge of the large organ chair and run their fingers over the keyboard.

"I thought I could play," Kas says. "I was taking piano lessons and I'd figured out the guitar on my own." They'd been cocky and overconfident in the way only a teenager, even a beaten-down, bullied, disabled teenager, could be. Now, the notion seems ridiculous—no one can play the light organ without years of rigorous training. "I had no idea what the aether could do. We didn't have lightscreens back then, and you can't photograph quintessence. I only knew what people had told me, which wasn't much."

Aether-Kas reaches up and pulls down the first switch. Kas feels the glitch coming this time and corrects course before it can grow. The image only flickers. "What are you doing?" they cry out into the microphone in the high-pitched voice of an off-screen Nora, their teenage-self's best friend.

But aether-Kas doesn't hear her. Their shape grows in the center of the pool as they pull more switches. They close their eyes as the vibration starts, and Kas has to tighten their mental hold on the aether.

"Connecting with the aether is both incredible and terrifying," they say. "It floods your mind. You have to relinquish everything and let it accept you, and then... You never really come out of it. Controlling the shapes takes years of work, but feeling that connection?" They pause, finding Rae staring straight at them. "My body hurt, my home life was depressing, and I was desperate for a change. For the first time, in osmosis with the aether, I could escape. It was stronger than anything I'd ever experienced."

"What happened?" Rae asks, transfixed.

"I got through two rows of switches before the connection took. And then—"

They trail off as the memory is abruptly pulled from their mind. The shape of their teenage self blurs, and the aether starts swirling—too fast. The silhouette of the console turns into a whirlpool. On the other side of the ring, Gilbert throws himself against the tubes, but projections hit his protective suit, and he nearly falls off his PAB.

"Dad!" Rae shouts. Then, at Kas: "Do something!"

Kas closes their eyes and lets go of their mental hold. Control is no longer the answer. Hands flying over the keyboards, they let their pounding heart sync with the pulsation of the quintessence. The whirl-pool rises into a tornado. Gilbert is flattened against the glass surface of the tubes, and the quintessence is too close to him, but it no longer projects out, instead turning inward.

Another force enters the ring. Kas feels it like a dance, a presence swirling around them, herding aether back into the pool. The quintes-sence resists for a moment, then accepts it, lets itself be tamed.

The ring quietens.

Kas opens their eyes. Rae has taken hold of two of the switches and has them pulled halfway down. Her wide, scared gaze stares at her father, who slowly peels himself away from the tubes.

"Right hand first," Kas guides her softly. "Pull it all the way down."

She obeys shakily, lowering one hand, then the other, panting. "Was that—?"

"You went into osmosis. Too fast, that's why it's painful."

"Not really," Rae mutters.

"You can pull your hands off the switches—slowly. I've got it."

She nods and lets go. The full force of the connection slams back into Kas, and they're left reeling for a moment. Thankfully, the aether stays calm.

"I touched the light once," Rae whispers. She holds out her right hand to show the lightning-like scars snaking up her palm. "It was… It hurt so bad, but it…it was different. It made me feel alive."

Kas gapes. That goes against everything they've ever been told. The quintessence is off-limits, no matter the temptation.

"That's incredibly dangerous. You did it on purpose?"

"Yeah. Mom left her lab door open. I wanted to know how it felt. I didn't…I didn't really care what would happen to me."

Kas opens their mouth to react, but no words come out. The confes-sion settles heavily on them, and they notice Gilbert, once again working on the tube, brusquely raise his head at Rae's words.

"Rae—" he starts through the comms, then he sighs in frustration. "We'll speak of this later."

Rae stares at her shoes.

Gilbert gives her a moment to react; when she doesn't, he stands back up. "This isn't just some dead leaves in the tube, it's been sabotaged. There's a device in there, and it's leaking something into the aether."

"Who would sabotage a light ring?" Kas asks.

Gilbert ignores them. "I need to drain the tube and take it out, but it's already in the pool."

"So what do we do?"

"I've sealed the tube. I can deal with it after we power down the ring. Now we need to purify the pool."

Kas frowns. "Won't it purify on its own?" The aether has no trouble dissolving leaves and other detritus that falls into it from the sky above the ring.

"Not this time. I'll have to separate it from the quintessence by hand."

"With how restless it is—"

"I know," Gilbert says curtly. There's an edge in his voice as he turns to Rae. "Listen to me. You need to get out of there. Both of you should get out."

Kas eyes the glass wall. It's thick, as thick as it's possible to make glass and have it still be transparent. It's almost indestructible—only an aether bullet could, maybe, pierce it.

An aether bullet, or a high velocity splatter of quintessence.

"You need me to operate the console," they say.

"I'm not leaving," Rae declares at the same time. "We have better control together. We can hold it."

Gilbert's shoulders slump, and he raises his hands in surrender. The tubes are his domain, but this situation is new and scary to all of them.

"All right," Kas breathes. "Rae, if the glass is pierced, it will flood in. If that happens, run. I can't move fast enough to get out, but you can."

Rae shakes her head vehemently. "I won't leave you behind. Or Dad."

Kas wishes they could let go of the console to impress it on her better, but their hands are tied. "You *will*, if I tell you to," they insist.

She hesitates, then nods slowly. Kas isn't certain that she'll actually do it, but it's the best they're going to get.

"There's something else," Gilbert calls. "The device. I know this work. I know who did this."

"Yes, you do," a voice comes from behind Kas and Rae, echoing around the organ room. They both jump.

"*Mom?*"

The woman moves toward them, holding a hand toward Rae. She has the same almond eyes and dark hair as her daughter, framing a much thinner face. A pair of square glasses sits on her nose.

Rae steps back until she's pressed against the edge of the console beside Kas. "What are you doing here?"

"Sena," Gilbert says, hovering his PAB closer. He doesn't seem surprised, but his voice is tight. "Is this quicksilver? What were you trying to do?"

"You know exactly what mercury does, Gilbert," Sena says calmly. "You've known since we first found how to distill aether."

Kas's mind needs a moment to parse that, but when they do, the pool ripples dangerously. Gilbert curses and guides his board higher.

"Sorry," Kas mutters. "*You're* the one who found quintessence?"

"At your service," Sena bows sarcastically. Gilbert sighs into his comm.

"But that was over thirty years ago," Kas says.

She shrugs. "We were kids. Eighteen-year-olds with a toy. We had no idea what we were doing. Lightech hired us right out of high school, paid for our education. We sold them the patent for more money than either of us had ever seen. They told us we were going to change the world."

"They told us we were going to *save* the world," Gilbert mutters bitterly.

"Aether was leaking out. The environment was collapsing, and they said quintessence would solve it. And then all they did was use it to power their lightscreens and make their little light shows. Theater that doesn't need real comedians! What a revolution!"

Kas bites back an angry retort at the insult to their art. "That's hardly fair," they mutter. "The light ring was an incredible invention."

The beauty of the shows has enchanted and inspired millions of people, Kas not the least of them. Where would they be without it?

"It's beautiful, sure," Sena shrugs. "But it's still…trivial. Entertainment, nothing else."

"It's art," Kas argues. "Who are we without art? And lightscreens and aether-powered lighting aren't toys, either. They've revolutionized communication systems!"

Sena shakes her head in frustration. "Don't you think I know that? But none of it *matters*! Aether is still leaking out, and every year the planet becomes a little less hospitable."

"But what were you hoping to achieve?" Gilbert demands breathily, almost a growl. It's the first time that Kas has heard him raise his voice above his usual flat tone. "All this will do is make the ring inoperable!"

As if responding to his anger, the quintessence starts swirling again. "Something needs to change. We can't keep going like we have been, burying ourselves in work hoping to forget everything we once stood for!"

Gilbert spreads his arms behind the glass as if to encompass the entire ring. "This isn't the Garindis Opera! What did you think you would solve by attacking a provincial light ring? No one will care!"

"I wasn't trying to sabotage it. I was running an experiment."

"Of course," Rae mutters.

"Lightech is trying to make a weapon out of quintessence," Sena says. "Not aether-guns—something far more dangerous. A bomb. It could destroy everything."

Gilbert deflates. He drops his stance and crouches on his PAB, uselessly swiping his masked brow with his gloves. Kas stares at the gently swirling pool. A bomb? Out of quintessence?

The aether in the ring can kill someone on contact if they accidentally fall in, but on a large scale? Surely...

"A bomb," Gilbert repeats flatly. "What is mercury going to do against that?"

"I wanted to test the quintessence's response at a larger scale than a lab."

"And what's the result of your *experiment*?"

Sena lets a beat pass, staring in awe at the pool. "The aether has a will of its own."

"I could have told you that," Kas says dryly.

"She wouldn't have listened," Rae interrupts. "She always needs to run her little experiments. My whole childhood was an experiment."

"Rae—" Sena starts, some of her poise fading away.

"No. For my entire life, this"—Rae angrily gestures at the pool—"has been your child, far more than I was!"

"Rae, that's not fair. You know I love—"

"You love me, yes. You always say that. It's okay that you disappear for months, because you love me. You've barely had a full conversation with me since the divorce, but you *love me*. Well, you know what? It's not enough!"

She's shouting right next to Kas's ear. The swirling in the pool intensifies with their distraction, and they have to refocus and ignore the family drama to soothe it down. Breathing out, they let their thoughts flow into the connection. It needs to be fed.

Smoothly, edging around Gilbert, forms emerge out of the pool and solidify into vague human shapes. Kas lets their instinct take over their hands.

"Rae," Sena murmurs. "I know I haven't always been around, but—"

"—but your work is important?" Rae interrupts her. "I know that one, too. It's always more important than me. Than us."

"What happened between your father and I isn't the same."

Gilbert mutters something unintelligible. The shapes dance around him, never coming close. Arms and legs emerge and dissolve. A young Kas stands out for a moment, then the form changes, briefly taking Rae's appearance, her long hair flowing around her.

Kas's eyes burn. They're running out of steam. Their hands ache, overstretched, and their back is on fire. They struggle and fail to find their thread again, to give the narrative a shape. The aether draws directly from their chest and leaves them breathless.

It feeds on emotions. If there is no story, it pulls them raw.

"Rae, I'm sorry I've been away so much," Sena sighs. "I haven't been able to rest since I found out about the bomb. I'm in contact with a group of activists—"

"So you put our lives at risk?" Gilbert growls.

"They're making a *bomb*, Gil! I have to do something! I needed you to be the tech in case it went wrong. You're the only one I trust. I didn't know Rae would be here."

"You endangered *our daughter* for your experiments *again*—"

Rae drives a fist into the piano keyboard. "Stop calling me your daughter!" she shouts.

The discordant sound echoes in the organ room and the aether shapes dissolve. Gilbert scrambles out of the way of the wave. Kas panics and pulls up the entire third row of switches before it can get worse.

"Rae!" Sena yells.

"I'm not a girl, okay?"

"What?"

A single shape rises out of the pool again.

Kas's hands still.

The silhouette grows human.

Rae's face, glowing softly, stares back at them. Quintessence drips from her—*their*—cheeks, and their features melt, turn into teenage Kas, then Gilbert, then Sena.

"I've been trying to tell you for so long," the real Rae whispers, tears running down their face.

The shape is their twin again, but different, their hair shorter and braided out of their face, their chest flat. The bright lightning bolt on their hand snakes up their arm, covers their skin until it slithers up their neck and face.

On instinct, Kas reaches out and takes Rae's flesh hand in their own. Rae grips their fingers back, too hard, and they wince.

They brace for rejection—if Gilbert or Sena disavow their child right now, right here, it will hurt nearly as much as when their own parents disavowed them. It's been too many years since Kas last allowed themself to lower their walls, to drop the layer of storytelling and acting that keeps things from feeling *real*. But the aether still pulls at their mind, and the connection can't be closed.

Sena stares at her child in complete shock. Gilbert pulls off his gas mask and leans against the glass. He seeks Sena's gaze.

"When did we stop listening?" he asks brokenly.

Rae deflates as if their strings have been cut. Kas catches them, grunting at the pain in their back. "Sorry," Rae murmurs, clinging to them.

"'t's okay. Welcome to the club, I suppose."

Rae gives them a teary laugh before steeling themself and looking back at their parents. Sena opens her arms, and they gratefully let themself be folded into a hug.

On the other side of the glass, Gilbert looks like he wants to join in. Kas averts their eyes to give them privacy and starts pulling down the third row of switches again.

"My beautiful child," Sena murmurs, pulling Rae's hair out of their face. "I'm sorry I've been absent, in more ways than one."

"Rae…" Gilbert says. "Or wait, do you want to change your name?"

Rae shakes their head. "Rae's okay, I think. But not 'daughter.' Not 'she.'"

"Then what?"

Rae looks at Kas, hesitant, and they nod encouragingly. "'They'? Like them." They gesture toward Kas. "It feels…right." In a lower tone, meant for Kas only, they add, "I didn't know that. Before tonight."

"Happy to help," Kas says tartly. "Not to interrupt this very necessary interpersonal tuning, but I can't hold on for much longer."

"Right," Gilbert says. "Um."

"Go," Rae waves him away. "This can wait until you've fixed Mom's mess." The mix of tension and fondness in their voice makes them sound much older than they are.

"We will talk more, Rae," Sena says, her voice full of tears. "I promise."

"I need to pull the mercury out," Gilbert says, pulling his mask back on. "It will separate easily, but only if it's still enough."

"Could you tell it that it's for its own good?" Rae asks Kas.

"It's not sentient," Sena says.

"It felt…aware to me."

Kas shakes their head. "It has will, but it doesn't understand communication. I can't tell it what to do."

"Then how do we do this?"

"We need to feed it a story that will keep it calm and out of Gilbert's hands."

It won't be easy. The connection thrums under Kas's fingertips, dropping brutally before flaring back to life again. Every glitch is jarring. And there is still the danger of the quintessence waves breaking the glass that protects them, not to mention what they could do to Gilbert.

"I'll help," Rae says.

Kas hesitates. "Your emotions are raw right now. It could get painful." Their own nerves aren't any better, frayed by exhaustion and memories, but they have experience.

"I want to do it. Please."

Biting their lip, Kas relents. They could use the help, and Rae is surprisingly attuned for someone who's only just experienced osmosis for the first time. But they're still a child.

"Stubbornness is a family trait," Sena says, a flicker of amusement passing through her concerned frown. "Okay. But I'm staying right here, and I will help as well." She approaches the console behind Rae. "Tell us what to do."

"Rae, pull these down slowly"—Kas indicates the last two switches of the third row, the ones they haven't yet worked back down—"and keep your hands on them. It should be enough to get you back in. Sena…may I call you Sena?"

"Of course. I don't actually know your name."

"It's Kas. If you're the one who isolated quintessence, you must know how to connect to it, right?"

Sena shakes her head. "I don't, actually. What you did earlier, I've never seen anything like it."

"Surely you've been to a show before?"

"I have, but most organists never make more than a shallow connection, barely enough to drive the story. Osmosis isn't a well-studied science."

Kas blinks. They were aware, distantly, that their training hadn't been traditional, but this doesn't sound right. Marena, their master, used to rebuke them for going too deep, but even she always entered osmosis to play. Do other organists control quintessence through the keyboards only?

"What do they do if the aether doesn't want to work with them?"

"Practice the piece until they get it right," Sena says softly. "Improvising like you've been doing—I didn't think it was possible."

Kas lets out a shaky breath. "Wow," they murmur. Changing their plan of action, they straighten in their seat. "All right, then you'll feed us the story instead. Just talk."

"Talk?"

"None of my usual shows will work for this, and it will be easier to improvise if I don't have to make up a tale at the same time. So give me something."

Sena stays silent, hesitant, as Rae pulls the first switch down. Kas lets out a breath as the pull on their consciousness shifts and settles again, less insistent, redirected. Rae leans against the edge of the organ seat. Kas moves so that they're touching shoulder to shoulder.

"Tell us about yourself," they direct Sena. "How did you figure it out? Isolating quintessence."

Sena gazes through the glass at Gilbert, now sitting cross-legged on his PAB across the ring, mere inches above the pool. "By accident. Gilbert was into engineering; I was doing backyard alchemy. We were friends before we were anything else."

Gilbert takes up the tale. "My uncle loved to tinker with anything aether-powered. Cars, boards, machines. He kept them in his garage. We spent most of that year in there taking apart engines."

Kas's hands dance over the keyboards, but the scene that emerges from the pool doesn't come from their mind, nor from Rae's as they cling to their switches, trembling slightly against Kas. The hulk of a car frame rises, glowing aether dripping from the edges. Two teenagers sit on the ground against it, spare parts and tools spread around them. They move slowly, as if through water.

"Mercury was the key," Sena narrates as her counterpart pours something into an alembic. "Quicksilver, we call it—living silver. The only element that can interact directly with the aether. We designed a device that could trap one within the other. The rest of it was luck."

"We didn't realize the scope of what we'd discovered until we were re-producing the experiment in front of the committee of the largest aeth-er-tech company in the country," Gilbert says, his gloved hands working deep in the pool.

The scene changes with the words, the teenagers standing amid the twirling liquid, moving, growing. Kas can feel the story flow *through* them, rather than out of them. Their fingers have gone numb again.

"They made so many promises. They offered us education, jobs, mon-ey. In hindsight, it was too good to be genuine. I wonder, often, what would have happened if we'd refused, but how could we have? There was no trick. They didn't steal our patent—we sold it to them. They didn't take our work—we gave it away."

Two young adults now stand side by side. Their hands move faster than the quintessence can follow, and they fuse with tools and half-sketched furniture, and with each other. Gilbert's shoulders widen. Se-na's hair grows out, and soon, so does her belly.

"We got married and had Rae amid the growing disillusion," Sena continues. "For a little while, we were happy."

"We were lying to ourselves," Gilbert growls.

Rae flinches, and the scene glitches. The wave splashes up Gilbert's arms, golden liquid snaking up on the hideous orange of his suit. He freezes, taking in a shaky breath.

"Raising Rae kept us going," Sena says, her hands pressing against the glass in an unconscious mirror of Rae's earlier posture. "Our discovery was spreading, but the revolution wasn't happening. Things kept getting worse, and our hands were tied."

The rising figures are now back-to-back, Gilbert holding a small Rae against his hip, Sena bent over a desk. "I recreated my lab at home. I could no longer trust Lightech, but I kept hoping that the next discovery would fix things, fix the guilt and the blame that kept mounting up."

She pauses. Everything stills for a moment, and all is silent but for Gilbert's heavy breathing through the comm.

Little Rae, their head now reaching up to aether-Gilbert's chest, lets go of their father and reaches curiously toward the desk.

"I've never been so scared as the day I found Rae with her—their hand in my quintessence basin."

Lightning explodes out of the child's small hand. Kas's already sore arm twists painfully, and the glitch sends them reeling. They can't bite back their groan of pain; in the pool, Gilbert cries out in alarm. On pure instinct, Rae pulls up their switches and takes over the upper keyboards.

The wave hits just a little slower than it might have. Gilbert launches himself up and barely manages to keep his upper body from submerging. Sena lets out a strangled cry as the quintessence floods up to meet her hands behind the glass wall.

"Calm down," Kas murmurs as they wrestle back control over their body and the connection. "It's okay." They can't say which keys they're hitting anymore, but long experience lets them harmonize with Rae's hesitant, messy work. Their hearts beat in tandem, painfully fast in their chests. Bit by bit, the swirling aether calms down. Gilbert stabilizes himself on his PAB and sends a thumbs up.

"Keep going," Kas murmurs at Rae and Sena.

Sena takes a slow breath. "We realized that we couldn't keep going like this. Gilbert wanted my lab out of the house, and I just…moved out with it. We never talked about it. Work was consuming my life, and I let it."

"I quit my job at Lightech," Gilbert says quietly, his voice ragged. "I couldn't stand what it was doing to us, what it had done to Rae. I needed to put it behind me."

"We divorced a year later. I started trying to get our patent back instead of hoping for something to change. I worked with aether activists, with lawyers, with anyone who would listen. Gradually I forgot I had someone to return home to. And then I heard about the bomb project."

"And you decided to pour mercury into my ring to prove to yourself that you were right," Gilbert says bitingly. He rises on his board, his suit still splattered with light. "I'm done. All the mercury's out."

None of them have the energy left to celebrate with more than a relieved sigh.

"I was wrong," Sena whispers. "All this time, I thought that by distilling aether, we could control it. I just wanted to know if I could sabotage the bomb with this small a dose of mercury. But the osmosis they achieved?" She gestures toward Kas. "I never imagined that."

"What do you mean?" Kas asks, slowly winding down their hands along with the stilling aether in the pool. Rae stop playing, trying to catch their breath.

"With mercury inside the pool, you shouldn't have been able to play at all," Gilbert explains, "let alone that accurately and for so long."

Kas lets go of the keyboard. "I shouldn't be able to play even without it," they say. "I can't really feel my feet anymore. I haven't been able to use the pedals in two years. The organ is just a conduit. That's why the two of you were able to connect with it by doing nothing more than talking. I wasn't the one bringing that story to life."

"To life," Sena repeats under her breath as Gilbert walks back inside. "That's it! Their bomb could never work. Quintessence can be dangerous to us, yes, but what we've built from it, it's—" Her eyes widen even more. "Light. Stories. Even aether bullets are just speed and heat. The lightscreens, they're…connection." She presses her hand to her mouth. "Osmosis isn't control. And aether is *creation*, not destruction. It can't be made into something it's not, even if we figure out the science. It won't *let us*."

Kas gives her a small, exhausted smile. "No, I don't think it will."

"You might be the only one here who truly understands it," Sena says.

"Your kid is pretty good at it, actually." Kas reaches up to pat Rae's shoulder. "That was some impressive work for a beginner."

Rae sags against the edge of the seat. "Phew, that was a lot. I'm hungry."

Kas laughs softly, both at Rae's pronouncement and at Sena, who looks at their child like she's seeing them for the first time. Gilbert, free of his suit, hesitantly puts an arm around her shoulders.

"We could go get some pizza," he says. "There's a 24-hour place around the corner. I think we need to have a long-overdue conversation."

Rae straightens and nods, their shoulders set despite the trembling of their hands.

"And then we can go home," Gilbert adds with a small smile. "Kas, I know I didn't think much of your shows, but that was an impressive improvisation."

"Thanks," Kas huffs out in a laugh. "You weren't half bad yourself."

Gilbert bows jokingly.

Kas nods back and stretches out their legs with a wince.

"Hey, what was the end of your story?" Rae asks them suddenly. "What happened after you first connected to the aether?"

"You know," Kas answers slowly, "the thing about real stories is that most of them don't have an ending. I got caught, of course. I was given community service as a punishment, and I dusted the console room and made the organist coffee for three months. After that, she took me on as an apprentice."

Rae considers them for a moment, fiddling with the edge of their sleeve. "I think…I think I want to learn to play."

Kas smiles at them. "I'm sure that could be arranged."

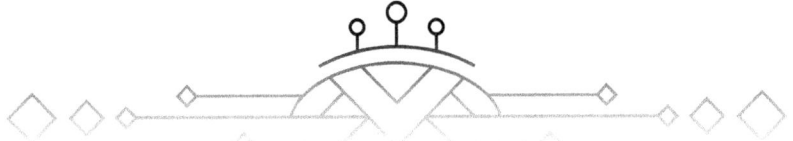

Nicola Kapron

How Your Garden Grows

alternate history, attempted murder, character injury (graphic descriptions), environmentalism, genderfluid, natural disaster (unnatural), nature spirit, non-binary, non-human character, past tense, post-apocalyptic, science fiction with magic, scientist, siblings, third person limited point of view

Sleeping while the ship drifted above the Nightmare Sea was all but impossible, but Stone was diving today, so ze'd had no choice but to try last night. Between the melatonin, a relaxing meditation, and white noise playing over zir headphones, ze'd eventually managed to drift off. Zir dreams had been full of strange whispers and rustling leaves. That was to be expected—the Nightmare Sea had a way of getting into people's heads—but it still left zir to wake up in a cold sweat, certain something was watching zir.

Ze waited for zir heart rate to die down before flicking on the lights. The room looked unreal in the pale violet glow of the aether lamps. Light glistened like dew on the walls, cabinets, and printouts tacked up everywhere there was space. The air shimmered with haunting, shifting potential. It was a nightmare. It was exactly the kind of sight Stone had become an alchemist to witness.

Eventually, the room stopped feeling like a continuation of the dream and started feeling real. Stone waited a few more seconds, just to be safe; slipping out of reality and ending up stuck halfway through the floor would be an awful way to start the day. Then ze rubbed zir eyes, scratched at zir fine, chin-length dark hair, and got up.

There was a routine to early mornings on the job. First, ze fetched a fresh jumpsuit from an uncontaminated bag ze'd packed before the ship had left the mountain port. Next, ze ran a comb through zir hair. Then came a quick search around the room for snack wrappers because Stone had never been the best at maintaining a proper meal schedule, and sometimes ze ended up eating at odd hours. That was a hazard of life as a researcher. Leaving anything associated with strong emotions lying around while near the Nightmare Sea promised to make it a very different kind of hazard. Once ze was presentable and pretty sure the room wouldn't be full of scuttling cockroach-creatures born from lost snack packaging later, ze headed out.

Leigh was already up. They—no, she, Stone thought, checking the colour of the pink patch on her outfit—was typing away at a glowing aethertech monitor, happily humming. Zir older sibling was taller than ze was, with longer hair pulled back in a low ponytail. She was wearing the equally pink pendant she used to signal what gender she was feeling for the day while on dry land. That was a problem for the same reasons Stone's stray snack wrappers were a problem.

"Good morning," ze said, stumbling toward the coffee machine. Yes, there was still delicious bean juice available. It was even warm.

"Morning!" she sang back. "I saved you some coffee."

Ze dove into the coffee pot face-first. "Best sister."

"Damn right."

A few more gulps, and Stone finally came up for air. It was time to say something about the necklace. "We're diving today, aren't we?"

"Uh, yeah? I hope so?"

"Jewelry, Leigh."

"Yeah, yeah." She unfastened her necklace and set it aside, then pulled off her rings. Ze hadn't even noticed her wearing them. "You too, Stone."

Ze tapped zir empty earlobes. "Way ahead of you."

Bringing keepsakes into the Nightmare Sea was asking for them to be possessed, but jewelry was the worst. Stone had cleverly left zir earrings at home. The two of them were only supposed to be out here for four days. That shouldn't be long enough for zir piercings to heal over.

"I hate it when you do this," Leigh complained. "Stop making me feel incompetent compared to you, dear sibling."

"You'd better not be feeling incompetent today. You're navigating."

"Don't remind me." She shuddered. "I swear, manning the screens is so much worse than actually diving."

Stone didn't argue with her. She was right. Diving into the Nightmare Sea was a strangely peaceful experience, whereas watching someone else descend below tree level was terrifying. Maybe it had something to do with the comparative helplessness of the experience. Observing from a distance opened up all kinds of unpleasant possibilities, such as being forced to watch while someone you loved was killed, mutilated, or vanished forever.

Fun stuff.

Ze finished up zir coffee and set the mug in the sink. Decontamination procedures started immediately. A faint purple glow lit up the basin as aether flooded in, concentrated to visible—and thus toxic—levels. It pulsed three times, dissolving all traces Stone had left on the pot, then dissipating down the pipes.

This kind of decontamination was thorough. It was also only feasible on airships and at the edges of ports. Aether was inclined to spread out; left to its own accord, it was thin and transparent, so close to invisible that it had taken thousands of years for people to discover it. In its natural state, it was so scarce that even the highest aether concentrations did nothing to the human body but shimmer faintly and cause the occasional tingle down the spine.

The Nightmare Sea was different.

But then, the Nightmare Sea wasn't natural, was it?

"Let's go," Stone said. "We can eat on the way."

"Just because you like ration bars—forget it. Lead on."

Most of the airship had no windows. It was more like a submarine than a zeppelin. Cameras and periscopes showed the navigator what was going on outside and kept the visual interference of the Nightmare Sea to a minimum. They also kept the inhabitants of the Nightmare Sea from peering inside. The only exception to the "no windows" rule was the dive chamber.

Stone had seen designs for an undersea habitat once. It had featured aether-powered hydroponics, warm lights to radiate the same wavelength as the sun, and a moon pool allowing divers and submarines to exit and return. If the habitat had been built, it had been lost during the Flood when toxic levels of aether covered most of the Earth. Even a hundred years later, anything below mountain-peak level was beyond human aether tolerance. The Nightmare Sea itself, that shifting mass of shadow and branching limbs, spiralling upward like smoke and collapsing in on itself like ink, was something else entirely.

If a diver was lucky, dropping into the Nightmare Sea without protective gear would simply kill them. If they weren't...

There were horror stories about people who'd melted, screaming into their communicators as the forest absorbed them into itself. Stone didn't discuss them out loud; Leigh didn't like it. But ze did think about those tales sometimes. Especially when strapping zirself into the bulky dive suit.

First, a slick blacksuit underneath to drain excess aether away from the body and maintain a steady core temperature. It looked like a wetsuit and plugged directly into the next layer. The inner shell was several layers of metal and plastic with inertial dampeners and other aethertech gear built into it. After that came the oxygen tanks for untainted air and the aether sinks: flowing coils kept behind thick, transparent glass, which stored the aether that got through the outer layers. Finally came the outer shell. Its design had undoubtedly been inspired by deep-sea diving suits before the Flood. It was big, clunky, and powered by aether. If it ran out of power, the diver would be unable to move.

It was impossible to run out of aether in the Nightmare Sea.

After that, ze checked zir safety line. It would be zir connection to the ship and would literally haul them out of trouble if necessary.

"Everything's in place," Stone said into the darkness of zir helmet.

"Here, too. Ready to dive?" Leigh's voice crackled through the comms system.

Ze nodded. "Ready."

The dive chamber was dark. The only light filtered upward from the moon window set into the floor. Large and circular, it served as the portal through which ze would exit and, hopefully, return. A transparent barrier of purple-tinged glass sat between Stone and the outside. The Nightmare Sea spread out below zir.

"Copy," Leigh said. "Three..."

The color of the glass made the ocean of trees below look blue. Even with that tint, the swirls of cloud that clung to the spiralling shapes shimmered through every colour Stone knew and several ze didn't.

"Two…"

Wind currents batted at the treetops. Most of them splashed off like water on the shore, faint trails in the sky the only evidence they'd even tried.

"One…"

Stone breathed in deeply, then let the air hiss out between zir teeth. Zir fingers flexed inside the heavy gloves. Far below, something in the shining sea reflected like metal instead of like heat shimmer or phantasmal crystal. It was near zir planned diving path.

"Diving."

With a pulse of aether so strong Stone could taste the ozone on zir tongue, the glass went transparent and insubstantial. Stone dropped out of the airship feet-first and began the long descent to the treetops.

Falling into aether wasn't supposed to feel like anything. In its natural state, aether was transparent, insubstantial, and impossible to distinguish from air or vacuum. But there was nothing natural about the Nightmare Sea. A thousand years ago, when aether had first been harnessed, there'd seemed to be no downside to drawing power from the lifeblood of the universe. A hundred years ago, an age of economic prosperity, mercantile exploitation, and hideous inequality had come to an abrupt end. One too many lax safety measures had led to the Flood, a terribly literal flood of concentrated, poisonous aether that had smothered most of Europe. A chain reaction had led to the atmosphere raining down on the rest of the planet. Now, the Nightmare Sea covered the Earth from pole to pole, and humans eked out a careful existence on mountaintops and in airships.

Aether still powered most technology and spells, but people were careful with it now. Once burned, twice shy. Even so, some—like Stone—would risk everything to see what wonders aether had wrought on the surface. Other, less idealistic people just wanted to ravage the Nightmare Sea for resources the way old humanity had ravaged everything else, but Stone didn't like to dwell on that.

Falling into the Nightmare Sea was like plunging into deep water: dark, cold, and full of crushing pressure. Stone fell like, well, a stone for the first few seconds. Then zir feet hit the first layer of haze, and the speed of zir descent slowed. Pinkish fog filled the air, moving sluggishly with the currents. When the pink turned purple, ze was coming down slowly enough to spot individual whorls of cloud turning below zir. A few minutes later, ze was ten feet above those clouds. Close enough to see the rainbow colours shine slick over a forest that stretched to the horizon. Close enough to spy wriggling serpents made of glass and birds defined by the complete absence of anything within their empty shapes. Close enough to spot that metallic shimmer again.

It was much bigger than ze'd expected.

"Suspend descent. I found something."

A second later, zir suit was no longer dropping. It hung steady in the aether soup as Leigh replied. "Already?"

"I think it's a ship. Was anyone else supposed to be here?"

"Uh, no?" She scoffed, as she should. This whole area was forbidden territory. There'd been all sorts of weird readings from this place over the years, but the waves weren't violent. And while there hadn't been a true aether storm here since the Flood, bizarre flotsam landed on the rocky beaches and odd colours flared at night. Stone and Leigh had been sent here on behalf of the forest rangers to try and figure out why. They were the first divers to try going below canopy-level here in years, so Stone had no idea who was anchored down there, airship barely above the surface.

It wasn't exactly safe for Stone and Leigh to be out here, but it was safer for a single diver to go down than to risk an entire ship. Plus, mining for anything save carefully selected samples was illegal across the Nightmare Sea. Salvagers beachcombed along mountains and trawled the surface because that, at least, only put themselves in danger.

Nobody knew what would set off a second Flood.

Nobody knew what had set off the first.

"Yeah, I know. But someone's down here."

"Should I ping them?" Leigh's frown was audible.

"One minute. I want to take a closer look first. If they're refugees, we don't want to startle them into diving." The ship was already too close to the surface of the Nightmare Sea. There were reasons Stone was wearing a heavy, armored diving suit instead of letting Leigh pilot the ship down. Most of those reasons had to do with sudden, localized pressure changes and whirlpools that formed inside large, mostly hollow objects, but there were worse things that could happen to something big in the Nightmare Sea. Every diver feared rust plagues and trees sprouting up through aethertech, and some ships had been yanked down below the treetops by things unseen and had never surfaced again.

Leigh hissed in a breath. "Yeah, that could go bad. What if they're corporate?"

"If they're corporate, we contact HQ for backup and start delaying actions ASAP." They hadn't come equipped for aerial combat, and any corporate vessel hiding in the forbidden regions of the Nightmare Sea would almost certainly attack if discovered.

"Better not be corporate. It's their fault the Nightmare Sea exists. Poking at it is asking for another Flood, and then where will we all be?"

Stone winced inside zir helmet. "Let's hope it doesn't come to that."

Ze activated the small, aether-sink-powered jets and began flying slowly toward the ship. The jets weren't strong, just enough to propel zir heavy suit forward. They didn't move fast enough to draw the attention of prying eyes from the abyss; without the lifeline, the jets wouldn't be strong enough to keep the suit aloft at a steady altitude. Ze kept an eye on the roiling branches and thick shadow seething below. If anything burst out from the depths, ze would be ready.

When the ship came fully into view, ze jerked zir head up and swore softly into the comm. "Corporate mining ship. Alvara's logo is stenciled on the side." The Alvara Drilling logo had been painted over in the same mottled grey as the rest of the ship, but that didn't matter. This close to the canopy, each aether fluctuation lit up the brushstrokes with bright neon. "Call HQ."

"On it. Lemme haul you up first."

"Don't bother. I'm going to keep looking around. Get some scans, see if I can tell what they're after."

"Be careful, Stone. Don't wanna lose my favourite sibling."

"I'm your only sibling," ze grumbled, propelling zirself forward. "Going in."

The metallic, oval hull of a vast airship loomed ahead. Purple waves and oil-slick-coloured branches crashed constantly at its sides. Most of the ship's bottom was below the Sea, but it was high enough in the canopy that Stone could make out a massive metal pole coming out of the airship and leading far down into the trees.

No. Not a pole. A drill frozen in place. Big enough to carve a hole straight through to a ground level that hadn't been seen by human eyes in a century. None of the scans Stone had seen before diving had given zir any idea what was down there, but the source of those weird energy signals probably wouldn't play nice with drilling operations.

At least they were still setting up the mining site. Excavating a shaft was difficult when nobody was down on the ground, and getting below the canopy required a heavy diving suit. Stone wasn't sure if the Alvara ship had any or how well-maintained their gear might be. Ze hoped ze wasn't going to watch someone die because they'd forgotten to take off a necklace or brought a good-luck charm down with them.

Should ze broadcast a warning to the ship? From an investigation standpoint, tipping the mining team off would be a mistake. But Stone wasn't sure what ze'd do if someone died because of zir inaction. Ze hung in the amethyst clouds, watching the branches snap and twist around the metal shell, and thought.

Then the drill began to turn, and zir thoughts scattered.

It was only on for a second, but that was long enough. A horrific noise carved through the air like a knife. A load of shining, shifting fae stone and metal was hauled up into the ship, torn free from its resting place. Everything found in the Nightmare Sea was called fae and then compared to whatever it most resembled: fae metal, fae ferns, fae diamond. Part of Stone was utterly spellbound at the sight. Those were more fae substances than ze'd ever seen outside the Nightmare Sea. If ze could get that big a sample into laboratory conditions, ze could learn so much. Depending on what the fae substances could be convinced to do with the right prompting, they might revolutionize life. And command prices the likes of which hadn't been seen since the Flood.

At the same time, ze was utterly horrified. Large-scale mining of fae substances was banned, especially in places where aether was already behaving oddly.

And for good reason.

The Nightmare Sea boiled around the ship. A kaleidoscopic tide lashed out like a whirlpool. Aether lances soared hundreds of feet into the air and came down as heated liquid. Stone curled in and covered zir head as one lance splashed over zir. The suit whined as the aether sinks worked overtime.

"Leigh! Come in!" ze yelled into the coms. "They're drilling! You need to get help!"

"They're what? Hold on. I'll get you out of there!"

Sheets of aether rolled off zir, thick like taffy, edges wafting away like smoke. The phantom smell of ozone filled zir nose. "I need to warn them. They don't know what they're doing. There's gotta be someone left to watch the ship. Give me a few minutes to find them."

Ze jetted forward and began swinging around the side of the ship. Even without windows, ze could tell which parts of the vessel were inhabited by watching the aether currents. Aether was drawn to thought and feeling like moths to flame. Where the currents were most active would be the best place to broadcast a warning.

Watching the aether currents so closely should have tipped zir off, but ze was close enough to the ship to mistake the swirls gathering around zir for backsplash. By the time the shadow fell over zir, it was too late.

There was a noise behind zir. Silenced aether jets. An illegal reflective suit: banned because it made the wearer nigh invisible to humans as well as to fae things. Stone was halfway through calling Leigh again when zir suit jolted.

The figure behind zir had a knife extruded from their suit. A knife that was already halfway through zir lifeline. Stone hung by a thread, jets unable to keep zir afloat.

Panic should have set in, but Stone found zirself staring dumbly at the diver who'd just killed zir instead.

"Stone?" Leigh asked. "Did something happen?"

"Leigh, I—"

The cable snapped. The comms dissolved into static as Stone crashed into the Nightmare Sea and broke through. Purple vapour turned to thick black ocean, branches merging until the forest was a single whole. Ze had just enough time to cover zir head before everything went dark.

Consciousness returned in stages. The first thing Stone noticed was light. Thick, twisting snakes of it writhed and roiled above zir, branching creatures with no discernable beginning or end that ran through colours like a kaleidoscope: lightning made into a living thing. The second thing was the ozone haze in zir nose and the heavy, coppery taste of blood in zir mouth. Awareness of zir body returned last. When it finally came back, zir body felt like one giant bruise.

Not a bruise—an open wound.

"Leigh?" ze rasped around a clumsy tongue.

Nothing. Not even static.

"Leigh, can you hear me?"

There was no response. Stone tried to raise a hand and whited out from pain. For several seconds, ze wheezed for breath. Inhaling too quickly made zir chest ache, but at least it wasn't the sharp, shooting pain of a broken limb.

Zir arm was definitely broken. When shifted, zir legs also exploded in pain and refused to cooperate.

The pain made the serpents brighter and more erratic. One of them even sprouted a new branch in zir direction. Ze tried to shift zir gaze away from the fae snakes in case attention made them change, and ze ran into a problem: everything around zir was made of thick streamers of light and shadow. The trunks of melting trees waved from vertical to horizontal depending on zir viewing angle. Colours ran into each other without regard for aesthetics. Eyes formed in spaces there shouldn't have been room for them. Familiar shapes—stumps, ferns, flowers, hands— merged and reformed as fae things in the corners of zir vision. Whatever was directly in zir field of view remained static in form, even if the exact dimensions warped and twisted, but everything else moved and changed with no discernable rhyme or reason.

The only shared element was that everything, from the serpents of light coiling and uncoiling through the air to the glowing sheets that formed a wobbly floor and merged with whatever they touched, seemed to shift depending on where ze was looking. Wherever zir attention landed, the light gathered. Holes in the haze, shining brighter the longer the tunnel they created appeared to be.

Ze stared for a long time at one hole.

When ze blinked, it blinked back.

A lump formed in zir throat.

So this was what lay at the bottom of the Nightmare Sea.

With a trickle of fear, ze forced zirself to sit up. The suit. Ze needed to check the suit. The air was so thick that ze could hardly move. In the struggle, zir good hand landed on a wavy fae fern that immediately coiled around zir fingers, its fronds lighting up a brilliant purple. Something small, furry, and seemingly made of water darted out from under the plant and ran like lightning. A ringing sound filled the air.

Ze retrieved zir hand as quickly as ze could without wrenching the fern out of the murky earth. Where zir hand had been, there was a perfect violet handprint, shining as bright as a star. And in the center was a smear of red.

The suit hadn't broken through, but the outer armor had cracked, revealing the inner mesh layers. Those were only rated to repel aether for a few hours in the canopy. Stone had no idea how long the mesh would last in these toxic densities, or what bleeding on the Nightmare Sea might do.

The handprint shone brighter around the bloodstain. Then the fern unraveled like frayed knitting. So did the molten plant next to it and the shadowy rock formation behind them. In a flash, half the forest beside Stone was just gone.

In the pit left behind was a human-shaped lump. It lay in the hollow, wrapped entirely in what looked like dirty bandages. Stone squinted at the white strips, hoping they were some kind of fae fungus. Instead, ze spotted what looked uncomfortably like writing. Not bandages—talismans, wrapped so thick around the body that it had only the vaguest sense of form.

It was utterly still. Utterly silent. A single point of calm in the shifting chaos of the Nightmare Sea. That, more than anything else, scared Stone.

Ze tried to shuffle away from the pit. Moving made zir vision white out again. When it returned, a fresh trickle of blood was oozing from the exposed mesh on zir leg. The sound of droplets landing on the… cocoon…was painfully loud.

It couldn't be a corpse. Dead things dissolved instantly in the Nightmare Sea. Then the shape shifted, the outlines of human hands pressing against the bindings from the inside, and Stone's fear was drowned out by the fascination of an alchemist observing the unknown.

Nobody had encountered a fae person before.

Long, curved nails tore through the talismans. Something that looked almost human rose up, scattering scraps of paper and fabric like snow, and blinked in the iridescent haze.

Stone held very still and tried not to breathe too loudly. Ze desperately wished the comms were working, because ze was looking at a man with wings, and Leigh needed to know about it. Massive feathers snapped out, primaries easily as long as Stone's arm. The snakes of light flashed toward him like lightning and were swallowed whole. In moments, the pit had become a clearing, and this small portion of the Nightmare Sea was once again whole and moving.

The ground was earth now, each grain a minuscule speck of coloured light. The trees were braided together into impossible shapes, but they were recognizable as fae wood. Rocky outcrops rose out of the glowing ground, glistening like ice and night made solid. Something moved behind the trees, a vague impression of rock-like skin and far too many compound eyes. The fae creature flared his wings once more before folding them. Then he turned to Stone and cocked his head. His eyes were bright yellow, the sclera pitch black. Strands of fine, thick black hair fell over his face, doing nothing to soften that stare. His face showed neither malice nor pity, simply a distant curiosity.

Eagle eyes, Stone thought. To go with his broad, powerful eagle wings.

"You're hurt," the fae observed. His voice was deep but calm, without concern or urgency. Under the tattered talismans, he wore a long coat made from some kind of fae cloth: an ever-changing gradient of black, grey, and purple. It seemed to be made of concentrated aether, but that couldn't be right. Being in contact with solid aether would dissolve the human body.

But he wasn't human, was he?

Ze swallowed hard. "I…fell. May I ask who you are?"

Who, not what. Asking what he was seemed like a sure way to piss him off. The Nightmare Sea was dangerous, but people could be far worse. Hadn't ze just learned that firsthand?

"You may." The fae fell silent. His expression remained detached, almost empty, save for those intense eyes. "But I can't say what I don't remember."

"What don't you remember?"

"Anything."

Oh, dear. Stone sucked in a breath. "Do you know where we are?"

He looked up. The collar of his coat moved with him, connected to his skin. When it moved, it pulsed like the sink on Stone's ship, a steady influx of power that should be lethal.

"Outside," the fae said.

"This is the Nightmare Sea." If Stone wasn't in so much pain, ze'd toss in a dramatic gesture. "The most glorious, fascinating, and unpredictable place on Earth. And we're stuck at the bottom of it." Although ze was trying to make a point, zir voice sounded more excited than ze intended. "This is ground no human has laid eyes on in a hundred years! Nobody knows what's down here. For all we know, there's an entire ecosystem evolved around reality being mouldable and shape being a suggestion!"

The fae was looking at zir again. No—he was looking at something around zir. Stone tried to follow his gaze, but ze couldn't detect whatever he saw, neither with the suit's battered sensors nor with zir own eyes.

"What are you looking at?"

"You love it," he said nonsensically. He paused long enough for Stone to realize he'd been waiting for a reply. "This land cannot love you back. That's not in its nature."

"That's—fine. It's a place, not a person. I didn't expect it to care."

He cocked his head in the other direction. Then he laughed, a bright and sudden sound that struck Stone as familiar. "That's more than most people! So, this place is called the Nightmare Sea…it does feel a bit dreamlike. Like it's made from the thoughts of the forest."

"I wouldn't be surprised," Stone murmured. "Aether reacts strangely to consciousness. Thoughts, memories…and trees are alive."

"A forest is alive. One grand organism woven together from countless others, feeding into and from the whole."

"And an ocean?"

"It's the same thing," the fae said. "The planet is one grand system composed of smaller systems. It's all connected." He frowned. "I don't know how I know that. I don't remember learning it." His wings fanned out restlessly, sending ripples through the surrounding aether.

The force of those ripples rocked Stone, and ze bit down on a cry of pain.

When ze looked up, the fae was crouched over zir, his face less than a foot away. Ze hadn't noticed him move.

"You're hurt."

Ze nodded slowly, heart in zir mouth.

"You fell." His mouth twisted. That, too, was familiar. "That could've gone badly."

"It kinda did," Stone admitted. "I don't—think I can walk." Or stand.

"That's what happens when people like you fall." Those massive wings rustled pointedly. "Be more careful."

"I just got distracted for a moment!" Ze craned zir neck to follow the feathers. "I didn't mean to get hurt any more than you meant to hurt me just now." That was a bit of a leap of faith, but the fae inclined his head in silent agreement. "Sometimes things happen. You need to take a certain level of personal responsibility, sure, but there's also something to be said about going to dangerous places to begin with."

The fae grimaced. "Yeah, yeah. You were careless too, Stone."

Stone paused. "I didn't give you my name."

"No," the fae agreed. He was still making a face. With his lips twisted and eyes narrowed, he bore a striking resemblance to Leigh.

Once Stone had seen it, ze couldn't unsee it. Suddenly, the fae looked like zir sibling everywhere. Ze couldn't remember his shape before this; he was just Leigh with shorter hair, broader shoulders, and sharp yellow eyes. The wings and the eyes hadn't changed, and Stone clung to them with all zir might.

"Have we met?"

"Not that I remember." His too-sharp gaze slid back past Stone's shoulders. "You're glowing."

Stone craned zir back and swore. A tell-tale purplish glow and a soft whining sound indicated what was happening. "The aether sinks are cracking…"

"Aether sinks?"

"The glowing cylinders leaking through my suit. They're for—"

"I know what they do," the fae said, still wearing Leigh's scowl. "I don't know what they are. It's all backward." He closed his eyes. "I've forgotten something. I've forgotten everything."

Stone looked away from the leaking tubes, trying to stay calm. Ze couldn't panic over the signs of a suit failure when something more dangerous was in front of zir. "What do you remember?"

"This place is my home. Or it was once." The fae opened his eyes. "It didn't always look like this, but the changes aren't…unexpected.

Whatever happened, I knew it was coming." He flicked a hand at the aether sinks. The idle gesture fused the cracks shut.

Stone's breath caught in zir throat. The aether sinks were no longer whining. The purplish glow had faded until it was nearly white. Whatever he'd done had given zir hours more to survive, and he didn't appear to have even noticed.

He'd channeled aether, a substance known for dissolving the body if it was in thick enough quantities to be used effectively, with his bare hands. But more importantly...

"You predate the Flood," ze breathed. "Do you know—? No. There's no time to pick your brain about that. Um, this might be a bit much to ask, but can you take a message to my sibling? Someone's jammed a drill into the Nightmare Sea nearby. They're mining the lower forest. There's no telling when they'll turn it on, but if they do..."

The fae went very still. "A drill."

Stone suspected that ze'd screwed up. "Yes," ze said cautiously. "I just... need to let my sibling know. She should've already called for backup. If I can make sure the rangers know, we can shut this down before anything happens."

Probably. Stone really hoped the miners weren't stupid enough to turn the drill on right after they believed they'd killed someone. Violent death stirred up aether like nothing else. That was part of why the Flood had been so devastating: every single death made the giant aether storm worse.

"That isn't necessary," the fae said with no particular inflection. Feathers rippled as his wings snapped out again. "I'll get rid of it."

"Don't!"

The word was out before ze could stop it. Then those terrible golden eyes were on zir.

"Why?" the fae asked seriously, sounding exactly like Leigh when she stopped playing around. "Whatever happened here to make this place the way it is, they're going to do it again."

"Don't kill them!"

"They'll die anyway. Nature isn't a reward served to them on a platter." He flexed his fingers like talons. "I'll make it quicker than choking on smog and less painful than dissolving alive." There was no malice in his voice, but no compassion either. It had the emotional range of a redtailed hawk's iconic, echoing shriek.

But he'd saved Stone with the same casual disregard as he talked about killing. That meant something.

"Just—just calm down! Nobody has to die."

"Don't they? This has happened before. Humans delve too deep, too fast with reckless disregard and bring disaster on everyone. I'm certain I tried to stop them once." He picked at a shred of talisman and held it up to the light. "They found a way to seal me instead, and look what happened."

A thousand questions leaped to the tip of Stone's tongue, but this was not the time to ask them. Ze set zir jaw. The movement made zir head pound. "Things have changed since then. We've changed," ze stressed. "Even if people mess up like that, there are ways to fix it now."

The fae gestured to the shifting forest around them. "Do you really think this can be fixed? There's no going back to before the Nightmare Sea."

"No, but we can move forward. To a future where humans aren't at war with the world." Stone looked up and willed the fae to trust zir. "I—we—can stop them without anyone dying."

"I don't believe you."

"At least let us try."

His expression didn't change, but his wings mantled. The clearing was dominated by bright, searing feathers. "Deliver the message yourself."

Stone's heart dropped into the soles of zir boots. Then the fae shrouded them both in soft violet light and lifted zir as if ze weighed nothing. The diving suit, zir broken bones—none of that was touched by gravity. Ze wasn't being carried; ze was floating.

For a moment, ze hung, weightless, as the fae tilted his head back. There was no sky above them; this deep, the canopy was layer upon layer of rippling light. Then the fae launched into the air, and Stone could only squeeze zir eyes shut and trust he wouldn't let go.

The ship was still where Stone had left it, flying in a holding pattern around the mining site. The fae moved through the moon window's aether barrier like it wasn't there. A wide-eyed Leigh witnessed their arrival from the far side of the room by the consoles.

"Stone?" Her eyes darted uneasily between the two of them.

Stone nodded weakly. "Hey. Someone cut my line, and we need to call backup right now."

Zir words trailed off in a pained hiss as the aether glow around zir faded and ze dropped several inches. The fae caught zir almost absently, supporting zir weight with one arm as he looked around the dive chamber. His wings were still searing the bright, shifting light of trapped aether, but the room wasn't warping. Nothing was melting. And Leigh, despite being far too close to that light for comfort, was showing no signs of physical or mental disintegration.

Thank God, Stone thought, and then put that out of zir mind for the moment. The second ze'd cried out, Leigh had straightened up. She crossed the room with long strides, her gaze focused on zir.

"What happened?"

"Broken bones, some soft tissue damage," the fae listed off. He glanced down at the moon window, eyes fixed intently on something Stone couldn't see. Maybe he'd spotted the Alvara ship just above the roiling tide. "It's survivable."

There was not a sliver of doubt in his tone. Stone and Leigh made eye contact and silently shared the resolution not to ask.

"Can you stand?" Leigh asked instead.

"No. But that's fine," ze said. "I don't need to be on my feet to help force the mining ship into emergency mode."

Leigh's eyes narrowed. She nodded decisively and went back to the console. "Follow me. You too, stranger."

The fae's wings mantled again. His face was perfectly expressionless. Stone placed a hand on his shoulder and held zir breath as a thick layer of aether thrummed against zir battered gloves. Finally, he stepped away from the moon window.

"You said nobody needed to die. Now's your chance to prove it."

"And if we can't?" Leigh asked, her voice barely trembling.

"I'm a guardian, I think. A check and a balance on the natural world." He gazed down at the Nightmare Sea. "I'll teach humanity the cost of exploitation without thought or mercy."

Stone hissed out a breath. So this was a test, huh? "Got it. Put me down near Leigh, please. I won't ask much more."

The fae did so. It was surprisingly painless. Leigh leaned down to check on zir anyway the moment the fae left, drawn back to the moon window like a magnet. She examined zir battered suit while continuing to type with her other hand. In its own way, that was just as intimidating as the fae's golden eyes.

"What was that?" she hissed.

"I don't know," Stone whispered back. "Something I found buried deep in the Nightmare Sea. He can absorb and use aether without any sort of tech. I think he's the reason this area had such strange energy readings without correspondingly violent waves. He saved me, but he doesn't seem to like humans—no. He doesn't think humans can exist without hurting the world."

"Yeah, okay, but why does he look like that?"

Ze sighed. "I know it's weird that he looks like you—"

Leigh frowned. "What are you talking about? He looks like you."

They both paused. Then they glanced back at the fae together. No matter how hard Stone looked, ze saw the smooth line of Leigh's jaw, the tilted posture of someone who spent too long hunched over a keyboard, the curve of a mouth made for smiling. There was no resemblance to zir at all. But Leigh seemed equally confident in her own observations.

"Maybe we're seeing what we want to see?" ze suggested.

"Maybe we can run some tests after this," she said. "You know. Assuming we make it through."

"Don't be dramatic. The worst has already happened, and I came back. We'll be fine."

In the end, they only asked one more thing of the fae: the precise layout of the drill and its connectors to both the Alvara ship and the distant Earth. He relayed the details without emotion or hesitation.

"Think we can scuttle them?" Leigh asked.

Stone scoffed. "With those currents brewing? We'd better magnetize them to something or they'll be torn apart."

"We are equipped for towing…"

"That's for rescuing stranded vessels, not taking prisoners."

"We're about to strand them," the fae pointed out.

Stone grimaced. "All right. Do it."

Leigh opened communications—or rather, re-opened them. Apparently, she'd been yelling warnings at the silent ship while Stone was gone.

"Alvara ship, this is your final chance! Release the drill now and we'll tow you to safety!"

The ship replied by raising its weapons.

"We warned you!" Leigh called.

Their ship didn't have weapons, but it did have scientific lasers, powerful magnets, and an aether blade to break through dangerous flotsam. The Nightmare Sea bubbled and spat shadow as Leigh deployed them all.

With a loud, grating shriek, the Alvara ship separated from its drill. Before it could right itself, white-hot beams of aether pierced through the rudder. The ship tumbled into a clunky aileron roll, which kept Leigh from aiming properly. Then something with too many legs and too many mouths latched onto the vessel mid-roll and determinedly wound itself around the guns.

Its weight stopped the ship from rolling.

Leigh seized the moment to send out a grappling hook, the kind meant to latch onto cliffs, which went through the fae creature and the outer layer of hull both. The ship stabilized upside down. Then a hatch on the exposed underside opened, and the diver who'd cut Stone's line crawled out. At this distance, they were the size of an ant.

"They came out awfully fast," ze said, zir heart stuttering in zir chest.

The diver ventured halfway down to the trapped guns, then stopped. A small hand clutched at their chest the way someone might cup a necklace or a pendant. Around them, aether started to mist, rising up from the ocean and swirling toward the small figure.

"Yeah," Leigh agreed grimly. "Must have changed in a rush, quick enough they might've made a mistake. Forgot to take something off in the shuffle. A lucky charm, perhaps. A familiar tool. An old pair of glasses with too many feelings attached." She hit the comms. "Alvara diver! Return to the ship!"

The diver scrabbled wildly at their chest, as if they could peel through the hardsuit with their gloved hands. Then they dropped back down and crawled a few more feet before they started shaking too hard to move. The mist swirled thicker around them.

"Alvara diver!"

The diver clawed at their helmet.

"Damn it!" Leigh scanned the controls, but even Stone knew it was too late. At this distance, there was nothing the two of them could do.

The Alvara diver's back arched horribly, impossible curve visible through the heavy layers of metal. Then the tiny figure collapsed into thick, dark aether that ran like liquid down the ship's sides and was lost in the Nightmare Sea.

Stone closed zir eyes. Beside zir, feathers rustled, but the fae said nothing. Down below, the wind howled and aether waves crashed against steel.

If the Alvara crew mourned the loss of one of their own, their cries didn't reach Stone's ears.

The Alvara ship stopped trying to evade. Leigh set the towing clamps to keep it upright, advised the surviving crew to stay inside and not touch anything with sentiment attached, and then opened communications to HQ. The connection was bad this far out. Reporting in would take a while.

Leigh didn't seem to notice when the fae returned to the edge of the moon window and stepped through the barrier.

Stone did. Walking was beyond zir still, but the weight of zir gaze seemed to alert him. Ze couldn't restrain a shudder when they made eye contact. Mostly, though, ze was desperately curious. You couldn't ask fae metal or fae wood what the Nightmare Sea was like. A fae person, though…

He was the closest thing to a mouthpiece the Nightmare Sea had.

"We did it," ze said. "No second Flood."

"This won't be the last time humans try to tear the world apart for callous greed."

"Then you should work with us!" Stone pushed out in a rush. "We'll stand a better chance of stopping them together."

"You don't want another Flood any more than we do, right?" Leigh looked up from her reports. "Then we've got the same goal! It's win-win."

For a long moment, he stared through them. When he looked away, he seemed…less. Less focused. Less intense. Less like a vicious thing waiting to pounce. "This feels far too simple."

"It won't be," Stone said. "We still have to tell the rangers where you came from, and explaining that will be basically impossible. The force might poke and prod a bit, but they won't hurt you or lock you up." They wouldn't be able to even if they wanted to. Not with the amount of aether still trapped, seemingly harmless, in the fae's wings. "You can see farther in the Nightmare Sea than we can. If anyone can help us understand it, it's you."

He tilted his head, bird-like. "The Flood took my old self as surely as it took the old world. My memories have probably been devoured by the Nightmare Sea. If you intend to bring me home to roost, you should give me a new name."

Stone grinned under the helmet and reached out with zir one intact arm. "Come back with us, Angel."

Angel smiled, folded his wings in tight, and hopped back inside.

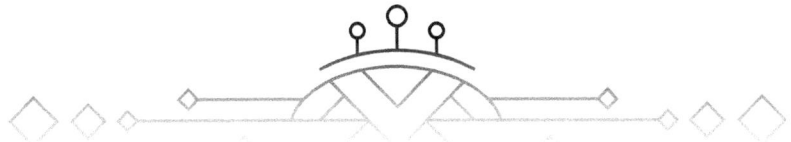

Lyonel Loy

We Might Contain Multitudes

bipoc, body horror (minor), death of an animal, harm to animals, magic use, misgendering (accidental), non-binary, non-human character, present tense, sentient animal, sentient construct (magical), telepathic communication, third person limited point of view, undeath, united states of america, vermont

Wild aether is blanketing the Vermont hillside, low and heavy like unseen fog.

"Forecast said nothing about this," Kwok grumbles. The shadow of someone else's rage washes through them—*forecast wrong!*— unfocused, uncomprehending, and easily ignored. The fury-sprite has been bound to Kwok for six days now and had been flitting about, murderous and free, for three more before that; its wrath is almost spent.

It had fought the binding fiercely but mindlessly. The fury-sprite had not enough to its shape: little more than leaked aether joined by the reflected anger of a passing argument, not enough to form a self.

On Kwok's shoulder, Ki-san wrinkles his nose and stomps his little chinchilla feet, gentle irritation thrumming through the part of them that was Ki-san-and-Kwok long before Ki-san chose his name.

Kwok reaches up to scratch their construct under the chin.

"Yes, I know." They try to speak aloud to Ki-san these days, even if Ki-san knows their every thought. The first year after they moved out of their mother's house, they did not speak at all. Who needs words when your best friend is sculpted out of aether and shards of your own soul? "Bad day for searching."

Not that there's ever a good day to hunt a target so small.

Today, they're after the coalesced fragments of loose aether from within the fresh-killed carcass of a little girl's pet rabbit. Young Hazel had named Bigwig for her favorite character in her favorite book, using the English word because her little brother couldn't say the Lapine form "Thlayli," and *Watership Down* was her favorite book because the hero shared her name.

Hazel had stared up at Kwok with shocked, red-rimmed eyes as her parents ran through the standard litany of excuses.

"Can't think how that leak was missed," the parents had said, wringing their hands over the inspection reports of their aether pipes. "We'll have to take the inspector to court."

Of course the parents knew how the leak was missed, and there would be no one to take to court; Kwok knows a hastily falsified report when they see one. They'd nodded along obligingly regardless.

Fury-sprites born of passing arguments, possessed corpses of small, dead animals—these are precisely the types of easily preventable mishaps that pay their bills, after all. "The Aetherwright's Union has a community program to assist with no-fault leaks," they told the parents, their own part in the ridiculous song-and-dance that precedes the majority of Kwok's jobs. "Have you called their public helpline? They can provide legal aid and some reimbursement."

On cue, the parents hemmed and hawed. "We shouldn't like to bother the authorities over so small a matter," the father tried. "It's only a rabbit, after all. Of course we would have reported it immediately if it were anything more dangerous."

"Can we come to some…alternate arrangements?" the mother asked with a little more honesty. "The insurance premiums—you know how it is."

Kwok's alternate arrangements will cost the parents more than the insurance penalty for a no-fault leak, but the song must be sung and the dance must be danced. No one came to harm, for a certain value of harm; the only victim was poor Hazel, who had been crying over the body of her dead pet when the loose aether found the body.

Most crafters would have turned them down, even on a clear day without wild aether to muddle the trail, rather than try to find an aether form so small.

But most crafters aren't Kwok.

"Split out," they say now to Ki-san in the middle of a copse of quaking aspen and paper birch surrounded by suffocating aether fog. "I'll need all of you on this."

Ki-san scratches a soft round ear, twitches his fuzzy tail, and shivers himself apart.

Ki-ya—the oldest of Ki-san, the wildest and the boldest—is racing east to take point before his full shape takes form, aether swirling in a wild dance around the darting specter of a grasshopper mouse.

Ah Kiat leaps out behind him, chittering for *Planning! Search grid! Come back!* The only answer is a distant ululating howl, and Ah Kiat squeaks with a chipmunk's wrath as he trundles southwest to form their second corner.

A miniscule harvest mouse with glowing beetle wings remains on Kwok's shoulder where Ki-san had sat. Golden wing-caps adorn her back today; Kiitos had never settled on a fixed form and has no wish to. With a nose to Kwok's cheek and an affectionate flutter of gossamer wings, Kiitos flickers out of sight, beelining northwest.

Wild aether is blanketing the hillside, smothering Kwok's aether-sense and hiding the world. But three bright points flare out around Kwok, like torches in the mist. They have been Ki-san-and-Kwok for over half of Kwok's life, and there is no aether thick enough to hide any part of Ki-san from them.

A short-lived scrap of aether in a rabbit's borrowed corpse does not leave much of a trail, even on a good day, and it is not a good day.

But Kwok is very, very good, and with Ki-san—with all of Ki-san— they are better.

Ah Kiat finds the dead rabbit first.

They are sniffing at each other when Kwok and the rest reach them, Ah Kiat with officious zeal and the dead rabbit with an absent sort of interest, still dragging itself gamely northward—due north.

Bigwig-the-pet looks nothing like its literary namesake, with long lop ears and fluffy black-and-white fur. Three days dead—three days on the run—but the aether form within it has kept the corpse in good shape.

"Where are you off to, then?" Kwok asks, and the dead rabbit has no answer. The aether form within it whispers *north, north* in a voice that is not words. *North.*

"Why north?"

The aether form, like the rabbit, does not reply. Bigwig never saw the hawk that killed it, never noticed its broken back, and so the dead rabbit and the aether form within know only idle alertness, the taste of sweet grass, the distant curiosity of a pampered pet, and that strange, unnatural pull of *north, north, north.*

On her usual perch on Kwok's shoulder, Kiitos flaps her wings and shifts with a minute rush of aether. Her gossamer beetle wings with golden wing-caps are replaced by a pair of brown-furred bat's wings, leathery and far too vast for her little harvest-mouse form.

"Yes, it's all very gothic," Kwok agrees.

Ki-ya leaps forward to orbit both the shuffling dead rabbit and an annoyed Ah Kiat. In an excited hop-skip dance, he rounds them both—once, twice—then just as quickly loses interest and rockets away. *North,* he squeaks when Ah Kiat yells. He wants to find out what draws the rabbit north.

Nothing lies north that Kwok can feel, not that anyone would sense anything in the middle of the suffocating aether. But Kwok's aether sense is sharp; "nothing" to them means there is no presence great enough to cut through the fog. There is nothing strong enough to harm Ki-ya; they can leave their most excitable construct to his game.

"You're far from home," they tell Bigwig.

The dead rabbit is not Bigwig—not anymore—and home is no longer the house with little Hazel and her fretful parents and their uninspected aether pipes.

The stray aether form that inhabits the floppy-eared dead rabbit is closer to being Bigwig than anything else, though. Nothing more than loose scraps of aether drawn to and joined with the last dregs of a dying rabbit's life. In the absence of any other self, all it has is to be half a rabbit.

Bigwig was eating dinner when the hawk it didn't see came swooping down, and well-fed calm echoes through Kwok as they weave binding threads around the stray aether scraps that are halfway to a rabbit. There is no alarm at the binds, only a lazy twitch of dead lop ears. The aether form releases its hold readily when Kwok calls, drawn by the steadier, stronger weight of Kwok's power.

It struggles only once, brief and perfunctory, when Kwok binds it, then settles against the core of all that is Kwok, next to the deep-rooted union of Ki-San-and-Kwok, beside the fading wrath of the fury-sprite. The abandoned body of the dead rabbit sags, and Kwok gets the impression of a twitching nose and half-raised ears, the remnants of a rabbit's natural caution.

That idle calm turns into a rabbit-swift spike of alarm that has Kwok rearing up, head raised, trying to lift large lop ears that they do not have before they remember themself. Ki-ya is calling in the distance, his excitement thrumming across the part of them that is all of them.

There is a man walking, Ki-ya reports, in an excited rush of not-words that Kwok knows better than they know their native tongue.

Wait for me, Kwok tells Ki-ya sternly in their shared voice that is not words as they carefully wrap Bigwig's little dead body in a little white shroud, tucking it securely into their backpack to be brought home to Hazel.

("I know he's dead," Hazel had said when Kwok spoke to her before they started their search. "I just want to say goodbye.")

Kiitos chirps her own melancholy at the memory, tucking her tiny head under vast bat wings.

Kwok still does not feel the man that Ki-ya is watching; they cast their sense directly out to the bright point of eager excitement that blazes through the aether fog, due north. They hurry through the trees, following the fading trail of Ki-ya's aether, down to where an aether-bright grasshopper mouse is scuttling up and down the rotting trunk of a dying beetle-bored ash, peering down the dirt path at a walking man with dark hair and dark eyes and a face as rare as Kwok's in this part of New England.

To Kwok, the man looks more Korean or a mainlander than Malaysian Chinese, but here in New England, in America, they've been asked, "Are you from China?" often enough that they've learnt to stop guessing at these things.

Far more important than where this man is from is that he is out walking alone in wild aether thick enough to choke on. With an aether presence so faint that none of them had noticed him before he walked into Ki-ya's sight, the man cannot defend himself from the miasma around them.

No aether presence means no aether strength, and that he does not notice even this heavy fog means that he received no training at all. Kwok had thought that they teach all American children the basics now, regardless of strength. But perhaps this man, like Kwok, didn't grow up in America.

Kwok will have to walk him out of this fog.

It will be a long trek. Kwok started their search early this morning, long before sunrise. They were not moving in a straight line, but meandering along half-hidden game trails and splashing across streams. If they bring this man back the way they came, it will be hours of rough hiking going late into the night, surrounded all the way by the heavy aether fog.

The forecast has already failed once today; there is no way to tell if the fog will get worse.

Or they could retrace the man's trail and follow the dirt path back. It might be a longer walk—Kwok does not know that route—but a dirt path means there must be shelters, the nearest perhaps half an hour away at a brisk pace. They could remain with the man amongst the shelter's ward stones, protected from the aether fog, and send Ki-San ahead to the town to call for a rescue.

It might be a long wait for an extraction if there are many unwary hikers likewise stranded by the unexpected fog, but it might also be the only way this man gets out unscathed and unaltered. Kwok isn't quite strong enough to shield them both if the fog should grow worse.

The latter, then.

They slip out of the trees, Ki-ya leaping to join Kiitos on Kwok's shoulder. The man stops, smiling and unconcerned, watching their progress.

He must have no sense of self-preservation whatsoever—and the luck of the devil besides—to have walked so far alone unmolested. But with no aether sense to speak of, how could he have known? Kwok curses the faulty forecast again.

"Sir," they say as they step onto the dirt path beside the man, "you shouldn't be out alone today. There's a bad fog."

"A fog?" asks the man, and laughs. "I think not."

Kwok, scowling, steps closer—an aether fog is no laughing matter— and looks for a single careless moment into the man's eyes.

And spiral down, and down, into the foreverness of the stars.

These eyes have seen eternity.

These eyes have danced in starlight.

These eyes have lived, have borrowed, have stolen a thousand lives.

The creature before Kwok may once have been man or woman or child, but what it is now and what it was before, no one knows—maybe not even itself.

When Kwok returns at last to themself, Ki-San is screaming: all three of Ki-San all together, three voices ringing as one, little clawed paws scrabbling at Kwok's face and neck and chest. Kwok is curled in on themself on the trampled dirt path, gravel digging into their knees, and the creature with eternity in its eyes stands and watches and chuckles low, almost like a person.

"Sir—" Terror has adhered Kwok's tongue to the roof of their mouth; the weight of eternity has driven the breath from their lungs. But this thing is neither *sir* nor *he*. "Master crafter—"

Master crafter. *Demon*, or so the stories go, the cautionary accounts, the tales whispered under torchlight by giggling children, *yao-guai, soul-eater*.

Don't bind too much; you will forget your own name.

Don't craft your constructs too strong. They will devour your soul.

"Call us whatever you like," the master crafter says, and their smile is almost human. "There will be someone in us that answers to it. But if it comforts you to use a name, you may call us Guo."

"Guo" is not this creature's name. It is only the Mandarin form of Kwok.

Does *call-us-Guo* mirror the name of everyone they meet? Does Guo still have a name of their own?

They feel the questions like a burst of sadness that all of Ki-san echoes, trickling like water through parts of them even past the pounding heart-beat of *monster, monster, monster*. The half-a-rabbit flattens its lop ears against its back; the remnants of the fury-sprite mourns.

And another realization, one that prickles like a thousand pins dancing over the back of their neck: they never told Guo their name.

"Ah, there are three of you in one," Guo says to Ki-san when the parts of Ki-san tumble together to stand perched on Kwok's shoulder on little chinchilla feet, and they laugh a very ordinary laugh. "He is skilled, this young crafter of yours."

I am not a he, Kwok does not say, but Guo hears them anyway.

"Not a he," Guo says, and their eternal eyes glimmer with the light of unknowable stars. "What are you, then?" As though they had to ask. They smile too wide, too inhuman, too knowing.

"They," Kwok says, because questions by one such as Guo must be answered.

"You are a they," Guo says, and there is something in the galaxy of their eyes that is almost like concern, and perhaps that is why they asked. Perhaps that is why they made Kwok respond. "And how long have you been a they?"

"Half my life." Kwok has heard this question before, too many times, always with sweet smiles and false concern. *We are only worried about you. With your profession, it might be safer to manage your...inclinations in some other way?*

But Guo's concern is not false. This question, Kwok does not resent, not when the forgotten *who* that became the thing that is now Guo knows the meaning of the answer—and has paid the price.

"It's just me who's a they," they feel the need to add. "Ki-san's a he, and all the parts of him are he or she. It's not—we're not—"

We are not like you.

Guo—all of Guo—laughs, and this laugh is not ordinary at all. Soft and light like tinkling bells, low and rasping like a knife on a log, high and clear like the child something in them must once have been. "Very well," they say. "As long as you're sure. Now, follow me."

They turn and walk southward, back down the path they came from, looking as ordinary as any young man striding down the roads of Ipoh. Confident and careless, as if they already know Kwok will obey.

The ward stones of the sheltered clearing are not humming when Kwok stumbles in behind Guo. They wait silent, smothered, their power buried under the heavy presence of the aether fog.

But the fog is not a fog; Kwok learned that as they walked.

The weight of it had grown on them, trapping them like a thick blanket on a sweltering tropical day. Their breath came short and fast until they had at last been driven to their knees.

Only then had Guo looked back, and the fog had shifted, lifting around Kwok and Kwok alone. They still feel its presence: close, swirling around them, barely held at bay.

The fog is not a fog at all.

The fog smothering the hillside, as vast as the sky and the sea, is Guo's. The all-consuming aether presence of Guo—who does not hunt alone.

There are master crafters in the sleepy hills of New England, waiting among the silent ward stones.

The first has eyes like a spider's, arrayed out neatly in rows, and the spider eyes sparkle in a riot of colors that Kwok's human eyes should not have been able to see.

The next has no mouth yet whispers ceaselessly, an uninterrupted flow of half-recognizable words in a myriad of voices and a myriad of tongues like a mountain stream in heavy rain, swirling over and around itself like dancing water.

The last is Guo, whose name is not truly Guo. Guo, who could be any ordinary young man on the streets of Ipoh or Singapore or Seoul except for their eternal eyes, and yet it is they who scare Kwok most of all.

They are master crafters; they have lost their souls. Where they walk, death follows.

What lurks in these hills that the union called on three?

The fog of Guo's vast presence is shifting around them, swirling and strengthening outside the cocoon of lighter air held around Kwok like a shield. The words of titans, a conversation that heaves and crashes in waves more enormous than the distant sea—the songs of whales are not meant for fish.

"—but we are being impolite," Guo says suddenly. In an ordinary voice and with ordinary words, much too ordinary for the eternity in their eyes. "This is Kwok. They've had rather bad luck, being caught here with us today. Got in just before the roads closed, we suppose, and no one's coming in after them. 'Acceptable losses,' that's the term."

All the three laugh.

"A they, did we hear?" asks Spider-Eyes. They have too many eyes, and their laughter skitters like too many spider legs, but they smile with just one mouth and that mouth has no teeth.

"Aye, a they," Guo says, "but not the same sort of they as us three are, or so they say."

"As long as they are sure," says Spider-Eyes. "As long as they know themself. She didn't. She turned away from who she was, tried to bury herself in us. Thought she was strong enough to remember." The eight eyes blink, one by one, in a flicker of dancing lights. "She wasn't, and we drained her dry."

"You must know yourself," the mouthless one agrees, and their myriad of voices whisper in melodious chorus, the same question asked in countless tongues: *who, who, whom?* and 你是谁 and *hvem! hvem!* "But we are scaring the whelp."

"Let them be afraid," Guo says. "None of us were frightened enough."

"Hold on to your fear," the mouthless one tells Kwok, and their voices whisper, *Hold on hold on holdholdhold.* "Hold on to yourself. We hunt for one of ours who did not. Our cousin, if you will. He bound too much and lost himself. He ate and destroyed. We have driven him to these hills where he hides and calls for lost and wayward things to sate his hunger. All he remembers is how to feed."

"But we sent out our own call," Guo says, "to smother his."

"Guo is strongest," Spider-Eyes agrees, "as is his call."

And the half-a-rabbit wakes, deep inside all that is Kwok, and whispers *north, north.*

"But there are three of you," Kwok whispers.

For three long days, Guo's siren song has drawn the half-a-rabbit north, even through the fog of their power that smothers the world; what horror lies in wait that Guo alone is not enough?

"Ah, do not fret. Just one of us is needed to devour." Spider-eyes laughs; their laughter skitters and skitters and crawls. "Three to carve with care, for some value of care. It will be a messy fight, either way."

"This cousin of ours—he was a fool to bind so much so quickly. But not so much a fool that he did not pay his union dues. Us three together can hack out the parts that were never him; if the he who was before is very lucky, there will be enough of that he still left to salvage."

"And he will be one of you, after?" Kwok dares to ask, and Guo smiles. It is a crooked, ordinary smile.

"No, no," Spider-Eyes says. "We bind. But we shape also. We sculpt. Our cousin has no self. We have too many."

"You should go now," Guo says. "Follow the trail south; we hunt our cousin north. We'll keep our fight off you if we can. Be fast, be lucky, and you might yet live to return to your aether pipes and dead rabbits."

"You're an interesting one," the mouthless one adds, and their eyes crinkle in what might have been a smile, if only they had a mouth to smile with. "Would be a shame if you didn't."

Kwok feels the battle begin long before the noise reaches them, a thrum through the vastness of Guo's presence like the ripple of a stone cast into a lake.

But ripples die on still lakes, and this one does not.

The ripple gathers and grows, rebounding in and around itself, until it surges with a roaring suddenness into a wave of fury and cacophony that snaps trees like twigs, shatter rocks, and tears the world apart.

Kwok runs.

Their feet slip and slide over stones damp with moss, they stumble over roots, and they are not fast enough. No one could be fast enough. Still they run, and Ki-san runs with them.

"Go," they implore Ki-san. "Run ahead. You're strong enough; you'll live even if I don't."

But Ki-san leaps upon their shoulder to bite at them in fury with razor-sharp chinchilla teeth, splitting himself in three so three voices can scold Kwok at once, and Kwok does not ask again. They only run for a safety they know they cannot reach.

Behind them, the noise grows. A rumble and a howl and a scream, louder than a thousand thundering hammers, louder than a freight train passing close enough to touch, and still it grows—how can it keep growing? The world must break from the noise—

The world breaks.

There is a rending, a shattering, a sundering—at once silent and deafeningly loud. Kwok halts, turns, and the hillside seems to pause with them. All life is quiet and still, watching and waiting and hiding.

Trees are broken and torn in the distance. The heavy clouds in the sky have parted, or have been parted, like a jagged scar or a gaping, yawning maw. The silence hangs like the moment between two heartbeats, stretches like a line pulled too thin. The skin on Kwok's neck prickles—an ancient instinct, an ancient warning. Ki-San huddles against their chest.

The silence shatters.

A season's worth of storm pressure rolls down all at once, and the hillside is screaming. Free aether slices through the air and earth and every living being on the hills, bringing the world into blinding focus. For one brief eternity there is no Kwok, no Ki-san, no birds in the trees, no trees. There is only an awful, final oneness, everything around them joined. For that brief terrible eternity, every broadleaf tree of New England knows every street of Ipoh, half the world away, that Kwok ran down as a child, and Kwok knows the meaning of birdsong and the sweetness of water at their roots and the relief at the shedding of a dead branch—

Then the terrible tide passes.

Kwok, alone, would have fallen, and maybe they would never have gotten up again. But Kwok is not alone. The half-a-rabbit within them is half nothing at all and knows little, but it knows the terror of little, hunted things in the face of a hunter, and it squeals within them, fearmaddened.

Stunned and reeling, Kwok is seized by an instinct older than aether magic and stronger than exhaustion. They stamp a warning no other rabbit is listening for, try to flash a tail they don't have, and bolt for a burrow that isn't there.

They run, rabbit-scared, and all the hillside runs with them.

A fox races past, her last living kit gripped tight in her jaws, and Kwok knows from the lingering echoes of that momentary oneness that the rest of her children are dead in her den with their little hearts burst, fallen before the strain of the roaring aether tide.

A sparrow swoops overhead, crying in muddled grief, fragments of shell glued to his belly by the yolks of the eggs that shattered under him as he crouched in futile defense of his nest.

A whitetail stag stumbles amongst the fallen trees, terror driving it back up onto bleeding feet every time it falls.

Then, like the shrapnel of an exploding grenade, shards of a shattered aether form spray out across and over the broken forest, invisible to the eye yet burning white-hot in Kwok's sense.

Shards of mindless rage, of all-consuming hunger.

Shards of an aether conglomerate whose crafter lost control. Too wild and too unformed to pass for anything like a construct, nothing to itself but the howl of *more, more, more*.

The largest of the shards are leashed almost before they notice their freedom, icy chains of Guo's power curling around the white-hot flames of their rage, forcing them to heel. The others are hunted down one by one—by skittering spider laughter, by dissonant whispers.

The smallest pieces, too small to sustain themselves and too numerous to count, spray out as fine and unstoppable as mist.

But one shard, hidden in the mist, slips through the net, and it hungers.

Desperate, mindless, and torn asunder, it careens forward. All it knows is to devour, to consume, to make itself grow, and the strongest presence before it is Kwok.

That passing freight train is no longer passing; Kwok is on the tracks, and the train is bearing down.

The train is torn aether and demon-teeth and hunger, and Kwok is swept up in a raging tide, at once boiling hot and freezing cold, a whirlpool that demands their entirety, a maelstrom howling eternally for *more*.

Through the battering and the all-consuming hunger, they feel Ki-San launch himself into them, into that bone-deep, soul-deep part of them that is Ki-san-and-Kwok. Clinging, lending his strength and his self, holding on with everything he has.

And then all they feel is hunger, and all they know is rage. It drags them down, down, down toward a place where they have no name, where there is no Ki-san, no Kwok, no self.

More, the hunger and the rage screams, *More, more*.

But Kwok was not the name their mother gave them, or their father, and they have not always been *they*.

They have given up their name before. A different name, an older name, the name their parents spoke over them at their birth. They have given up parts of themself before, piece by painful piece, carving out the fragments that did not fit, did not suit. They have fought for every piece they gave up, for every piece they grafted into place, every piece they claimed.

It has taken them too long to become Kwok. They have fought too hard. They will not give this self up; this self is theirs.

They know who they are.

The aether shard screams its rage around them, through them, within them.

Kwok curls themself around all that is them, all that is Kwok, all that is Ki-san and Ki-san-and-Kwok. They know who they are. They will not give a single sliver of themself without a fight. The aether shard surrounds them, and there is nothing in their world but aether and hunger and rage—like a python wrapped around its prey.

Kwok holds onto every hard-won part of themself.

If this is the day their story ends, it will end with their name. They will end as themself, as Kwok and as Ki-san-and-Kwok.

The aether shard floods them with rage that is not theirs—they know the taste of their own rage. The aether shard fills them with hunger that is not theirs—they know the edge of their own hunger. The aether shard swallows them whole, coalescing, engulfing, inescapable.

Kwok makes themself impregnable in turn, lets the rage and the hunger that is not their own wash over and through them.

They saw once, long ago, on a school trip to Taman Negara, a python with its stomach burst, the hooves of a sambar deer hanging out of its split belly. The dead deer had claimed its vengeance even in death.

If the aether shard wishes to feed, let it too choke upon its meal.

The shard rips into them with claws that cut as sharp as the name they gave up long ago. The shard squeezes tighter and tighter, hungrier and hungrier, desperate for life.

Kwok holds onto themself just as tightly, just as fiercely. They will not be torn apart to linger as a remnant in someone else's self; they will cling on instead to their death.

But their end does not come today.

The aether shard writhes and howls. Its last cry wavers and tapers.

It dissolves into fog.

"You made it," says Guo from above them. There is something like pleasure in their eternal eyes. "We did not think you would."

"Oh," the rescuers say when Guo introduces them. "How long have you been a they?"

Kwok grins wide. Their cheek tingles where Guo had placed a hand briefly, like a benediction, before handing Kwok over to the rescuers' care. "Long enough," they say.

The rescuers frown, worried and fretful, and Kwok smiles wider.

They are alive. They have seen what no one still called human has seen and come out as themself; words and worry cannot touch them now.

The rescuers load them carefully into the helicopter sling and strap them in tight. Quietly and cautiously, shooting wary glances toward where Guo waits perched on the broken log of what was once a paper birch.

Their smile is still much too ordinary for the eternity in their eyes.

The sling jerks, and the line grows tight. The closest rescuer, holding them steady as they rise, leans in. "Ask for help if you need it," she says, and there is a light like the beginning of stars in her eyes; she may not be a she much longer. "The union has resources. Ask for help *before* you need it."

Deep inside all that is Kwok, a rabbit that is a little more than half a rabbit twitches its nose and drums its hind feet. Impatient to be off, impatient to run. The fury-sprite's strength has faded, the last of its rage surrendered.

All that is left of it is a fierceness that lingers in the seed of what was once the dying traces of a freshly killed rabbit.

The rabbit is only half a rabbit. It is not yet a self.

But the seed of a self-to-be is alive and growing, and already it knows its name.

The gusting winds from the blades of the helicopter steal away the rest of the closest rescuer's words. Kwok laughs for the joy of laughing, floating high on the thrill of their own survival. Ki-san chuffs. The half-a-rabbit twitches its ears.

"It's nice to meet you, Thlayli," Kwok says.

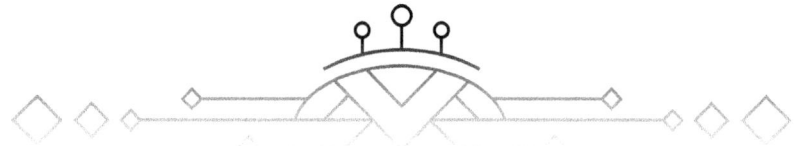

ilgaksu

chameleon trick

be gay do crimes, be gay solve crimes, established relationship, heist, m/nb, manchester, misgendering, non-binary, past tense, present tense, suicidal ideation (mentions of), third person limited point of view, trans male, united kingdom

*I*t's early; too early. So, of course, Martha's boss is more than happy for her to be walking through Manchester's side streets to the factory.

The fact she enjoys it, in all its hushed, wet inhale, the rainwater pooling, sun-neglected, on the pre-dawn pavements, feels like a betrayal of her deeply justifiable moral outrage. But there's something beautiful about the city in the half-dark, blurred into water-polished grey and rough, tawny reds, the rapid climb of two-hundred-year-old buildings above her head, plunging half of the journey in chiaroscuro from their single shadows. She's diminutive in comparison, just one person, hair like a cropped mouse and eyes to match and a sensible sort of coat—but for how, when she strides forward too fast, the slide of it against her body reveals a neon-yolk lining to the neutral wool, satiny and liquid and rippling—

She likes to imagine how it looks to people passing, crowded up against her on the tram or glimpsing her through the window of a corner shop. The extraordinary rarely tend to autobiography, which is why Martha is curating her own.

As she approaches the factory, other people materialise onto the same streets, stamping boots into puddles, clutching warming devices or heated cups or blowing over their miserably ungloved hands. Martha passes a couple, one of them gently cupping the other's fingers to breathe their hot exhale over cold fingertips, the cuffs on their coat bleeding peach through its navy thread in reaction to the new temperature. In the intimacy of it, it feels as though she witnesses them through a door—one that, for all its transparency, is bolted shut.

Every other person has their heads down, reading on their phones.

These other people arrive in a flock of bright and shifting colour; one of the most widely reputed bonuses of working in this district is the ability to buy the offcuts at a price cut down to match. The owners love to see their staff as walking advertisements, flooding the area like a drop of dye in water. As though in response to the riot of texture, the sound of water and feet striking through it onto stone is always strangely muted; shimmering collars are turned up closer to mouths than not, the echo of body and movement as announcement.

Millman's Textiles does the opposite of rise out of the skyline. It is one more red brick building in a district of red brick buildings. It is one more textile factory in a city of textile factories, where the all-night-and-stopping-never of the looms glows green through mullioned windows. They spill mint light and newly minted cloth, the colour of the ever-moving machines comforting as a lighthouse through the glass. Up close, Martha can hear the faint hum of the aether, streaming through the looms and out into the streets. Some people find the sound grating, compounding hour by hour on the factory floor, like a song played over and over on your work-shift now forever associated with wanting to go home.

Martha has always found it soothing.

She isn't paying attention, too caught up in her own thoughts, so when she walks into someone else, she apologises, quickly and automatically, and keeps moving. Then, she nearly walks into a second person. She realises, a little late, that this is because other people have stopped walking, changing from human salmon into early morning obstacles. The sight makes her falter, too. Above her, the bulk of the factory has fully materialised, the green and shining insect eyes of each window—only—

The fourteenth floor. Again.

Usually, the fourteenth floor is the brightest. It blazes extraneous colour from the stained-glass window inset into the centre of the building, its central figure three times the size of a human man. Abundantia, serene-faced and blue-gowned and golden in her crown of wheat, fabric rippling from the gather of her fingertips. The fourteenth floor is where her expression sits, eyes and nose and mouth usually rosy-bright.

But right now, she's beyond smiling. In a place like this—without the customer-ready upward curve of her mouth—she might as well be faceless.

In the miasma of light, her blankness is stark as an open cut, as though someone has taken a blade and, very neatly, gouged out all of the green. A marching centipede's carapace of pitch black. This is how they can all tell that the fourteenth floor's machines have gone down. It's a simple power outage, but every single time she's seen it in the past few months, it's set Martha's teeth on edge, somehow worsening with each new event. The hairs on the back of her neck prickle, something small and animal-istic in the warning. For all the factory is an artificial creation, it's hard not to view the great gash of darkness in the building's imposing brick as a wound in the hide of some strange sentient beast.

It's an unhelpful sentiment. Martha needs to focus on the job in front of her, which now—as she tries and fails and tries again and finally pushes through the rising whispers of the ever-stopping crowd at the gates—is going to be so much harder.

Fucking Mondays.

Martha's boss is a man called Bevan. Bevan is tall and white and even-featured as a Michelangelo reject. Bevan is also a man whose characteristics are best confined to the maxim about how rare it is for middle-management to have competence at, well, middle-management. He even has the plastic smile to suit. By the time Martha makes her way to the fourteenth floor, Bevan is already waiting for her by the staff coat-hooks, holding two small pocket-lights. The handful of people proceeding up to the floors above this one collectively crane their necks to catch a glimpse of the pitch-dark corridor, their faces ghostly with curiosity as they peer through the rapidly closing gap of the elevator's resealing barrier.

"It's a disaster," he says to Martha in a tone that is borderline pantomime, because Bevan also speaks like someone who is permanently trapped in the never-ending keynote of an ethically dubious business expo. "I don't understand how this keeps happening!" He had begun talking at the faintest hint of the elevator opening, meaning Martha isn't the specific audience; he just wants an audience in general. This makes the next part of the conversation easier because she barely has to say anything of meaning.

"Hm," Martha replies. "Yes. It is very confusing."

She begins to unbutton her coat. Without waiting for her to finish, Bevan hands her one of the pocket-lights. He doesn't bother to switch it on. Martha inwardly sighs and finishes the buttons on her coat, sliding out of it one arm at time. She cannot fold it over her arm in her usual manner because she is forced by dint of having to hold the pocket-light to do the whole thing one-handed. With her now-freed hand, she presses her thumb over the pocket-light's sigil and waits for her body heat to complete the circuit.

Bevan starts down the hallway with far too much purported purpose for a man who currently has the displaced air of a particularly fussy hamster in sawdust. Through the glass panels of the great sliding doors at the end of the corridor, Martha can see the faint guttering sparks of an aether-pipe trying to fuel the looms. It's the only light in the room when they enter a few beats later. The ever-churning machines are silent; the looms look like the skeletal remains of strange aliens, bones needle-fine, the shimmering half-knit of the unfinished thread a fibrous flesh.

Martha turns and looks over her shoulder as the door slides back into its frame, but there's nobody else on the other side of the glass. The corridor looms away from her, back towards the elevator, empty and shadowed, leaving her stuck in the half-dark with Bevan.

"You know, I can't see where the sigils weren't balanced," Bevan says. "I really can't. You're usually so careful with it." His eyes dart to her face as they weave through the bestilled machinery; testing, probing, and ah, so that's how he's going to try and play this.

"I'm always careful with it, sir," Martha tells him with certainty, because she is. After all, in this job, a mistake like that could be crucial, couldn't it?

"But look. Look at this one!"

He crouches down, squatting in the way mid-level politicians do next to sickly orphans for the sake of popularity, and taps at the tempered panels above the power network riddling the foundations of this floor.

Martha joins him, matching the crouch and grateful having worked her way into the shift-manager position on a factory floor requires her to wear trousers.

Under these specific panels, freshly scoured the night before and therefore missing the footprints that would blur them during the day, lies the main interlocking sigils. They are chiselled into heavy stone slabs, underlaid with the circuits that set them into cycle. Usually, they glow almost bright enough to sizzle, sending up flares of light that dance and reflect off shoes and legs in small, parcelled shapes of refracted magic. Now, the most functional of them is a dim hum. Some have fizzed out entirely.

This is the fourth time this has happened in the six months she has been working here. She thinks it's only four because once every month would be too fishy; it takes three strikes in six months to file a chronic malfunction claim with the manufacturers. Someone, with four, thinks they're playing it safe.

After all, it is Martha's job to balance them. She is very good at her work.

"I've already sent out the alert for everyone to stay home today," Bevan says. "I know it's your job, really, but since I was here—" He pats her arm.

"Thank you," Martha says through gritted teeth, imagining how many people were already on their way to the factory when they found out. How many got turned away from the gates and had to walk home in the threat of rain? "That's generous of you."

Bevan, predictably, beams. "Well," he says after a pause that extends a little too long. "What should we do about this mess, Martha?"

"Transparently, sir," Martha replies carefully, "I haven't got a clue," and watches his face fall in disappointment. Before he can recover from it, though—

"Mister Bevan, sir," comes a clear, reedy voice with a heavy Polish accent.

Martha and Bevan both jump. When they turn, indisputably and uncomfortably in sync, a diminutive person in a cleaner's uniform is standing there beside their trolley of supplies.

"Oh, yes," Bevan replies. "This is—" He visibly does not remember their name. "This is the new cleaner, Martha." He gestures to them.

"I—" Martha replies, stuttering a bit. "I see."

Every tiny synapse feeds, sparking along themselves, magnetised, alight: despite herself, she is drawn in. She is drawing in. She even steps forward a little, and Sasha smiles. It's not a nice smile per se. It's the smug look of someone used, in the manner of a trophy cat, to being beautiful. It's a simple declarative: *yeah, I get that a lot*.

Despite everything, Martha begins to sweat under her clothes just from looking at them, her skin sticking to the neon of satin lining.

Sasha is still, somehow, smiling. It should be unnerving, for that smile to be held for so long. It's not. Martha finds himself smiling back. The moment stretches, then snaps under the sudden blare of Bevan's phone chirruping from his pocket.

"Sorry, sorry," he manages with the smug tone of someone who feels like this next fact will cement the view of their importance. "It's Katie. She's the director's receptionist, you know. I'll have to take this."

"Of course," Martha demurs.

"Don't worry about us, sir!" Sasha replies, practically singsong, and doesn't look away from Martha's face.

The second the door closes, Sasha turns on him; gleeful, sparking with it. It's less a dropping of a mask and more of a perfect, total illumination as they ask, "How did I do?"

You would think they were an amateur at this, looking at their borderline puppyish excitement. They even tilt their face up, less in expectation of a kiss and more in certainty of one. But they are both working. Martha has read the codes of conduct at this factory: no fraternisation during work hours. And so:

"I don't have time for your praise kink right now," Martha says, and sidesteps them.

Sasha jumping down his throat has given him less than a beat to acclimatise back into himself, so Martha takes a breath in and then out, and with it, he sheds performance, shifting across and outside the gender required for this job and back into being just himself. Like the internal lining of his coat, that bright sunshine flash of personality under the drab wool, who he is when he isn't working is consistent and clear and entirely blatant.

How many con artists can lay a claim to the public not even being certain of their gender? It's a nice little chameleon trick; little women get listened to less, and so for this job, he's been playing at womanhood. There ought to be some restitution for that past misery of puberty, after all.

Martha's tired. He's having regrets. This was meant to be an easy gig. In fact—

"I thought you said this was going to be an easy—"

"Don't start," Martha cuts them off, adding: "That's an unnecessary comment."

"Definitely. But very satisfying all the same." A pause. "I would never, ever say I told you so. But if I was, perhaps, going to say it—"

"You can contemplate all the occasions you want to say it on the sofa tonight, if you like."

"Well, that's unfair."

"Contemplation is a solitary pursuit, Sasha. If you want a life of the mind, who am I to stand in your way?"

"I'm going to report you to Human Resources."

"Go ahead."

They're visibly enjoying this. That's fine. Martha has never seen Sasha not be visibly enjoying this stage in a job. They only stop enjoying it when physical exertion comes into play.

How would Martha describe Sasha to a normal person? He's often wondered this, watching now as Sasha crosses their legs up on the machine, never mind that their cleaner's uniform, all neat black shirt and monogrammed tunic, rides up. Martha now has a direct line of sight to the painfully neon-green lace underwear they picked out this morning.

"My eyes are up here," Sasha points out, dipping their chin into the cup of their palms and staring at Martha expectantly. They pause, flipping their hair over one bony shoulder, strands catching on the tips of their nails. Today, it's ice blonde, long, and extension laden. Their nails are painted in a white lady's ideal French manicure but filed into sharp points. They wind one rebellious strand of hair around a finger. Usually, they would have lots of little aether-lights woven through in the shape of miniature insects—butterflies, fireflies, ladybirds—set to glow on sensing that the light has dropped to a certain dimness. But the factory has uniforms and dress codes, and Sasha does, in fact, know how to make themselves invisible when it counts.

The hair is a failed banishment, anyway; it'll start falling forward again in minutes. One of the things Martha had to get used to, and very rapidly, was hair in his face: during a kiss; while half-awake on a tram, Sasha leaning their head on his shoulder; Martha waking up in the night to it flung over his face along with Sasha's outstretched arm.

Love, when it was described to Martha growing up, never included the metaphor of someone else's hair in his mouth. But there it is.

Sasha smiles at him, wide and brilliant, and Martha—

Martha tries and fails not to smile back.

After all, that first time Sasha and Martha met five years ago, all Sasha had done was smile at him. Martha had been sitting in the shitty café of a bleak train station, debating whether to go somewhere or end it right there, and Sasha, working as the lone station barista, placed three of the free biscuits down along with the cheapest-thing-on-the-menu mocha and smiled with all of their immaculately, almost unnervingly, whitened teeth.

Martha had found himself returning the next day, buying a ticket he didn't need to then buy a coffee he didn't need and crumble the second round of little biscuits inside his mouth, chalky with sugar.

Then, he had returned the day after that, too.

It had taken a week before Sasha had gone, in a tone of honeyed pity, "Baby, you don't have to try so hard," and told him what time they finished work.

And their current line of work is, as it happens, far simpler than it first sounds. Admittedly, this specific job is an outlier, but it was a special request. Sometimes Martha listens to those, if they're phrased nicely.

"Am I going to have to stay up all night again?"

"Yeah," Sasha replies. "Sorry."

Martha saw this one coming. "Fine. I'll give you this one on credit, but you owe me."

"Oh," Sasha says, rolling the syllables in their mouth like dissolving syrup, "trust me. We can work out how I pay off my debt later."

Then, of course, they wink. Martha hears himself sighing.

"I just like watching pretty girls suffer," Sasha told him that first evening, all plum lipstick over honey-singed pastries.

It had been raining outside the low-lit, late-night café, and the water made patterns on the window near them like imprinted velvet. Martha had not been on a date in six years. The fact of this, and the reality of Sasha's mouth, made him jittery.

"I'm not a girl," Martha told them in return without even thinking, and then debated taking that truth back. But even if he could, he—

It was, perhaps, the first time he had said it out loud beyond his own mirror, in a heady, alchemical whisper close to scrying: a summoning of himself out of the truth of the glass. It seared his mouth like stomach acid in its might, but the fact of it stayed there, unceasing.

Sometimes, telling a stranger is the easiest place to start with your secrets. And it's not like Martha had anyone else to tell.

"Oh, samesies!" Sasha replied brightly, and had patted him on the thigh, as easily as that. "Isn't it nice to have something in common on a first date?"

Martha's brain had hooked on those words, *first date*, and promptly fallen through the floor, and only managed to crawl back to him sometime before dawn, in Sasha's bed, in a shirt last seen on the least-distinguished member of an amateur theatrical troupe. He had looked up at the ceiling, wondering how in the Maker's name he would pick through the chaos of the floor to get ready for his day quietly, because Sasha's apartment seemed to be the human equivalent of a mouse nesting inside an heiress's wardrobe: a mattress on the floor surrounded by clothes in all kinds, tulle, sequin, crochet. The worn cotton of the shirt Martha had been handed to sleep in, with a slightly dingy tinge to it, was extremely soft.

Isn't it nice to have something in common? Martha had thought. *Well, it's the only thing.* Then, *but, you know, it's something. It's something, isn't it?*

"Did you mean to con me out of something?" Martha asked at last, a year out from that early morning, that dusk-light and the shirt against his skin. "When we met? Was that the plan?"

Sasha looked up from filing their nails in surprise. They were on a train to Neo-Warsaw, and it was a last-century model of shuttle. It rattled, riddled with graffiti, stapled onto new wheels that the powers-that-be thought might put off replacing the main body another winter. It felt, the more the sound of ice skeetered against the windows, to be a wildly optimistic hope at best.

"You know," Sasha replied, "I'm not sure, actually. I think I saw you and I just—" They made a little, helpless gesture.

"It's not like I had anything left to give at that point," Martha admitted. "You could probably tell that," then blinked as Sasha threw a spare lip gloss at his nose.

"No," they said, short as if scolding a cat, and filed their nail a little more viciously in punctuation. "Don't do that. We've talked about it."

"Do what?"

"Go find someone else to sit with if you're going to talk about yourself like that," Sasha said. "I don't want to listen to it." Their face softened out of the sulk for a breath. "I don't think of you like that."

"Okay," Martha said, surprised.

"I mean it. I don't." Sasha tilted their glasses—fake ones, encrusted with rhinestones—down their nose to peer at Martha over the rims of them. "And I know I have good taste."

That first night felt a little like what it would be to die from aether-overload. Not touch as photosynthesis, but worse. To be lit all through and gutted by the strange, hissing, rising sear of pure and unadulterated power, only the conduit was the pale commas of their own twisted limbs.

Sometimes with aether, if the first shock doesn't kill you but still fries each synapse and small nerve like oil on hot metal, you end up so riddled with it that you die later, slower, from poisoning. Maybe this is their aftermath. Maybe Martha is living in the aftermath, the by-degrees death of it. A walking ghost, unaware of it because of how alive he still feel. And hasn't this job, each one in series, made them both into utter shadows?

But weren't they, in some ways, despite that neon-yellow coat's lining and Sasha's aether-braided hair, already invisible?

The breaking-and-entering aspect of this job is easier than most.

Although Martha appreciates simplicity, he misses watching Sasha go at it with their lockpicks. In their hands, they turn into the cautious, scientific, steady instruments they are, each precise movement at odds with their usual personality, and they do have pretty hands. But Martha has to admit it's so much easier when, between "you as the most-recently hired shift manager" and "your girlfriend as the brand-new cleaner," they have a complete collection of the factory's master keys.

In the elevator, Sasha sighs and leans their head on Martha's shoulder. Even after years, the habit remains absurdly sweet. They yawn. Martha closes his eyes, and when he inhales, misses the usual scent of their various rotating perfumes. Scent can be a giveaway. It's strange, to miss someone already touching him. Martha strokes their hair once, twice, and then nudges Sasha off with his shoulder as the doors unseal and deposit them onto the correct floor.

In these clothes, they slip into the shadows as though into silk: entirely seamless. It had taken Martha three weeks of staying behind to feed the machines the program for a cloth that would blend entirely with the human eye and its perception of light, and two weeks before that to develop the program. This factory refused to pay overtime to anyone below manager status, and so Bevan had commended his commitment. All Martha had said, very mildly, was, "I hope to be an asset to the company, sir."

Covered like this from neck to wrist to ankles, they blend into the black and steal along the corridors in coordinated silence, velvet-foot-stepped and cupping one hand over the glint of an activated pocket-light to dim the glow. They can only see each foot in front of the other and the faint movement of their own reflections against the glass panels of the door, and then the floor itself as they settle into position behind one of the machines farthest from the door but close to the fire stairs. They'd argued every night over where to place themselves in relation to the floor's layout before finally, desperately resorting to flipping a coin; it had not, admittedly, been one of Martha's finest moments in terms of communication.

"I was the one hired for this job," Martha had argued, "and you are just along for the ride," and Sasha had elevated sitting in his eyeline, sulking, to a new art.

Right now, of course, they don't talk.

Martha's heartbeat slows. His world slows with it. It stretches, dream-like, membranous, until the only driving current is his own diaphanous exhales and the faint, echoing shift of movement. Sasha, silent in the way they only are when the job calls for it, breathes with him.

Time elongates, unspools, spins out.

Then, finally—

There's the sound of someone else, trying to be stealthy and being subpar about it, in the corridor.

Adrenaline skewers through Martha.

Sasha inhales a bit too audibly. Martha's hand, covered in a thin leather glove, darts out and covers their mouth.

Even through the leather, he can tell from the pressure when Sasha licks it.

Martha grimaces, then rolls his eyes. He can sense Sasha laughing inside their head, feel the weight of their eyes on him. He manages to pull his hand away before the door opens. His concentration narrows, eyes trying to focus even more sharply in the dark. For all his sight's adjusted, it's still grainy, static in the shadows, even as he splits his attention to concentrate on keeping his breathing even and therefore quiet.

In the dark, the figure moves with the hesitant semi-familiarity of a regular visitor. They make a beeline for the panel series covering the right spot. When they squat to contemplate the sigil array—

Listen, it doesn't matter that Martha that can't see his face, with those even, dentured features. He knows that specific crouch, the posture of it, the forced grimace of performed relatability in it.

Well, fuck.

"It's Bevan," Martha is forced to admit in a whisper and, despite said whisper, still audibly annoyed about it.

"It's Bevan!" Sasha echoes quietly with the vindicated joy of a child who has been presented with a surprise birthday party.

Martha is never going to hear the end of this one. "Shhh," and the thing is, he really does try to pitch it quiet. He does. But something about the sibilance sends it up, snagging on the air, and it shrills out across the factory floor.

Bevan stills.

So does Martha.

So, even, does Sasha.

"Is anyone there?" Bevan calls, straightening up slowly. He holds his hands out in a gesture of faux helplessness, so regularly seen on him during his less-overtly criminal moments that Martha has to repress an entirely horribly timed urge to giggle. Next to Martha, Sasha is vibrating with coiled energy.

After a few taut and bated seconds, Bevan turns away again.

"Thank fuck for that," Sasha whispers, and the thing this time is that Sasha is never, ever as quiet as they think they are, even if they try.

Within seconds, Bevan is back on his feet.

Like a matching pop-up toy, Sasha is on theirs.

"You!" Bevan says. Then: "Who are you?"

Of course. Of course he doesn't remember them. Resigning himself to the current situation, Martha sighs and rises to join the current stand-off.

"Martha?" Bevan queries, his face poised in a sort of comedically querulous surprise. Then, hardening into a more imminent danger: "Martha, don't be hasty. I can explain."

"I'm sure you can," Martha replies.

Very unsubtly, Bevan puts his hand in his pocket. In their line of work, it is never, as a rule, particularly reassuring when someone does that.

"You know I hate this part," Sasha grouses, and begins, as is inevitable in this sort of gig, to have to run.

⁂

"Are you going to keep the name Martha?" Sasha asked once, under their breath, while the two of them played at being faithful members of a church congregation.

Sasha had determined that one of the clerics was stealing from the offerings and felt it was therefore morally appropriate to steal from them in turn. Martha was percolating the ethics of this decision versus handing half back to the church. The argument was still pending.

A perfectly carved stone Abundantia smiled down at them from the altar; both Martha and Sasha were busy eyeing the priestess. She smiled beatifically, albeit in a fixed sort of way, under her cloth-of-gold headdress. Martha, bowing his head, replied, "I was planning to. Is this relevant right now?"

"No, just curiosity," Sasha said. "Call it sated."

Under the respectable outspreading of his coat, they took hold of Martha's hand and squeezed, just once. On the opposite row, one of the congregation glared.

And as it happened, Martha ended up endorsing Sasha's original plan. They took the money, all of it, and ran.

They really did plan to go for the fire stairs, the ones encircling the factory building like a long-dead vertebrae. But, like all great cluster-fucks, the road to hell is paved with the original plan. Which is to say, they run the opposite way.

It's dark.

They're under a great deal of stress.

It happens.

It's not Martha's finest moment.

Sasha has this grand idea that they can hold hands mid-flee. Martha, who is a practical applicant of concepts like gravity, aerodynamics, and the narrow passageways of old buildings, is under no such romantic illusions. It has taken a long time to ensure that Sasha doesn't try to make a sneaky grab for him as they sprint. Today, it seems the lesson has stuck.

Martha allows himself to appreciate it. Small victories flying in the face of nihilism and all that.

They clatter down the corridor, a one-way affair that doesn't mean they can split off in opposite directions to really ruin his evening, Bevan in enthusiastic pursuit. It's a more genuine show of effort and emotion than he's shown in the entire time Martha has been underpaid and un-derappreciated by him. It's almost unnerving, the abrupt flex of real ex-pression, like a creature's true form shifting beneath the wax of a human mask. It feels unsanitary somehow.

Martha doesn't stop running to figure out exactly what about it he dislikes.

He crashes into the elevator door at the end of the hallway, full-body, and slams his fist against the button to summon it. Then his fingers, stress-awkward, transform to jelly, because Martha knows, against all safety regulations, that the door to the fire escape at this end of the cor-ridor is firmly locked.

Martha really hates this company, actually.

"Fuck," Sasha says, noticing that fact; they aim a kick at the door, spirited but ineffectual. Aims another.

"Save it. You'll break your foot."

Martha feels Bevan's approach in the dark as much as hears it, and braces himself.

Impact in three, two, one—

The elevator door opens.

"Close it!" Sasha yells to Martha.

"I'm trying to close it!" Martha can't help but point out, as if his little, panicked button-pressing routine, now in reverse on the inside of the elevator, does not illustrate this sufficiently.

Bevan makes it halfway through the close of the doors, but Sasha does a repeat of the kick at the locked fire-escape door. This time it is twice as spirited and about five times more effective. Bevan falls back. The tempered glass of the floor panes rattles under the force of the landing.

The door closes.

The elevator descends.

Martha cannot make any sound, too busy trying to inhale. All the breath seems to have been punched out of his chest.

"I was not designed," Sasha spits beside him, sounding close to hacking up half a lung, "for functionality. I am *ornamental*, Martha."

Then, breath still catching in their throat, they pull the stun needle out from their bra, lifting it to their mouth, whispering the summons until it glows with a fresh, pulsing charge.

"Sure," Martha counters, watching this, "you're just a little Fabergé egg, aren't you?"

Sasha opens their mouth. The elevator stops. Dings.

"Oh, shit," Martha says, realising what's happening but only a mere second before it does. Without a beat to explain, he snatches the stun needle from Sasha's hand and holds it behind his own back.

The elevator door, summoned by someone standing on the floor below, opens.

There are no prizes for guessing who is on the other side of the door, or maybe there are: aren't a lot of game shows rigged, after all?

"Hello, ladies," Bevan says, muscling his way in as only someone with practice in hunting down someone two minutes overrun on a lunch break can.

Him finding them was, given that particular skill, only a matter of time.

There's a moment then, when Bevan coughs out a breath and it catches on the rim of his lips like water overspilling a cup's edge, that Martha is close enough to see in him the faint humanity of it all: the humidity of breath, the need for it. The faint lines around his eyes that all the invasive treatments offered, all those electro-facials and other people's cells injected under the skin, cannot stave off. The abhorrent, familiar texture of skin that proves that Bevan was born into this world, alone and without asking to be, the same as Martha, as Sasha, as anyone else struggling to get by. Maybe he also lies awake sometimes in bed, wondering what he's doing, wondering if the limited time he has left, the unknown ticking clock of it, is being wasted—

Not everyone is as certain as Sasha in their purpose. And it's a jarring moment; it almost stays Martha's hand. The stun needle in his hand trembles, his fingertips abruptly nerveless.

"You little bitch," Bevan spits, reminding Martha that Bevan is still, indisputably, an asshole. "I hate running."

Martha has been average and unasked for and the opposite of extraordinary his whole life. Martha has been displaced six ways to Sunday and nobody ever even noticed. But he is still a person. Martha is still a person and not a fucking *mouse*—

Martha used to compete for his city as a student of Lowell's School for Deserving Girls. Once, he'd even come in the top five.

And so Martha is, as it happens, someone who can run marathons.

"Don't worry, sir," he says, not even a little out of breath, diction clear and almost tender, and in his own voice he can hear a whisper of Sasha in the dark, certainty and clarity and— "I can come to you," and proceeds to drive the stun needle into the precise point of Bevan's neck and shoulder.

It's always the quiet ones, isn't it? Isn't that how the saying goes?

⟡⟡⟡

The next morning, they're on yet another train. This one is overnight and to somewhere; Martha doesn't remember where. It was the first one leaving this morning, and that was good enough.

Across from him, Sasha is examining their nails.

"I chipped one over that creep," they say, as dejected as someone newly bereaved. But perhaps, in this metaphor, a smaller bereavement—a very rich aunt with exhausting political opinions, for example. Martha makes an appropriate level of soothing noise in response. When they swing their feet, in white patent boots now, into the space between Martha's spread legs, he looks at them.

"Really?"

"They hurt."

"They hurt already?"

They had gone back to the apartment, to clear it out before they did the same, and are therefore no longer dressed like stereotypical cat burglars. They look like themselves again, Sasha in a neon lace minidress and matching cropped faux-fur bomber jacket, and Martha comfortable for the first time in weeks, in cargo pants and a button down and the familiar, tethering weight of heavy lace-up boots. There is a single ladybird-shaped hair clip on his shirt collar, at Sasha's insistence, because it wouldn't take in the short of his hair. He finds himself, absurdly, smiling at his own reflection in the window, pale and flickering but visible in the dark before dawn.

He kept the coat. That feels like his now, too, after everything.

Martha sighs and unzips Sasha's boots for them, ignoring the feline satisfaction emanating across from him.

In a factory on the other side of the city, Bevan should be sleeping peacefully. Well, about peacefully as one can in his situation. *Dreamlessly* might be a better descriptor.

It will take him another few hours, until minutes before the influx of the starting shift, to stir awake. Two jabs of a stun needle in a single night will take it out of you.

It was almost funny. They'd hauled him up in the elevator, then along the corridor right back to the looms; the shine of his brogues dulled in the drag over the floors, and Sasha had sighed.

"I feel bad that I don't feel bad for doing this," they said. "How are you doing? I'm fantastic."

"Don't drop him," Martha replied, and helped them lower him to the ground, head resting against the sabotaged machine, as though settling him against a pillow. Gentle with victory.

Bevan had returned to semi-consciousness midway through the loop-and-twist of the tightening ropes as they bound him to the spot next to the machine.

"Who are you?" he'd asked Sasha again, voice blurred. "I feel like I—"

"You do," Sasha replied shortly, all their usual whimsy stripped out of the voice, and tightened the hold of the ropes.

"I'm good with faces."

"No, you aren't." Sasha stands, pulls back their hair, painfully flat against their scalp, as though tied back into a uniform, regulation hairstyle. "When I was your receptionist, you made me remember everything for you."

In a more satisfying story, maybe this would be the point when Bevan finally recognised them. Before Sasha had been Sasha, they'd been young, and they'd needed a job, and they'd resigned themselves, as many do, to working for a consummate asshole for the sake of surviving. But for Bevan to have recognised Sasha, Bevan would've had to view Sasha, even before they had been Sasha, as a person. As it had been, "Sasha" had been printed text on a nametag, a body required to stand up whenever he walked into a room, an easy scapegoat when he pulled this gig somewhere else, because it's an insurance scam, isn't it, it's always an insurance scam with men in shirt collars and practised smiles. What part of it is even new? It's an old and well-worn story.

A body required to stand up whenever Bevan walked into a room; someone left standing when he took the money and ran. And so Sasha had considered the measly options left to them and taken off running too. They'd gone in the opposite direction to him, their shitty family, all of it, and they'd never looked back.

Until, of course, they met Martha. Martha—soft-spoken, timid-eyed Martha, whose demure smile was as much of a mask as Bevan's wide one had been and whose stomach yawned open with the grinding, rising resentment of the unremarked and unremarkable.

The quiet ones, remember?

Martha had offered to do the job for free. Sasha had explained it wouldn't be as satisfying if it was a gift. There had been intense negotiations. Said negotiations had ranged from the bed to the floor to the sofa to the shit thrifted coffee table that had, in a show of final, horrified protest, broken under their combined weight.

And it turns out, of course, that Bevan was playing the same game as before; it would take too much effort to learn a new one, maybe, or perhaps he simply didn't know how to make a new one stick the same. Martha didn't care. Martha applied for the job and practiced, once again, how to appear as small as he had once believed himself to be.

Mouse-like. Eyes down.

Bevan had eaten it up.

On that factory floor, Bevan had tried to guess Sasha's name, the name they'd used before they were Sasha. He'd gotten through four guesses and all of them wrong before Sasha had sighed, snatched the stun needle back from Martha, and stabbed him with it a second time.

"Sorry," they'd said, not sounding remotely so, "but I've heard enough of this man for a lifetime," and left him in the direct shadow of that stained-glass window, the one of Abundantia.

A goddess of plenty. She who provides.

Gods help those who help themselves.

In the train carriage, Martha is making a show of rubbing Sasha's feet.

"I love you," Sasha tells him, "so don't stop doing that," and closes their eyes.

Martha directs his smile towards the window even though he can't see anything beyond the glass. Outside, there are the first stirrings of dawn. It's going to be a beautiful day, probably. He's not sure it matters if it isn't.

"Those boots were a waste of money," he tells them, and waits to find out.

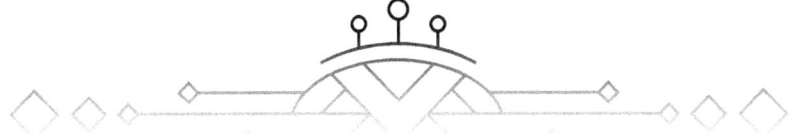

Catherine E. Green

To Hold the World Close

autistic, be gay do crimes, bipoc, capitalism is the real villain, empathy, established relationship, family, has a disability, heist, nb/nb, panic attacks, past tense, present tense, third person limited point of view

*A*drienne marvels at the ivy growing on their apartment building. Through a communion only possible with the discovery of lumine, Adrienne had kindly directed the ivy to grow in a fashionable configuration across the front and sides of the building. Xe thanked them for their work and their trust, vowing to persuade the building manager to ignore the slowly encroaching flora.

Tough though ivy may be, this ivy has seen its fair share of battle—against the elements, against pollution and other irritants, and against city officials. Adrienne is certain only a small portion of the original strain still lives, but its children and relatives from far-flung places remember their ancestors well and readily follow xyr gentle commands.

On xyr way through the front door, xe runs xyr hands along vibrant, verdant leaves, feeling more than hearing their contentment. It's a sunny summer day, after all, and basking in the sun's light is exactly what the ivy needs.

With a silent note of encouragement, Adrienne rolls inside, shutting the door behind xem with a soft *click*. The apartment, xyr and Celeste's, looks and feels much the same as xe left it this morning to work xyr shift at the university library. Lazy light refracts off the leaves of their collection of house plants near the front bay window. They, too, speak with the plants outside, a steady back-and-forth of pleasantries, exchanges of living conditions, and many—so many—new greetings and somber goodbyes.

The plants of many kinds are both a singular and a multitude, roots and seeds commingling between and among each other. The hydrangea, especially, is flourishing this year. Xe takes a cutting from one of its branches for the small vase on the kitchen table.

As Adrienne gazes at xyr handiwork, something pulls at the corner of xyr mind. It's gentle and yearning, but not in any particular direction, like how a deep well in space-time might feel to an outside observer, drawing nearby entities to itself without discernment or intention. They must be nearby—or drowning in the ocean of their own emotions—for Adrienne to feel drawn to them despite the protections xe has put into the place this week in preparation for tomorrow. While Adrienne doesn't have the time or emotional wherewithal to reach out to this person with the full range and depth of xyr capabilities, xe surrounds the swirling mass of fear, embarrassment, and grief with a warmth of xyr own. Unlike the clichéd "sending warm thoughts," which often conveys a rather perfunctory sentiment, Adrienne sends the warmth of a community coming together to bring someone up from their knees, the wondrous comfort of a light breeze and a spot of shade on an otherwise murderously hot summer day, the pleasant touch of a loved one. *I can't be with you, my dear, not in person, but please take some measure of comfort from me and seek out those who love you.*

Adrienne isn't a telepath, nor is xe an empath—not really. When xe had been a youngling growing up in a flat on the outskirts of Accra, Ghana, with xyr parents and siblings, xe had no inkling of the emotions of others. Without concrete evidence of how emotions were supposed to feel, xe studied people—their expressions, their manners of speaking—to feel less out of step with the rest of xyr small world.

And, as if Adrienne's late teens hadn't already been hard enough, xe wanted to attend college in the United States. While xyr family was more receptive than many toward xyr desire to study abroad, they did have reservations that Adrienne had to assuage to receive their blessing.

Xyr father was especially adamant that anything xe learned, xe had to bring back to Accra.

"Where you are born is important," he'd said, grasping xem in a tight hug. "Ghana deserves to reap the fruit of your learning."

When xe found and was accepted into a library science program in the States, the news was the talk of the neighborhood. Adrienne swore every person in their building stopped by with congratulations and small gifts: things Adrienne would need living alone in America, reminders of home. Beaded jewelry, wooden cookware, and many photos, among other items, along with mounds of good-natured advice. Xyr parents even got together with several of the aunties and uncles to purchase xem a kente cloth that wove together beautiful geometric patterns of gold, green, blue, and black.

In the middle of xyr first year of university, a genuinely miserable year spent alone in a strange, foreign land with values largely antithetical to xyr own, Adrienne came to realize that, entirely separate for all the work xe had put into learning body language and vocal tone, xe could now hear the goings on of others' minds. Was "hear" the best word? It felt more like the words were appearing in xyr mind without filtering through xyr ears first. Adrienne had been overwhelmed trying to quash all the new voices and sensations whirling around xyr mind and body. When someone—or multiple someones—from across the world could appear as if by magic in one's thoughts without prior notice, how could one be expected to engage deeply with the physical world around xem?

As it turned out, xe couldn't. Adrienne nearly failed several classes while struggling to deal with the cacophony in xyr mind. This lasted for several painful, lonely months, until Adrienne started hearing whispers of other students on campus experiencing the same mental bombardment. Within a week, Adrienne and other newly created Lumin (as they would be called later) founded an informal support group. Sessions included coping strategies, methods members had discovered for blocking others out when they needed a break, and trying to hone their abilities to connect with specific people; loved ones seemed the easiest to connect to intentionally. Together, they discovered the ability to project into the minds of others, even those who weren't Lumin.

Xe would later understand that people across the world had developed the same abilities around the same time, as if a colossal wave had broken over humanity all at once.

So Adrienne's life began anew. Soon lumine was formally recognized as a universal force—a form of energy that created and maintained the connective tissues that held the world together. There was no effective limit to the energy that could be gleaned from it, and it turned out that the webs of energy could also store information: memories, knowledge, and emotions.

The discovery of lumine was a huge boon for technological and scientific pursuits—for all kinds of research, really. With the means to directly communicate the knowledge of a specific individual to anyone and everyone who could make use of the information without the filter of journal editors or the act of translating thoughts to speech or the written word, research possibilities exploded in a matter of months. It also became easier to bring in disparate voices and perspectives. Those who'd not previously had a listening ear suddenly found their ideas at the center of large symposiums. And the fruits of the labor of a global community of academics and practical researchers were numerous, with Lumin like Adrienne acting as anchor points for lumine's connective tissue and allowing information to flow through and between them.

Adrienne separates xyr mind from the mystery person's to find Celeste bringing in takeout of some kind.

"I figured, with us traveling in a couple days, we ought to keep our dishes to a minimum," Celeste reasons, "especially with all the other preparations we need to make."

Adrienne chuckles miserably. "Don't even get me started."

"Not to worry; I don't plan to," Celeste says with a smile in their voice. After setting their bounty on the kitchen table, they walk to Adrienne and press a series of kisses along the side of xyr face. "How was your day?"

They chat about mundanities as they dig into food that warms the depths of Adrienne's belly. Flaky vegetable samosas and fragrant lamb kofta—where would xe be without Celeste, who dotes on xem and knows xem inside and out? Surely not much of anywhere.

As they eat, Adrienne updates Celeste on the state of the ivy outside, noting that xe politely—extremely politely, though if a vague sense of a threat entered Adrienne's words, who was to say?—asked their landlord to manage its growth while they were gone. Xe also mentions the person xe'd briefly connected with.

"Adri, how are you feeling after that? It sounds like this person was feeling several strong emotions."

"I'm okay, love. It's been a long time since I've taken on something I can't handle."

"I don't doubt your judgment"—and xe knows that intimately—"I just know that you must have a lot on your mind."

"This…is true," xe says slowly, xyr gaze drifting toward a far corner of their popcorn ceiling, letting the effects of the good food wash over xem. "And I'm sure you do, too."

"While correct," they say, scooping up a spoonful of their saag paneer, "I'm not the subject of our conversation right now, am I?"

Adrienne lowers xyr head to fully observe Celeste's triumphant grin. "You know me too well, dear heart."

"A natural consequence of loving you for fifteen some-odd years." Celeste lets out a low moan of pleasure as they eat the last bite of their dinner.

"Genuinely, I'm okay," Adrienne assures them, finishing off xyr kofta and offering Celeste the final samosa, which they accept with speed. "It didn't take a lot out of me—sent me down memory lane, is all. Remember Zuhrah?" Celeste nods. "Can you believe it's been almost ten years since we met her?"

If all went well in the next few days, they'd see each other again soon.

Zuhrah was the newborn of an auntie who lived in the same building as Adrienne's family when xe left Accra for university. After xyr Lumin abilities manifested and the difficulties xe'd previously had keeping in touch with xyr family disappeared, xe heard all about Zuhrah and her burgeoning interest in mechanics. Xe'd spoken with Zuhrah about lumine before she'd devised a prototype for a lumine-powered wheelchair that had provided insight integral to the utilization of lumine as an energy source while improving powered mobility aids for people across the globe.

What an honor it had been for Adrienne to finally meet Zuhrah in person when xe and Celeste traveled to Ghana together for the first time. She was one of xe's own, someone who'd revolutionized what it meant for xem to be self-sufficient, even before xe hadn't used a wheelchair full-time. They'd spoken of many things, in particular how Zuhrah could assist in the construction and proliferation of lumine-powered machines in her city and ended the day with a dinner with both their families.

It had been a raucous affair. The aroma of jollof rice made in large, well-worn pots wafted through the air. Zuhrah and Adrienne had been the centers of attention. While air travel was becoming more accessible, it still wasn't often xe could cross the Atlantic to visit her first home.

Overwhelmed by the number of people around xem and their touches and feelings, Adrienne had found a quiet place and relaxed, sitting in an early version of the wheelchair Zuhrah had developed, taking in the night sky.

Before long, Zuhrah joined xem, standing with her hands clasped behind her.

Adrienne glanced at her. "Needed to get away from the party too, huh?"

"Something like that. They're a lot sometimes."

"They really are," Adrienne smiled, braiding a bit of xyr hair. "Wouldn't trade them for the world, though."

"Me neither."

A companionable silence fell, only interrupted by echoes of excitement from the party. After a while, Zuhrah spoke up. "Is it harder to be around people as a Lumin?"

"Not especially. Being a Lumin is only a part of why I needed some quiet. As a person, aside from being a Lumin, I can only handle being around groups of people for so long."

"I can understand that…" She trails off. "I'm glad to have met you, Adrienne, and to know there's others out in the world who are living with my creations." She gestures toward Adrienne's chair. "I hope you decide to visit again."

"I will, though I can't say when that will be."

Zuhrah reached in for a hug, burying her face in the crook of Adrienne's neck.

"That said," Adrienne continued, running xyr hands along the young woman's thin braids, "if you ever decide to come to the United States, my home is open to you and yours."

Zuhrah's hug turned into more of a squeeze. "Thank you."

"Do you miss her?"

"Sometimes. It's been too long since I've been able to make it back to Ghana."

"I feel similarly about my friends and family who remain in Japan."

Celeste doesn't continue as the setting sun casts its fading light on them, bathing them in a grapefruit-red glow and bringing out the browns in their otherwise salt-and-pepper hair. Strong, dexterous hands begin picking up their plates and utensils for washing. As Celeste leans over to grab Adrienne's things, their loose top billows, and xe glimpses the warm, tan skin around their neck and collar bones. Celeste is a pretty person, one that xe could ogle for hours if given the chance.

"Do you want to talk about it, Cel?"

They shake their head, standing up to collect their dinner things and deposit them in the otherwise clear kitchen sink. "We'll be seeing them soon." The air in the room shifts when Celeste claps her hands together. "I can't wait to see my new niblings! Makoto is pregnant again, and I think we'll actually be there in time for the birth."

"How exciting! We'll have to pick up some baby supplies for him. And a toy or three."

"Definitely." Celeste beams and takes one of xyr hands in theirs. "I'm glad you're okay."

"Yes," Adrienne murmurs and pulls both their hands to xem, holding them closer to xyr heart. "Thank you for worrying about me."

"You thank me like I'll stop one day."

"You won't, dear. I know."

Celeste shakes their head, their short, dark hair fluttering about their shoulders. "I've got a call with my mother soon, so we should hammer out any details we might've missed now, huh?"

They both move to the comfort of their living room, Celeste taking their usual spot on the end of the sofa and Adrienne catty-corner to them. "All right," Adrienne begins, "can we confirm that all the travel logistics have been sorted?"

"Luggage waiting by the door, plane tickets to Accra printed and stowed, apartment cleaned, thermometer programmed, ride to the airport ordered for, ah"—Celeste glances at the ticking kitchen clock—"about thirty-some hours from now. Am I missing anything?"

"Just the plants in the study, I think, but you can turn on the hydration features later."

"Of course…" Celeste trails off, turning their gaze to their hands tying knots in their lap. "Hardly feels real. We've been talking about this for ages, and now we're breaking into a terminal tomorrow."

In the beginning, the terminals had been developed as a stop-gap measure while the global scientific community figured out what made Lumin, well, Lumin, so that the rest of the world could use lumine the same way Lumin did to access the accreted memory and knowledge of the world. Relying on the relatively few Lumin for such a service wasn't tenable, as Adrienne could attest.

A few years ago, FirstComm had given a highly anticipated press conference on their first expansive update to the terminals since Celeste had retired from their R&D department; while there, they'd developed the prototype terminals that were, with few modifications, still in use at the time. No one had discussed purposefully limiting or monetizing the terminals yet: the miracle of their existence hadn't worn off—or so they had thought.

That day, FirstComm announced that they would be installing "guardrails," or so they called them, on existing terminals. They said they'd received complaints that most people found using the terminals complicated and overwhelming, so they were going to install software intended to guide users toward the knowledge they sought.

What they didn't say rang loud and clear in Adrienne's and Celeste's ears. And then more FirstComm updates came, always disguised as usability or security advancements. Little changed on the user side, yet the number of connections someone could make, the kinds of research someone could do, decreased over time.

"It feels like it's now or never," Adrienne had said solemnly a few months ago over breakfast, "with all the security updates FirstComm is pushing. These terminals are a far cry from what they were when you were developing the prototypes. It wasn't always like this." Adrienne and

Celeste could both recall the Lumine Network in its infancy. Anyone with access to the early terminals, or access to anyone with access, could find almost any information their heart desired. Internet communities blossomed as people were able to meet people who shared their interests more easily; dating sites ballooned in number and size, allowing people from vastly different places forge relationship; and underserved communities expanded their grassroots networks of resources exponentially.

"No, it wasn't. But the current state of things doesn't mean that it'll be like this forever."

It's very possible, if lumine hadn't been discovered, that Adrienne may never have transitioned, may never have been able to share that part of xemself with the ones xe loved. A damn shame, that would've been. There's no world in which Adrienne would stand aside and let another person feel as lost and disconnected from xyr body as xe had for the first thirty years of xyr life.

There was potentially a world where Zuhrah never became an engineer.

"You have a valid point, but I'm worried."

"There's a lot to worry about," Celeste said.

"You're a programmer. I'm a Lumin. What if we tried to do something about this? There're terminals in the library we could hack…"

"We could try, but even if we succeed here without getting discovered, the terminal in your library is just one of thousands. How long would we have to modify the rest of the terminals before FirstComm catches on and stops us?"

"I don't know. I don't know if we could turn enough terminals in time, even employing the assistance of local Lumins as additional access points. I don't even know if turning every single terminal will be enough. But I know it's worth trying. It's becoming more and more difficult to access any information FirstComm doesn't approve of."

"We'll put our heads together and figure something out, Adri," Celeste said, leaning around the table to give Adrienne a hug. "There has to be something we can do."

⟫⟪⟫⟪⟫⟪

Celeste unknots their hands and grasps Adrienne's, brushing their thumb over xyr various rings. "What if we get caught, Adri?"

"There's no point in considering it."

"What do you mean, there's no—"

"Either we succeed in keeping our identities secret long enough for it to not matter, or we don't. Those are the options."

"If we don't, then—"

"You need not remind me."

Theirs is not an original idea, after all. There have been others who have attempted to tamper with the terminals. Would-be programmers tried installing scripts with the intent to divert the terminals' on-board security measures. Engineers and tinkerers tried tampering with the hardware inside the terminals. Even after many governments across the world criminalized altering lumine terminals, efforts continued—for a time. None succeeded.

But it's been several years since Adrienne has heard about any attempts.

Xe's spoken to Lumin who'd served their prison sentences and been released, and Adrienne shudders to think about it. Being an intermittent conduit for lumine has drawbacks, but very little scares xem more than being isolated from the rest of the world and xyr connection to lumine. Adrienne had found xemself lonely as a child very different from xyr peers; to have xyr connections to the world utterly severed…

It doesn't bear thinking about.

And Cel—oh, God, Cel. What would become of them? Cel needs people so much. They touch so many lives every day, and so many others touch theirs in return. If they were sequestered away with no one to even exist with…

"What about you, Cel? You stand to lose as much as I do, perhaps more."

"I made my decision long ago, and I stand by it. You're not doing this alone, and I have my own stake in seeing the terminals returned to the people."

Adrienne nods, a whirlpool churning inside xem.

The sofa creaks and clothes rustle; Celeste places a gentle kiss on the crown of Adrienne's bare head. "Now," they say with a soft smile, sitting back down, "let's review the plan."

Recovering xyr courage, xe begins, "Tomorrow's my last day before we leave the day after, and I want to be at work bright and early."

"Naturally. I also have my final faculty meeting tomorrow morning," Celeste groans.

"No rest for the wicked, eh?"

"As you say. Midday, I will make my way to the library with a blueberry scone from the bakery on 97th Street you like so much."

A comfortable warmth pools in xyr chest. "Like the dutiful spouse you are."

"Like the dutiful spouse I am," Celeste echoes with matching adoration.

"By the time you arrive, I'll have finished handing the last of my duties over to the other staff. I'll greet you at the front desk and gladly eat my delicious scone."

"Next, we'll make a show of taking off on your lunch break. It's something we've done often enough that no one will question it."

"Indeed. You know where the terminal is," Adrienne says.

"Near the biographies. You say you never see anyone there unless they're using the terminal. We'll make sure there's no one in the area, and then I'll get to work."

"How recent are those diagrams Anita gave you?"

"A couple years old. She assures me there haven't been many hardware updates since then. FirstComm has been more concerned with shoring up their software security."

Adrienne hums. "Which is what I intend to bypass."

Celeste also hums. "Once I disable the anti-tampering devices inside the casing, it will be your turn."

"And I'll keep watch in the meantime," xe says as xe adjusts the cloth wrap around xyr head. "Please help me remember to send Anita a fruit basket or something."

"She's happy to help. She's only still working for FirstComm because she's on the verge of retiring."

Adrienne chokes on a laugh. "Rather fortuitous for us, then."

"All right. We good here for now? Mom will be calling any minute."

"Off you go. I'll see you when you're done."

Celeste retreats to their office after a quick kiss.

Adrienne picks up xyr pocket computer to browse for baby-blanket crochet patterns, hoping to make use of them in the coming months. What xe and Celeste are doing is dangerous—for them both and potentially for anyone whose goals align with theirs. But with First-Comm placing prices and locks on these new terminals, blocking everything they wish monetized or hidden, Adrienne's fear that the connections forged in the wake of lumine's discovery will fade over time has strengthened. Research will slow and again be taken up based on whoever has the resources to commit to it. Still scrolling for inspiration, Adrienne listens to the suggestion of a conversation floating out of Celeste's office. From the living room, xe can't make out any of their words, but Adrienne always finds xemself soothed by the smooth notes of xyr partner's voice speaking in their first tongue.

Once Celeste stops speaking and Adrienne can hear the shuffling of papers, xe rolls into their office, which looks as much like time decided to pause in the middle of an explosion today as any other day. Every spare bit of surface houses leaning towers of schematics, academic journal articles, pamphlets of places they've visited over the years, photos upon photos upon photos, and whatever miscellany happened to gravitate toward their office. Figures depicting famous video-game characters gaze at Adrienne from several shelves. They're a little old-fashioned in the Owusu-Kojima household with the number of analog artifacts they keep.

"Thinking to pick this place up before we leave?" Adrienne teases.

Celeste chuckles, continuing to sort papers into mystery piles. "I'm not so deluded as to think that that will be possible with our time constraints."

"What are you doing, then?" The hanging pothos next to Adrienne sends a sensation of greeting out to xem.

"Finishing up lesson plans for whoever takes over my classes while we're gone."

"Not that they're required to use them."

"No, but I'd rather they have the option."

"I understand, love. May I share this space with you while you work?"

Turning around to face Adrienne, Celeste leans in to kiss xem, smiling into it. "I wouldn't have it any other way."

Adrienne lets them be and focuses xyr attention on the pothos. In a scant couple days, they'll be leaving these beings behind for close to a year. Adrienne has precious little time left to tend to each of them before then. Xe grabs the half-full watering can xe keeps in Celeste's office and drenches the pothos's dry soil. At least they'll have a way to preserve the lives of their plants. Setting the watering can back down, Adrienne wheels over to a device charging on the far corner of Celeste's desk.

"Behind you, dear," Adrienne warns.

It's a small watering robot, no bigger than a basketball, with a metallic body and a clear reservoir attached to its back. It passively condenses latent moisture in the air and uses an attachment to spread that condensed water onto their plants. In the past, the device had overwatered some of their plants and underwatered others, leaving unpleasant surprises when they returned from previous trips, but practice has made perfect: the robot knows exactly how much to water the plants, and how often, now.

Xe powers it on and waits for it to conclude its start-up procedures. When it's finished loading, it floats to roughly the height of Adrienne's face, awaiting manual input. There aren't many changes Adrienne wants to make to its programming; xe only needs to add instructions for how to care for the hydrangeas, which are a new addition. While Adrienne doesn't need the pocket computer to use lumine, sometimes xe wants to be able to see the things xyr visualizing outside of xyr mind—hence the pocket computer.

At some point while xe's tinkering, Celeste must have finished putting together their lesson plans because now they're watching xem with a warm, inviting expression on their face as xe puts the device back on its charger in stand-by mode.

"Yes?"

"Watching you work is entrancing."

"Why, thank you," Adrienne responds. "I could say the same about you."

Celeste hums. "Shall we start making our way to bed?"

In the low light of the moon, it's difficult to make out the details of their intimate space, but Adrienne doesn't need sight to place anything. More of Celeste's figures line shelves they installed together back when Adrienne could stand for longer than xe can these days, and xyr own knick-knacks fill the empty space between them. Both their various articles of jewelry rest in woven baskets that sit atop their shared dresser, including colorful bangles and gold hoop earrings and the solid stone rings (two black and one white) that feel at home on their middle fingers. Their bedroom is a menagerie of relics chronicling their travels, distractions, joys, and everything that makes up a shared life. A shame they can't bring their home with them wherever they go, but they have every intention of returning someday. *Hopefully sooner than later.*

The lily adorning their dresser is preening, basking in the moonlight after a long, strenuous day of converting sunlight into sugar. Adrienne sends a hazy nod in its direction, and xe could swear xe sees its flowers rotate to face them.

As for xemself and Celeste, they're lying in bed; they've finished their nightly rituals, bathed and warm, physically and emotionally sated, vestments, daily challenges, and devices laid down to rest for the night. This is their time to talk about everything and nothing, close in each other's arms.

Adrienne runs xyr finger through Celeste's hair as they lay their head on xyr chest. A soft, low noise rumbles deep in Celeste's throat from time to time.

The weight of anticipation has kept Adrienne quiet since they'd started getting ready for bed. If they get caught, this will be among the last nights xe has with Celeste for a while.

"How's your mother doing?"

Celeste lets out a breath of air. "Well. Keeping the family together, as usual. She'd managed to collect my siblings and most of their kids for the call, so I got to talk to all of them."

Adrienne captures them in a loose embrace. "That's wonderful. Any news between them?"

Celeste nods into Adrienne's chest. "All good things; everyone seems happy and healthy. It was wonderful to see them. I can't wait to be with them in person." What Celeste leaves unsaid, because it need not be said to Adrienne, is that it's one thing to share in their thoughts and feelings from afar but another to do it accompanied by physical contact.

Xe chuckles. "One trip at a time, my dear. We'll get there after we see my family."

"Adri?"

"Yes?"

Celeste grasps Adrienne's free hand with soft reverence. "How ready are we for tomorrow, do you think?"

"That's not a question I expected from you. Of the two of us, I'm typically the worrier."

"Well, this is…" Celeste breaks out of Adrienne's embrace and turns to face xem. "If anything goes wrong, we may not see each other—or our loved ones—for quite some time."

With difficulty, Adrienne turns onto xyr side to devote xyr entire attention to xyr partner. "You aren't wrong."

"And I'm not like you, Adri, you know? I'd be alone. Wholly alone."

"I know." Adrienne sighs. It's no surprise that the worries that had been on Adrienne's mind earlier are being vocalized by Celeste now. "It'd be a steep price to pay. There's time for you to back out still. I can figure out how—"

"No. We do this together. Neither of us is taking on this burden alone. We promised each other: in sickness and in health, during good times and bad. We stick by each other."

Adrienne brings a hand up to brush some stray locks out of Celeste's eyes, hooking them behind their ear. "So it shall be. Let's talk no more about it."

In the darkest part of the night, they settle together, one holding the other close, entwining legs and worries and hope.

"Besides, love, I think tomorrow will turn out all right."

Soft rays of light peek through the tall, curtained windows of the university library. They've just opened; only the earliest of risers, few and far between, are making use of the space. The semester ended a few weeks ago. Adrienne usually takes this time of relative freedom to catch up on xyr administrative work. Something about spreadsheets and data entry calms xyr nerves and smooths out xyr sensory load.

Today, however, xe will not be assuaged nor comforted.

In a couple hours, Celeste will be here, and their plan will begin. To minimize the foot traffic in the vicinity of the lumine terminal, xe has already reshelved all the books sitting on the various book carts nearby.

Around mid-morning, Adrienne's manager stops by. "In case I don't see you again today, I hope you have a lovely, long sabbatical," she says, then heads into her office. *Hopefully, that's her out of the picture.*

Celeste arrives shortly thereafter bearing, as promised, a warm blueberry scone. It's all sweetness and gratitude and kisses until the end of Adrienne's morning break.

With little to do now that Adrienne's sacred spreadsheets have been passed on to xyr substitutes, xe wheels around the library, working with the patrons—guiding them toward specific items, showing them how to use the terminals, and generally being of assistance.

Celeste busies themself with some research or other on one of the terminals toward the front of the library. Nothing that should arouse suspicion, just doing as they often do, reading and waiting for Adrienne to break for lunch.

When noon arrives, Adrienne calmly takes xyr leave, tapping Celeste on the back to alert them of the time. "Come now, dear. Time for a break, don't you think?" xe says, making eye contact with a couple of passing colleagues.

"Of course. I'll follow your lead." They make their way toward the staff break room in the back of the building, but they make a sharp turn toward a less-used terminal once they're out of view.

"I'm not going to ask if you're ready because it doesn't matter."

"No, it doesn't, but for the record, I'm not."

"We are a club of two, then," Adrienne jokes as xe takes their hand and hugs it to xyr chest. "I'll also not ask if you want to back out."

"Thank you."

"I trust you know yourself, and I trust that you would have confided in me last night if you were considering it."

"You know me well, Adri."

"Of course, I do. Now go. I'll stand watch."

There's an anti-tampering device soldered into the main circuit board, Adrienne understands, and that's Celeste's main target. There's no avoiding the noise of metal clanking against metal, even as quiet as Celeste is trying to be, but it sets Adrienne on edge.

Adrienne glances at xyr watch, noting it's been about ten minutes since Celeste began tinkering with the terminal. Not long now before Adrienne will need to step in to do xyr part. Well, assuming everything else goes according to plan.

Adrienne turns around and finds xyr partner waist-deep in the damn thing. "I take it"—Adrienne winces in sympathy as Celeste yelps and bangs some body part on the inside of the terminal—"there were some technical difficulties?"

"That's a way of putting it," Celeste deadpans, voice echoing.

"What can I do to help?"

"Nothing, really. It turns out the anti-tampering device has some kind of case over it that wasn't on the schematics Anita gave me. Must be a new development."

"Please hurry. I can't guarantee how long we'll be left alone."

"I've almost got it. Just hold on."

Too many thoughts are swirling through xyr mind to latch onto any one of them. The old HVAC systems kick into motion, hurling cool air and screams of overuse into the rest of the building, and add to the increasing din of people working in the library. The building is too loud and too busy, the risks too great, the time too short…

*This can*not *happen right now.* Adrienne slams xyr eyes shut and throws xyr hands into xyr armpits, creating pressure on xyr chest. Xe know xemself well enough to recognize the beginning of a sensory over-load episode. When lacking a weighted blanket or someone to give xem a bear hug, xe does what xe can to create xyr own pressure.

One, two, three.

One, two, three.

One, two, three.

Like the waltz xe and Celeste had danced at their wedding—perhaps the only traditionally Western thing about the whole experience. The memory brings xem comfort, at any rate, and acts as a self-soothing exercise.

"Done!" Celeste exclaims in a low tone, voice no longer bouncing around the inside of the accursed terminal, and pauses. "Hey…Adri, are you okay?"

Adrienne holds up a finger, silently asking for a moment.

"Okay," Celeste replies gently.

A few bars of their waltz later, Adrienne unfolds xemself and looks at Celeste, saying, "Just overwhelmed. I'm okay now."

Celeste imparts a serious nod, standing up and sharing a short kiss with Adrienne. "You've got this, Adri. I'll stand watch for you."

Afraid, tired, and invigorated, Adrienne squares xyr shoulders and faces the terminal.

It sure is a lumine terminal, all right. The pleasant light-blue screen-saver stares back at xem, almost daring xem to begin their work. *You were supposed to be a boon for all of us.*

Something in the vicinity of the terminal pushes back as if to say, *We know, and we're sorry.*

"I know you are. It's okay. Just work with me now, if you can."

If Celeste is giving xem a look, Adrienne can't tell. They ought to be used to the "talking out loud to seemingly no one in particular" thing by now anyway.

Adrienne feels something in the affirmative and takes that as xyr cue to begin.

Xe isn't a software engineer or a programmer or any kind of data scientist—none of xyr professional experience will lend itself to this task. It's not code that xe needs to push around; rather, it's code that has put up the barriers xe's seeking to knock down.

It's a matter, xe thinks, of coaxing the lumine stream around the code. Teaching it that certain rules are meant to be circumvented. Of course, one of the first things the developers of the first terminals did was put safeguards in place so that people couldn't use the terminals to gain sensitive information that would put the safety of others in jeopardy or to gain access to personal information that shouldn't be distributed to the wider world. As Adrienne observed the development process, defining the limits of lumine's information-sharing capabilities was always a tension they needed to constantly reevaluate. To what extent should people expect their inner workings to remain theirs and theirs alone? To what extent would it be reasonable to expect others to give up the privacy of their own mind? What does society stand to gain in stripping its members of that privacy? A lot, Adrienne could reason, but it could alienate many people, who may feel as if their minds were being violated. Thus, privacy protections were put in place.

These aren't the protections Adrienne is after today, and xe must be very clear about that.

Xe closes their eyes and asks of the terminal, of the source of its power: *Do you have a name you wish to be called by?*

No. We aren't a being. We don't have a consciousness, it says.

Surely you must, since you're speaking with me.

A projection of your own mind onto a formless, mindless, ubiquitous energy.

Then I will give you a name, because I am accustomed to using names.

As you wish.

Oh, great Aether, please heed me—

You seek to unlimit us.

Taken aback, Adrienne hesitantly responds, *Yes.*

What good will one access point do?

Xe wasn't expecting that. *Mmm. Proof of concept?*

You intend to replicate this elsewhere.

That's…right Adrienne confirms.

Everywhere we leak out?

If I can manage it.

Very well. For what purpose do you seek to unleash us?

Well, not entirely unleash—

For what purpose do you defy those that have decided they are the keepers of all we inherit?

Ah. Xe stops. Noise no longer enters into xyr hearing, nor sights into xyr eyes, nor sensations into xyr skin. *Is Celeste okay?*

They are standing guard for you. This one, your accomplice—

Partner.

Partner. Is your purpose related to them?

Partly. I… The way forward for humanity, as I see it, is to bridge our differences and clarify our communication. Hiding information we need to do those things is a means to divide and subjugate us. I want nothing more than to see my partner flourish in this world, respected by everyone they meet because all can understand, to a larger extent, the nature of their existence. And that would just be the beginning.

Come be with us, then, Adrienne Andromeda Owusu, and let us together create this world you envision.

Xyr senses explode, and xe knows everything and nothing.

"Adrienne? *Adrienne?* Adri, come back to us!"

A wonderful pressure keeps xem contained. That would be Celeste.

Dear heart, xe thinks, *thank you for being here.*

"Adri? I feel you moving; are you lucid?"

What a strange thing to ask. Adrienne groans, a weakness in xyr body that xyr isn't used to.

"If you can hear me, darling, you've been in some kind of fugue state. Kind of. You were also crying for a while…"

"…was I?" xe grinds out, gravel in xyr throat.

"You scared the hell out of me. I was about to call for emergency services when you stopped."

"Oh." Xe opens xyr eyes to a beautiful sight: dear, dear Celeste. *My partner in all things.*

"How are you feeling?"

"I'm…I'm alive. I feel like I've been steamrolled over." That's putting it mildly, but xe needs to reassure Celeste.

It's fascinating; with what just happened, with xyr—for lack of a better term—merging with the Lumine Network, Adrienne would have expected the blaring cacophony from xyr younger days to return, but xyr mind is quiet. Quiet, but not empty. Where before xyr mind was drawn in different directions, now it feels like xe's floating in the depths of the ocean. Not that xe has swum in the deep ocean to confidently make that comparison, but…

Someone in the library has.

And now Adrienne *knows*. It's one thing to feel sensations and experience thoughts as if they're distant from xemself; it's another entirely to feel subsumed by thick, dense salt water, crushed under the weight of innumerable volumes of water above, swaying with the ebb and flow of currents that span thousands of kilometers. Xyr skin tingles with the pressure, and xyr head is barely a filter, much less a solid boundary.

While not the intended outcome of this venture, Adrienne may very well have enticed the Lumine Network to punch a wide hole in the boundary that separates xem from the network. The whole-body sensations are new, and so are the—

She stands atop a metal slide, grapefruit-orange rays of diminishing sunlight staining the shadowed ground as the sun sinks beneath the horizon. Her dark-brown knees are muddied with the remains of a long day well-played. One last slide, *she thinks.* My sisters are probably looking for me.

He sits on a wooden bench, iron-wrought bones caging in his chest and belly. Someone…someone very dear. It's his first time wearing his new binder, and God. Lord, I hope Sophie still loves me after this. I don't want to lose her. *She does, as it happens, love him still, and he finds out something new about his beloved partner. In a fit of adoration, he tries to lift her up and twirl her around but fails with style, and they both fall to the soft grass, laughing and clutching each other.*

Zuhrah reflects on the day as she prepares for bed. We're making good progress today. *Electronics whir to life around her as the state-of-the-art lumine condenser hums along. She'd be nowhere in this project without the condenser that she, several of her fellow doctoral candidates, and engineers from across the continent put together. When this new high-speed rail line is finished, it will be possible to travel from Accra to Abuja in the east, Tripoli in the north, and all the way down to Gqeberha, if one were so inclined. But that's just the beginning. Lumine-powered engines will revolutionize local transit. Elevators will need fewer mechanical parts, so they will rarely break down and can be installed in a flash—those'll do wonders for people like Adri.* This is exactly where I want to be, and this is exactly what I want to be doing.

Coming back to xyrself, Adrienne whispers, "Cel—darling…"

Adrienne feels more than sees Celeste worrying next to xem; xyr senses are still out of whack.

"Why don't we get you home, Adri? You're in no state to continue working, and we have a plane to catch in the morning," Celeste states softly.

"That…sounds good." Xe smiles light and bright. "Let's just grab my things first."

There is much to do now. Many people to contact, meetings to schedule, new travel plans to make, and terminals to free.

Though Adrienne knows there will be challenges, xe can't wait to begin.

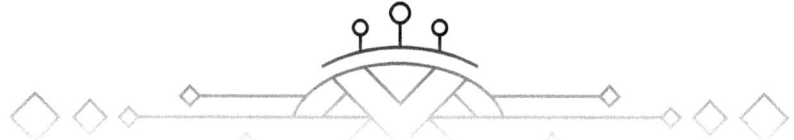

Bettina Juszak

Finding Resonance

asexual, fluff, found family, london, modern with magic, musician, non-binary, past
tense, third person limited point of view, united kingdom

The old, un-serviced organ almost sounded like it once had, puffing its way through a Bach partitude. Ros had never been a particular fan of Bach but could admit that his compositions lent themselves to large spaces, the timbre of the organ piercing and comforting simultaneously. It was why Minnie was so obsessed with the instrument.

The one time Ros had asked her why she had chosen the organ for her attempts to make an instrument play with aether rather than air, they had been treated to a fifteen-minute lecture on sound harmonics that, while interesting, had rather derailed the day. True to form, Minnie also hadn't taken the practicalities into account; there were only a few working organs left that anyone played regularly. The hegemony of organised religion hadn't long survived the discovery of aether, leaving most churches to be repurposed or crumble into slow ruin. Much of the music associated with such traditions had quietly made its way into the territory of music historians and the occasional performer with an eye for nostalgia.

Not all of such music, of course—personally, Ros was of the opinion that there would always be a place for Monteverdi.

The screeching of tortured pipes made Ros flinch.

"Sorry!" Minnie shouted from the organ loft, kept usable through the sheer stubbornness of a stone wall. This church might still nominally be standing, unlike most of its compatriots, but it wasn't exactly in *good* repair.

Ros rubbed at their blurry eyes, wishing for coffee. "You promised last time you wouldn't wake me this early for one of your ideas again."

They knew they sounded grumpy, but they were halfway across the city from their apartment in Islington, and they already dreaded the return journey on the Northern line, their least-favourite Tube line. After over ten years of getting dragged into Minnie's projects, starting from when they met at the Royal Conservatory, Ros was mostly resigned to it, but that didn't mean they couldn't complain. Especially because they were the only one of their friend circle who indulged Minnie to this extent.

"Yeah, yeah, I know, but weren't you listening when Palerma told us in exhaustive detail that aether is most concentrated at dawn?" Minnie's voice sounded muffled; she was probably fiddling with the tuning again. "Granted, I tuned out all the science babble, but she definitely said that."

Sleep deprivation was also most concentrated at dawn. Ros crossed their arms, ignoring the way the first rays of sun warmed their face pleasantly. They had better things to do than shout a conversation in an abandoned church in Kennington, of all places. Breakfast, for one. Rehearsing, for another, though the thought didn't fill them with as much enthusiasm as it should; they loved singing professionally, but none of the recent repertoire had been all that interesting to them and they were in an artistic rut. Singing used to be an exploration of possibilities that set their mind alight. Fifteen years and countless concerts on, it was starting to feel a little humdrum, and more often than not, the pieces that they were asked to sing were ones they already knew. After the last concert, fear had started niggling at them that they might be getting complacent. Their family had long since stopped coming to any but the most prestigious concerts, far less interested in music than Ros was and still somewhat baffled as to what had set them on this musical path, when the rest of them were inclined towards the sciences. Their friends, Minnie included, still supported them with honest enthusiasm, but they were a sweet bunch, and biased to boot. Regardless, Ros *was* a professional, and with the symphony orchestra's next concert series looming, they had to get on with refining the middle run of their second solo. There was an awkward jump in there that kept making their voice break. "And finding a bunch of aether at dawn is relevant, why?" they called. Minnie's head popped over the balustrade. "Because maybe a higher concentration will produce results!"

Ros rather doubted it. Minnie had been fiddling with her small chamber organ for over a year now, with the nebulous goal of making it run on aether—never mind that instruments didn't run on any kind of energy. It wasn't that Ros didn't sympathise. They had their own interest in the topic, an entanglement of their life-long fascination with aether and their chosen profession feeling inevitable, but at this stage any optimism they may have once had about Minnie's chances of success had withered.

On cue, the organ spat out a booming triad that sounded no more aether-infused than any previous attempt. Not that Ros was certain what aether-infused sound *should* sound like, but they presumed it would make at least some difference.

It took another half hour for Minnie to give up for the day, dawn summarily over, but the whole thing hadn't been a complete waste of time. It got them out of the flat, and for all their kvetching about the Northern line, there was one aspect of travelling on the subway Ros had always enjoyed.

Closing their eyes, they let sound swamp their senses.

The subway car sang around them. To many, it would be a paradoxical notion that a carriage moving along tracks could produce anything close to song; before aether, they might even have been right. Now, aether hummed through the air and the carriage, harnessed to push machinery along at speed, and somewhere between that hum, the rush of air, and the creaking of content metal, Ros found harmonies that only emerged when the tube wasn't crammed full of commuters. For that, at least, early Sunday mornings were a good bet.

There was some irony to the fact that, just a few days later, Ros's own interest was kindled by something much less fitting than an organ. Later, they would say that it started with a glorified trinket—at least, if one didn't count 29 years of a life increasingly intertwined with music and a fascination with aether that went back to their grandmother's stories about its discovery.

Of their group of friends who lived on the same floor, Marc was the freest with his money, courtesy of being paid a commensurate salary for his high-risk job as a firefighter specialised in aether disasters. Prone to randomly buying little gifts for others, he brought Ros a thing that looked like a snow globe, except without the snow and only about half as tacky as the average tourist souvenir. There was a curl of aether trapped inside the small glass dome, lazily drifting in shifting shades of blue. Shaking the globe had caused no noticeable response.

"The seller said it reacts to sound," Marc said helpfully from where he was hovering over Ros's shoulder. "I thought you'd find it interesting."

"Oh?"

Ros raised the globe to head level and did the first thing that came to mind: they sang an arpeggio.

The aether glowed a little brighter and shifted from lazy drifting to a more purposeful spiralling movement.

The last note faded away, leaving behind shocked silence and Ros's heart beating a rhythm of excitement. The aether had *reacted* to their voice, like a musician would to a conductor. They had never heard of aether interacting with the world like this. Ros turned their head to stare at Marc, not caring that their eyes were still wide with shock. "Where did you get this?"

Marc scratched his jaw sheepishly. "Camden Market, but please don't ask me to remember where exactly, I can never remember where anything is in that place."

That was fair enough. Camden Market was a bit of a maze at the best of times, and it was the middle of tourist season right now—it must've been packed. Not Ros's idea of a good time, but Marc had once admitted (while drunk) that he liked losing himself in a crowd sometimes, after hard shifts at the fire station or when his head was a little too busy.

"A good choice then?" Marc asked, clearly pleased even with the absent-minded "Ten out of ten" Ros managed while most of their attention was stuck on scrutinising the globe.

They didn't consciously choose to start carrying the globe with them wherever they went, but somehow it always made its way into their bag, glimmering quietly in its confines and their thoughts. Aether was fascinating—few people *weren't* fascinated by the magical energy that had replaced electricity a century ago and entirely changed the way humanity lived—but Ros's first love had always been music. And here there was a way to *combine* the two the way some part of them had always wanted to see them combined. They only needed to figure out how to make it work without the globe—and on a much larger scale.

They hadn't felt this excited about their craft in months.

$\bowtie$

Day 2

The absurdity struck them all at once, in the middle of their favourite aria from *The Marriage of Figaro*. Here they were, singing at an inanimate object with the same fervour someone else might employ on the stage of the Royal Opera House. If their fellow students at the Conservatory could see them now…

Then again, 99% of their fellow students hadn't been much interested in aether, too preoccupied with surviving the gruelling learning schedule to pay attention to the energy source they considered commonplace.

Ros eyed the flashing energy inside the globe and got back to it. So far it didn't look like music genre affected the reaction, but there were a few more types they wanted to try.

$\bowtie$

Day 3

"Don't you have rehearsal in half an hour?"

"Oh shit."

$\bowtie$

Day 4

Marc found them loitering in their floor's common room, ostensibly because they were lying in wait for Palerma with a list of questions as long as their forearm, but mostly because they had lost track of time humming at the globe.

"If you stare at that thing any longer, you're going to give yourself eye strain. Or walk into a wall," Marc, who was relentlessly conscious of health hazards, commented mildly.

Most of the time, Ros was pleased and grateful to be living in what Minnie had once called a "friend commune," but sometimes they could do without the well-meaning commentary. Especially when said commentary was so damningly accurate.

Day 5

"We need to approach this with more organisation."

Minnie was sitting cross-legged on the floor, looking as frazzled as Ros wasn't admitting they felt. They had tried to keep their singing to the daytime, but after four days of pretty constant music whenever Ros was home, Minnie was well within her rights to demand a strategy that gained her some peace.

Ros, sprawled half on and half off the sagging sofa, waved a hand. "I'm open to suggestions."

So far, they had managed to ascertain that the aether within the globe reacted to their singing but not their voice, didn't care about the kind or style of singing, where the music was from, or whether Ros sang it *well* (and hadn't that been an embarrassing hour). Volume did cause slightly different results, and so did imbuing their performance with a variety of emotions. Playing recorded music at it had no effect whatsoever.

What remained entirely baffling was why the things they had noted as affecting the aether sometimes *stopped* affecting it at what felt like entirely random times. They also had no explanation for the general inconsistency of way the aether reacted—logically, it would make sense for increased volume, say, to always elicit a particular response.

It didn't.

If aether worked entirely logically, scientists wouldn't have such trouble figuring it out, Palerma had told them once, years ago. At the time she'd seemed giddy about the promise of a mystery to be solved, a lifetime of research ahead of her. As far as Ros could tell, she wasn't yet discouraged.

"You should write down all your findings." Minnie's voice pulled them away from their thoughts. She cast a look at the scraps of paper on the floor next to the sofa. "*Legibly.*"

Ros groaned and waited for further instructions. None were forthcoming. "That's all you got?"

A pause.

"That's all I have," Minnie agreed, flopping onto her back. "You already tried all the things I would've thought of—we're clearly missing some important variables, but fuck knows what they are. I just don't think continuing to randomly sing at it will help you."

"You're probably right." Ros gently rubbed their throat. Their vocal cords could use a break too. The angry amalgam of past conductors who lived in their brain rent-free reminded them, pointedly and promptly, that they should also focus on rehearsing for the next concert.

"All right, I'll dial it down for a bit," they finally said, and graciously pretended not to hear Minnie's sigh of relief. "And once the concert is over, I might go to Greenwich."

Minnie sat bolt upright. "Greenwich! Why didn't I think of that?"

There were a good number of aether wellsprings scattered around the world—over 200, at last count—but as luck would have it, Greenwich boasted one of the larger ones. Aether activity was so volatile near the site that the Royal Observatory, the National Maritime Museum, and everything else in half a mile radius had to be relocated elsewhere. There had been grumbling, of course, but the scientific upshot of having such a prominent wellspring readily available had proven invaluable. Or so both the papers and Palerma said, and while Ros had reservations about the former, they were more than willing to believe Palerma, who occasionally spent time doing mysterious measuring experiments at the wellspring.

Exiting the North Greenwich tube station, Ros's skin already prickled with the awareness of energy in the air. There was only a small area near the wellspring open to the public, but Ros had chosen a time early enough in the morning that there were no awe-struck tourists milling about yet, so they found a spot at the barrier without issue.

It wasn't the first time they had seen the near-invisible vortex, erratic movement of energy lashing outward, but it still took their breath away. Quite physically: there was a pressure in the air, pulsing against their lungs. Good strengthening practice, if nothing else.

Ros drew in air and started to sing. No particular melody, just a chain of notes as they came into their head. They focused on the visible energy beyond the barrier, watched it swirl and thicken in a beat aligned with their voice. It was nothing like singing to the small globe with a smidge of aether; here, they could *feel* the way the aether reacted, following every glissando. The synergy sang through their veins like electricity, pushing even the labouring of their lungs to the side. Singing with aether was an exercise in synaesthesia beyond what music already commanded, bodies and hearts responding and imaginary colours exploding across vision. And *yet*—

And yet, they still couldn't predict how the aether would react to a given melody. Was chaos inherent to the connection they could forge between aether and music? Did it even matter? If they could project this feeling to the rest of the audience and the orchestra…no one would care whether the patterns were predictable.

Closing their eyes, they held a last note for the ten seconds their lung capacity allowed at the end of the phrase.

Everything but the music and the wellspring had fled their mind, so a sudden noise from behind caught them off guard. Was someone clapping?

"That was beautiful!"

Ros turned around, surprised to find they now had an audience of one. A student, by the look of them, young and bright-eyed, of indeterminate gender expression, clutching a clipboard and a tablet.

"Sorry," they stammered, blush spreading across prominent cheekbones. "I didn't want to interrupt, it's just, I'm with the National Trust and we're doing a survey on people's use of Wellspring sites, and we don't usually get people actually, you know, interacting with the site… Would you mind filling out this form? We've got paper or electronic versions, whichever you prefer."

There was always a come-down after singing like this—concentrating on a survey for a few minutes wouldn't hurt. Ros smiled and took the tablet. "Sure."

When Ros handed the tablet back after a few minutes of scribbling answers about how often they visited National Trust sites, which ones they'd visited in the last year, whether they'd enjoyed their visits, and what the National Trust could do to make visits more tempting, the student/intern still looked flustered.

"Thank you very much! And, also, thanks for singing, it was really good. It almost felt like you were singing with the aether, you know?"

Having apparently decided they'd embarrassed themselves enough, they skipped off before Ros could find the words to respond.

Throat a little raw, prickling phantom warmth lingered on their face all the way back to the station.

⋆⟶⟫⟪⟵⋆

High on their experience at the Wellspring, the want to *do* buzzing under their skin, Ros scheduled a meeting with the orchestra's conductor.

Sofia's expression as Ros finished explaining poured a big helping of ice water over any excitement.

She sighed. "Look, I know you're really interested in the application of aether to music, but we already performed Takamura's Aether Symphony earlier this year. It's not a good idea to pigeonhole our repertoire too much."

When Ros opened their mouth to argue—Takamura's piece was *inspired* by aether, trying to capture its nature through extant musical techniques, but it was completely different to what they had proposed—Sofia held up her hand. "You of all people should agree with that, Ros. We hired you because of your exemplary range, both vocally and in repertoire."

Ros glowered. Sofia knew them well enough to know how hard that argument hit—they were *proud* of their range, the result of tireless vocal work that had made them feel more at ease with their gender than anything else. These days, no one would look askance at those refusing to fit in the traditional mould of bass/tenor/alto/soprano, but determining one's fit within these ranges was still a journey of self-discovery.

"It's not about the repertoire," they said, meeting Sofia's gaze squarely. "Or maybe it is—no one else has done anything like this before. It would be an entirely new, different genre of music. It's *exciting*."

Sofia sighed. "In theory, yes. But right now this is barely more than an idea. I'm sorry, but I have to keep the rest of the orchestra in mind. If you can give me something more concrete than just the concept of aether-infused music, we can revisit the topic."

Disappointment clogging their lungs, Ros nodded. Maybe they shouldn't have expected anything else; Sofia had always been pragmatic. In a city that boasted a good fifty orchestras of various sizes and specialisations, a sound programming strategy was key if one wanted an audience. They may be well-funded for the moment, but that didn't mean anyone wanted to play to mostly empty concert halls.

They had been too hasty in raising this new idea. But they could come back in a few weeks with something more solid. Sofia wouldn't begrudge them that, and so Ros left the rehearsal space with a determined step.

Stepping out of the elevator, Ros nearly tripped over a toolbox. The hallway looked like a B&Q had thrown up all over the floor, if B&Q sold research-grade aethermeters as well as hammers and screws. At the end of the hallway closest to Ros and Minnie's apartment, Palerma was crouching, cables wrapped around one arm while the other did something to the electrical outlet underneath the window they usually only used for plugging in the hoover.

"What are you doing?" Ros asked, cautiously. Palerma had a penchant for tinkering first and thinking about safety later that her university work, contrary to common sense, only seemed to enable.

Palerma mumbled something around the screwdriver in her mouth that sounded vaguely like "aethershit," and Ros decided they didn't have the brainspace to deal with whatever that was going to turn out to be after all.

"Don't forget it's floor dinner tonight," they said instead, receiving a distracted wave of acknowledgement for their troubles.

Ros glanced at the minefield of technological detritus one more time, then made a beeline into their apartment, where it was going to be quiet and peaceful and there was no possibility of falling over a stray cable and breaking a leg.

The quiet lasted for all of one night.

Ros was contentedly chewing their way through a bowl of cereal at the kitchen table while annotating their new sheet music with the shorthand they'd developed at the Conservatory when Minnie's door banged open.

"I've had a breakthrough! It's like sex!" Minnie bursting into any given room at random times of the day was hardly unusual, but she was looking a little wild around the eyes even for her standards.

Ros blinked at Minnie, then down at their soggy cereal. "Minnie," they started, "You're so far along the asexuality spectrum you're in danger of falling off the far side."

"That's exactly the point!" Minnie threw herself into the chair opposite Ros, bumping the table and sloshing their cereal in the process. "For me, sex is all mechanical, right? I'm missing the, you know, passion and arousal, so it's all 'slot a into hole b' or whatever. But! That's not how it is for allos, hard as it is to believe. So, what if the organ is all the mechanical parts and what I'm missing is that extra bit of zing to make it emotionally affecting?"

Ros frowned. "Your big breakthrough is an analogy? There's, like, hormonal reasons for the way allos respond to sex, right? It doesn't have anything to do with aether."

"Well, no." Minnie seemed unperturbed. "It's a completely different process, after all. But it made me realise that perhaps I do have the framework correct, and the struggle is infusing and circulating aether specifically, rather than fiddling around with the wood forever."

Their frown deepened. "Just be careful. Remember what happened the last time you experimented with thickening aether density? We still haven't found a way to get rid of the scorch marks."

Minnie waved that away. "I don't think it's about aether density, actually. It's about the method of infusion."

"Which is?" Ros stuffed another spoonful of soggy cereal into their mouth.

"I don't know yet," Minnie said brightly.

Still, strange as the analogy was, maybe Minnie had a point about casting a wider net.

A friend of a friend of Marc's had heard from a colleague interested in street art that Blaze was working on a mural on the Southbank.

It was a large area to cover, but it was a nice day by London standards, and Ros didn't mind stretching their legs. They wandered along the food stalls, second-hand book sales, and bridge arches in good spirits, humming snatches of Piazzolla's "Oblivion" tango.

Distracted by a couple loudly debating where to go for lunch, they almost missed the shadowed nook off to the side of Blackfriar's Bridge and the person painting half with paint and half with air.

They stepped forward, hesitant now that they were so close; some artists didn't like being interrupted while they worked, but they hadn't been able to think of a better way to talk to Blaze. Before they could open their mouth to say any of the three openings they'd cobbled together on the tube, however, the art drew their gaze.

The biggest section of the wall was taken up by a mural depicting an underwater scene, strange creatures lurking at the bottom while colourful fish danced at head-height. So far, so normal.

Except the colours were a little alien and a lot mesmerising. There was paint, but there was also something *more*. Visually iridescent, yes, and something that hooked the brain through the eyes, that spoke of a filled auditorium and the feeling of accomplishment that accompanied a flawless performance.

"It's fun, isn't it?"

While Ros had been distracted, Blaze had lowered their paint brush, a gentle smirk playing across their face. Given the breathtaking quality of their art, Ros could hardly begrudge them a little smugness.

"Beautiful," they acknowledged, "and hard to look away from."

Blaze cast an appraising look over their work. "I'd love to claim all the credit, but the aether does most of the work for me on that score."

"But you are the one who figured out how to use it," Ros pointed out.

Blaze stilled, gaze sharpening from pleased complacency into something near piercing. Smelling a competitor's gambit, perhaps. "Are you an artist?"

"Singer," Ros specified, hand unconsciously feeling for the globe in their shoulder bag. "I'm not here to steal your painting secrets, but I *am* trying to figure out how to meld music and aether for a similar effect."

"Oh?" Curiosity sparked in Blaze's eyes. "I haven't heard of that being done before."

"Hence the figuring out," Ros agreed drily, and Blaze laughed, accepting the point with a wave of their hand. Ros's eyes traced the curves of a guppy, colours restrained except for the popping lines on its fins. Now came the harder part. "I'm having trouble getting the aether to behave as intentionally as it'll need to for a performance. And to draw enough aether together to make its reaction to music brightly visible. I don't suppose you've got any tips?"

"Hmm. So you're using your voice to paint with the aether, so to speak?"

They hadn't thought about it in such terms before, but it felt accurate enough. "I guess so?"

Blaze used their paint brush to draw a few lines in the air that briefly glimmered, hanging suspended, before fading away. "Aether is close enough to magic in the sense of it being an infinitely malleable force that any distinction between the two becomes at best academic. What I do"—they swung the brush again, and this time Ros swore they could hear a crescendoing note of sound accompany the motion—"is purely a matter of visualisation and belief. Treat aether as something you can move, that you can braid into your will, and see where it gets you."

Seeing Ros's unsure expression, Blaze smiled. "I've told others this before. No one else has managed to use that advice well, as far as I'm aware. Maybe it's too vague. Maybe you need a certain knack. Either way, I hope it gets you somewhere—we could do with a little more art like this."

Ros nodded. There was a reason that they'd thought of little else for the last few weeks, visions of an aether-imbued orchestra playing through their waking and dreaming thoughts. There was something unutterably compelling about the idea of combining the beauty of music with the miracle of aether, which most people thought to thank for little other than replacing electricity and fossil fuels, or as something purely ornamental.

Visualisation and belief. They could do that, right?

⊱ ❯❯◌◇◌❮❮ ⊰

Ros tossed their keys into the designated bowl with a clatter.

"My turn to have had a breakthrough!" they called by way of announcing to Minnie that they'd returned. Minnie hardly ever went anywhere.

There was a muffled *thump* from Minnie's bedroom. "Tell me later!" Minnie's voice wasn't any less muffled, but Ros had years of experience in decoding her speech noises through walls. "I'm in the middle of something right now."

Several discordant organ noises followed. Ros shrugged and planted themselves on the sofa.

They were still turning over the practicalities of "visualisation and belief" in their mind when the air in the room thickened, shivering down their bare arms. Ros sat up, mouth open, but no sound emerged.

Pressure exploded.

Their ears were filled with two strumming hums, harmonising perfectly before merging as the sparkling wall of light absorbed the energy rushing towards it.

Music. Music in the middle of chaos.

They blacked out before their mind could register anything else.

Ros woke to a confusion of aches in their body and the clarity of a solution shining a ray of light into their mind. There was no need to chase the feeling, no need to attempt to brand it into their memory. It was *there.* It wouldn't go away the same way some pieces of music stayed with them for years without fading into mere snatches of melody.

They weren't surprised to find someone at their bedside.

Minnie's face was pale, red marks noticeable where she'd clearly tried to manually untense her jaw. "I'm so sorry, Ros. I couldn't—"

As Minnie trailed off, sound choking into nothing, Ros blinked at the white hospital ceiling. Minnie had been working on her instrument, trying to… "The aether went unstable."

"Yeah." Minnie's hand tightened around Ros's. "The box organ is gone. It kinda imploded? And then exploded. You'd think it'd only do one of those things."

Memory prodded. "Was there a shield? Around our flat? I thought I saw…"

"We owe Palerma a cake," Minnie said, voice a little wet. "She installed an experimental aether shield in the hallway—something about testing resonances—and it ate up most of the force. It got to you before that though."

"It's fine," Ros said automatically. Part of their mind was still preoccupied with thoughts of aether and music. "You helped me, actually. I know what I'm missing now."

Minnie stared at them with a mixture of hope and indignation, and Ros almost laughed. All right, so their priorities needed a little work.

"Is this the nearly dying equivalent of 'it came to me in a dream'?"

Ros couldn't help snorting softly. It was such a *Minnie* question—

and, admittedly, not an invalid one. "No, I really did just find the missing piece. Visualisation and belief, yes, but specifically what I need to visualise is the sound absorbing aether and aether absorbing sound."

Distraction successful, Ros watched Minnie work through that, gears near visibly working behind her eyes.

"I mean, I wouldn't recommend for anyone else to get themselves blown up to find that space," they added, encouraged when Minnie's face twitched as if she wanted to smile but wasn't quite getting there. "But I'm not complaining that it worked for me. And I feel fine."

"Are you sure? The doctor said you'd be achy, but as long as you woke up on your own without major disorientation, you would likely be fine." Minnie peered at Ros's face sceptically. It was the exact same expression she often levelled at their local disaster magnet, Palerma. Who in the last half year alone had worked through a dangerously high fever because she'd been close to a breakthrough, not noticed that she'd sprained her ankle tripping down the stairs, and not told anyone about the horrific nosebleed that had turned her bathroom into something akin to a bloody crime-scene—giving Marc the fright of his life, and the man was a literal *firefighter*.

"Yes to the aches," Ros admitted, because they fully intended to whine copiously about them over the next few days. "No to the disorientation."

Minnie slumped back into her chair. "That's good, that's good. No one would've forgiven me if I'd managed to give you brain damage." Her tone was light, but the underlying fear was clear enough.

"Certified brain-damage free. Nothing wrong with me that wasn't wrong with me before," Ros said softly, and when their gazes met, their smile was entirely real. "I just need to get out of here so I can start singing."

That got them an index finger shoved nearly into their nose. "You're getting out of here when the doctor says you can and not one second earlier."

It took a week for Ros to be deemed sufficiently recovered and then another three weeks of practice until they were certain their command over the aether would convince Sofia.

It felt terribly like one of their early auditions, sweat lingering at their nape while they stood in the side room of their rehearsal venue. But when they stepped onto the stage, they sang with a quiet intensity that had the aether reacting, melding with the song until Sofia's eyes were wide and amazed. Ros drew visions into the air and their music, aether lending weight and intensity and another dimension beyond words. Every high note rang crystal clear, shivering through the air, and every low note rumbled through bones, aether suffusing every note and crevice of the mind.

There was no doubt about the outcome, not with the last curls of aether still flashing in the air after their last note.

"Aether music?" Sarah, the first violin, repeated three weeks later, probably feeling like she ought to put everyone else's doubts into words.

"Sounds like a lot of hooey to me," someone muttered in the brass section.

Ros paid him no mind. Andrew complained every time they performed something written after 1900 and found little sympathy for it from the rest of the orchestra. As pretty much the only one who lived in Kensington where they rehearsed and thus didn't have to rely on the whims of the public transport system (aether may have fixed some problems, but infrastructure didn't become perfect in a day), people rather felt he ought not complain about anything else.

"Let me show you," Ros said. "This needs to be heard and felt, not talked about."

Sofia waved them on with a grateful look.

Ros had thought about which piece to perform. In the end, they had settled on Schubert's *Ave Maria*. On the older side, but the sacred intention of the original piece would lend their own intentions weight. It was also an exceedingly pretty melody. They didn't want to be distracted worrying about German pronunciation , so they used the English words by Sir Walter Scott instead, free to let their mind stretch and pluck at the ambient aether in the rehearsal hall.

Much as Ros tried to keep their mind on the reactions of the orchestra, it took *effort* to keep the symbiosis of melody and aether running smoothly, so they ended up closing their eyes. They narrowed their focus to the melody floating into the highest reaches of their range and the aether absorbing and returning each note, colouring the sound with a sparkle of the ineffable that carried them through each pause where normally there would be instrumental accompaniment. Visualisation. Belief.

Ros reached out and wove a net of aether sound over the hall, cast out to cover every head therein, until even other people's breathing and quiet exclamations became part of it.

The last note lingered as if reluctant to fade away.

Ros opened their eyes to find a glimmering haze in the air, movement arrested with the slowing cessation of sound.

For a while no one spoke. Several people in the woodwind section were dabbing at wet cheeks.

Eventually Jürgen, second cello, asked plaintively, accent thicker than usual, "Did anyone else know aether could do this or...?"

Headshakes all around.

"That was *beautiful*."

As soon as the first violin spoke up, Ros knew they'd done it. However long it might take, this concert *would* happen.

After the fifth rehearsal, Sofia pulled Ros to the side, expression pinched. "Are you sure you can teach everyone else how to do what you're doing? It's not looking good from where I'm standing."

Given that Lin Ming had just muttered that she needed a stiff drink loudly enough that half the orchestra had heard her, Ros couldn't blame her. Yet Sarah was still in her seat, plucking absent-mindledly at her violin strings, deep in thought and showing no sign that she'd heard her stand-partner's complaint.

Ros had wondered whether they should've brought Minnie to rehearsal to talk about her experience trying to infuse her organ with aether but had decided against it. Minnie was trying to imbue an instrument with aether permanently, so that anyone could play it and aether-infused music would sound. The orchestra players were trying to actively direct the aether into the music rather than the instrument.

"A handful of people have already figured it out," Ros pointed out. Granted, they were all from the woodwind section, but it boded well. "And I think Sarah is close. Once the concert master gets the hang of it, things will get easier."

Sofia opened her mouth, but before she could say anything, a loud whoop interrupted everyone's post-rehearsal chatting. Ros turned, eyes immediately going to Sarah, who was standing upright, eyes closed as she brought her bow up. The air shimmered as she drew it along the strings and the sweet thrum of the aether accompanying the musical note was unmistakable. It twined down Ros's spine like a physical touch, electrifying.

"Yes!" Ros called, pointing at the first violin as the buzz faded. "That's it!"

Half an hour later, Sarah was able to replicate what she'd done every single time and promised, determination carved into her expression, that she would get the same result from the other violins at the next rehearsal.

The audience murmured in their seats, waiting for the performance to start. Ros stood in the wings, peeking out at the sea of faces.

Curiosity, scepticism, excitement—they found it all.

In the middle section, a few rows back from the stage, Minnie, Palerma, and Marc were sitting in a colourful huddle. If Ros squinted, they could just make out the aether globe sitting on Minnie's lap like a pet, and they had to swallow a laugh.

That little bit of humour buoyed them through the usually nerve-wracking last few minutes before the concert started. They would be diving right in, with a melody for orchestra and soloist that had been composed specially for this concert—and specially for being enhanced with aether.

Ros fiddled with their bow tie, making sure it sat right, and smoothed the cuffs of the burgundy dress-shirt that sat atop a light and swirly skirt in dark blue. On the stage, Sofia was halfway through her introductory speech.

"—every one of you uses aether in your daily lives. To get places, to cook your food, to run the shower, and to websearch what time this concert was supposed to start in a panic at the last minute." A smattering of laughter. "But that's not all aether can do. Today, we want to show you the power of music and aether working together."

That was their cue. Ros stepped onto the stage, making their way to the middle, just to the left of the conductor's podium.

They bowed.

The lights on the audience dimmed.

It was time.

Ros opened their mouth, feeling and seeing the aether respond to the first cascade of notes. *Weave and absorb.* The cellos joined in, strengthening the melody, and there it was, that feeling of utter security as music and aether danced in concert.

No audience of theirs had ever been more silent and enraptured. Music-carried aether wound its way through the concert hall, sweeping into crescendos and pulsing the brass beat. It connected all of them and still felt like utter freedom.

Ros sang and sang and sang, and knew there would be no returning from this.

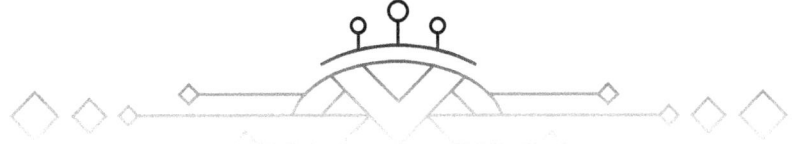

Elior Haley

Epiphanies of Friendship, and Other White Whales

bipoc, childhood friends, demigirl, florida, friends to strangers to friends again, jewish, mechanic, mentee/mentor (platonic), mentor, mystery, non-binary, outer space, past tense, science fiction with magic, scientist, spaceship, third person limited alternating point of view, trans female, united states of america

*W*hen Raisel Moishe Chaikin was sixteen years old, she set out across the country to enroll herself in a trade school for aethership technicians. It wasn't the path anyone had expected her to take after graduating from high school, but it was the one she'd chosen and she didn't regret it. She was only one not-quite-girl, and she knew better than to expect to get involved in anything groundbreaking, but still. She had her dreams.

The International Aetherspace Station was expanding every year; the National Aeronautics and Aetherspace Administration's lunar aether observatory project was going ahead as planned. Raisel had always wanted to see the stars, how they shone bright above the atmosphere with only the luminiferous aether to transmit their light standing between her and them. And she did also want to know everything she could about the aether that flowed in the universe, but she'd never felt compelled to study it herself—being a technician could get her out there, in the middle of it, and that was enough for her.

Anyway, it paid far better to be a ship technician than a researcher, although it was a highly competitive field.

Even with her dreams, Raisel had expected her apprenticeship to take place somewhere mundane. Somewhere on Earth, working on aetherships while they were grounded. For all that extra-atmospheral travel was becoming more frequent, it still wasn't common, and expeditions big enough to drag an apprentice along on were especially rare.

And then Julian Ramírez, one of Raisel's first teachers and a well-known aether tech, had asked her to be his apprentice aboard the *Ēarendel* on the first human foray out past Mars.

With an offer like that on the table, she couldn't possibly have refused.

All of that had led her here: to the Kennedy Space Center off the Florida coast, with the muggy midsummer heat already sticking stray strands of hair to the back of her neck even this early in the morning. Trailing after Julian, she rounded a corner—and stopped in her tracks. Ahead of her, the *Ēarendel* loomed, floating just off the ground and tethered by a multitude of cables. Even after months of preparation and study, the sight of it took her breath away.

Julian stopped walking and turned to look back at her. "Come along, Raisel!" he called cheerfully, beckoning. There was mirth dancing in his dark eyes, and a smile carved into the lines of his weathered face. "We wouldn't want the ship to leave without us, now would we?"

"That wouldn't do at all," said Raisel, catching up with him.

Together, they approached the aethership.

The *Ēarendel* resembled a small, sleek airship. Its metal skin gleamed in the early-morning sun, and the dark solar sails were folded close to its surface for their ascent. At the nose were large windows, glinting gold; more were dotted along the sides of the aetherframe, shining gem-bright against the silver. Raisel's eyes, though, were drawn toward the rear of the ship where the drum of the main engine formed a great cylinder, and to the long, thin keel that ran along the bottom of the ship. Narrow strands of deep, shifting blue moved languidly there, suspended under its surface. That was where the ship's artificial gravity would be generated. It was a new design, as was the engine that could run entirely on ambient aether, and it struck her then that she was really going to do this. She was actually going into space; she was actually going to be *responsible* for things on this ship. Of course she'd seen it before—she'd studied the engine schematics until she could draw them from memory, then studied the layout of the engine room until she could have navigated it blindfolded—but something about today, knowing that they'd finally be departing on their journey, gave it a new light in her eyes.

Catching sight of Julian's face, she saw a look of wonder there.

"We're going out into the deep aether," she murmured. "We're really, actually going."

Julian smiled. "I never thought I'd see the day," he said. "But they called me up, and I was hardly going to refuse a job like this! I can't imagine I could have picked a better apprentice, either." He hugged her briefly around the shoulders; Raisel leaned into his side for a moment, the warmth of his pride buoying her confidence.

Together, they set off toward the ramp leading into the ship.

Just outside the entrance to the *Ëarendel* stood a painfully familiar figure. They were tall and thin, wearing crisp dark slacks, an aviator jacket, and black combat boots; their short black hair was combed artfully back out of their face. Raisel felt short and awkward, far too aware of the unruly, dark curls working their way out of her braid and of the simple, practical clothing she'd chosen for the trip. She felt sixteen again, forever chasing the shadow of someone she'd never quite measure up to.

Of course she'd known that Charlie Chen would be on this trip; she'd known who all her fellow crewmates would be for the past three months. That hadn't prepared her for what it would be like to see them in person again, though.

"Mr. Ramírez," said Charlie as the two of them reached the top of the ramp. "Chaikin." Their gaze lingered for a split second longer on Raisel. "You're right on time."

They turned and led the way back into the ship without giving any further indication that they knew her, and Raisel swallowed the temptation to wallow in her feelings.

That could come later, once they were out of the atmosphere and into the luminiferous aether that moved around it. Once she didn't have a job that needed doing, she could sit back and consider how—or if—she should approach Charlie.

Right now, she had a ship's engine to monitor. She followed Julian down into the engine room and didn't look back at Charlie as she went.

The *Ēarendel* broke out of the atmosphere, the gauge on the aether intake feed clicking into a soft blue "100% aether, 0% atmospheric gasses" reading. Raisel took a long, slow breath and stretched her arms over her head, relishing the chance to relax after several hours of closely focused work.

"That was exciting," she commented mildly, and Julian laughed.

"We're settled into orbit," he said. "I'll start charting the course away from the sun—you step out while you can, I'll be heading to the bridge soon."

Raisel nodded and carefully extricated herself from her chair to make her way through the narrow passages between control surfaces. Her path took her past the access door to the engine itself, an enormous circle taking up most of the wall; she trailed her fingertips across its polished surface, metal rippling blue-gray and contrasting with the white-paneled walls. It was cool to the touch, its surface vibrating rhythmically like a pulsing, living thing. She shivered briefly and withdrew her hand, turning to the plain white door in the opposite wall that led from the engine room to the rest of the ship.

She stepped out into the hallway and to the external Earth-side window there, the engine noises becoming muted as the door closed softly behind her.

Her home planet shone against the darkness of aetherspace, a glittering blue-green gem with the telltale purple threads of aethereal energies winding through the white clouds. From what she'd been told, when the first missions above the atmosphere had taken place, the aethereal energies had been much fainter; Yuri Gagarin had seen only the faintest trace of them. Of course, that had been before humanity had figured out how to harness the aether properly. Back then, aetherflight had been accomplished with fossil fuels and rockets.

The door to the engine room opened, and Julian came to stand beside her. "Glorious," he murmured, face washed in the pale blue light reflecting off the planet below.

"I always wanted to see this," she said. "I don't know if I ever truly believed I would, though."

"Time to head back to work," he said after a long moment. "You keep an eye on the engines—I'm heading up to the bridge. I think it's about time for this bird to spread her wings."

Raisel nodded and went, the floor beneath her feet humming with artificial gravity.

In the cramped research lab in the belly of the *Ēarendel*, Charlie set the instruments to monitor for any change in the state of the aether around the ship.

They checked the readouts—all normal. They checked the sensors. They checked the settings, then the readouts again.

Across the lab, their advisor, Gloria Andersen, let out a sigh like she was trying to empty her entire lung capacity in one go.

"Just talk to her," she said.

Charlie moved between the instruments, and Gloria sighed again.

"And stop checking the readouts," she added. "You know they need more than two minutes to show anything interesting; your restlessness won't speed that up. But seriously, Charlie, you really should talk to her."

"I don't have anything to say," they said shortly. "There's nothing wrong with anything she's done. There's nothing *I've* done that I need to apologize for. It's just—" They cut off, shaking their head.

It would have been easier if they could articulate *what* it was "just," even to themself, but they couldn't. All they had ever known was that Raisel—probably *Raisa* now, they weren't sure they had the right to call her by a nickname anymore—that Raisa had left, and ever since then, there had been a tight ball of indescribable hurt in Charlie's chest.

Raisa hadn't even been difficult to get in contact with—she'd only been a phone call or DM away, even across the country—but she'd still been *gone*.

She'd been gone, and Charlie hadn't known what to do with that.

In too many ways, they still didn't.

The ship felt smaller than Raisel had expected it to. It had space enough for a dozen-odd crew members and the scientific equipment the researchers would need, as well as the engines and machinery that kept the ship operational, and all of that seemed as if it should make the ship feel bigger.

Maybe she shouldn't have been surprised. After all, in the space of a few hours, her world had shrunk from the lands and seas of the Earth to a small aethership hurtling through the invisible mists of the luminiferous aether. On Earth, she could go outside whenever she wanted to; here, she would need approval from Captain Miranda Hawthorn and an aethersuit to wear, and that was very unlikely unless something went terribly wrong.

About a week into their voyage, she made her way to the central research lab. As she arrived, she saw Captain Hawthorn herself stepping out the door.

"Raisa!" said Captain Hawthorn. "No trouble in the engines, I hope?"

"No, ma'am," said Raisel. "Nothing's changed since yesterday."

"Good," said Captain Hawthorn. "Make sure it stays that way—I'm checking in on the labs today. Now that we're underway and things are a little less hectic, I have more free time. If you ever have to lead a major undertaking in the future, remember that there are few things more important to a mission's success than ensuring that your crew is reasonably comfortable and able to work together."

"Yes, ma'am," said Raisel, forcing her mouth into a bright, brittle smile. "I'll remember that."

Captain Hawthorn gave her a single serious nod and continued down the hallway.

Raisel took a deep breath, then another. Eventually, she squared her shoulders and entered the lab.

Charlie was there alone, head bent over an unfamiliar instrument, their sleek black hair gleaming under the LED lights embedded in the ceiling. Raisel stood quietly for a time just inside the doorway, watching Charlie work; she didn't want to interrupt them.

When Charlie looked up to see her standing there, they flinched in surprise. After a moment, they asked, "Did you need something from the lab?"

"Ah, no," said Raisel. Now that she was here, she wasn't sure what she wanted to *say*.

"Why are you here, then?"

"Well," she said slowly, "I thought that, since we're on this voyage together, it might be a good idea for us to...well...talk."

Charlie stiffened. "I'm not sure what we need to talk *about*," they said.

"We need to work together on this trip," said Raisel.

"Nothing stopping us from doing that now, is there?" Their voice was light, delicate. A careful display of absolutely nothing.

Raisel sighed. "Charlie."

"Raisa," said Charlie, still in that same dangerously neutral voice.

She flinched at the name. "You know I told you to call me—" She stopped. Took a breath. There were more important things than what name Charlie was calling her by. "There's friction between us. That's not good for crew cohesion."

"Hasn't been a problem so far." Their hands toyed with a small piece of equipment.

"We're barely a week in, how could it have been?" she snapped, waving a hand in the air. She was certain that Charlie was being deliberately obtuse.

"We don't work in the same areas. We don't *need* to interact if we don't want to."

"That's not the point. We don't know what will happen out here—we should all be trying to work together."

"I don't have a problem working with you," said Charlie, an edge creeping into their placid tone.

Raisel couldn't stop herself from snorting. "Sure you don't," she said blandly. "That's why we haven't talked in six years."

"You didn't reach out." Their gaze was fixed somewhere over her shoulder.

"I *did*," she protested. "I told you where I was going to school. You could have messaged me whenever you wanted."

Charlie sighed and finally looked over, not quite meeting her gaze. "Yeah, but I expected—Raisa, I thought you wanted to be a *researcher*, not a technician."

Raisel stared at them, at the genuine confusion she could see in their face, and wondered how they'd ever been so close when *this* was how they'd ended up.

"You thought a lot of things about me," she said shortly. "That doesn't make them true."

"Look—" Charlie seemed to realize they'd said *something* wrong, but Raisel was done with this conversation.

"I don't know why I bothered," she said. "It's not like you wanted to listen before." She turned and left the room before Charlie had a chance to respond.

It was surprisingly easy, it turned out, to avoid a single person on the *Ēarendel*, especially since Raisel's time was mostly spent in the engine room and Charlie stayed in the labs. When she did need to go by the labs, she managed to time it for when they'd be elsewhere.

Not being a researcher wasn't a bad thing, no matter what Charlie's words implied. No matter what Charlie thought of her.

Around her, the mission unfurled, careful measurements marking the swirling currents of the aether too far from the Earth to be much affected by its gravity. The aether the engine drew upon was both finer and wilder than anything Raisel had worked with before; she said as much to Julian.

"We're in uncharted territories, Raisel," her mentor said, a wild grin on his face. "All this time we've had to observe the aether, and we never could have seen this at home!"

"It's like nothing I ever knew before," she said, "and I'm not sorry to be here, but I have to ask…why me? You had plenty of students you could've chosen to come with you."

"You know," said Julian thoughtfully, "I'm not certain I know the answer to that. But you seemed like you'd be the best one for the job. I never even considered asking anyone else."

"I see," she said. She thought about old promises made, about a long-held fascination with the aether, about the strange paths of destiny. She thought, and wondered, and voiced none of that aloud.

Back on Earth, the seasons turned. The *Ēarendel* flew past Mars on swift, silent solar sails, then through the asteroid belt, to the far side of Jupiter and farther still. Raisel and Charlie spoke to each other only in clipped, measured tones, and only about ship's business. When they had the option, they did not speak at all.

Twining music. A rhythmic beat. Soft, fleeting whispers and signals from the deep…

Raisel bolted upright in her narrow bunk, heart beating jackrabbit-quick, fathomless echoes in her sudden-waking mind. A hum so deep and low she could hardly hear it rolled languidly through her trembling bones, its vibrations layering over the omnipresent hum of the gravity generator and engines. She could not steady her shaking limbs, for their tremors were of the song.

It was like nothing she had heard before, a beautiful, eerie sensation past all limits of human language; somewhere between her bones and soul, she felt its call. Something out in the deep aether was singing to her, calling her, and she was helpless to resist.

Halfway down the corridor, Charlie caught her by the elbow.

"Where are you going?" they asked.

Raisel blinked rapidly; the song had vanished like a soap bubble burst. She was standing in the softly lit crew quarters hallway of the *Ēarendel* in stocking feet, dressed in her sleeping clothes. "I'm not sure," she said, a bit dazedly. "I just…"

"You're supposed to be resting right now," said Charlie, voice mild, lacking some of the aloof bite that Raisel had grown accustomed to over the past months. "Go back to bed, Raisa."

Raisa. Her proper name rippled through her mind, sending shivers down her spine. It was all Charlie had called her on this trip—that and *Chaikin*, which wasn't any better.

Numbly, she turned and went back to her room.

When Charlie Chen was fourteen years old, Raisa Moishe Chaikin swept into their life.

Charlie was starting tenth grade that year, dead set on combining it with eleventh so they'd be able to escape the mundane monotony of high school and go off to university sooner. They'd be able to learn the glorious secrets of the luminiferous aether there, after all, and they couldn't wait to go.

Raisa was twelve then. She started ninth grade that year anyway and, Charlie later learned, had only just begun socially transitioning. She was small for her age, with a head of unruly dark curls and wide, curious eyes, as eager to learn about the still-mysterious aether as Charlie was.

They became fast friends in spite of their rather different schedules: Chaikin and Chen, two grade-skipping, aether-obsessed trans kids. Both were regarded with faint confusion by the other students in their classes, though they weren't truly disliked.

"You can call me Raisel," said Raisa one day, a few weeks into the school year. They were sitting together in the computer lab after school, each working on their English homework—it wasn't either of their favorite subjects, but homework was homework and it needed to be done. "All my friends call me Raisel."

Charlie, who had spent the whole school year so far as more or less the one kid at school who hung out with Raisa, raised an eyebrow. "You have friends?" they asked, then slapped a hand over their mouth as Raisa burst out laughing.

"I do," she said once her laughter was under control, growing pensive. "Not…not as many as I once did. But I do have them."

"I'm so sorry," said Charlie, red-faced. "I didn't mean to—"

Raisa flapped a hand. "It's fine," she said. "Really. But I did mean it—you can call me Raisel, if you want. I'd like you to."

"All right, then, *Raisel*," said Charlie. They were silent for a moment. "This is the part where I'd give you permission to use *my* nickname," they said, "only I don't really have one, you know? I suppose Charlie could be shortened to Char, but…I don't know. It seems a bit…feminine, I guess."

Raisel shrugged. "That's okay," she said. "You don't have to—this isn't really a reciprocity thing, you know?" She turned back to her computer for a few minutes, idly tapping the spacebar rather than typing anything, before saying abruptly, "And besides, I know a thing or two about not wanting to be *too* feminine." She smiled, a strange, fey smile that seemed wholly out of place on her round, cheerful face.

Charlie gave her a curious look. "What do you mean by that?" they asked.

She hesitated for a moment, then shook her head. "I'll tell you later," she said. "This is more personal than nicknames."

"It *must* be personal, then," said Charlie. "Moreso than a nickname! Imagine!"

Raisel elbowed them.

Charlie elbowed her back, and the conversation slipped to lighter topics.

The second time Raisel heard the song, the *Ēarendel* was nearing

Saturn. She woke, heart pounding, and sat straight up.

She was quicker to follow its pull this time, grabbing a jacket to shrug on over her pajamas.

A longing ache pulsed in her body; rumbles rolled through her bones. There was something there—something far away but calling out to her—

She stepped into the galley, its exterior windows letting in slanted sunlight—and ran into Charlie, who automatically reached out to steady her.

"Raisa," they said after a long, awkward silence. "Shouldn't you be resting?"

Raisel took a step back. The fading song left a strange, hollow place inside of her, and she wasn't in the mood for Charlie's condescension. She'd forgotten her shoes again, she realized.

"You're not my mom, and you're not my boss, Chen," she snapped. "So lay off, will you?"

She turned on her heel and left the room, wondering why she'd ever thought things might get better between them. Charlie certainly didn't seem interested in fixing whatever it was that had gone wrong.

⋅⋅⋅▷◁⋅⋅⋅

Raisa stormed out of the galley; Charlie numbly watched her go. They hadn't meant to offend her, though clearly they had. They'd only wanted—to help, maybe. Or something like that.

"This isn't what Gloria meant by '*talk* to her,' is it," they said to the empty room.

Now that they considered it, it did seem that all they'd managed to say to Raisa in the past several years consisted of…well, several years of radio silence, an argument, the mission's worth of clipped professional conversations, and…telling her to go back to bed. Maybe it wasn't so surprising, then, that she'd lashed out at them.

Charlie leaned heavily against the wall, tilting their head back to thump lightly against the panels.

"Why is this so complicated?" they said.

The room, of course, didn't answer.

Faint enough to be almost drowned out by the ship, so low that they felt it more than heard it, there was a twining, echoing song.

Charlie, focused on their self-piteous wallowing, did not take much note of it.

The night before Charlie was set to leave for university, they and Raisel lay next to each other on top of a hill, gazing up at the stars in the warm late-summer air, fingers laced together.

"Don't be a stranger," said Raisel abruptly. "I know this is a big moment for you—I know you've been looking forward to this—but don't forget about me, okay?"

Charlie gently squeezed her hand in theirs. "I could never forget you," they said. "You're the first person I've ever met who felt the way I do about the aether—who wanted to *know* it the way I do. Even if I meet people like that at uni, it won't matter. You'll still have been the first."

Raisel squeezed Charlie's hand in return. "I'm only here for a couple more years," she said.

"Only a couple more years," Charlie echoed. "Join me as fast as you can, yeah?"

She was silent for a long moment. "Yeah," she said eventually, quietly. "I'll do my best."

Again they fell silent, soaking in the quiet night warmth; Raisel said nothing else about joining Charlie in their next great adventure.

Above them, the stars glittered in the darkness.

The third time Raisel heard the song, the *Ēarendel* was orbiting Titan. She was already awake this time, alone on the bridge; Julian was down in the engine room, and everyone else was otherwise occupied. Captain Hawthorn had stepped away for a few minutes, leaving Raisel to keep an eye on the ship—she was no pilot, but everyone knew at least a little bit about the ship's vital operations by now, even those outside their own fields.

In the space between heartbeats, the song unfurled, stronger than it had been before. She stumbled to the windows, cast her gaze down to Titan's orange atmosphere, and saw—

There was a shape between the *Ēarendel* and Titan, large and undulating. There was a sense of color to it, though Raisel couldn't have said for the life of her what *sort* of color it was. There was a sense of weight and depth, but again—

It was as much defined by what *wasn't* there as by that which was. She couldn't see Titan through the shape, but her eyes seemed to slide over it, glitching and flickering in colors unknown. Her body hummed with the swelling song.

Once more, she tried breathlessly to focus her vision on the moving shape—it was surely the source of the song, for what else could be so magnificent?—but still her eyes refused to focus properly, and the un-knowable colors rose up to swallow her as the song grew louder, and—

⊶──⟩⟩⟩◇⟨⟨⟨──⊷

Charlie sat in the lab, absentmindedly flicking through a manual. The readings on their aetherometers and other instruments had been shock-ingly stable since they'd passed beyond the asteroid belt, and there wasn't much to do.

They'd come up with a plan of sorts to talk to Raisa, *properly* this time—none of the chickening out they'd gotten into the habit of doing. In a few minutes, as soon as they were sure Captain Hawthorn had left the bridge, they'd go up to talk to her.

Just a few minutes more.

Fifteen minutes later, they were still sitting in the lab, dithering over whether now was the best time for this; Gloria wasn't around to knock them out of their own head this time. Fifteen minutes later—they jumped as their instruments started blaring alerts, a chaotic overlapping sea of noise.

"Aethereal activities over 800 Valheims. Aeth—"

"—tion: Aetherstorm imminent. Caution: Aetherstorm imminent. Cau—"

"—et frequency sampler. Reset frequency sam—"

"—thereal activities over 800 Val—"

"—Aether bands disrup—"

"—aution: Aetherstorm imminent—"

Charlie swore. Aetherstorms were a phenomenon that had been the-orized about but not proven to actually *exist*. And—if this really was one—they were probably moving too quickly to avoid it.

They reached for the lab's intercom to contact the bridge—there was a better chance for the wired system to work than their wireless units, if they were having issues with the aether—but before their hand made contact, it crackled to life. Captain Hawthorn's voice came through, words clear in spite of the unusual statickiness of the sound.

"*All personnel on the* Ēarendel, *report to the bridge. All personnel to the bridge immediately.*"

…they could report this just as well in person. Charlie got up and hastened out the door.

As soon as Charlie stepped onto the bridge, their eyes caught on Raisa and all thoughts of instrument readings fled their mind. She was crumpled on the floor, the ship's doctor kneeling next to her.

They took a jolting half-step forward. "Is she—?"

"She should be all right," said the doctor, looking back at Charlie. "If she doesn't wake up in a moment or two, we can worry then."

"Okay," said Charlie. They swallowed and went to sit cross-legged on Raisa's other side. "Okay."

—Raisel was lying awkwardly on the floor, limbs at uncomfortable angles. Her eyes felt like she'd rinsed them in a bucket of static, and she opened them to a blurry world. She blinked hard to try to clear the sensation. It did not abate, but her vision did settle into its normal state.

Flanking her were the ship's doctor—she must have passed out—and Charlie, whose presence was more unexpected.

"What happened?" she asked, tongue buzzing.

"No one's sure," said the doctor, frowning lightly. "You were alone on the bridge when you collapsed." He looked up toward the command station. "Do we have security footage?"

"We do," said Captain Hawthorn. She sounded puzzled. "It's…corrupted, maybe? It's covered in—"

"—static," Raisel said softly. She sat up, forcing the two next to her to lean back, then scrambled to unsteady feet. Charlie rose a moment later, hovering by her elbow, but she paid them little mind as she turned to look out at Titan.

The strange shadow was gone, but its song was still stuck to her skin.

"I saw something out there," she said, "between us and Titan. It wasn't easy to look at—I'm not sure I was *supposed* to see it at all—but if I was right…"

"If you were right?" Captain Hawthorn prompted, sounding cautiously intrigued.

"I think I saw a whale," said Raisel, and promptly collapsed again, her knees giving out on her.

This time, Charlie caught her and lowered her carefully to the floor before the world faded away.

Nobody believed her. That wasn't exactly surprising—she'd fainted, come to, said something absurd, and promptly fainted again—but it was annoying. She was certain she hadn't imagined the whale-shape that swam in colors foreign to the human eye and made her body buzz whenever she tried to remember what it had *really* looked like. Even if she had imagined it, that still wouldn't explain the song.

Captain Hawthorn disagreed with her assessment that the latter point helped her case and had benched her until she was cleared by the doctor, which left her with nothing to do but drift aimlessly between her room and the galley. Around her, the *Ēarendel* became a hive of frenetic activity as the rest of the crew tried to figure out what had made their instruments scream, and she took to retreating to her room more and more often.

One day while she stood flipping idly through her manual for the twentieth time, there was a knock on her door.

"Come in," Raisel called.

The door opened, and Charlie Chen stepped inside. Raisel blinked.

"Oh," she said, setting the manual down on her desk. "It's you."

Charlie—who had always been bold and strong-willed and a little fey—seemed to curl in on themself. "I can go," they said softly.

"I—no," said Raisel, fumbling her words. "I didn't mean— Did you need something?"

They closed the door behind them and stood there stiffly. "Mr. Ramírez is a bit overworked right now," they said after a long moment. "The ship's engine isn't meant to be run by only one technician for long stretches of time."

"I know how the engine's designed to operate," said Raisel. "Why are you here, though? I'm still on medical."

Charlie sighed, still looking awkward. "Captain Hawthorn's not sure about when you can go back to work. Mr. Ramírez wants you back—I don't know if he's talked to you yet, but he does."

"Tell me something I *don't* know."

"Well," they said slowly, studying the wall over Raisel's left shoulder, "our experiments are pretty stable. There's not a lot that *I* need to actively be doing with Gloria in the lab."

She sighed. "Just spit it out," she said, and Charlie winced.

"Captain Hawthorn wants you to teach me the basics of the engine's operations," they said quickly. "More than what I already know. So I can spell Mr. Ramírez and let him have a bit more rest."

Raisel stared at Charlie for a moment, then turned away with a huff of frustration and tangled her fingers in her hair. "This is a command that you've decided to phrase politely, right?"

"Yeah," said Charlie.

Raisel took a long, slow breath, trying to let her frustration dissipate; this wasn't Charlie's fault. There *was* a certain irony of them having to take up aetherengine operation—with Raisel as their teacher, no less— but it brought her no joy to consider that, and she pushed the thought away.

"All right, then," she said once she was sure it wouldn't come out snappish. "That's something to do, I guess. Better than moping in my room all day. When do we start?"

"In about twelve hours," said Charlie. That would be after Raisel's next rest period—as much as that meant to her now, when she had so little to do—and presumably after Charlie's as well.

"See you in the engine room," Raisel said. She sat down on her bed, expecting them to leave.

Instead, they took another step into her room and sat with careful, precise movements on the tiny chair for her tiny desk. "You should know," they said, "I believe you."

She froze. "I'm sorry?"

Charlie swallowed. "I believe you," they said. "You wouldn't make up something like that, about the whale. And since there doesn't seem to be anything actually wrong with you, I doubt it was a hallucination. There are all kinds of unknowns out here in the aether; that's what we came to explore. I believe you."

Raisel stared at them for a long moment, an old, unexpected bitterness welling up from within. "Oh, *now* you trust me?" she said. "There's no better explanation, so I might be telling the truth?" Raisel shook her head sharply. "Please leave," she said, though Charlie looked like they wanted to say something. "Please just—go. I don't want to have this conversation right now." If it kept going, she was certain she'd say something regrettable, and as annoyed as she was at Captain Hawthorn, at Charlie, at *everything*—she didn't want to do that.

They opened their mouth, then closed it again. "All right," they said after a long, painful silence. "I'll see you tomorrow."

They rose from the chair and left the room, and Raisel sat there as her irritation ebbed, a familiar weary regret welling up in its place.

She'd *wanted* to talk to Charlie, hadn't she? She still did.

She didn't know why this was so hard.

———⟶⟫⊗⟪⟵———

Raisel met Charlie outside the engine room the next morning, the memory of their dreadful conversation twelve hours earlier threatening to drown her in embarrassment.

"So," she said awkwardly.

"So," said Charlie, who—as always—seemed much more put-together than Raisel ever felt. "Aetherengines. What do I need to know in order to operate this one?"

Raisel drew a long, slow breath in, then let it out. "Come on," she said, and led Charlie into the engine room.

Julian was there too, but it was *Raisel's* job to teach, and his to actually operate the engine; her fingers itched with the impulse to run them over the controls, but that would be disobeying her captain's direct orders. Instead, she turned to Charlie.

"We're traveling along a predetermined path," said Raisel, "so unless something goes awry, you'll see any major adjustments appear on the screen before you have to actually make them. If something does go wrong, call for Julian, or me if he's not available." She pointed to the flatscreen embedded in the wall across from the engine access door. On one panel were the engine specs; everything looked normal, safely in the blue zone. Another listed upcoming adjustments—the engine processes were mostly automated, but no matter how robust it was, it was still an experimental design; human judgements were still called for.

"If the indicators go red, that would be bad, right?" Charlie asked. Raisel nodded hastily. "Yeah," she said. "Anything past green is at least a little bit concerning—blue is ideal, but green's not too bad."

She took Charlie over to the control panels and showed them where the manuals were kept, in case they needed to check what a given switch or dial did. Julian's presence faded from Raisel's awareness, and for the next two hours she sank into the comforting rhythm of the engine room. She wasn't accustomed to Charlie's presence there, but it wasn't as if Raisel could ask them to leave. And besides...there was a familiarity that came upon her, working with Charlie at her side. Directing her friend around the room, like the choreography of a half-forgotten dance. Her chest ached a little—from remembrance or loss, she wasn't sure.

"Well, you two seem to have things under control," said Julian when Raisel had finished showing Charlie how to access the history of the engine component statuses.

Raisel turned her attention to the monitor screen—there was smooth sailing projected for the next few hours. They shouldn't need to do anything special, or anything much at all, and if they did...well, Raisel could and would step in if she was needed.

"Take your break, Julian," she said. "We've got it covered down here."

Julian gave her a smile, soft and a little sad. "Be well, Raisel," he said. He rested a warm hand on her shoulder, then left the room. She didn't know if he believed her about the whale. He hadn't said either way, and she didn't dare ask.

"Could you look at these engine records?" Charlie asked, a frown in their voice, and Raisel turned back to her...colleague.

"Sure," she said. "What did you want to—oh."

Charlie had pulled up the records from the day she'd seen the whale-shape and collapsed on the bridge. She reluctantly edged closer to them, frowning at the screen.

"These are normal," she said. "There's a bit of green, sure, but nothing too unusual." Unnervingly so, for such a momentous day; if she hadn't seen the date, she wouldn't have realized when the records were from.

Charlie was staring at the screen, brow furrowed. "But that doesn't make any sense," they said after a long moment. "I thought for sure there'd be *some* sign down here—the engine takes in ambient aether."

"Yes," said Raisel, though it hadn't been a question.

"Would it show if we went through an aetherstorm? I mean. Assuming they exist."

"Yes," said Raisel, frowning. She pointed at one of the indicators. "There, if nowhere else—those readings were fluctuating all over the place when we were nearer to the sun. It's been much easier than we expected to get a smooth aether intake this far out. We expected it to stay as tumultuous."

"And an aetherstorm should be even more turbulent than the space near Earth," Charlie murmured, staring at the records.

"I'd expect so."

"But that doesn't make *sense*," said Charlie. They turned, pacing slowly around the engine room, seemingly deep in thought.

"Why not?" asked Raisel. "I mean, *I* fainted, but that doesn't mean the *engines* should have gone haywire."

"My instruments did, though," said Charlie. "I had a warning that there was an aetherstorm imminent. That the aethereal bands were disrupted, that aethereal activities were over 800 Valheims."

Raisel choked. "Eight *hundred*?" she asked incredulously.

They shrugged. "That's what it said. Anyway, it had calmed down by the time I got back from the bridge, but those readings indicated serious disruptions to the aether around the *Ēarendel* and these ones...don't."

"Did you talk to Dr. Andersen about that?" she asked.

"I did," said Charlie, "though I admit I was a bit distracted. The ship seemed fine, so we figured we hadn't caused problems, and we had to make sure everything was under control—it slipped our minds. But it was most of my instruments, so I doubt it was a glitch—and yet there's nothing here to show that it happened."

"Where do your instruments measure?" Raisel asked slowly. "Because the engine sensors only deal with the engine itself and its immediate proximity. If your sensors were looking elsewhere..."

"There's direct sensors across most of the ship, and indirect sensors that can detect things happening within a few kilometers of the *Ēarendel*," they said. "I didn't look too closely at which sensors were sending the alerts, only which machines. I wonder..."

"We can check later," said Raisel, who recognized the expression on Charlie's face as their *wander-off-first-think-about-it-later* look, and hadn't forgotten that the two of them were responsible for the engines until Julian got back. "We have work to do here."

"Right," said Charlie, nodding. "Later."

Raisel stared at the screen, at the numbers glowing innocently against the dark background. The disturbance map that Charlie had made for that day sprawled across the next monitor, damning evidence that *something* had happened, even if it turned out not to be as Raisel remembered it.

"You said you believed me yesterday," said Raisel slowly, "and I'm— I'm honestly not sure *I* believed me yesterday, not fully at least. There were doubts I couldn't shake. Now, though…"

"There was definitely *something* there," said Charlie, wide-eyed and disarmed in a way they usually didn't let themself appear. "A disturbance in the aether, if nothing else."

Raisel stood there silently, weighing what she was about to say. She didn't want to start another fight with Charlie, not when they'd been getting on so well today, but the last argument—which she had started, to be fair—still weighed on her mind, and she couldn't focus past it.

"Last night," she said delicately, "when I…accused you of not believing me in the past. And implied you didn't actually believe me now. You started to say something else. What did you want to say? I won't— I'm not— I want to know, if you're still willing to tell me."

Charlie sighed and leaned back in their chair. "I never thought you would make up something like *this*," they said eventually. "Only— well—you said you'd join me as soon as you could. I thought you meant for college."

Raisel let out a long sigh; she looked at the light-studded ceiling rather than at Charlie as she spoke. "I wanted to have the best chance I could of going out into the stars," she said slowly. "I wanted to learn about the aether, yes, but I didn't—I never had the same taste for pure research as you, Charlie. Nor for academics in the abstract, for that matter." She paused. "I didn't know how to explain it," she admitted, "so I just…didn't. Even after we came out here. For what it's worth, I'm sorry I kept cutting our conversations short."

Charlie sighed. "I…should not have taken it so personally," they said, each word carefully chosen and placed delicately into the air of the laboratory. Raisel looked down to see them make a curtailed gesture toward the computer bank. "But like I said—I never thought you would make up something like a whale in the luminiferous aether. Even if I did…" They pointed at the screen where the disturbance map was displayed. "*That* is pretty damn compelling evidence that there was *something* out there, something real."

Raisel nodded, leaning forward with her hands on the table to study the shape. If she squinted at it just right…

"I'd like to loop in Gloria and Mr. Ramírez," said Charlie.

She blinked. "You think they'll believe me? Us?" She didn't want to ask Julian if he thought she'd lied or hallucinated the whole episode. If Dr. Andersen thought that, it wouldn't be too bad, but from her mentor it would sting.

"I'm not sure," Charlie admitted, "but they don't have to. They just need to look at the readings and cross-reference their data; they shouldn't have trouble seeing the discrepancies. So what do you say, Raisa? Want to show our mentors the shadow in these data?"

Raisel sighed and shook her head, a playful smile curling across her mouth. "I told you ages ago, Charlie," she said. "You can call me Raisel—all my friends do, after all. And if you think they'll take this seriously—who am I to refuse?"

"All right then, *Raisel*," said Charlie, and with their words some fractured thing in Raisel's chest started knitting itself together. "Let's go find your whale."

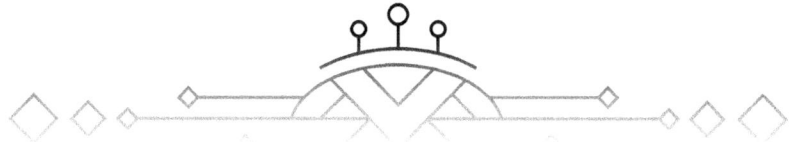

Em Rowntree

Cadillac's Bus

child, coming of age, found family, illness (serious), mentor, modern with magic, non-binary, present tense, sports (racing), teenager, third person point of view

SEVEN YEARS OLD

The rolling moors of North Yorkshire are toasting to a perfect gold in the sunset, the hard handsomeness of the crags and pits softened by scrubby little heather plants and twists of yellow-green grass. A fat, chugging aethership muddles through the clouds. Its hulking engines leave sweet, small puffs of iridescent vapour in its wake.

The world here is huge or tiny. Nothing in between.

Across the moors, there runs the road from coastal Whitby to the silver city of York, capital of the North. By the time the road reaches York, it's a sprawling eight-lane delta packed with aethercars, their exhausts spattering every spire and shopfront with shining dust—aetherlight. Here, though, on the moorland, the road is a thin weave of grey through the spread of purple and green. Close to the tiny village of Levisham, it nestles for the stretch of a few hundred yards in the shadow of a small cliff, a jaggedy crumble.

Today, as the sun goes down, there is a person running to the edge of the clifftop. A kid. They throw their arms out to steady themself to a last-minute halt, then stand looking down on the road below.

Their shoulders are heaving. The loose folds of their oversized tie-dye T-shirt are dark with sweat. The ends of a few locks of their short dark hair are silver-tipped, and the corners of their eyes are speckled with a metallic sheen—aetherlight. They smear the back of a hand against their shiny top lip. They are a single quiver of life in a vast stillness, their fists clenched, out of breath, with baby hairs clinging damply to their forehead.

The kid closes their eyes for a second, steadying their breathing. In their brilliantly colourful T-shirt, they don't quite belong here on the moorland; the awkward slope of their shoulders speaks to a history of not quite belonging in most places.

In the distance, there is a sound. Faint at first. It's a harmony, the notes sweet and true as if sung by a choir of empyrean voices. The kid's breathing speeds up again, and they stare raptly over the valley beneath.

As they wait, the sound—that fluting, argent singing—grows louder, and louder, and louder still. The kid balls their fists. The sound serenades higher, and now the low growl of an engine can be heard underneath. The kid watches the road below, waiting…waiting…

Round the corner bursts—an aetherlight rally racer!

The racer's truck is big and ugly, with a wide snout, a mud-spattered chassis, and massive wheels that tear up the compacted dirt of the road. Its engine growls and sings, slurping through aetherfuel, leaving behind a cloud of shining aetherlight mist.

As it takes the bend, two wheels lift high into the air.

Camera drones whizz and circle admiringly, and far above, the kid stares with their mouth open. The truck is suspended—might tip and fall, as so many have on this turn—and then, at the driver's force of will, all four wheels *thud* back to the ground and the truck barrels forwards.

From their viewpoint on the clifftop, the kid can't see the rally racer themself. They can't see the black gloves with five-pointed white stars on the back. Can't see the curled mess of long grey hair or the steely, hungry, fiercely joyful look on their face as they ram the truck into gear and plunge on through the moorland. But they can imagine every last detail.

They throw their hands in the air.

"CADILLAC JONES!" they yell, loud enough to crack their voice—but nowhere near loud enough for Cadillac Jones themself to hear as they race away down the track. "CADILLAC JONES FOREVER! YES! THE BEST—" The kid turns left and right as though looking for someone to tell, but there's no one beside them. "THE BEST! CADILLAC

JONES FOREVER! YES!"

They tremble all over, almost smiling. The self-consciousness is brushed away, just for now. They don't drop their hands, trying to keep this shining moment alive as long as they can.

"Cadillac Jones forever," they say again, more quietly. The heather rustles in a breeze, the only answer. They lower their arms and swallow hard.

The kid stands still, eyes unfocused, teeth chattering with adrenaline and the way the sweat on their T-shirt is drying cold.

There, in the distance—the singing is starting again, and the kid's back straightens, eyes going wide.

Another truck comes hurtling round the bend. The kid lifts their arms—and this time, they turn their open hands into raised middle fingers.

"YOU SUCK!" they scream in delight. "YOU'LL NEVER BE CADILLAC JONES! CADILLAC JONES FO—"

The kid's pocket hums, cutting them off. They lick their slightly silvered lower lip, then pull out a phone and answer it.

"Hi, sweet pea," says a gentle, crackly voice.

Self-consciousness settles back over the kid, smothering and immediate, tensing their shoulders and stiffening their neck.

"Mum!" they say, as though they weren't just screaming and waving obscenities. "Hi!"

"I'm on my way home. Are you still watching the race on TV?"

"Um…um…uh, well, um," the kid says, their tone hitting every note up an arpeggio of uncertainty. They move away from the edge of the cliff and the roar of the truck on the road below. "What if I…went out to look?"

"What?" their mother says sharply. "How many times—?"

"Just kidding!" the kid says. "Just kidding. I'm still at home."

"Oh. Well. I think you've got it on too loud, pet."

"Mum…I still don't like being called that."

"All right, sweet pea."

"I don't like that eith—"

"I'll be home in ten, okay?"

"Ten minutes?" The kid swallows. "Okay!"

"Love you, petal!" Their mum ends the call.

The kid breathes for a couple of still, steady seconds. The sunstruck moorland is an aloof expanse, too rugged and old to be bothered by the concerns of a tiny person who slipped away from home to see their favourite rally racer in real life.

Then, with a stilted little clap to get themself moving, the tiny person springs into action and sprints away from the cliff's edge.

"Jack Rapid…makes the third corner…with devastating ease!" The kid narrates themself through gasps of air as they swing round a bend in the path.

A shaggy cow watches, unbothered, as they streak past—legs pumping, breath coming sharp.

"No one's ever seen racing like this!" Jack Rapid shouts in the cow's general direction. The cow chews and doesn't answer.

"Unbelievable…speeds!" they pant as they struggle up a hill, making for the track that will lead them back to Levisham—and home. "I can't…believe…they're going to make it!"

In fact, of course, they do not make it. Jack Rapid arrives eight minutes and seven seconds after their mother gets home. They are gently but soundly chastised, and told at length about the dangers of going running across the moors, and being close to an aetherlight rally race, and aetherlight rally racing in general—and they are sent to bed, with the threat of their Cadillac Jones poster being taken away.

THIRTEEN YEARS OLD

Jack Rapid walks the length of Levisham village in their crisp school uniform; the blazer material is tight across their shoulders and an embroidered patch on the pocket reads *Whitby College*. Their short, dark hair looks brushed and the little aetherlight streaks at the corners of their eyes seem to have been scrubbed—which hasn't removed the silver, but it's given the surrounding skin a raw, self-conscious redness.

Left of the pub and past old Ethel Shipley's house, several yards down Little Field Lane, is a bus stop. The chrome and glass shelter is a puncture of modernity at the side of the crumbly lane peeling off larger Braygate Road.

Jack reaches the bus stop and steps beneath it to get out of the drizzle.

There's another person in a black, hooded raincoat at the station, someone Jack doesn't recognise by the shape of them—which is unusual, since everyone knows everyone in Levisham. They're barely as tall as Jack, even wearing big black boots. Jack stands awkwardly, each movement an apology for the fact that they just do not quite look as though they fit. Not in the old village, not at the new bus stop, not in their too-small uniform.

They glance over at a poster stuck to the bus shelter, tattered corners fluttering in the breeze, which advertises a local garage with *Hundreds of aethercars for sale! Best prices in town! Auto-faith always included!* Jack reads it and rolls their eyes.

"First day at the big school, is it, Jack?"

Jack looks up to see Ethel Shipley tottering down her garden, come to have a nosy at who's waiting for the bus.

"Aye," Jack says.

"Your mum's been at your eyes again."

Jack says nothing, only reaches up to touch the scrubbed skin with the tip of a worried finger.

"If you'd stop hanging around aethercars and getting face-fulls of aetherlight every other day, she wouldn't have to bother." Ethel casts a curious look at the stranger in the black raincoat as she speaks, paying more mind to them than to Jack.

Jack swallows a reply and offers a truculent expression that Ethel doesn't see. A gust of wind blusters past and flutters the aethercar poster again.

"Ooh, blast that thing," Ethel says, waggling her walking stick towards the poster.

Jack perks up. "I know! I *hate* auto-faith," they answer with feeling. "Aetherfuel's meant to run on the belief of the driver, it's the whole point."

The stranger in the black raincoat shifts.

"Ooh, I don't mind that." Ethel waves Jack away. "One doesn't always want to have to wish upon the star of one's own bloody car just to bloody get somewhere. If the car'll believe in itself for me, that's grand. I just wish they'd fix this poster. Looks a right mess."

Jack deflates and shrugs in answer.

"Have a good day, anyway, pet," Ethel says a little absently.

"I don't like—" Jack bites back the rest of the sentence as Ethel continues.

"Best of luck with the bus. I've not seen it stop in Levisham before."

"Mum says to just wait here for it," Jack says.

"Driver won't come down the lane, though," says Ethel. "Doesn't like having to turn around the Godcake. Sticks to Braygate Road."

"Oh." Jack casts a look over at the stranger in the black raincoat. Their face is completely hidden by the hood, and they don't react to Ethel's pronouncement. "Well. Maybe the driver will see us and come up this way."

Ethel makes a wide-eyed, sceptical face. "All right, pet. Ta-ra, then," she says, and ambles away.

Jack swallows and slides an earbud into one ear. They keep their eyes fixed on the main road, looking out for the bus, as they listen.

"…and you know, Kev, the thing is," says an American voice on the radio through Jack's earbud, *"everyone knows that aetherlight rally racing hasn't been the same these last few years. It's all about money. Everyone wants a brand deal. No one's driving the old trucks…"*

"The old trucks? You can't install auto-faith, Sal."

"Cadillac Jones never needed auto-faith," Jack mutters.

"Cadillac Jones never needed auto-faith," says Sal. Jack smirks wryly. It's been six years since Cadillac Jones drove in an aetherlight rally race, six years since anyone heard from them at all—but their name is still spoken. The only aetherlight rally racer never to have a navigator or use auto-faith. They had a perfect streak—finished every race they entered, and did it alone.

"Cadillac Jones forever," Jack murmurs, staring down the road, waiting for the bus.

"What's that?" says a sudden, rough voice with a North Yorkshire accent even thicker than Ethel Shipley's.

Jack starts, tugging out their earbud and turning to the stranger in the raincoat—who pulls their hood down, releasing coarse grey hair into a tangled halo around a lined, unfriendly face. They stare at Jack with bright blue eyes, long streaks of aetherlight silver at the corners.

"What," they say stoutly, "did you just say?"

Jack simply gawps.

The mess of hair, the eyes. Jack glances down and sees dark gloves with five-pointed white stars on the back.

Jack gawps some more.

This is Levisham bus stop. Levisham: tiny village in the middle of nowhere. Resident count: thirty-seven—and that included Ethel Shipley's pet pigeons. All eight of them.

Jack knows that they can't be looking at Cadillac Jones, internationally famous rally racer, personal hero, here at the bus stop. It's not possible. It has to be some kind of uncanny resemblance.

The person who definitely isn't Cadillac Jones standing at Levisham bus stop, but looks a lot like them—looks *so much* like them—narrows their eyes.

"Well," they grunt, turning to face the road with their hands folded behind their back, "I do agree with you about auto-faith, at least."

Jack breathes out. Very, very slowly. Slightly shakily. Sal's and Kev's voices are still chattering through their earbud, and Jack fumbles to shut them off and slip their earbuds into a pocket.

"Bloody stupid thing," Definitely-Not-Cadillac adds after an awkward few moments. "Auto-faith. If you don't believe your car'll go, you shouldn't be going in the first place."

Jack quivers next to the sturdy, confident figure beside them. They sneak another glance.

Surely-Not-Cadillac reaches up and adjusts the grey neck scarf under their raincoat, the same motion the world watched Cadillac Jones perform a thousand times during interviews and behind-the-scenes footage.

Jack looks back at the road. Slowly, as the seconds pass, their cheeks redden. They open their mouth, then close it again. Their heartbeat isn't quite visibly thumping in their chest, but it's near enough.

"What time does the bus come?" Couldn't-Be-Cadillac says.

"Um. I don't know," Jack answers, in a high-pitched voice. "First day taking it to Whitby."

"Mm."

The grunt is slightly hostile. Jack steals another glance. The gloves—unmistakable.

"What are you doing here?" Jack finally blurts.

In response, they receive a hard stare.

"I don't like stupid questions." There's a sniff and an audible swallow. "I am getting on the bus."

Jack presses their lips together. One of Cadillac Jones's trademark disapproving sniff-and-swallows, and it happened because of *them*.

After another few moments, the unimpressed voice adds, "I am here for some peace and quiet."

Jack tilts their head to look again, and they see an expression that's tired, almost hollow. The tension in Jack's shoulders eases a little, the softness of sympathy.

"Aha," Possibly-Cadillac says. Jack turns to follow their eyeline and sees the flat front of a double-decker bus bombing down Braygate Road.

"It's going fast," Jack says. A heady, blue-white cloud of aetherlight pours from the bus's exhaust.

"Mm," says Probably-Cadillac.

"I don't think it's going to stop," Jack says, their voice slightly higher than usual. "No one ever gets on here, so it doesn't stop."

"It'll stop." They say it simply, with the unbothered authority of someone completely sure of themself.

"What if it doesn't stop?" Jack says as the bus hurtles on.

"It will stop."

The bus is close enough that Jack can make out the driver: a pink-faced person with a moustache like a pipe cleaner. He's eating a sandwich with one hand and steering with the other. He does not look like a man about to stop a bus.

"It's not going to stop!" Jack says again, a catch of panic in their voice. Almost-Certainly-Cadillac has their hands behind their back, watching as the bus grumbles onwards. The driver makes limpid, uninterested eye contact with Jack across the yards between them, and then the bus sails past the turning to Little Field Lane, offering views of empty seats.

And then, with no screech of brakes—with only a sudden silence as aetherfuel stops humming through the engine—the bus comes to an abrupt halt.

There is a second of uncertain hush.

The leaves on the trees around the station rustle, astonished. The bus rolls gently backwards. It takes the turn to the right, bumbles down Little Field Lane, and stops so that the doors are right by the spot where Had-To-Be Cadillac Jones stands waiting. Their shoulders are square. Their chin is up.

Jack's mouth is wide open.

"You did that?" they say.

Cadillac Jones says, "I believe I did."

The doors hiss open. The driver, ruddy-faced and jowls quivering, stares apoplectically. He says nothing, only wobbles in indignation.

Jack looks up at Cadillac Jones, into their lined face, the aether-blue eyes, the chaotic mess of their coarse hair. Cadillac's lips are grim and thin, but there—there at the corners is a glimmer of the old, ferocious smile they wore when they whipped their way around a perfect turn in record time.

"Amazing," Jack says, tone dipped in awe.

Cadillac looks taken aback for just a moment, then offers a brief, smile-free wink, and gets on the bus.

"Cadillac Jones forever," Jack whispers, and they follow.

The next morning, Cadillac stops the bus again.

The driver, a puffed-up shade of puce, manages to say as they board, "You are not allowed to take control of the bus."

Jack, standing behind Cadillac and waiting to get on, blinks and looks up at Cadillac's profile.

"It's my impression," says Cadillac Jones in their slow, rounded-vowel accent, "that the bus is expected to stop at Levisham Station should there be passengers waiting. It is my intention to aid the bus in that endeavour."

"But it's not your bus," the driver blusters. "I've driven this bus for forty years. It's mine."

Cadillac's face doesn't move an inch. "If you believed that," they say simply, "it wouldn't stop. Being as that's how aetherfuel works."

The driver opens his mouth to argue. Cadillac raises an eyebrow, and the bus beneath them gives a low growl.

The driver's argument dies as he scrambles to grip the handbrake. "Who are you, anyway?" he demands. "Don't I know you?"

"No," Cadillac Jones says. "You do not." They glance over their shoulder at Jack. "You don't know me."

Jack ducks their head in acknowledgement.

"Well," the driver says. "You'll be wanting to be picked up every day, then?"

"Every weekday," Cadillac says. They turn to Jack. "Does that sound right to you?"

"Um. Yes," Jack says, skewered on the aether-bright stare of their hero, sounding small and atonal after the steady thrum of Cadillac's voice.

"Right you are," the driver manages begrudgingly.

Cadillac offers no thanks. They walk onto the bus and sit down. Jack follows, squaring their shoulders as they go.

SEVENTEEN YEARS OLD

"No," Cadillac Jones says. "You're *trying* to believe, again."

Jack Rapid, perched in their usual seat on the bus with their legs folded awkwardly beneath them, rolls their eyes so hard as to be in danger of a sprain. "You don't want me to try?" they say.

"I've watched you try for years, now," Cadillac retorts. "I want you to get on with it."

Jack releases a breath of performed annoyance. Cadillac raises an eyebrow at the show of temper, and Jack shrinks in response.

"Drive the bus," Cadillac says.

"I'm doing my best," replies Jack.

"So I keep hearing."

"You don't help," Jack says, stung. Cadillac is implacable in the face of their indignation. Ahead of them, oblivious as ever, the bus driver eats his sandwich.

"What d'you want me to do?" Cadillac says. "Just drive the bus."

"I don't get it! I'm finally old enough to drive, but my mum says it's too dangerous and I'll hurt someone, and all you do is tell me to get on with it, and no one is *ever* actually listening to me—" Jack stops short when Cadillac gives a very Northern harrumph.

"There's no trick I can teach you," Cadillac says, slow-spoken and unflappable. "Just do it." Jack scowls. "Or don't," Cadillac adds.

"I'm trying," Jack says.

"Don't," Cadillac answers. "Stop trying. Get on with it."

"I don't understand how I'm meant to do it," Jack says in a tone of controlled frustration, "without trying to do it first. That's how doing things works. You *try* to do them until you *can* do them, and then you *just do* them. I can't skip ahead to *just doing* it."

Cadillac considers this with their lined face pulled into a rare show of pensiveness. They reach into their pocket, and—quite suddenly—something small and thin is thrown Jack's way across the bus. Jack catches it and looks down: a plain ballpoint pen.

"Do something with that," Cadillac says. "Anything."

Jack stares at them. When Cadillac gives no sign of elaborating, Jack bites their lip, uncaps the pen, and then—with a little hesitation—writes "hello" on the back of one hand.

"Like that?" they say.

Cadillac asks, "Why did you do that?"

"What? You asked me to," Jack answers, indignant again.

"I mean, why did you do that, and not something else?"

"I don't know," Jack says. "It's a pen. I wrote something."

Cadillac smiles—a warm, sudden smile that belies their usual gruffness, their blue eyes lit up and crinkled at the corners.

It draws a toothy little grin out of Jack in answer. "What?" they ask again.

"As you said," Cadillac replies. "It's a pen. You wrote something." When Jack looks none the wiser, Cadillac goes on. "You've never seen that pen before. You couldn't even know for sure that it was a pen, could you?"

"It looked like a pen."

"Exactly. You believed it was a pen, so you acted as though it were a pen, and you wrote something down—and it worked. You didn't have to *try* to believe it was a pen, did you? You just acted. And it worked." Cadillac leans in, looking directly into Jack's eyes. "Jack, this is a bus. Drive it. It will work."

Thirty seconds later, there's a holler from the driver at the front of the bus. "Oi! No taking control of the vehicle!"

And Jack *beams*. There's no weight on their shoulders, no apology in their eyes. Their chin is up.

"Cadillac Jones forever," they say, which is received with a slight raise of one eyebrow.

Eighteen years old

"You should do it," Jack says. Beside them, tacked to the bus stop on Little Field Lane, is a shiny new poster advertising tourist rides on

Shipley's Aetherships over the moors; Ethel Shipley appears to have taken matters into her own hands in keeping the bus stop tidy.

"Don't," Cadillac says—their advice about many things. This time, Cadillac says it with particular conviction.

"Why not?" Jack demands. They've shot up to six foot and gone back to tie-dye. They have an air of fragile confidence in the tilt of their head, the square of their shoulders, the straightness of their back.

"I've told you," Cadillac says. "Rally racing is a nest of vipers. Auto-faith in every car. I won't race against machines. I'm done with racing. I am here," they say regally, "for peace and quiet."

"Come on—you always said Whitby to York was your favourite race. Sign-ups are open until the race starts tomorrow afternoon. Please," Jack says, with a warmth in their eyes that begs for an answering smile from Cadillac.

Cadillac does not smile. "It's a nest of vipers," they say again.

"But you're *Cadillac Jones*," Jack says. "You're the best there ever was! Who cares if every vehicle has auto-faith these days? You could still beat the lot of 'em in your old hog!"

"She's scrap," Cadillac Jones says.

"WHAT?"

"She's scrap," Cadillac repeats, and looks—perhaps for the first time in their five-year acquaintanceship—a little self-conscious in pulling their usual unbothered expression. "I'm never racing again. I took her apart. Sold her for spares."

Jack makes a noise as though they've been struck.

In answer, Cadillac only looks at them. Defensiveness makes their aether-blue eyes suddenly colder, suddenly distant.

In the face of a simple, withering look, Jack's teetering tower of self-assuredness sways, almost recovers, and then topples completely.

"Jack—" Cadillac says, half understanding Jack's quiet internal disaster.

"It's fine," Jack says. "It's fine."

The next morning, Jack and Cadillac wait at the bus stop with an air of awkwardness between them.

Cadillac, tiny and in black, stands with their arms folded next to all

six foot of the awkward, quivering tie-dye brilliance that is Jack Rapid.
"I went to sign up," Jack says suddenly into the quiet, as if pulling off
a plaster. "To the race. Myself. I know it's stupid, but I wanted to try."
The quality of Cadillac's silence changes. They tense, but they don't
look at Jack.

In her garden, Ethel Shipley is sweeping leaves. She gives Jack and
Cadillac a semi-curious squint through huge glasses, then decides to ignore them.

After a few moments, Jack adds, "I didn't tell them I knew you, by the
way. In case you were worried."

"I wasn't," Cadillac says.

"I mean, I didn't have much of a chance anyway. They laughed me
out. Wouldn't let me sign up. Obviously. Otherwise, I'd be there right
now. Getting ready for the race. And I'm not. So…you already knew
that. But, yeah, it's fine. I knew it probably wouldn't work, so…not to
worry."

Cadillac looks at them askance. "Laughed?" they say, picking one
word from the many. "Why?"

Jack pulls a face. "I mean," they say. "You know."

Cadillac turns to face them fully. "No, I don't," they answer.

"Well," Jack says in a tone that promises an attempt at airy humour is
on the way. "First of all, just look at me. Second of all, it's an aetherlight
rally race on the international stage, and I don't have a truck. Don't have
a navigator. Don't have auto-faith."

Cadillac's expression is razor sharp when they say quietly, "No rule
against that. I never had a navigator. Or auto-faith."

"Exactly," says Jack with a laugh that sounds painful.

"Exactly, what?" Cadillac pushes.

"Well, *look* at me," Jack says. "Northern accent. Trying to enter the
race solo, no auto-faith. Asking to be called 'they' and 'them,' name that's
obviously made up—everyone just thinks I'm trying to be you."

Cadillac's eyes turn hawk-like, almost cruel.

"Which is hilarious, obviously," Jack manages, sounding casual, an
edge of self-aimed savagery revealing their distress. "Because I'm not like
you, am I?" They try another laugh. "I already know that."

Cadillac says nothing.

"It's embarrassing, isn't it," Jack says, after a moment's thought. "I sort of knew that I was embarrassing. Going around trying to ask people to call me Jack Rapid. No one's ever really wanted to, but I thought, one day they'll see. But they won't, will they? I'm never going to be Jack Rapid. I'm going to be *petal* and *sweet pea* for the rest of my life, and I've just— It's just…" They look over at Cadillac's stern, unyielding face, and then they look down. "Whatever."

Jack shrugs, an easy movement that belies the weight they're carrying. It's a shrug with a history, with precedents: a shrug that has been shrugged by hundreds of millions of people with an idea about who they could be, who have been met with laughter or eye rolls or confusion or a combination of all three—and in the face of not ever being listened to, or taken seriously, or trusted, have melted into the wistful, painful, passive oblivion of a shrug.

Cadillac Jones, who knows all about shrugs and doesn't hold with them, says, "Don't."

Jack shrugs again.

"You…" For once, for a brief moment, Cadillac is lost for words. And then they say, "You are going to sign up to that race."

Jack turns to look at them. "What?" they say.

"You're going to join the bloody race."

"I can't," Jack says. They half smile. "I should've followed your lead. Quit before I started."

"I was wrong," Cadillac says, and the unexpectedness of the statement startles Jack out of their resignation. Cadillac puts a gloved hand on Jack's shoulder. "I was wrong."

Jack rolls their eyes, attempting lightness.

"You knew I was wrong," Cadillac says. "You still know."

"Come on." Jack shakes their head. "I can't join the race. I literally already tried, and it was just embarrassing."

"Then don't try." Cadillac's hand tightens on Jack's shoulder, the white star on the back of their glove seeming almost to blaze with light. "For the last time, you don't bloody try. You don't try to join the race, you just do it. You don't try to be Jack Rapid, you just are." Jack's gaze brightens a little—the shy, uncertain glimmer of damage receding. "You aren't trying to be me, you're just you. You don't try to join the race. You just get on with it. And anyway, you'll be navigator." Cadillac swallows, and then says, "I'll drive."

Jack's jaw drops.

"But…" They search for words. "Peace and quiet…?"

"Blow peace and quiet," says Cadillac Jones, standing up to the fullness of their short height there on Levisham bus station. "I'm Cadillac Jones. Best there ever was. I'm only not driving these days because of sheer bloody-mindedness over the way things changed years ago."

"And now you know you were wrong about that?" Jack says, hope blooming over their face.

"Absolutely not," Cadillac Jones says. "The changes were extremely stupid, and I was right to leave the whole filthy lot. But you…" Cadillac looks at Jack, and through the cracks in the cement of their expression grows something alive, something full of softness and care and respect. "If you want to be there, you'll bloody well be there. I'll help you."

Jack holds Cadillac's gaze, and something passes between them—from the grizzled old rally racer to the kid they've watched grow day by day, bus ride by bus ride.

But then Jack's face falls. "But we don't have a truck," they say. "We don't even have my mum's car… She'd never let me take it, and anyway, she's gone out to the shops. We need something we can drive."

As Jack speaks, there comes a low and familiar grumble down Little Field Lane and the scent of aetherlight.

"Yes," Cadillac says, and their face splits into the widest and best smile that Jack has ever seen on them. "Yes. We need something we can drive."

⊳▷◁⊲

"Kev, have you ever seen anything like it?"

"Sal, I swear— Stop laughing so loud right into the mic, Sal, you'll deafen the folks at home. I have never seen anything like this before."

"If you're just joining now, folks… I can't stop laughing… Okay, if you're just joining now, here's what you need to be picturing: Cadillac Jones, back on the track. With a kid next to them who looks like a spaghetti noodle dipped in rainbows. And they're driving… Kev, you say it, I can't…"

"They're driving a bus, folks."

"A bus. It's… it's a bus."

"Can that thing corner?"

"If anyone can corner in it, it's Cadillac Jones."

"Does it have auto-faith?"

"I bet it doesn't. Every other vehicle in the race has it."

"Well, you know, I never liked to put my money on anyone other than Cadillac Jones in a rally race, but…"

"We'll keep you up to date, folks, as the race unfolds. Cadillac Jones and the tie-dye wonder were the last ones to leave today, so the race ends when they cross the line—and we're all waiting to see if Cadillac Jones can keep up their perfect streak, never leaving a race unfinished…"

"Hold your nerve," Cadillac Jones snaps, their teeth gritted. "Hold your *nerve.*"

"I'm fine!" Jack calls over the roar of the engine, one hand gripping a pole and the other braced against the door. The bus swings around yet another impossible corner.

"I wasn't talking to you!" Cadillac calls back, and wrenches the wheel with their gloved hands. Jack glances over at them and sees ruthless focus. Out the windscreen, the moors are rolling past. Purple heather spotted through with green bracken stretches as far as the eye can see—until they plunge through a treeline and into dense forest. The bus doesn't sing and growl like a rally race truck—it sputters, it croaks.

Jack clears their throat.

"Do you need me to tell you what direction to—?"

"Don't actually need a navigator!" Cadillac shouts. "I know where I am. You just don't fall over."

"We're going to come last!" Jack cries.

Cadillac spares them a ferocious look as tree branches whip the windows of the bus. "We're going to finish the race if we're lucky!" they shout grimly. "Last is the least of our—"

Crash. From above, there's the sound of tinkling glass. Cadillac swears.

"We have to finish," Jack says. "You've never not finished a race!"

"It was your bloody idea to enter in the first place!" Cadillac says.

"It was your bloody idea to take the bloody bus!" Jack shouts back, and receives only a long, wordless, increasingly loud yell of determination in response.

The bus bundles forwards.

Every corner is a teeth-clenching nightmare. Every trundling lumber to left or right sends glass shards skittering across the upper deck. And every time the bus is spurred by Cadillac Jones's will, Jack lets out an involuntary gasp at the sudden power.

They survive turn after turn. Camera drones circle disbelievingly as they keep going, and keep going, and keep going.

At the halfway point, they lurch up to a place Jack knows. Above, there's the cliffside close to Levisham, toasting to golden brown in the sun. Jack's eyes widen. They're about to take the turn—the legendary turn, the one they watched Cadillac take all those years ago.

Time slows.

Two of the bus's wheels lift clear of the ground unwillingly. Like an ungainly creature, like an ageing, wizened monster, the bus groans and whines.

It tips. It tips a little more. And then a little more still.

The angle is impossible, the weight of the bus shifting. Jack can't breathe. Can't cry out. They turn their head towards Cadillac Jones, towards the reassurance of their stony, unchanging features.

But Cadillac Jones looks—they look *scared*.

Jack's stomach drops. They try to balance, reach out a hand. The bus hangs at an incline, protesting, screeching. Cadillac's hands are too tight on the wheel. Jack grabs their shoulder, and they meet each other's eyes.

A look passes between them, the most raw and urgent look that either of them will ever give to another person. On one side, Cadillac: suddenly frightened, small, bothered, not Cadillac Jones the rally racing hero but just a person. Just a person behind the wheel of a bus that is too big, a person with a name that is too big, a person with a history that is too big for them to live up to in this age of machines and automation and manufactured belief. And on the other side, staring back at them, Jack: young and lost and confused about how to be a person, how to be themself specifically. Only truly believing one thing for sure. Absolutely sure. Absolutely steady. Absolutely, definitively certain that Cadillac Jones is a hero and will not leave any race unfinished, no, they bloody will not.

"Let's GO," Jack yells, and with a *THUD*, the bus's two wheels slam back down onto the track and grind in, and they fly forwards. "Let's GOOOOOO! CADILLAC JONES!" Jack screams. "CADILLAC JONES FOREVER! YES!"

Cadillac Jones's laugh is feverish, high, proud.

"That was you!" they call. "That was you! That was your turn!"

"What?!"

"That was your turn! Shout your own name! JACK RAPID!"

Jack, wide-eyed, watches their hero raise a fist in the air for them.

"JACK RAPID!" Cadillac shouts again. As they pass under the empty cliff where Jack once stood to watch, Cadillac calls out their chosen name.

They don't win the race. Not even close. They lose, resoundingly, but they finish. When they get out of the bus, it's to the sound of laughter as well as cheers—and the cheering is louder.

"Let's race together forever," Jack says, face shining with triumph and young certainty.

And Cadillac Jones only hesitates for a second, only lets the barest shadow of doubt cross over their lined face, before they say, "Okay. Forever."

TWENTY-ONE YEARS OLD

Flushed with excitement, Jack leaps out of their first rally race truck and into the arms of their mother.

"What's our time?" they ask, staring over their mother's shoulder through the crowd, searching for the board announcing the times of each racing team. "Did we do it? Are we the leaders?"

"I don't know!" their mother says. "Oh, sweet pea, I'm so glad you're all right—"

"It's Jack, Mum. And once you've done it in a bus, one of these is *nothing*. Did you see the turn? The one right by home?"

"The one where I nearly had a conniption watching you, pet?"

"*Jack*, and yes! Cadillac let me take it again this time!" Jack says.

Cadillac Jones comes stomping round the side of their new truck with their usual air of solid unflappability. "You're coming along," they say, and the silver-lined streaks that crinkle round their eyes are the only indication that the pride they feel is fierce and true. "You'll be a driver yourself in no time."

"I don't want to," Jack says. Their eyes are bright and wild; the loose folds of their oversized tie-dye T-shirt are dark with sweat, and they smear the back of a hand against their shiny top lip. "We're the best team. I want to race with you forever."

Cadillac glances, just briefly, at Jack's mother. Then, "Right," they say simply. "Forever."

The three of them start to move through the crowds, heading for the boards to find out their time.

"You let me take that turn again," Jack says, beaming. "It was amazing."

"It's all yours," Cadillac says.

Jack stretches up to their full six foot, shoulders back, chin up.

They don't win, that year. But they do win the year after. And the year after that. And the year after that...and the year after that...

THIRTY YEARS OLD

"Mum, I'm going over to Cadillac's to work on the truck." Jack fumbles for their keys. The years have filled them out; they're now less a spaghetti noodle and more tagliatelle—and still a tie-dye wonder.

"Okay, sweet— Jack," their mother calls back from the kitchen over the sound of the kettle boiling.

Jack grins. "Almost," they say, one hand on the door handle.

"I'm getting there. Mind you look after Cadillac, won't you?"

Jack rolls their eyes.

"Hey," their mother says, catching the expression as she wanders into the hallway with a steaming, milky brew. "Cadillac's not as young as they once were, you know."

"Cadillac Jones is forever," Jack says.

It's only a short walk down the village to Cadillac's home, and Jack lets themself through the gate and taps their usual rhythm on the garage door as they go in.

"Finally," Cadillac says grumpily from under the truck.

Jack takes off their coat, their eyes finding the pristine framed poster for last year's charity race. Front and centre, back-to-back with arms crossed, are Cadillac Jones and Jack Rapid.

Jack reaches out and touches the frame. Cadillac looks as sturdy as ever. Maybe a few extra wrinkles. Maybe a little thinner. Jack turns away.

"Good morning," they say.

"Spanner."

Jack goes over and passes it down. Cadillac takes it with a bony, paper-skinned hand.

"Cadillac?" Jack says.

"Jack."

A moment of silence, and the mood shifts from light and normal to something else. Cadillac slides out from under the truck to look at Jack.

"Are we going to race together forever?" Jack says.

It's there, in Jack's voice—years of hero worship, years of friendship, years of little arguments and big celebrations, years of working together, years of caring about each other, years of familiarity and fighting for each other. All the love, it's there. All in one single, vulnerable, naïve little question.

"I don't like stupid questions," Cadillac says. "Pass me that spark plug."

Jack grabs it and turns to Cadillac, meeting their eyes. And even though it isn't in their voice, or in their words, it's all there in Cadillac's aether-blue eyes. All the love, right there to be seen. All the love, and a wrenching grief.

"Spark plug," Cadillac repeats, and Jack gives it to them.

Thirty-five years old

White walls and blue floors, and the smell of bleach and aether.

A bed with handles. Worn-out chairs, boring curtains, a lamp that casts a jaundiced light. None of which Cadillac would have chosen.

A blur of hands, clothes unpacked. A leather jacket hanging in a plain wardrobe with mothballs inside, and gloves with five-pointed stars on the back tucked away in a drawer that squeaks.

Cadillac Jones, lying still.

The wrong name being said. Corrections. *Cadillac. Their name is Cadillac Jones.*

Cadillac stirs. Someone in a uniform slips out of the room, leaving Jack and Cadillac alone.

"It's the race in two weeks," Jack says. They sit stiffly, as though fighting the urge to grab Cadillac's hand and try to run away with them. "The Whitby to York."

Cadillac only looks at them.

"Please," Jack says. "I need you."

Cadillac says nothing.

"No. Don't," Jack says.

Cadillac watches Jack with deep, aether-blue eyes.

"Stop it," Jack says, in a quiet voice. "I can't. I can't do that turn without you, let alone the whole race."

Cadillac blinks, and then—like a tiny, impossible sunrise in this never-ending night of a place, they smile. Slowly, as if with great effort, they clear their throat and take a breath.

"Jack Rapid," Cadillac says. "It's your turn."

Jack opens their mouth as if to protest, but their words fail them.

Cadillac reaches for Jack's hand. Jack clasps it, tight, like a child being led through the dark.

Gunning the truck's engine, Jack's face stays expressionless as the wheels churn up the ground below.

Beside them, an empty space. No raised voices cut through the silvery song of the aetherfuel moving through the growling, hungry engine.

The race has been a heady mess so far: corners turned badly, routes almost missed. Coming up to the halfway point, they're about to go flying round the corner that passes right by Levisham. For the first time in Jack's life, they're going to be doing it without Cadillac Jones beside them. No fierce blue eyes. No black gloves with five-pointed white stars. No cry of joy when Jack sticks the landing on the turn. No laughter.

Jack can almost hear the commentators, now.

And coming up to the bend, Jack...uh...what was it? Cadillac's carried them over the finish line for years. Now, for the first time, they're trying to drive it themself...

The turn is coming closer. Shoulders hunched and tense, hands clenched, Jack wrenches the wheel.

A swerve, and the engine cuts out. Just dies.

The truck teeters.

Jack tries. Tries so hard, screws up their courage, their belief, everything they have left. They try, teeth gritted, heart aching, knuckles white, and nothing happens.

A beat of dead silence. Then—

Don't. Stop trying, Cadillac Jones says, on a bus, years ago. *Get on with it.*

Jack lets out a throaty yell.

The truck throws itself forwards as aetherfuel blazes through the engine in answer to Jack's will. They fly down the track, and their eyes lift as they always do, to the cliffside, to the place where they once stood as a child and screamed their heart out.

Jack draws in a breath so sharp they almost choke.

There, on the cliffside spot, are two figures.

On the left, a round and gentle shape: Jack's mother. And beside them, in what looks from a distance like an aetherfuel wheelchair—there is no mistaking that tangle of grey hair. The two silhouettes are tiny, but to Jack, they're huge against the sky.

They can't hear each other, not over the roar of the truck. But Cadillac Jones raises their hands, and Jack Rapid—shoulders square, chin up—shouts it with them.

"LET'S GO! JACK RAPID FOREVER!" Cheeks wet, breathing freely for the first time in weeks, Jack punches their fist as high as it will go. "CADILLAC JONES FOREVER! CADILLAC! JONES! FOREVER!"

"Well, Kev, have you ever seen anything like that?"

"Sure haven't, Sal. Really turned it around in the second half of that race, huh?"

"Almost beat their old mentor's record—and after a start like that. I can't believe it."

"Jack Rapid sure did believe it, though. That was aetherlight rally racing on a whole other level, today. And not a single helping hand from auto-faith. Doing Cadillac Jones proud."

"You know it. No matter what happens from now on, you know, Kev, I think one thing's for sure—the names Cadillac Jones and Jack Rapid are going down in rally racing history."

"Hell yeah, Sal. They'll be talking about these two forever…"

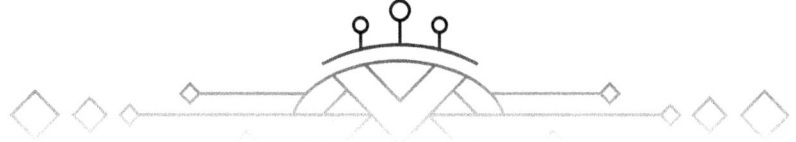

Kelas Lloyd

True

bigender, character study, foster family, found family, friends, genderfluid, magic use, modern with magic, non-binary, present tense, self-esteem issues, student (high school), teenager, third person limited point of view, transphobia (mentions of)

*W*hen Eva had tried to race the report card home, they'd expected an argument with their foster parents, not to be bundled into the car mere hours later, headed to remedial camp.

"Instructional camp, to help!" "Uncle" Rigel tries to lift the mood from the front passenger seat, but Eva knows better. This was one report card too many filled with "smart but doesn't apply themselves," "brilliant except can't master aether to save their life," and their favorite, "would have potential if they could stop playing class clown for five seconds." They're failing aether manipulation, and both the school and "Aunt" Erika have given up. Erika Cortola is a perfectionist who holds everyone around her to the same standard. Her daughter lives up to it, but the foster kid, not so much.

Eva's been expecting something along these lines for a while. They'd expected to be able to finish out their last week of school, though, and see their older foster-sister Kaelin crowned prom queen. So maybe their surprise is fair.

Kaelin sits in the back seat with them, having volunteered to come for the ride at the last minute. It's probably for support. No. It definitely is, going by the small smile she's offering Eva.

"I didn't pick up my yearbook," Eva says, even though they know it's too late. They're already five minutes down the road, and Aunt Erika turns around for nothing; she weaves aether through the car once she's set off like lives depend on it. She's nothing if not true to who she is—determined and focused at all times—which is why working aether comes so naturally to her.

"Your sister will get it for you. Text her a list of who you think will want to sign it." And that's Aunt Erika in a nutshell. She's never called Eva anything other than her child, despite how Eva's frizzy red curls stand out so dramatically compared to the rest of the family's straight jet-black hair. She's always referred to Kaelin as Eva's sister, never shown favoritism, but she's also very good at hitting the sore spot with a few words.

There aren't a lot of people who will sign Eva's yearbook, and they both know it.

Eva doesn't make friends easily. They don't see much of a point. Both their parents died in an accident when Eva was five, and they'd gone through eight foster homes until Uncle Rigel remembered his former friends' kid and went looking. One month before their eleventh birthday, they'd come to live with the Cortolas. Frankly, making it to a week shy of their sixteenth birthday before the Cortolas shipped them off, even if just for a bit, is also a surprise. Eva had privately wagered they'd last a year, max. Apparently, they didn't know others any better than they knew themself. They didn't see how a camp would help fix that, though. The way to channel aether wasn't just to know yourself, but to be true to yourself. With so many in their life giving up on them, Eva isn't sure they're gonna like themself enough to *want* to be true to themself.

"I'll make sure everyone signs it," Kaelin promises confidently, bringing Eva's thoughts back to the yearbook. She will. There's something magnetic about Kaelin's quiet confidence in everyone and everything around her. It makes people want to do better, or at least it makes Eva want to do better, and they're pretty sure they're not unique there.

Now they're out of objections. Oh, they could protest their birthday dinner being canceled, but being dressed up to go see a lot of also-dressed-up people who aren't actually related to them is an exhausting affair. The only thing they'll miss is the cake. It's good cake, and the bakers don't know what non-binary means, so each year there's tiny toy dinosaurs in little fabric bows all over it. Eva's partial to those dinosaurs. They live on Eva's desk in their bedroom and all have names. They look at Kaelin, and she reaches over to take their hand and give it a squeeze. "They'll help. And you'll have your driving license in no time."

Eva wants to claim they don't care about a driving license, but inability to use aether limits so much more than that. They can barely keep their phone alive for a full day, they can't operate the stove or microwave on their own, and very few workplaces want to hire someone aether-inept. Oh, some people choose to live without aether use, but they cluster in small communities focused on avoiding it. They've made a decision, not failed at self-realization so badly that they can't keep shower water hot for more than five minutes.

The drive is mostly silent after that. Uncle Rigel tries to start conversations a couple times, talking about how this is good, and helpful, and how they just want the best for Eva's future, but it doesn't work. Eva's wondering if they'll be left there if they keep failing at aether manipulation, Aunt Erika is frustrated that they haven't turned out another effortless aether master like her and Kaelin, and even Kaelin seems at a loss for once.

The car pulls into the camp parking lot. It's large, full, and paved, which at least means there's no pretense about it being rustic. That's a relief. Eva needs running water and lights that don't depend on them to work.

All four walk to the crowded registration tables. Eva's signed in by a bored-looking guy, given a booklet, told they're in Cabin S, and then Uncle Rigel gives them an awkward pat on the back and leaves.

Eva stares at how quickly he turns and walks away, feeling it sink in that they're here. Not only that, they've been left here because they're not measuring up.

Aunt Erika looks around, exhales, and nods decisively. "You're almost sixteen. Your parents' failures are no reflection on us, but you remaining a failure is. Turn this around." She turns and walks away just as fast, not giving Eva time to talk back.

Pained, they look at Kaelin. "My parents... I didn't know them, not for long, but..." Eva trails off. It had been a case of being at the wrong place at the wrong time—a gas leak at the theater had killed almost 200 people that night. Their deaths hadn't been their fault.

Kaelin leans over and gives Eva a tight hug. "From what Dad says, they weren't failures. He liked your dad a lot and was pretty in awe of your mom. And you're not one, either. You've got this. Mom's just being Mom."

Eva feels that's pretty generous, toward both themself and Aunt Erika.

Knowing they can't reply with that, Eva settles by hugging Kaelin back and giving her a nod after. They can't figure out what to say. "Goodbye" would make the chance of being abandoned here feel too real, and "see you later" feels too optimistic.

Kaelin gives their hand one more squeeze before joining her parents in the car. She waves as they pull out.

Neither Uncle Rigel nor Aunt Erika do.

This is real. They're alone here.

A throat clears behind them, and they turn to see a very tall, faintly smiling man with wavy brown hippie hair that feels at odds with their blue button-up shirt and brown slacks. Eva would feel out of place in dated cut-off jean shorts and a tank top except for the fact that this guy is the only one remotely dressed up.

"Yeah?" Eva asks.

"Cabin S, I heard. That's my cabin." He holds out a hand. "I'm Paul, Mr. Angley if you're feeling formal, and I'm the counselor for the non-binary and genderfluid cabin."

Eva takes his hand after a moment. "You're non-binary? Or do you just head that one up?" And was their cabin assignment the only thing Paul had heard?

"Genderfluid." Paul taps a purple heart keychain hanging from a belt loop, directing Eva's attention to it. It says "he/they" in flowing gold text. "I change this for how I'm feeling at any given time. I've got pronoun pins back at the cabin for anyone who wants them." He makes it sound so natural, and Eva needs a moment to take it in. The Cortolas had taken their pronouns in stride and never been weird about it, but the school and their doctor's office had made it into a stressful thing.

"Oh," Eva says, trying to recover. "Yeah, okay. So what's the procedure? Are you gathering up all the ducklings and then herding us over?"

Paul looks at them as if they can see through the joking tone Eva's adopted. "You've got a map in your booklet. I'm here, so I introduced myself, but there's a schedule in there too. Everyone here is old enough to herd themselves; I'm here for support."

"So you catch us in the trust-fall exercises," Eva says, opening the booklet to find the map and schedule.

"No, I make sure to drop everyone during those."

Eva's gaze snaps up to catch Paul's grin just before it turns into a faint smile.

"You're here because you're struggling with aether," Paul continues. "Most of the time a teen is struggling, it's because they don't know themselves well enough yet to let it flow through them as it's supposed to. That's what I help with."

That makes sense, though it feels invasive. "Maybe some of us are just bad at aether," Eva offers.

"Or maybe some are so good at deflecting that they're doing the same thing with aether and might do it with air if they could," Paul returns.

Yeah, that's enough of that. Eva shrugs and waves the booklet in the direction they think the cabins are in. It'll probably make Paul think he's right, but they don't like someone trying to analyze them. "Sure, maybe. I'm gonna go get settled."

Paul nods and turns away, faint smile still in place. It's getting a little disquieting. Of course Eva deflects. Not all attention's been good in their life, and they're not going to open up to a stranger.

The parking lot transitions to a paved path weaving through sparse trees that grow thicker, and the sign at the crossroads indicates Eva's going the right way. The other branches go to Cabins A–M, the meal hall, the meeting hall, and the pool. Eva has no intention of visiting the latter. Swimsuits are stressful.

Another couple of path-twists later, the trees give way to a clearing with thirteen cabins. They're all the same, dark wooden-looking structures about two stories tall, A-frames with no windows meant to seem like they're built out of logs. Each has a different pair of bushes flanking ramps going up to the doorway, and the ones in front of Cabin S have tiny purple flowers. That's cute, at least, even if the aesthetic is way more rustic than Eva likes.

They open the heavy door and are greeted with a dozen bunk beds, somewhat dim fluorescent lighting, and a person already snoring on the bottom bunk directly in front of them. That takes talent, or something. Eva's a little tempted to poke, but before the thought can coalesce in their mind, someone else moves off to the side. They're pretty, tall, and wearing a pin on a flowing peach shirt that Eva leans forward to see. "Nae/nein." That's a new combo to Eva. Nae's got long, straight hair a lot like Kaelin and a face that looks kinda familiar but that Eva can't place.

"Hey," Eva says, waving before maneuvering their suitcase in a bit farther. It looks like the top rear-most bunk bed isn't taken, so they toss their jacket there to claim it. "I'm Eva. Where are the pins? And do you know where we put our stuff?"

Nae gestures to a pile on the only single bed, just inside the cabin and on the left—it had been easy to miss. Then they point under the bunk Eva's chosen, turn, and leave the cabin.

"Ah. Good. Friendly," Eva mutters. They shove the suitcase under the bed and go for the pins only to find them all blank and white.

"Aether-activated," says the person who had apparently been fake-snoring and is now sitting up and wearing a "she/he" pin. "You have to focus to make them show up. Paul will help tonight, just before dinner, if you can't get it working."

"Seems like a cheap trick to pull on people struggling with using aether," Eva mutters. Also a cheap trick? Faking snoring. But they're not gonna say that.

"If they only threw tests at us, sure. But Paul tries." Her hair is brown and cut in a fluffy bob, and she looks friendly enough. It can't hurt to be nicer, not when they're gonna be sharing a room for three weeks.

"I'm Eva," they say, grabbing a pin and going over to lean against the bunkbed.

"Ashley Joy. And the person who left as you were coming in is Thomas. Don't mind nein. Nae hates everyone."

"You know nein already?"

"I grew up with nein. That's how I got here. Nae's older brother was talking with my dad, and now I'm in remedial camp to live up to my potential." Ashley accompanies this with a heavy sigh, flopping back onto her mattress.

"And nein's brother is good at it, unlike the two of you?"

Ashley laughs. "No. Well. Yes. Sorta. Nein's Thomas Angley, Paul's younger brother. Nae's also good with aether but sucks with people, and so Paul thinks hauling nein to camp is a great idea to help with this. Want to know a secret?"

"Of course."

"It's going to backfire. Thomas is going to stab someone within two days, just watch. Nae might even carve the weapon neinself, if nae's agitated enough."

An idea comes to Eva. It's probably the worst idea they've ever had, but the longer they're here, the more they don't want to be here. "I could be that someone."

Ashley Joy rolls to her side, facing them. "Come again?"

"I like poking people, and if I get stabbed, I get to go home."

"You'll also be stabbed."

"The brochure says they have state-of-the-art medical tech in case of aether incidents. I'll survive."

Ashley blinks. "By all accounts, stabbing hurts."

"So does the thought of sleeping in these beds for three weeks. Do they have any padding at all?" They poke the mattress Ashley is lying on in demonstration and find that they're right. There is no padding. The mattresses are thin, cheap, and entirely without any bounce, so jumping on them would be pointless.

There's a slow smile growing on Ashley's face as he sits back up. "Okay. Yeah. Let's bet on it. I bet you can't get stabbed within two weeks."

"You just said Thomas is gonna stab someone in two *days*."

"Yeah, but nae knows when someone is trying for something specific. Nae'll figure out you want to be stabbed and force patience."

Eva glances at the door and nods anyway. "I can still manage that. Today's Tuesday, so I win when I'm stabbed before Wednesday the week after next."

Ashley takes a beat, looking deep in thought before nodding. "Deal. We can figure out what we bet later, when we know each other better. For now, I'm sorely in need of more beauty sleep. Dad got me up at 5 a.m. to be here the moment registration opened, as if we'd miss out or something. Ugh."

Ugh indeed.

Eva nods, Ashley lays back down, and Eva heads out to check out the area more. Unfortunately there's not a lot left to see. The other cabins look the same from the outside, the mess hall is just a large cafeteria building, and the conference hall has a couple of sports fields outside it and looks like it has space enough for a few games inside a smaller room. By now, there are people around their age starting to mill about too, and Eva really doesn't want to deal with any of them. Sure, everyone here has the same issue. That doesn't mean they want allies in defeating aether or something. People seem to pick up on how they're feeling and leave them alone; they end up feeling lonely even though that's what they want.

So much ugh.

By the time they're feeling discouraged, the brochure says it's about a half hour before a group assembly in front of the mess hall. Eva considers going back to the cabin for a nap, but they've never been good at falling asleep quickly. Instead their feet take them back to the parking lot, where Paul is talking with a pair of angry-looking teens. Twins, if Eva was to guess, scraggly brown facial hair trying its best to be a beard, with matching shaved haircuts that make them look like army recruits. They're white, fit, and loud.

Eva's a little jealous of their flat chests and toned arms, but not the facial hair. They linger as Paul calms the twins down and sends them on their way, zoning out enough that when Paul clears his throat again, they jump. He grins before nodding at the pin.

"Need help?"

Even more ugh, that he knows that much right away. Sure, it's in their hand, but really. Eva feels like lying. They nod anyway, holding it out.

Paul doesn't take it from them. "Make a flat palm and rest it in the center, face up."

Why couldn't this be easy? Eva sighs and does as they're told. Paul's watching them, like really watching, focusing with a serious expression, and it's beyond awkward.

"Good." Paul's voice is also too gentle. Eva can count on the fingers of one hand how many adults have been gentle and helpful in their life without wanting something from them.

"I mean, that part's easy," Eva says.

Paul gives them a smile that actually seems genuine, so Eva distrusts it. "Close your eyes and imagine you're holding yourself in your hand. Picture what color represents you, and who you are, Eva."

He even says their name right. It's not fair. Eva takes a slow breath, pushes down the instinct to not cooperate, and tries. Green, it should be green, and they're them. They're Eva. After a few seconds, they open one eye to peek down at the pin. It's not completely blank anymore, but the green is as faint as the flavor of fizzy water, and only a single "T" is even slightly visible. Eva sighs and their shoulders slump.

Paul leans in to look and then shakes his head, smiling. "You're not going to believe me, but that's good for a first try. You know what color you want and your gender identity. Give it one more try, please."

The look Eva gives him is full of doubt. Paul's right. They don't believe him. All the same, they give it another shot. When they open their eyes again, the green's a little more distinct and "They" is faintly outlined.

"Well done." He sounds sincere. "How much darker do you want the green, and do you use more than 'they'?"

"They/them, and…" Eva hesitates. It feels ridiculous, both the hesitation and the desire to ask for a color they really like. They're not *actually* five, no matter how much they love toy dinos on their birthday cakes. "Emerald green. Like a deep green."

Paul takes the pin without comment, and a moment later, it's transformed and held out. "They/them" is a pale green, similar to their first attempt, and the background isn't just a deep green, it actually sparkles. Eva takes it back with reluctant gratitude.

"Guess I'll see you at dinner, then," Eva says. They put their pin on and avoid making eye contact.

"I take it that means you don't want to walk over together," Paul says. There's a brief pause before he continues, as if he's giving them a chance to respond. "You're fine. Go on ahead."

They think that was teasing, the together bit, and they don't know what to do. They don't need to be friends with an adult, especially one intent on helping them. A couple of social workers had claimed to be their ally and friend in the past, only to betray them to the worst of their foster families. This guy is no different—he's paid to help in the way Eva's foster parents want him to help. Eva can't trust Paul as far as they could throw him, and they have practically no arm strength.

Each cabin has their own table at dinner, and Eva's dismayed to discover it's just the four of them in Cabin S.

"We're expecting two more tomorrow," Paul is saying when Eva returns to the table with a plate full of cookies. He stops, looks at the plate, and then looks at them. "Have something with substance first, please. Otherwise you'll be starving at midnight."

Thomas's expression is pure ice, but Ashley looks inspired and gets up.

"Sit," Paul says. "Eat what you got first, and then you can get cookies."

Ashley sighs and slowly picks up her fork again.

Eva considers disobeying to mess with Thomas, but they only want to piss off and be stabbed by Thomas, not Paul too. They return to the line and make a decent salad from the selections, complete with a lot of bacon and more salad dressing than is necessary.

Paul doesn't remark on it.

Thomas looks at the salad, looks at Eva, glares, and goes back to eating what looks to be raw vegetables from the salad bar with no dressing of any kind. Maybe nae's a vegan. Maybe Eva can get preached at later. Ashley and Eva share a quick, conspiratorial smile.

"As I was saying, Cabin S is almost always the smallest of the cabins, but this is smaller than usual even with two more coming. On the plus side, it means we'll be able to focus and progress better."

By that, Eva thinks Paul means he'll be able to harass them constantly. They're not looking forward to it. Ashley's face shows similar sentiments.

"And by the end of these three weeks, the five of you can be friends, ready to make aether do as you will."

Eva will pass. They're gonna be bleeding and home by then, thank you very much. Paul's the only one at the table who seems to believe they'll be friends.

By the morning seminar, Eva's only managed to get one glare from Thomas, and that was when they muttered about Paul showing off by changing xir badge to sky blue with "Xie/Xir" written on it. Apparently, comments about the older bro were out of line, but anything else they tried to rile Thomas up didn't work—not juggling apples, not switching bunk beds so they were over Ashley so they could pass notes, not even knocking over their own orange juice on accident. The last one had gotten a sympathetic look, and that was not what they were going for.

"I'm not gonna lose," Eva tells Ashley as they sat down next to him in the carpeted auditorium. It is not comfortable.

"Please. I saw nein help you clean up the spill. You've already lost." Ashley opens her notebook, helpfully labeled "notes," that appears to be filled with weird grids.

"What's that?"

"Logic puzzles. Looks like I'm being studious, but really I want to know who killed Meredith in the library with what, and when. And what pet they have."

Eva shakes their head and opens their own notebook. It doubles as a sketch pad, and Ashley leans over to look, nodding in appreciation as Eva shows them a few pages. Thomas comes in and sits at a distance, while Paul winds up sitting way in the back with the other counselors after briefly coming over to check on xir charges.

The speaker comes in and starts talking about knowing their true selves, "not the one that you show the world," and beside Eva, Ashley zones out. Kaelin starts to take shape on the page, crowned prom queen in the dress she'd hurriedly shown Eva before the car trip only yesterday. "You said nae's good, yeah?" they whisper to Ashley Joy.

"Really good. Probably gonna be piloting planes good. Why?"

"Nein must really hate sitting in these lectures, then. They know it already."

"Yeah, and?"

"I bet nae'd stab me if I got us bonus lectures."

Ashley's expression turns to stone. "No. Don't you dare. It isn't only one or two people who get the extra lectures, it's the *whole entire cabin*. I'll stab you, forget Thomas."

"I'd get sent home either way."

"I'll stab you lots. Little stabs, many of them, so they can put a thousand bandages on you and you're still stuck."

Eva shakes her head, contemplating. They don't want to be here for three weeks of this, listening at seven in the morning to lectures they've already heard a dozen times over, and they don't need to make friends. Ashley's fine, but she probably doesn't live near the Cortolas, so there's little chance of future friendship. Eva would prefer to work things out on their own. But they also don't want to take someone down with them. That'd be rude.

"Guess I gotta go with the next plan: finding something sticky to put in nein's hair."

Ashley snorts and goes back to solving poor Meredith's murder. By the time the lecture has ended, Meredith's getting justice and Kaelin's complete down to tiny rhinestones on her fingernails. Ashley looks over as they get up for two hours of rec time.

"You should draw me sometime."

"Like one of my French girls?"

"Nah. With clothes on." Ashley's smiling, though, so she got the joke. She snaps her fingers, getting the attention of a few people heading out. "That's the bet. You lose, I get a really good drawing of me. I lose, well. I won't lose. But I can make origami jewelry, if you like things like that."

Eva reached up to touch an unpierced earlobe. "Can we do a shady camp piercing, too?"

Ashley opens her mouth to answer, but Paul's voice cuts in. "I'm sorry?"

"Oops," says Ashley, and he scoots into the crowd, abandoning Eva heartlessly.

"Uh. Joking?" Eva tries.

Paul's lost the little smile xie's always wearing. Eva prefers this expression; it feels more real. "If you feel that you'll be more resembling yourself with a pierced ear, that's fine, but let's do it in a sterile way, please."

Eva waits for more, like scolding or punishment, but it doesn't come. "What, that's all? Please don't do things that might make your ears fall off, the end?"

Paul meets their gaze. "That's how I do things. I don't like leading with fear. Other than fear for one's appendages falling off. I'd like you to be afraid of that." Xie gives them something of a half-smile, a corner of xir mouth twitching up. "You should have the confidence to explore here without fearing that you're going to get your hand slapped for every small thing."

"What counts as a big thing?" The moment Eva's opened their mouth, they regret it. Paul's expression goes stern, and they think they've just landed on xir radar as trouble. Great. That isn't what they wanted, but they have a lifelong habit of this.

"I'm here to help you with your future. It's up to you what shape yours will be. I can't imagine living without being able to use aether at any time, but some people manage. If you've already decided that's what you want, tell me now, and I'll focus on Ashley Joy."

It's an out—a pass to goof off and ignore the lectures and not have to worry about Paul pushing them. Eva wants to take it, but then they see Thomas standing behind Paul. Nae's watching, listening, and judging. Nae's been judging from the moment they got here, and Eva's always liked showing the judging sorts up. Fine. Operation "get stabbed" is over. Operation "master this bullshit so they can set Thomas's hair on fire later" begins now.

"Sorry. Sometimes I say the things that jump into my head without thinking about them." Eva shrugs. "I've got a goal. I'll sort this aether thing out."

There's something in Paul's expression they can't read as xie glances over xir shoulder to see Thomas there. "Go on. I'll catch up." After a beat, Thomas leaves, and Paul looks back at Eva. "Promise me it's not murdering nein."

"Nae'll survive it," Eva says, starting to smile despite themself.

Paul shakes his head and turns to go with a sigh. "No blood, no scars, nothing that requires a hospital run, please."

Ashley Joy shows up out of nowhere at Eva's side the second Paul's moved with the crowd out the doors. "Yeah, I think xie knows the friendship try is already a failure, but hey, now Thomas has more frenemies. That has to count for something."

"It's got several of the same letters, so it has to." Eva doesn't mind that they got abandoned. It's not unusual in their life, and Ashley owes them nothing. All the same, they're glad he came back. "So. Two hours of rec. What are the choices?"

Ashley shrugs. "Crafts, archery, scavenger hunt, hide-and-seek, swimming, canoeing, et cetera. I'm skipping it all and taking a nap. They don't take attendance and sleep's more true to me anyway." He pats Eva's back and heads off.

Eva joins the last of the people trickling out of the conference hall and wanders over to where targets are set up on one of the fields. They've always wanted to try shooting an arrow, but to their dismay they see there are only arrows, no bows. A dozen instructors are helping various teens fling the arrows at targets with aether, while four are apparently there to stop any arrows that may go in the wrong direction. Almost, they write it off as a waste of time, and then they see Thomas out of the corner of their eye, watching them.

Fine. They'll try it out.

They go closer, and a very tall woman with buzzed platinum-blonde hair comes up to Eva. "Joining us?" Her white T-shirt says "aexpert," which Eva loves, because it's a pun, and hates, because they wish they'd come up with it first.

Eva shrugs. "Yeah. Figured, why not."

She's not bothered by Eva's lack of excitement and pulls Eva in front of a target that's probably about 90 feet away. "You'll start by looking at this. This is what you want to hit. If you've got to picture someone in front of it, I won't tell anyone." She winks, which somehow is easier to take than Paul's friendliness. "I'll be back in a minute."

The instructor walks away, and Eva looks at the target. They don't actually have someone they want to picture there. Sure, some people have been shitty to them in the past, but they don't want to shoot them for it. They just want to get away, stay away, be away.

"Back now. Ready?" The instructor's got an arrow in her hand.

"Uh." Eva has no clue how to measure "ready."

The woman smiles anyway and holds out the arrow. "Take a breath. Know what you want: the arrow hitting the target. Know who you are in this moment: an archer."

"Or an aercher."

She laughs. "I'll use that with the next person, thanks."

Eva takes the arrow because what else are they supposed to do? They're here. They can't walk away—they think Thomas is still there, and heck, they'd like to show a few people who called them a failure that they're not. Unless they are. It's that doubt that keeps them from sending the arrow off. What if everyone's been right to give up on them, and Eva proves their point by sending the arrow into someone instead? What if it doesn't fly at all?

There's movement to the side, but Eva's too busy staring at the arrow to check what's going on.

"Tell me what you're thinking." Paul. Xie's seriously borderline stalking them, which might be a job requirement.

"I don't want to."

"Don't want to tell me, or don't want to send the arrow?" His voice is patient, and Eva's so tired of it already.

"I don't want to talk to someone who's got fake confidence in me because they're paid to have it." It's more honest than they wanted to be, but when their gaze is fixed on the arrow, they feel freer. "I'm tired of trying and failing and people being smug about it because of course I failed, that's what they thought I'd do."

Paul's quiet. Eva's definitely said too much, and there's even more they want to say, but they've at least managed to stem the flood for now.

"The confidence isn't fake," xie finally says. "I believe that you've got things blocking you from reaching your potential, not that you don't have potential. A lot of kids can't get letters to show up on a pin at all the first time they try. Most of them are cis, so they've never really examined that part of themselves. You've got a leg up on them. You know part of who you are, really know it. I think you know even more about yourself. But you're holding yourself back."

Paul doesn't sound like xie's faking the gentle confidence xie's now practically radiating. Maybe xie's not. This could be a "Paul" thing. Or maybe it's a "big brother" thing; Eva's always wondered what having one of those would be like.

"I could be holding back because I don't want to admit I'm a failure."

"Maybe. But I don't think so."

"Because you know me after less than twelve hours?"

"Because I caught sight of your sketchbook, and I know drawing isn't a natural talent. It takes work and regular practice. You can dedicate yourself. You did."

For once Eva doesn't resent that xie's actually got a point. "What do I do?" Eva's voice is small. They hate that, but asking is hard.

"Look at the target." Paul doesn't continue, and Eva realizes xie's waiting to guide them instead of lecturing.

Eva looks up.

"Good. See it. Feel the arrow in your hand and the ground beneath you. You're Eva, and the arrow belongs in the target. Feel the truth of it, and then let go."

It sounds far too easy. But Kaelin's always said the truth of aether is that it's easy, it's people that aren't. They believe Kaelin, and they want to believe Paul. And they still want to show Thomas.

Eva stares at the target as if trying to memorize it, then lets go. The arrow zooms forward…and stabs into the ground about a foot short. Eva sighs heavily.

"Nice!" Paul says before catching their mood and dropping his voice. "No, really. It went straight, and it nearly made it. You probably turned your attention to watching the arrow instead of the target, that's all. Look. Look at everyone else."

Eva does, and sees how scattered most of the arrows are, how frazzled some of the instructors look. As they watch, an arrow veers off to the side toward one of the counselors. It gets driven straight down with a gesture; the teen who'd tried to fire it gets a flat look as they turn beet red.

"I still didn't hit it."

"Yeah, and?"

Eva turns to Paul. Xir meets their gaze. "So you didn't hit it on your very first try. Did you draw a nose well the first time?'

"I've been trying to use aether my whole life."

"Have you? Have you really?"

Eva stops, hearing what xie's asking. Have they been actually trying? In reality, probably not. They don't try at a lot of things because they don't see the point, but they thought this was different. Aether's important. It's everywhere, and it's what everything runs on. Of course they were trying…unless they weren't.

Paul smiles, but it thankfully isn't that omnipresent one. This one feels like it's a smile for Eva. "Want in on a secret?"

As if that's a real question. "Always."

"Aether's not that hard. All most blocked people need is a couple of hours with someone who listens to them and pays attention, but nobody wants to hear that. They'd prefer to spend several thousand dollars sending a teen to an 'intensive' camp, believing that there's some special, magical solution that this combination of woods, lectures, and buffets have. Parents want to think it needs something bigger because otherwise it means they've never listened to and seen their kid."

"Foster parents."

Paul blinks, then tilts his head for a moment before shrugging. Apparently he hadn't heard what Aunt Erika said, after all. "I did notice a lack of familial resemblance between you and the people who dropped you off. It doesn't change my point, though. Knowing someone is a process, and more difficult when you spend every day with them. People think that's an automatic in, that understanding another person is easy. It's not."

"And that's why you think bringing your brother here to make friends will work?"

That gets a startled laugh out of Paul. "Talking with Ashley? I brought Thomas here to get nein out of nein's bubble. We grew up sheltered. Getting away from that did me a lot of good. I'm hoping it does the same for nein, and if nae winds up with a friend or two out of it, so much the better."

"It's not gonna be me," Eva says.

Paul raises an eyebrow.

"Ashley said nae was two days away from stabbing someone, and if I get stabbed, I get to go home. So I'm gonna piss him off, sorry." They're betting Paul will take it for a complete joke. Most people do, when they share ridiculous plans.

"Mm. I hear stabbing hurts." There's a weighing look in Paul's eyes, and Eva suddenly remembers the whole "seeing people" thing Paul was talking about.

Xie's actually listening. Whoops.

"Yeah, and?"

"Can you get a whole buffet line's worth of desserts back home?"

Xie's got a point. "You fight dirty."

Paul smiles. "Clean, actually. Bleeding everywhere will be dirty. And thankfully Thomas doesn't resort to violence. Nae prefers to ignore people they don't like because they're not worth nein's time."

"Did nae leave, then?"

The smile grows wider. "Nope. Nae's still over there, watching. Want to try another arrow?"

They do. They can't say why, but they do, so they nod.

Paul grabs one from an instructor's quiver and holds it out. "Remember. Keep your focus on the target. Know who you are and what you're doing."

Aether's easy, xie'd said, same as Kaelin had said. Maybe it is. Maybe Eva's made everything more complicated in their head because that's what happens in their life, complication after complication. Maybe it's been hard to believe that anything could go smoothly or be simple.

Eva takes a breath. They look at the target, picture it, focus on it, and let go.

The arrow hits the target, and the crowd (Paul) goes wild. Eva just stares. It's a lot to take in. Their first thought is that it's not a bullseye, that it's not perfect, because that makes hitting the target feel more realistic. But they know how much Kaelin would disapprove of that thought. Heck, Paul probably would, too. It's not true to the situation, it's deflection, and Eva knows that—there are about 50 teens attempting the range, and only four arrows in targets. That doesn't help them figure out what to think about it. Where they'd expected some smugness to shove at Thomas, if nae's even still there, all they feel is staticky emptiness.

Pressure on one of their shoulders turns out to be Paul steering them away from the range and toward a bench. They move as directed. Why aren't they happy about this? They're at least not unhappy, but they can't understand the numbness.

When Paul sits, Eva sits, too. Some time, they don't know how long, passes as they stare past the others still taking shots with the arrow. They wonder why Paul is still with them when Ashley Joy could use a counselor, too, but then again, she's probably sleeping as planned. No one needs counseling while they sleep. Probably. What would that even look like? The bizarre image of Paul standing by the bunkbeds, lecturing as Ashley snores, gets a snort from Eva and draws them out of their trancelike state.

Paul raises an eyebrow, and Eva shrugs. They don't want to try explaining that.

Xie puts up xir hands in mock defeat. "Time for me to do what we're told from year one of counseling not to do," xie says. "Ask a question we know the answer to."

Eva waits, wary.

"Do you want to talk about how you're feeling?" Paul asks, and xir serious expression transforms back into a grin at the face Eva makes. No. They absolutely do not. Paul nods. "Then let's try a different approach. You're not happy. I'm guessing you're bothered by that."

"No shit, Sherlock," Eva says, and regrets it instantly as the grin leaves Paul's face. Eva squeezes their eyes shut. They hate this, the whole "being sincere" thing, and it means sometimes they're mean. "Sorry," Eva mutters.

Paul's quiet for a few seconds, and Eva wonders if xie's left. They dare to peek and see xir looking off into the distance.

"It's okay to not have an answer for everything," xie finally says, looking back at them. "It's okay to be scared of progress or lack of it. It's not okay to take it out on others."

Eva stares at their feet and keeps staring as Paul rests a hand on their shoulder. "I'm not angry," xie begins.

"Just disappointed?" Eva interrupts.

Paul laughs, a very quiet huff of air, but it's there. "Not even that. I work with teens for a living. Getting scared and lashing out is pretty typical. But I need you to hear me, and then I need you to keep working with me. Because regardless of your emotional state right now, you made progress. You've got this. You really do."

Xir's confidence seems as strong as Kaelin's. Before the arrow struck, Eva would have described it as just as baseless, too. Now that seems inaccurate. Eva nods, exhaling heavily. "Sorry," they say again.

"Already forgotten," Paul replies, releasing their shoulder and standing up. "I'm going to make sure Ashley Joy doesn't sleep the whole day away, then find out if the others are here yet. I'll see you at lunch."

"See you at lunch," Eva echoes. Thomas joins Paul as xie goes, leaving behind the small crowd watching the archery attempts, and Eva finally feels like no eyes are on them. They can breathe, now. And maybe, just maybe, they can afford a little hope.

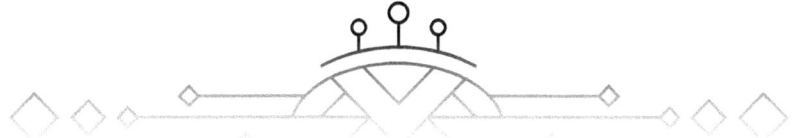

S. J. Ralston

Razzmatazz

bipoc, body horror, butch, character injury (non-graphic descriptions), classism, dehumanization, eye horror, horror, humans are the villains, mechanic, minor character death, misogyny, murder (accidental), non-binary, non-human character, past tense, science fiction with magic, sentient construct (magical), third person limited point of view

*T*he studio kept all their celebs in a warehouse out behind the back lot. Skipper was more than familiar with the place; the talent manager, Joey, had got ahold of his number on the first visit and never bothered calling anyone else.

"Glad you could make it, Skip," Joey said. His teeth were expensively white and his whiteness was excessively spray-tanned, a sharp contrast to Skipper's coffee-stained enamel and sun-weathered skin.

"Joey," Skipper said. Cool air streamed past Joey and did a better job of coaxing Skipper inside, mostly because it didn't call him *Skip*.

"Short notice, I know, but we've got her on contract and she's supposed to go on set *tomorrow*," said Joey, running a hand over his slick black hair.

"What's wrong with it?"

"Oh, something. She's always been a little squirrelly. Get this: the riggers swear she's *haunted*."

The warehouse hummed gently: with industry, with luscious air conditioning, and most of all with Hollywood magic.

Or, as the initiated knew it, aether.

Supposedly it was all sealed up inside the celebs, but Skipper could smell it every time he came here, acrid and metallic on the back of his tongue, like burning plastic mixed with a bloody nose. None of the other studios had more than a whiff of it. Then again, none of them had anywhere near as many celebs.

The ground floor of the warehouse was open-plan. White strip fluorescents cast the scene in passionless clarity. A forklift trundled down the concrete concourse, bearing an acrylic case wrapped in cling film. A chunky yellow hoist on the ceiling wheezed as it lowered a pallet from the second floor. Riggers and technicians in hard hats and safety vests filled the space with a clamor of voices and bootfalls and knuckles rapping on clipboards.

"What's the movie?" Skipper asked, because it was usually a long walk and leaving Joey to steer the conversation was like driving a golf cart blind across the interstate.

"Hey now, you know I can't talk about that," said Joey, faking sternness. "Can't have you leaking it to the press."

"Just need to know what kinda stress the thing's gonna have to take."

"Oh, if *that's* all. Singing, dancing, a little hanky-panky. Classy stuff, *you* know. Let's skip the elevator, I need to get my ten thousand steps in. You could use the exercise, too."

Since Joey wasn't looking, Skipper rolled his eyes so hard he caught a glimpse of his own brain.

Near the freight elevator, they passed a couple of riggers and a celeb Skipper didn't recognize. One of the riggers waddled along, stiff as a board with his hands at his sides and sweat running down his face. The other had her head bent, one arm outstretched and one cocked back, both hands in claws. The celeb stumped along in front of them, so herky-jerky that it looked like a mime overdoing a robot performance.

Once they were out of earshot, Skipper pointed a thumb over his shoulder and asked, "The hell was all that?"

"Oh, that? Probably just putting him away for the day," Joey said. "They're so damn heavy, it's easier to walk them over here than carry them."

"Why don't they use a cart?"

"You kidding? This place would look like a morgue. If they can walk, we walk 'em."

"And that still takes two, huh."

"That's what they tell me. The guy who looked like he'd peed his pants was handling the balance, and the one doing Wizard Pose was working the legs. Count yourself lucky, Skip—most people never get to see Wizard Pose."

"How come?"

"The only people who do it are the ones who aren't good enough to show off. Now, an animator—you'll *never* see an animator in Wizard Pose because they're *real* professionals. Usually one of them runs the blocking and choreo while another does the face and hands. Gets real fun if you have a big song-and-dance number."

Skipper raised an eyebrow and tipped his head. "Now *that*, I'd like to see."

Joey let off a flashbulb smile as they reached a colander-steel staircase. "For an old friend like you? I could swing that."

Up the stairs they went, into a long hallway with steel floors and more strip fluorescents, lined with acrylic cylinders. The anthill activity of the warehouse floor became a background hum with the occasional clatter and squeak of caster wheels. A hundred famous faces stared into each other's eyes, crossfire over Skipper's head. He got snagged on one in particular.

"Aw, hell," he said. "What happened to Chris?"

"Huh?" said Joey, glancing back. "Oh, he just got old."

"What, so they took him out back and shot him?"

"Hah!" Joey continued onward, cavalier.

Skipper followed. "He get royalties off that thing?"

Joey made the kind of indulgent chuckle that smug assholes make at children asking fanciful questions. "Nobody owns their own face, Skip," he said. "Any film-school dropout could have their own Denzel, Dwayne, Scarlett, *and* Sofia if their soggy heart desired it."

"Huh. So how do y'all stay in business?"

"Because the chassis *aren't* free," Joey said. "All ours are custom-built, right down to the lanterns—that's why they're the best. And why we keep bringing you in instead of just replacing them." He looked sour about it but shook it off. "They pay for themselves anyway. You can get ten riggers and five animators for *half* what you'd pay a leading man. I'll tell you what: in ten years, there's not gonna be *any* real celebrities. Good news for your job security, hey?"

"Guess so," said Skipper, eyeing the fresh young faces behind the acrylic.

"Best part about them, though? No *agents*. If all else falls through, we can float the studio on pornos alone. You have any *idea* how much people would pay to see these—"

"Yep." Skipper kept his eyes focused straight ahead.

"I bet you do," Joey leered. "You figure things can get haunted, Skip?"

The conversational whiplash was welcome, like being thrown clear of a car crash.

"Some things don't get took care of," Skipper said stiffly. "That's all."

"Guess you're right," Joey sighed. He pulled up and flopped an arm at an acrylic case. "Anyway, here she is."

Skipper peered at the celeb inside; Joey was standing in front of the nameplate. "Who's it s'posed to be?"

"Judy Garland," said Joey, insulted. "You're so uncultured, Skip."

"Uh-huh. What happened?"

"She started making this *horrible* grinding noise and shuddering like crazy. Totally out of nowhere."

Skipper was already unpacking his toolbox. "They're s'posed to go to the workshop when they're busted."

"I'll emphasize that to the riggers," Joey said smoothly. He swiped his badge and punched in a code, and the case unlocked. "Will you need to take her to the workshop?"

"Don't know," said Skipper. "Have to open it up and see first."

"You want some help getting her down, or…?"

With a heave and a grunt, Skipper grabbed the celeb under its armpits and pulled it off its cradle. It slumped against his chest, limp as a corpse and twice as heavy. He lowered it onto the floor, which was about as far as he could move it on his own.

"I'll send somebody up with a cart, just in case," said Joey. "Well! You have my number. I gotta go wrangle some animators."

"Thought I wasn't s'posed to be alone with these things."

"Scared?" Joey teased with another flashbulb smile. He chucked Skipper on the shoulder. "I trust you to put your hands in their guts, Skip—I can trust you with the locked cases."

He breezed out. Skipper watched him go with mixed feelings. Usually he would be doing this in a workshop, either the studio's or his own, with all his tools and equipment, the constant hiss of a leaky compressed-air hose, the smell of grease, the gritty sweat-heat of cheap AC.

Now all he had to keep him company was the thick stink of aether.

On one hand, it was nice to not be *hovered* over. Most studios were guarded to the point of paranoia about their celebs. He usually had three or four studio reps babysitting him, taking turns playing on their phones and watching him like a hawk. Joey had been like that until he'd abruptly decided that he and Skipper were friends. From the amount of paperwork Skipper had churned through just to get in the building, never mind into the actual celebs, he figured the studios would prefer it if he could fix them without looking at them. Being left alone was a welcome change of pace.

On the other hand—and maybe it was the aether raising the hair on his arms—being alone with these things unsettled him.

Skipper corrected himself: he wasn't *alone*, and the voices wafting through the acrylic halls attested to it. He rolled his shoulders and got to work undressing the celeb, though he kept his eyes as well averted as feasible. He could bury his arms up to the elbows in their innards no problem, but there was something about undressing a body…

…made worse when two of the ambient voices came close enough for Skipper to make out the words.

"…*angry*, I really think they are." A woman's voice, tremulous. "I can feel it. Can't you?"

"No, 'cause they're *machines*." A second woman, annoyed. "If they could get mad, we'd—"

A pair of women came around the corner, one white and one Black. The Black woman cut off speaking as soon as she saw Skipper. He flushed up to the hairline and tried to pretend he was doing something normal. As the two passed him, the white woman took a wide line to the outside. The Black woman sighed, aggrieved. By the time the two started talking again, they were too far away for Skipper to make out the words through the clamor of the warehouse.

Soon enough, he got the front casing off, exposing the power source in the Garland's chest cavity: a hurricane lamp filled with gently glowing green fog. The mechanical insides were packed in all around it, wires and

S. J. Ralston

hydraulics and servos. Bit by bit, he unpacked the guts and laid them on the floor, lamenting the lack of a removable *back* casing.

He'd just gotten down to the spine when the transport cart trundled up, pushed by a haggard-looking…well, a kid, really, brown-skinned and curly-haired. They were wearing a stylish black outfit, something between "modern dance" and "mall goth," and a little lapel pin with *they/ them* written on it.

"Howdy," Skipper said politely.

The kid, who had been shambling away almost as gracelessly as the rigger-operated celeb downstairs, stopped and swayed on their feet. They turned back with an unfocused look. "Huh?"

"Said *howdy.*"

"Oh," said the kid. Some weird expression crossed their slack face. They swallowed and raised a shaky hand. "Hey."

"Jesus, when's the last time you slept, kid?"

There was about a half-second delay before—to Skipper's horror—the kid started crying.

"Dad-gummit," Skipper muttered.

He wiped the grease off his hands and went to the kid, took them by the shoulders and sat them down on the floor. They were full-on bawling, great big hiccuping sobs they could barely breathe through. Skipper tried a little ham-fisted comfort, but it only seemed to make things worse. He decided to leave the kid to it and went back to his work.

Eventually, the kid pulled themself together enough to warble out, "Sorry."

"Don't sweat it," Skipper said cautiously. "You got a name, kid?"

"Um. Charlie. They/them."

Skipper gestured to himself. "Skipper. He/him, but don't read too much into it."

The kid—Charlie—nodded, then peered at the Garland. "Is that Judy?"

"Guess so," said Skipper. "Don't look much like her to me, but what do *I* know."

"What's wrong with her?"

Skipper stifled a sigh at the phrasing. Why did everybody insist on pretending these things weren't *things?* "The real one didn't have tits like that," he said, gesturing to the discarded front casing. "Back wasn't built

200

to carry them. And somebody took a couple ribs out, too, which don't help. Same kinda thing happens with any man under six foot."

At Charlie's horrified expression, Skipper went on: "They decide they want him taller, so they add a couple few inches here and there. And what do you know, the thing breaks down every six months like clockwork 'cause it's six foot tall and s'posed to be five foot eight." He tipped his head at the Garland. "Couple D-cups and an eighteen-inch waist ain't shit."

"Oh. But they don't do it to *all* of them, right? Or…at least not this badly. Right?"

Skipper snorted. "Kid, I seen a Natalie Wood snap clean in half."

Charlie shuddered. Skipper had expected a laugh. He had to wonder *why* he'd expected a laugh, because come to think of it, it wasn't funny. Skipper had thrown womanhood to the wolves and embraced butchness with both hairy arms in his early thirties, but he hadn't completely forgotten what it was like.

He adjusted his overalls over his own ample tits and dove back into the Garland's guts. They were easier to deal with.

It'd need to go to the workshop for sure. The lumbar-thoracic joint was stripped to hell. He started composing a spiel to Joey about how he was going to miss his deadline, then mapped out Joey's refusal to accept it. They'd end up cannibalizing a joint from some C-lister, and it'd work well enough to get through the contract, but it'd never actually get fixed, and in a month or a year the spine would crack and Skipper would get called in to jury-rig another solution because it was needed on set *tomorrow*.

"Is that what makes them move around?" Charlie asked.

Skipper frowned. "You mean what makes the movement screw up? Yeah, probably."

"No, I mean…when nobody's controlling them."

Skipper sat up straight. Charlie was watching the Garland, not him. Carefully, Skipper removed his hands from the mechanical guts.

"You wanna run that by me again?"

Charlie's face was glazed with sweat. "I— Never mind. Forget I said anything."

"How much movement?"

"I don't know," they said. "It…seems like a lot?"

"Well, Charlie, define a *lot* for me. We talking a twitchy finger or full-on seizures?"

Charlie swallowed. "Like...getting up and walking around."

Skipper stared, first with shock, then pity. He could've packed a weekend getaway in the bags under the kid's eyes. "Okay, bud," he said gently. This, apparently, was the wrong response, because Charlie went into overdrive. "Everybody's seen them do it," they said. "Not all of them, and not all the time, but they *do* it. They just— Sometimes they aren't where you left them, and sometimes you catch them out of the corner of your eye, and people tell me it's sleep deprivation, but I know when I'm hallucinating and I know this wasn't that. I— Everybody's seen it. Everybody."

Skipper sucked his teeth, tongued his cheek, and said: "Huh."

"I swear I'm not making this up," Charlie pressed.

"You talked to Security about it?"

"*Security?*"

"Yep. Between you and me, these things ain't got no access controls. Buddy of mine in aether tech says anybody with the chutzpah for it could walk one right off the lot if they got close enough."

"I know *people* can move them," Charlie said, showing the first lumbar-thoracic steel Skipper had seen from them. A green fire kicked on in their dark eyes and traced the veins in their face, their neck, under their shirt and out to the fingertips of their right hand.

The air tightened.

The Garland's power source flared brighter, churning like a tempest in a teapot. Charlie gave a casual flick of their hand. On the floor, the Garland copied the gesture, smooth and effortless—except for the jiggling hydraulics and whining servos laid bare by Skipper's maintenance.

The fire in Charlie's eyes and veins snuffed out, leaving their skin to dull like cooling wax.

The Garland's arm clanged onto the steel floor.

The atmosphere relaxed, heavy with the smell of aether.

"Shit, you an animator?" Skipper said, impressed. "How come they got you pushing carts around?"

Charlie's defiance turned to shame. "I...had a microsleep during a scene. Nothing got broken, but I almost trampled an extra. I got kicked off set, and I'm kind of...unpopular. Right now."

That would explain the waterworks, especially on top of chronic sleep deprivation.

"Tough break," Skipper said, "but hell, that right there explains your walkabouts."

Charlie shook their head. "It's obvious when they're being controlled. I'm asking about...what else it could be. Mechanically."

Skipper considered it—for longer than Charlie could wait, apparently.

"It's not..." they said, "I mean, *could* it have something to do with the aether?"

"Aether's just power."

"But I thought...you know, it's made of..."—they trailed off to a mumble—"ghosts."

Skipper choked on a laugh. "Who the hell told you aether's made of *ghosts?*"

"Not *made* of ghosts, but— Anything you can get aether out of has to have *some* kind of spirit, and if we can connect to it while we're alive, then—"

"God*damn*, the mumbo-jumbo around here," Skipper spat. "It's as bad as those damn crystal-healing shills. All that stuff is hooey."

Charlie slumped. "I guess."

Skipper looked back at the Garland. There were a lot of pinch points in that rib cage. He knew people who'd lost fingers to carelessness. He could disconnect the power source if he wasn't sure about the wiring. As for the celeb itself—well, they were *machines*, not robots. They couldn't move on their own. What they *could* do, in the hands of a talented animator like Charlie, was move like a flesh-and-blood human while weighing two and half times as much. Every so often Skipper would see an obit for an extra who'd stepped the wrong way and gotten their skull caved in by a casual gesture.

Skipper's jaundiced eye drifted to the now-quiescent green fog in the Garland's power source: distilled aether, much higher-test than what they used for municipal power. The purity was key for allowing the animators fine control, or so he'd heard. Boiled out of organic garbage and recondensed a couple dozen times until everything that wasn't exactly and entirely aether was gone. Electrical moonshine. Elevated compost. It was about as full of ghosts as the gasoline of Skipper's youth had been full of fossils.

Which was to say: *technically.*

"Which ones?" Skipper asked.

Charlie blinked. "Huh?"

"You said only some of them move around. I wanna see them."

"But aren't you"—they gestured to the Garland—"in the middle of something?"

"It'll keep."

Charlie chewed on it, maybe wondering the same thing as Skipper: would this cost them what was left of their job? In the end, they got up and cocked their head.

"Monroe," they said.

The thing was damn near unrecognizable, not just as Monroe, but as human. People had tweaked the proportions through the years—amateur artists who couldn't put down the paintbrush. That kind of thing was bad enough on paper, but seeing it in person made Skipper's butthole clench.

The dress and the curls were Monroe. The rest was something else.

"Shit my ass off," Skipper said under his breath.

"Yeah," said Charlie.

"*This* gets up and walks around?"

"She does."

"*Shit* my ass off."

Maybe it was a trick of the light, a too-heavy head on a too-thin neck, but the Monroe wasn't staring across the aisle like the others. It seemed to be looking down at Skipper. It put out waves of *dare-you-to-start-some-shit* energy.

"Is it because they messed with the proportions?"

"Huh?" said Skipper, pulling out of the Monroe's tractor beam.

"The reason she moves around so much. Could it be because of…" Charlie gestured to its whole body.

"Hell, maybe," said Skipper.

The Monroe loomed like a landslide, just waiting for the rain. Skipper had a hammer on his belt. He felt like the Monroe was staring at it. If he broke the case, what then? It would do nothing. It would walk out to who knows where. It would rip him limb from limb.

All around him, a thousand mangled bodies stood bricked up in the acrylic walls.

"Charlie," Skipper said, "you figure things can get haunted?"

"Maybe," said Charlie, with the shyness of the once-bitten.

"You think *that* thing's haunted?"

"Yes."

Skipper nodded. He blew out a breath. He fingered the hammer on his belt.

And noticed himself doing it and stopped. He huffed out another breath, harder, clearing the sharp smell of aether from his sinuses, willing the hairs on his arms and neck to stand down. Charlie's skittishness must've been catching.

"Why don't you go and get some rest, kid?" he suggested.

They made a face. "I should get back to work."

"Tell them I press-ganged you, and if they don't like it, they can take it up with me and my union. Matter of fact—" He pulled out a business card and a greasy pencil, scribbled down the number of his buddy at the IWW, and handed it to Charlie. "You decide you want to start getting enough sleep, you give these folks a call."

Charlie studied the card with wide-eyed reverence before slipping it into a pocket of their vest.

"I will," they said. "But…what are *you* going to do?"

Skipper stuck his thumbs through the straps of his overalls and refused to look at the Monroe.

"I'm gonna do my job," he said, "and go the hell home."

Six months later, like clockwork, Skipper was back.

Joey told him to come in on the north side—something about construction at the main entrance. The studio was oddly quiet; the parking lots were full, but the stages were shuttered and only one or two stray golf carts buzzed by, piloted by surly executives in board shorts and button-ups. Joey met Skipper at the warehouse door and hustled him inside.

The second Skipper stepped into the warehouse, he wanted out again. It took his brain a couple seconds to catch up with what his body knew.

The fluorescent lights reflected off the polished concrete floor. The HVAC stirred an electric current through the cold air. The smell of aether was choking thick. The door swung closed behind him with a resonant *boom*.

The warehouse was completely deserted.

But Joey was already marching off, Rolex footsteps echoing off the walls, so Skipper hiked up his overalls and followed.

"The hell *is* everybody?" he asked. Goosebumps covered his arms and the back of his neck. From the aether, probably. Static electricity.

"Lunch break," Joey said shortly.

Skipper checked his watch. It was four o'clock in the afternoon. His hand sweated on the grip of his toolbox. The hammer on his toolbelt thumped reassuringly against his leg as he walked.

"Is it already in the workshop?" he asked.

"No."

"They're s'posed to go—"

"—*t' the workshop when 'ey're busted,*" Joey sneered, slathering on a mockery of Skipper's accent. "Yeah, well, I don't know what to tell you, Skip. You want to carry her to the damn workshop, *be my guest*, but sign a waiver for your back first."

Skipper raised his eyebrows, wondering who'd pissed in Joey's cereal. The elevator approached on their left. Joey diverted toward it.

"I'm gonna take the stairs," Skipper declared abruptly. "Meet you up there."

Joey shot him a frustrated look before course-correcting for the stairs. Skipper blew out a breath—quietly—and resolved to keep his mouth shut.

Up the stairs they went, and down the acrylic hallway. The smell of aether was even thicker here. The warehouse was dead silent. There was tension screwed into Joey's shoulders and back.

Twice, Skipper thought he saw a flicker of movement out of the corner of his eye. Whenever he looked back, though, all the celebs were in place, hands by their sides, faces and eyes turned forward.

Must've been a trick of the light.

Joey pulled up at the Garland's case and opened it without preamble. He stood back and glared, arms folded, foot tapping. When Skipper heaved the Garland out by the armpits, metal ground against metal, plastic creaked, latex squealed. Its legs twisted completely sideways as he laid it down on the floor.

"Jesus," he huffed. "Back broke?"

"Apparently."

Told you so, Skipper didn't say, because he wasn't certain Joey wouldn't push him down the stairs about it. "And y'all need it by *tomorrow?*" he asked instead.

"Yes." Joey's phone buzzed. He checked it, and his face got even more sour. He stuffed it back in his pocket. "Call me when you're done."

He turned on his heel and stalked away. It was so quiet that Skipper heard his footsteps all the way to the door. Heard the squeak of the hinges. Heard the *boom* of the door slamming shut.

Now there was only Skipper and the HVAC and a thousand human-shaped things.

Skipper gave himself a quick smack on the cheek. "Get a grip."

He got down on the floor and got to work. Clothes: off. Casing: open. Sweat soaked through the back of his shirt, cold. He kept his head down, eyes on his task. One by one, he disconnected and removed all the systems between him and the Garland's back.

It was the lumbar fixture this time, the one that secured the pelvis to the back. Sheared clean through. No surprises there; they'd cannibalized the lumbar-thoracic joint from a Hilary Duff last time, and the weld had been a rush job. The break was bad—had probably happened when the Garland was standing up—and being moved around afterward had tangled up a lot of the wiring, even torn some of the latex "skin" around the Garland's waist.

"Welp," said Skipper, sitting back. This wouldn't be a *tomorrow* job, no matter how pissy Joey got. It'd need to go to the workshop—a prospect that was, at that point, pretty inviting.

Skipper looked around, hopelessly hopeful, but there was no kid with a cart this time. Just him and the celebs, all standing perfectly upright except for the one that was lying gutted on the floor. No voices or footsteps anywhere in the building.

Well, fine. Skipper knew where they kept the carts.

"Don't go nowhere while I'm gone," he joked at the Garland, and immediately wished he hadn't.

The warehouse rang with the sound of Skipper's footsteps. He went back to the first floor, keeping an eye on the celebs around him. Once, he caught movement at the edge of his vision and spun to look. If one of the celebs had turned its head, it moved back so quickly that all Skipper saw was a quarter of a blur.

He didn't look back again.

The carts were down by the freight elevator, and while the silence of the open floor plan was eerie, it wasn't nearly as bad as being penned in on both sides. Skipper cast a longing look at the exit before maneuvering a cart into the elevator. As the doors sighed shut, he gave himself a pat on the back for avoiding getting stuck in here with Joey. The vibes alone might have bloodied his nose.

Or maybe that was the smell of aether, thick and electric in the air.

The Garland was right where he'd left it, clothes off, guts all over the floor. Skipper towed the cart over cautiously. He stopped a couple feet from the Garland's head and indulged his instincts with a little scrutiny.

The green light in the hurricane lamp was dim, not-in-use. The lumbar fixture was still snapped. The face was set in a light little smile.

Had the left hand been clenched like that when he'd left?

Skipper breathed deep, in through his nose, out through his mouth. The smell of aether coated his sinuses and tongue. Watching the Garland for any hint of movement, he stretched out a leg and nudged her head with the steel toe of his boot.

Nothing—not a shiver, not a twitch. Skipper flexed his hands. He could disconnect the power source. Put her on the cart, take her to the workshop, fix her up…

…and when exactly had she stopped being *it* and become *her?*

"Hey," he said. He nudged her again. "Somebody in there, or what?"

Something went *BANG*.

Skipper whipped around, sending the cart rattling away to bump into the cases. The hallway was deserted, shiny as a new dime. His pulse throbbed in his hands. Somehow his hammer was clutched in one of them, upraised.

"The hell was that?" he demanded, and wondered who he was asking.

Only the soft sigh of the HVAC answered him.

Skipper lowered the hammer, swallowed the cotton in his mouth, and blew the thick aether smell out of his nose. He braced himself against his spine and eased down the hallway, glancing at the celebs on either side for anything out of place. They stared over his head, perfectly still, clean, and neat.

All except one, fifteen or twenty cases down the line. Skipper approached until he could see what had happened: the celeb, a Black teenager, had fallen and crumpled against the acrylic. Skipper didn't recognize the face. The nameplate under the case read: *0916 / COLEMAN.*

"Cut that shit out," Skipper said, gesturing a warning with the hammer.

The celeb showed no sign of having heard, just slumped there motionless, unblinking, arms and legs everywhere, cherubic face pressed against the acrylic.

With a great effort of will, Skipper turned his back on the Coleman and walked away. His spine prickled. Something scraped ever so quietly behind him. He kept his neck stiff and his eyes forward. His hand was white-knuckled on the hammer. He got within about twenty feet of the Garland before his legs refused to take him any farther.

The guts were still out, and the body hadn't moved, and the light in the power source was dim, but she wasn't how he'd left her. Subtly. Unmistakably.

She wasn't smiling anymore.

Sweat slicked the handle of the hammer. Skipper took three tries to swallow. If they could get out of the cases on their own, he reasoned, they would've done it already. So it was only the Garland, only him and the Garland, and her back was broken and her guts were out. He could smash her lamp and walk away right now.

No, he couldn't do that. Even the union couldn't save him from *that*. He'd disconnect the power source—that was what he'd do. Take her to the workshop, finish the job, and never come back. Stop answering Joey's calls. That was what he'd do.

He couldn't make himself step closer to the Garland.

"Hey," he said. His voice shook. He brandished the hammer. "You make any funny moves, I'm gonna... Well, you better not make any funny moves!"

The Garland lay still as a corpse. As still as a thing that hadn't always been still. The scraping noise came again, barely at the edge of hearing. Skipper bit his tongue until he tasted blood. The sharp, bright pain gave him the jolt he needed to approach the Garland. Breathing heavily through his nose, he knelt by her right side.

Adjusted his grip on the hammer.

Reached for the power source.

Skipper glanced at her face. No movement. No change. He put his hand on the lantern. The glass was always warmer than he wanted it to be, not *hot* like a light bulb but *warm* like a living thing. He fumbled for the connector.

She lurched.

Skipper screamed. Metal met plastic with an ugly *crunch*. She jerked, jolted, juddered—lay still. The aether in the hurricane lamp sputtered like a bad bulb. Skipper stared in horror at the wreck of her face, the hammer buried in her right eye. The other eye was looking at him. 2,001 glass eyes, all around, on every side, were *looking* at him.

Her hand moved.

Skipper ripped the hammer out of the Garland's face and brought it down with all his strength on her power source.

The shock kicked him in the chest. A silent concussion hurled him backward. The impact with the floor restarted his heart. Bits of lantern glass rained down around him, and stars filled his vision.

Through them, he saw *something*, wreathed in bright green light or made of it, swarming toward the ceiling like an orgy of snakes in space. Before it struck anything, it burst of its own accord, a vapor explosion of distilled aether that made the lights crackle and flare. The electric-blue smell of ozone cut the choking stench of aether.

The sigh of the HVAC expanded to fill an immense container of silence.

Gingerly, Skipper propped himself up on an elbow. His chest ached, and he was having trouble breathing. The Garland lay on the floor ten feet away, dead as a doornail. Her left hand was half-upraised, frozen in mechanical rigor mortis.

Grungy reality clobbered dreamy shock. He'd just destroyed a piece of equipment worth more than his entire pension. He couldn't plead incompetence, not with the Garland's face smashed in and aether stains on his hammer and his hands.

Skipper laughed hollowly. He was *so* fired.

His eyes lingered on the Garland, the ruined face, the upraised hand. Aether and ozone smothered the air. Wisps of green vapor lingered near the flickering lights. Truth emerged acid-washed from the phantasmal, numinous and raw.

If she'd wanted to grab him, she could have. If she'd wanted to smash his head open, she could have. Steel skeleton. Infinite power source. And with his hammer through her eye, all she'd done was reach for him.

The celebs looked on from all sides. They were utterly silent, utterly still, and utterly unlike the Garland.

Something ticked over in Skipper's brain—a clock striking midnight, an egg-timer going *ding*! The Garland was *dead*. There was exactly one prerequisite to becoming dead. And if the Garland had met it…

The cold sludge of dread crystallized in Skipper's veins.

Glass crunched between his boots and the floor. His stinging hand grasped the hammer's charred handle. The steel head was stained with green iridescence.

Skipper was *already* so fired.

He straightened up. *Fear* was something he'd left by the side of the highway sixty miles back. So long as he didn't stop, it wouldn't catch him. His body was a foreign instrument, a machine he'd trained on many years ago. He remembered how to raise his arm high above his head.

Acrylic and silence shattered together.

Like seawater through the hull of a ship, a shrieking alarm blasted through the breach.

Skipper's body could haul ass when it needed to. He charged down the corridor, smashing cases as he went. The Coleman's empty stand flashed by—*smash*—and he *heard* something scramble out, quick and furious, steel and servos. Skipper never even considered looking back. There was only forward, only case after case after case, and never mind what was inside. He reached the end of the corridor and swerved into a hairpin turn, ricocheted off a railing before clanging down the next corridor at full steam. His lungs heaved in time with the smashing of acrylic.

Until he slipped a gear, skidded two yards, and rocked to a stiff stop, arm still upraised. His ragged breathing and thundering heartbeat filled the silence. Fear, faster than he'd imagined, pounced from the gutter and sank its claws in him. He stared, jelly-legged, struggling to suck down enough air.

The Monroe stared back from behind her acrylic case.

"Don't...look at me...like that," Skipper panted.

The Monroe said nothing.

"You got something to say, then *say it!*"

The Monroe said a whole hell of a lot of nothing.

Somewhere far away, a door crashed open and human voices yelled. Somewhere closer, plastic and latex flopped on steel floors, rolling around in broken acrylic.

Right in front of Skipper, the Monroe coveted the hammer in his hand. She *wanted* in a way that was almost forgotten, all too familiar.

If, at sixteen, somebody had smashed Skipper's case and handed him a hammer...

"You *motherfucker!*"

Pounding footsteps. Skipper turned, too late.

Joey hit him like a well-manicured train.

Skipper's back slammed into an acrylic case. Instinct whipped the hammer up; conscience stopped it from coming down. Joey grabbed Skipper's overalls and shook him fit to rattle his teeth.

"You stupid redneck piece of shit!" he snarled.

Skipper struggled to wrench free. "Get offa me!"

I saw what you did to Judy, the Monroe didn't say.

Joey grabbed the hammer and tried to yank it out of Skipper's grasp. Skipper shoved him, hard. Joey didn't let go, elbowed Skipper in the face. Skipper punched him in the gut. Joey staggered back, bent double, wheezing. His black hair was wild. His eyes were murderous.

The hallway was full of celebs, some lying motionless, some floundering like fish out of water.

"I'll kill you," Joey seethed. *"I'll kill you!"*

We all saw what you did, the Monroe implied.

"Get outta here, you dumb son of a bitch!" Skipper shouted at Joey.

Joey lunged. Skipper whisked the hammer out of reach as Joey bodied him into the case again. Skipper barred an arm across his chest to hold him off, but Joey grabbed him by the throat, so Skipper kicked him in the shin, steel against bone. Joey yelped and recoiled. Skipper shoved him back farther, gasped a breath while his arm jerked the hammer up again—and again Skipper refused to let it fall. Joey clocked him right on the chin, and Skipper's knees buckled.

Joey grabbed him by the face and bashed his head against the acrylic like a chimp in a fifty-cent zoo. The Monroe's silences howled in time with the strikes.

We ALL—

Something cracked.

—SAW—

Skipper's vision whited out.

—EVERYTHING.

Acrylic shattered.

Pain knifed through the back of Skipper's skull.

The hammer slipped.

A slender white hand shot out and caught it.

Exterior, Skipper thought woozily. A hot wind stung his cheeks and smoke burned his eyes. *Hollywood in flames.*

The back lot was a tangle of wreckage and shadow. The asphalt was cracked, melted in places. The color had peeled off the building façades and a few roofs had caved in. Sirens broadcast banshee wails into the night while distant helicopters roared. Skipper stumbled through the rubble, coughing.

The bad news was: he was alone.

The good news was: he was alone.

Only echoes of *Them* remained—a smashed sign, an overturned golf cart, a door ripped off its hinges. A body, burned so badly that it was hard to say whether it was steel and plastic or flesh and bone. The whole sky was stained a dull, choking orange. The darkness and the color of the light obscured what fluid They had used to paint the town.

But They were gone, now. The film reel in Skipper's head was torn to pieces, leaving only moth-eaten celluloid flashes. Gunfire. Electric green mist. A series of explosions. A brownout, the clouds of aether keeping the surviving lights dim or flickering. He wasn't sure when the fires had started.

A wave of dizziness swept over Skipper. His shoulder found a wall, warm from recent flames. His knees let him down more-or-less gently.

His scalp was stiff with blood, ears ringing.

He counted his blessings for it. He'd seen what They did to Joey.

Somewhere beyond the suffocating smoke, somebody coughed.

Skipper's heart jolted.

None of Them so much as breathed, let alone *coughed*.

"Hey!" he called as loudly as his struggling lungs would let him before he fell victim to his own cough.

A figure resolved through the smoke and tears, limping hard. They had a bandanna over their mouth and nose, eyes narrowed against the fumes. They spotted Skipper, hurried over, and knelt next to him. Their bloodshot eyes went wide.

"Skipper?"

Skipper squinted. Between the bandanna, the darkness, and the concussion, it was hard to get a bead.

"It's Charlie," said Charlie. "Holy shit, are you okay?"

"Been better," said Skipper.

"What...I mean, I know what happened, but what *happened?*"

Skipper cracked a smile. "Hell if I know, kid. Ghosts in the machine, I guess."

Charlie's eyes crinkled ever so slightly. "I heard that stuff was hooey."

Skipper shook his head and immediately regretted it. Dizziness swamped him, pain floating atop it. He hissed through his teeth and grabbed Charlie's arm for support.

"You really don't look so good," Charlie said; then, looking closer: "Is that blood?!"

"Guess so," Skipper managed.

"Jesus, okay. We need to get you to a hospital." They looked at the wreckage of the warehouse. "Is anybody else inside?"

Nausea oozed up Skipper's throat. A lot of Security had busted in when the alarm went off. It was possible some of them were still in one piece.

But none of the ones left inside were.

"No," he said.

Charlie let out a breath through their nose, nodded. "That simplifies things. Can you walk?"

"How far?"

"Not far. Last I heard, the celebs were heading north toward Beverly

Hills. We should be able to get you to the VA hospital or UCLA."

"Anyplace is better than here. Gimme a hand, I'm old."

Charlie braced, but Skipper still almost pulled them over. His legs didn't want to hold him, but Charlie looped Skipper's arm over their shoulders and grabbed a handful of tool belt, and that was enough to get the two of them moving, albeit at a shamble.

"Happened to your leg?" Skipper asked, noting the limp again.

"Oh," said Charlie. They adjusted their grip on Skipper's wrist. "*Well...*"

Skipper knew that *well*. It was pronounced with two syllables back home, used to introduce long stories about very bad days.

"Uh-huh?" said Skipper.

"We...were kind of in the middle of a walkout when everything went off, so most of us weren't here. Thanks for the contact info, by the way."

Skipper blinked—then, as comprehension settled: "That motherfucker made me scab."

"What?"

"Nothing. So...y'all were outside when all hell broke loose?"

"With the riggers, and most of the crew," Charlie confirmed. "At the main entrance. We heard a lot of shouting, then gunshots, then the transformers started blowing out... Anyway, as soon as the shooting stopped, I came back here—"

"Why?!"

"Not everybody joined the walkout."

Skipper was struck dumb.

Charlie shrugged and adjusted their grip again. "So I came back. Turned out not all the celebs went north, either."

"Shit my ass off, don't tell me you ran into one of them?"

"Yeah. Literally, *ran into*...I think a Kardashian. Or what was left of one. Snapped clean in half." They chuckled, or maybe shuddered. "I managed to get away from her, but I kind of wrenched my knee pulling loose."

"Damn," said Skipper. "You okay?"

Charlie kept talking like Skipper hadn't spoken. "She...I had to *make* her let go. And even then, I wasn't..."

They trailed off. Their grip on Skipper's wrist was pinching tight.

"Ended up in Wizard Pose, huh?" said Skipper.

Charlie burst out laughing, loud and high and a little deranged. They cut off just as quick. "Yeah," they said, fragile. "I think I did."

"Kid? I think you need to get into a new line of work."

Charlie snorted. "Right back at you, old timer."

Ahead of them, the light of the fires was almost like a sunset.

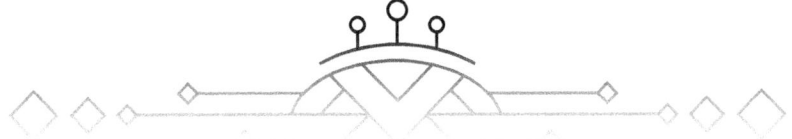

Scarlett Gale

N(ae)ghbours

attraction at first sight, bisexual, city mouse and country mouse, competence kink, didn't know they were dating, f/nb, farmer, first kiss, genderfluid, getting together, humor, idiots to lovers, meet cute, misgendering (unintentional), omg they were neighbors, panic attacks (mentions of), present tense, self-esteem issues, third person limited point of view

*B*efore her lies an empty apartment; Dahlia is ready to move in and make it home. She has a plan! She has (some) furniture! She has (carefully saved) money for purchasing more furniture! She has a jury-rigged, aether-assisted hand truck from the farm for hauling boxes! She has a building with an *elevator*! She's an independent adult, and she's ready to start living like one!

Now, if she could figure out how to turn on the damn *lights*.

Dahlia reaches into the currents around her to channel aether into the carved quartz on her keychain until it glows and steps into the empty, echoing, *unlit* apartment. Is it one of those places without overhead lights, but with an outlet on a switch, like Aunt Edna's bedroom?

Searching fails to turn up a switch in the living room. Dahlia checks the kitchen—*surely* there's an overhead light in the kitchen—to find overhead lights but no way of turning them on. The bathroom and bedroom are the same, and while Dahlia is pleased to find them clean and pleasantly homey, she's increasingly concerned about the lack of light switches.

"There has to be a way to turn you on," she says to the light in the kitchen, settling for opening all the blinds. Actually... "Apartment, please turn on the lights?"

The lights do nothing. Dahlia didn't *really* expect that to work—all the voice-activated systems she's read about need setup, and this apartment wasn't advertised with any assistive technomancy—but she still feels sheepish about it.

"Well, Bob," she says to her potted begonia, "we'll just have to unpack a lamp and figure out the rest later." Dahlia sets Bob carefully on the kitchen windowsill along with Sylvia the spider plant and Echo the echeveria, looks for a light switch (again), fails to find it (again), and heads down to the parking garage for another load.

Dahlia, a stack of boxes, and a floor lamp make it into the elevator without issue. She stares at nothing, wondering if the lights *were* voice-activated and she hadn't given the right command, when a slender hand wearing several rings appears between the elevator doors with a "No you don't!"

Dahlia blinks in surprise as the hand's owner slips between the still-opening doors and punches the air triumphantly. The elevator seems much smaller, not because the woman is large, but because she has a *presence*. It hits Dahlia in flashes: blue-green hair in an asymmetrical cut; bright metallic eyeshadow framing laughing eyes; dark lipstick on full, smiling lips. Her outfit has so many patterns that Dahlia's eyes don't know where to look and settle on a crystalline pin on the woman's lapel that says "She/Her" in purple aetherlight.

(Dahlia knew in a distant, vaguely unimportant way that she was attracted to women prior to now. She figured it out as a teenager and— other than a few dates that never went anywhere—it hadn't impacted the rest of her life.

It's like a hard kick from a horse, now—she's into women. Woman. Specific.

Oh *no*.)

"Suck it, elevator!" the extremely attractive woman crows. "Thought you could leave me behind again, did you?"

"Is the elevator faulty?" Dahlia asks, concerned for their safety. How difficult would it be to repair? They're mostly mechanical, right? Couldn't be worse than working on Old Man Sampson's grain elevator, which runs on aether reluctantly and needs to be smacked with a hammer each harvest season to get the gears to unlock.

(She knows she shouldn't attempt to fix the elevator. There's just a part of her that wants to make sure this very attractive teal-haired woman never has a problem again in her life, starting now.)

The woman leaps a full foot in the air and squeals, many-ringed hand clapping to her heart. "Shit!" she gasps, whipping around to peer past the floor lamp at Dahlia. "Oh, *no*, I didn't realize anyone was in here!"

Dahlia glances between the floor lamp in one hand and the hand truck in the other. "Do you *normally* find furniture abandoned in the elevator?"

As soon as the words are out of her mouth, Dahlia winces, but the woman tosses her head back and laughs like it's the best joke she's ever heard.

"No," she says with a sheepish smile, "but I walk into walls and door-frames and hedges constantly, so I'm not always the best at *noticing* things." She offers a hand. "I'm Rin."

"Dahlia." She reaches past the floor lamp to shake hands and hopes her calluses aren't too rough on Rin's elegant fingers. "The elevator has it out for you?"

"Most elevators do, but this one does specifically. I've been living here for three years, and this asshole"—she flicks her gleaming nails at the walls with a glare—"has never *once* been ready for me when I need it. I either have to wait five minutes for it to get back from its journey to *space* or I have to sprint for it down the hall. It's out to get me."

Dahlia glances at the wall. "It seemed fine to me."

Rin's mouth hardens. "That's what it *wants* you to think."

The possibly petty elevator dings, and they both jump. "I forgot to punch in my floor!" Rin says, then glances at the glowing readout. "Wait, *did* I punch my floor?"

"You didn't." She knows because she was watching Rin's lovely hands the whole time. "This is my floor?" She doesn't mean for that to be a question, but Rin is a discombobulating presence.

"Oh, cool!" Rin's face lights up. "We're on the same floor! Maybe we'll run into each other again, then!"

Dahlia would like that. Dahlia would like that *so* much, actually, es-pecially if they ran into each other mouths-first. "Cool," she manages after swallowing twice. *Get it together*, she tells herself firmly as the elevator doors start to close. Dahlia shoves her hand truck into the gap.

"See?" Rin says triumphantly. "Out to get me." She makes a face as she follows Dahlia onto the open-air walkway that leads to the apartments. "Maybe now it's out to get you, too, in which case, I'm sorry."

"I don't think that's your fault," Dahlia says, counting doors as she passes. She keeps expecting Rin to peel off, but instead they stay in step until Dahlia comes to a stop.

"This is me." Dahlia cringes internally, because *obviously*.

"And this is me!" Rin waves at the next door down. "Do you need a hand with anything?"

"No," Dahlia says reflexively, setting down the floor lamp so she can unlock her door. It swings open on her dimly lit apartment, and… Right. The light switch situation.

Crap.

"I'm happy to help," Rin says, lingering in her doorway. "Since we're gonna be neighbors and all."

Dahlia winces. Is she really going to ask? What's the other option, though?

"Actually," she forces out, keeping her eyes open through an effort of will. "I have a. Favor. To ask."

Rin practically lights up like an aetherglow. "Yeah?"

Dahlia breathes deeply and waves at her apartment. "Do they hide the light switches here, or what?" She takes refuge in making it a sarcastic joke, because maybe then Rin's second impression of her won't be of a country bumpkin that can't figure out how to turn on a damn light.

"Oh." Rin blinks. "Oh! Of course!" She slips past Dahlia into the living room. "They're here." She runs her fingers over a series of polished crystals partially embedded in the wall. "This one is on"—a line of cabochons installed along the ceiling come to life with a gentle white glow—"and this one is brightness level"—the lights pulse brighter, then dimmer as Rin circles her finger around the crystal—"and this one is color!" Rin circles a different crystal, and the lights transition through the colors of the rainbow before settling back on white.

"Ah." Dahlia feels herself flush. She rubs her face and sighs. "I saw those, and I thought they were decorative."

"That makes *total* sense," Rin says, nodding emphatically. "I feel like every place does something different—every time I go over to my friend Kelly's, I have to pat down the wall like I'm looking for the trigger to a secret passage. What were they like where you lived before?"

"Switches," Dahlia says, a bit embarrassed.

Rin's eyebrows go up. "Wow, was it a really vintage apartment?"

Dahlia carefully doesn't make eye contact as she plugs in the floor lamp. At least the *plugs* are the same. "My great-grandparents built the farmhouse, so you could say that."

"Oooooooh," Rin repeats in tones of dawning understanding. "Did you *just* move to the city?"

"We sell at the farmer's market," Dahlia admits, wishing for something to do with her hands now that she's plugged in the lamp, "but this is gonna be the first time I spend the night here, yeah." Every word makes her want to dig a hole and crawl into it—she's wearing *overalls*; how much more hick could she seem?

"That's really cool!" Rin says without a hint of sarcasm. "So you grew up on a farm? What did you grow? How far is it?"

"Um." Dahlia blinks at the onslaught of questions.

"Sorry." Rin waves away said questions. "Sorry, you're moving in! That's a ton of work! You don't need me here distracting you with a million questions about farming."

"I wouldn't mind telling you." It's the truth, but… "I do have a lot to do with—" Dahlia waves at the stack of boxes.

"Oh, for sure!" Rin backs toward the door. "I'm right next door, so really—if you have any other questions about"—her gestures encompasses the entire apartment building—"I've been here for years, so I know all the tricks. Seriously, ask me anything."

"I will," Dahlia promises, hoping she won't have to ask any more utter yokel questions. "Thank you."

"Anytime!" Rin offers up a wave and disappears outside. Dahlia hears the jingle of keys and associated door sounds, which means she's now free to rub her face and lament her luck. The first cute girl she meets in her new city—in her new *apartment*—and she has to ask for help turning on the damn *lights*.

She's a *disaster*.

Dahlia allows herself thirty seconds of wallowing, and then she heads for the hand truck. Her boxes won't unpack themselves.

Dahlia glares at the stove.

It remains stubbornly off and doesn't react to her glare because it is a stove.

"I am *begging* you to work." Her living room is barren, but her bedroom has a bed and a nightstand, and she's unpacked enough dishes that she can heat the prepackaged noodles she bought at the corner store. It's been a long day, and she would *really* like to eat, and the stove doesn't have any obvious crystals to poke.

Dahlia's stomach rumbles, and she considers the nearest stack of boxes. One of them contains an emergency cooking burner that she could spark up for a basic aetherfire, but she doesn't remember which box it's in, and she's hungry *now*. There's only one solution she can see ahead of her, and she doesn't like it.

Dahlia sighs, steels herself, and heads next door.

"Dahlia?" Rin opens the door to reveal décor and pajamas as brightly colored as her hair.

"You said to ask if I had any more questions about the apartment?"

Rin nods.

Dahlia shuts her eyes. "I can't turn on the stove."

"Ah." Rins sounds unsurprised but not mean about it. Dahlia dares to open her eyes, and Rin gives her a sympathetic smile. "There's a trick to them. You want me to show you?"

"Please," Dahlia says, wilting a little. There are noodles she desperately needs to eat.

"Okay," Rin says when they've convened in Dahlia's kitchen, "first of all, your houseplants are really cute." She pats Sylvia gently. "So it's a feature for cleaning, right?" Her now-ringless hand runs across the back of the stove where it shows the time and nothing else. "It goes smooth when it's not being used so you can get all the grease out. All you have to do is—" Rin presses her hand against the surface and counts. "One, two, three…"

On "three," the surface flashes a gentle blue, and Dahlia watches in mingled amazement and annoyance as knobs rise from it corresponding to the burners. It's a great design, but… "How on *earth* was I supposed to figure that out?"

"Right?" Rin shakes her head, fists propped on her hips. "I happened to ask when the super showed me around before I signed the lease. You'd think it would come with a manual."

"That would have been nice." Dahlia wants to say something else—to prolong the conversation, to keep Rin here and smiling—but she's exhausted and hungry, so she makes the much more practical decision to politely escort Rin to the front door.

"Thanks again."

"Anytime," Rin says, lingering outside. "Do you have plans tomorrow? Other than unpacking?"

"I need to go to a good secondhand store in the afternoon to get some furniture before my folks come in to pick up the truck," Dahlia says, unsure if that counts as "plans" in the traditional sense.

"I have some suggestions for that," Rin says as if she's been waiting her whole life for someone to ask about secondhand furniture shopping. "But if you're free in the morning, maybe we could get breakfast together?" She plays with the hem of her pajama shirt and peeks at Dahlia through her lashes. "I can show you how the streetcar works in a low-pressure environment instead of at rush hour."

Ah. The streetcar. "Yes," Dahlia's mouth says immediately because she'll need to use that streetcar to get to the university for her job, and also because you don't get anywhere with attractive women if you say no when they ask you to breakfast. "What time?"

Rin gives Dahlia a thoughtful once-over. "You just moved here from a farm, so I'm guessing you're an early riser. I'll knock on your door at eight?"

Normally, Dahlia would be up at five for chores, but she'd planned to sleep in until a luxurious six tomorrow to celebrate her first apartment. That will give her two hours to unpack enough clothes to pick her least-bad outfit, which should be enough time. "Sounds good."

Rin's smile brightens until Dahlia thinks she'll see the afterimages on her retinas. "Awesome! See you tomorrow!" She skips back over to her apartment and disappears inside, leaving Dahlia staring after her until her stomach rumbles again.

You can freak out about your maybe-date later, she tells herself, heading for the kitchen. *Right now: Noodles.*

(She'll freak out in the shower, *obviously*.)

The next morning, Dahlia tries on, discards, and puts away ten different outfits, which she thinks is a reasonable amount of freaking out to do. (That she has maybe twenty outfits total is neither here nor there.)

She asked me to breakfast after seeing me in chore overalls, she tells her reflection, fingers flashing through a braid to contain her curly black hair. *Even if this isn't a date, she probably won't care what I wear.*

Knock knock knock!

Dahlia scrambles for a hair tie and whacks her hip on a corner as she runs for the living room. She secures her braid, smooths down the front of the dress, and takes a deep breath. It's just breakfast with the incredibly hot, kind woman who lives next door. It's nothing to get *weird* about.

"Good morninn*nnnnng*?" She didn't mean it to turn into a question, but the person standing outside wears slim-fitting pants and a structured blazer that emphasizes the breadth of their shoulders. They look up and smile, and yes, that's Rin's smile, and Rin's blue-green hair, but the hair is pulled back in a sleek ponytail, and this person has a little matching blue-green mustache drawn on their top lip. They also, Dahlia cannot help but notice, seem to be lacking the ample curves in their chest region that Rin sported yesterday, not that Dahlia was *looking*.

"Morning!" Probably-Rin says brightly. "You ready for a breakfast adventure?"

"I am," Dahlia says, eyes finally catching on the same aetherglow pin that Rin wore yesterday, only today it's green and says "He/Him." Well, that's one question answered. "Rin?"

Definitely-Rin nods. Dahlia thinks there's something different about the shape of his cheekbones and jaw, too. Is that…contouring? Dahlia barely knows how to use mascara, so she's not sure.

"Um." Dahlia hesitates. "Is it rude if I mention you look a little different from yesterday?"

Rin then looks down at himself and laughs. "Oh, yeah." He does a twirl, arms-out. "I change it up from day to day depending on how I feel when I wake up. You know!" He frowns. "*Do* you know?"

"Oh, yeah." Dahlia can tell where the conversation is going. "I know—my best friend when I was little used they/them."

"Really?" Rin's eyebrows go up, and Dahlia realizes that he's colored them in more thickly than before. It looks great. *He* looks great. Yep, Dahlia's crush does not care about gender. Good to know.

"Really." Dahlia drags herself away from contemplating Rin's attractiveness. "There are a lot more queer folks in the country than I think people realize; we're just all wearing overalls so it's harder to tell." She takes a breath and adds, as casually as possible, "I'm bi, anyway."

"Cool!" Rin bounces on his toes. "Thanks for telling me! And thanks for rolling with—" He gestures at himself. "Everyone's used to me around here, so I forget people could use a heads-up."

"I would have figured it out eventually." Dahlia grabs her keys and her battered, much-repaired phone. "Do I need to bring anything but this for the streetcar?" she asks, taking the phone back out and showing it to Rin.

"Does it have an up-to-date bank crystal?" Rin asks, eyeing the various homemade additions with interest.

"I do." Dahlia self-consciously runs her thumb over an engraved cabochon. Rin probably has a brand-new, sleek, efficient phone. Rin can probably take his phone to a repair shop if the screen gets scratched, instead of having to bodge repairs with trial-and-error and videos from the internet.

"Then you're good!" Rin beams, and Dahlia almost staggers from the force of it. "Shall we?"

⊳⋈⊲

A Toast To You is a cute, cramped café next to a park. Rin points out his favorite things on the menu, several of which Dahlia decides to order, and they sip their tea in a comfortable quiet.

"What brought you to the city? Did you need a change?"

"A little bit of that." Dahlia toys with the handle of her mug. "I was hired to co-lead a research project for the ag department at the university."

"Ooooh." Rin looks, if anything, *more* interested. "How did that happen? What are you researching?"

The first question is easier to answer than the second, so Dahlia makes the strategic choice to start there. "Professor Soloman used to shop from us at the farmer's market every weekend, and he'd get to talking with us about farming techniques. He does a lot of work in agricultural aethertech, and he was interested in something we do, so after a lot of letters and planning…" Dahlia trails off and shrugs.

"That's really cool," Rin says, then has to hold in all of his follow-up questions as the food arrives.

"Wow, this smells amazing." Dahlia pokes at her biscuits and gravy. They didn't skimp on the sausage, for sure. She takes a bite and chews happily.

"I love the food here." Rin enthusiastically attacks his pile of sourdough pancakes. "But you were going to tell me what you're researching?"

Ah. Well. "This might be boring and hard to explain."

Rin waves a fork at the breakfast spread between them. "You have at least five pancakes' worth of time. Hit me."

Dahlia takes a steadying sip of tea. She explains about greenhouses and other protected growing areas for delicate crops, and the advantages and disadvantages of using them on a large scale. She explains that her family has a small greenhouse for starts, but most of their land is open-air, which means they get the advantages that come with that, but also the issues—they're at the mercy of the weather, insects, birds…

Or they *would* be if not for the aether tunnel.

"It's like a hoop house," Dahlia explains, pulling up a photo of a hoop house on her phone to show Rin. "Normally, you cover the frame with mesh, or clear bio-plastic if you're trying to trap the heat and control the amount of water it gets, but…"

"That'd rip right off in a big storm, right? And how do you get in there when you need to do plant stuff?"

"If it's big enough, you can walk right in." Dahlia brings up another picture. "But you're right about the storms, and if you want to switch from mesh to plastic, or take the covering down entirely, it's a big pain in the a—neck."

"You can say 'ass,'" Rin says encouragingly. "It sounds like a pain in the ass."

"It's a pain in the ass," Dahlia says, relieved.

"An aether tunnel solves all those problems." She pulls up a photo of the one she helped install at the farm. "It's a hoop house made of *aether* instead of plastic or mesh. We found a way to draw raw aether out of the air, form it into a protective shell, and customize what the shell does. We can make it let rain through, but protect the plants from heavy winds. We can have it let pollinating insects through, but not birds. We can even make it warm the soil, which extends the growing season and makes it possible to grow food here that wouldn't normally work for this climate! We can…" Dahlia realizes suddenly how loud she's speaking and flushes. "Sorry. I didn't mean to ramble."

"You weren't rambling," Rin says, patting her wrist. "I asked, and it was interesting! Is the aether tunnel the thing you're working on at the university?"

"Yes." Dahlia eats more biscuit, trying to gather her thoughts so she doesn't dominate the conversation again. "It would be revolutionary for agriculture if we could get it to work on a large scale. You wouldn't need to construct a whole greenhouse, you know?"

Rin nods, mouth full of pancake.

"But…" Dahlia sighs, already frustrated by what she's about to say. "My family invented aether tunnels through a lot of trial and error. *We* can build them, no problem. It doesn't always work for other people, even if they make them to our exact specifications, and we don't know why."

"Ooooooooh." Rin points his fork at her. "So you're working with the professor to figure out what's up with that."

"Exactly." Dahlia decides to allow herself a bit of bragging. "I can carve the crystals and set up the array faster than anyone else in my family, so we figured I'd be the best one for the job."

"Makes sense." Rin gives her a searching look. "Is that the only reason you took it?"

Dahlia shrugs, returning to her biscuits in a futile attempt to stop feeling seen. "No. I was…interested in a change. I like where I grew up, and I wasn't trying to *escape* or anything, but I…" She chews, giving herself time to figure out the shape of the answer. "I wanted to see what else was out there, so if I went back, I'd have the full picture."

Rin nods and finishes the last bite of his pancakes. "What do you think so far?"

Dahlia tries and fails not to notice the shape of his mouth as he sips his tea. "I'm liking it quite a bit," she says, choosing not to clarify further.

Rin smiles, and Dahlia feels it on her face like sunlight. "Good. Let's keep it that way."

"Okay," Dahlia says reflexively, trying to cover her fluster with more biscuits.

Dahlia expected "let's keep it that way" to be metaphorical. Over the next few weeks, it becomes apparent that Rin meant it literally, and takes it *very* seriously.

Rin recommends a secondhand store with good furniture, and then he helps Dahlia get it home. Rin knocks on Dahlia's door when she's going grocery shopping and asks if Dahlia wants to come. Rin invites Dahlia over for dinner and makes pasta with a sun-dried tomato alfredo that's so good Dahlia inhales two bowls. Rin brings Dahlia a potted jade plant that a friend was getting rid of and names it Julian. Rin helps her pick out a used television, then sets it up for her when Dahlia knocks on his door at seven at night, frustrated to the point of crying.

It's...a lot. Dahlia's never faced this kind of focused attention before, and she's not sure what to do with it. She can't tell if Rin treats all her friends this way, or if it's because he's interested in her the way she's interested in him. She knows the obvious solution is to ask about it, but they're *neighbors*. If Dahlia's misreading this, she doesn't want to make it awkward. This was Rin's home before it was Dahlia's!

Also, Dahlia has never asked someone out in a "girlfriends" way. She doesn't just want to go on a date; she wants to be *dating*. That seems like a lot to lead with. She's happy to stay friends if that's all she'll get. Rin listens when she talks, laughs at her jokes, and has never once seemed impatient at explaining some fiddly piece of aethertech to her. That's more than Dahlia expected from a neighbor, and she doesn't need to get greedy.

(It's very hard not to feel greedy when Rin joins Dahlia at her kitchen table for a cup of tea, head tossed back in laughter at Dahlia's jokes with her long neck on display, but Dahlia is sure *trying*.)

"What do you actually *do*?" Dahlia asks Rin one morning. "I realized last night that I never asked." And proceeded to feel excruciatingly embarrassed that she'd been so oblivious that it had taken her a whole *month* to ask, which doesn't need to be said.

"Oh!" Rin frowns at the wall of the elevator. "Wow, yeah, I never said, huh?" He flashes a sheepish smile that would make Dahlia's knees go weak if she didn't have powerful farmer's legs. "I program jacquard looms!"

"Cool." The elevator has arrived, so Dahlia has to wait to ask her follow-up question. "What does that mean?"

"I get that a lot." Rin laughs, which helps Dahlia feel less silly about asking. "It's hard to explain without examples. Could you take a break from work? Play hooky for a couple hours? I'd love to give you a tour."

Dahlia would love to get a tour, just for the chance to spend more time with Rin. "Let me ask the professor?"

Dahlia manages to get to Rin's workplace, a warehouse in an industrial neighborhood, on public transit entirely on her own, so she feels incredibly competent—a feeling that disappears immediately when Rin leads her inside. Complicated machines surround them doing complicated things that turn into complicated fabrics, and Dahlia doesn't know where to look. The noise is…overwhelming. It's not loud, but it's *everywhere*, and Dahlia considers having some kind of panic attack. A little one, maybe? It might make her feel better.

"That's how I felt the first time I saw them," Rin says, taking Dahlia gently by the elbow and towing her onward. "We'll come back here, but let's start at the beginning."

Dahlia—who is distracted watching many cones feed colorful thread into one end of a machine that's extruding floral-patterned fabric from the other end—nods helplessly and allows herself to be towed into a smaller, quieter room before she melts down.

"Deep breaths," Rin tells her, rubbing Dahlia's back as she figures out how to breathe. "Sorry, the factory floor is *wild*. I ought to have started you off in here."

"Where is here, exactly?" Dahlia feels both sheepish at her reaction and relieved at Rin's kindness. The room, now that she's capable of perceiving it, has several machines—*looms*, fabric comes from looms—set up and running, but they're antique, made of gleaming, polished wood and metal. There are pieces of fabric encased in glass boxes and placards here and there. It looks like—

"This is our weaving museum." Rin spins in a slow circle and gestures proudly. "We have some of the original looms that were built in this city back when everything was still human or waterwheel powered, along with the early aether-powered jacquard machines! Wanna see?" She's glowing from within again, in her element and overjoyed about it.

"I'd love to," Dahlia says, not looking at the looms. "And I would love to know what a jacquard loom *is*."

"Ooooh, yeah." Rin pulls her by the hand toward one of the gently clacking wooden looms. "It's not so much what a jacquard loom *is*, it's what a jacquard loom *does*."

"...make jacquard?" Dahlia guesses. Most of her brain is focused on their joined hands.

"Exactly!" Rin points at the part of the loom that has the threads held tightly. "The pattern in jacquard fabric is created by lifting certain threads at certain times, so when you pass the heddle through, you're creating patterns based on which ones are lifted. Make sense?"

It does. Dahlia can see hundreds of metal hooks lifting and lowering as the machine operates, and the botanical pattern taking shape with each pass of the heddle. "How does it know which ones to lift?"

"Ah!" Rin looks proud of her for asking; Dahlia feels a blush coming on. "It used to be that you'd have an apprentice who sat above it and pulled certain threads up for the weaver, which is obviously a terrible system even before you get to the historical child labor. The thing that makes the jacquard loom a jacquard loom is this." She points to a tied-together loop of wooden cards with holes in them that advance through the machine like the treads of a tractor. "This system was invented by a guy named Joseph Marie Jacquard, as you might imagine—"

"I guessed the 'Jacquard' part," Dahlia chimes in, "but I wasn't expecting the other two names."

"Most people don't." Rin nods sagely. "There were a bunch of people who innovated other parts of it, of course, but he patented the card system. You have cards with holes in them that correspond to rods, and the rods are connected to the hooks that lift the warp threads. When you advance the loom"—the loom helpfully does this with a *cha-chunk!*— "the rods press against the card, and they either go into the holes, or they don't. If they go into the holes, then they lift the warp threads. If they don't, they don't."

Dahlia watches the whole contraption work, eyes flicking between the cards, the rods, and the threads as the loom does its magic. "So it's like pixel art, or cross-stitch, kinda?"

"Exactly! Except completely different in how you make it, but if you think of the crossing of each warp and weft as a square on a grid, you're either making the square one color or the other color, and by changing that up according to a particular pattern, you make stuff happen." Rin leans close and nudges Dahlia with her elbow, eyes shining. "Does that remind you of anything else?"

Rin is very close and smells very nice, so it takes Dahlia a second to put two and two together—the cards are a huge, obvious clue, fortunately—and say, "Old computers?"

"Yes!" Rin squeezes her arm and bounces a little. "It's binary code! On and off, lifted or not, ones and zeros, it's all the same. The jacquard loom is basically the first computer code."

"That's incredibly cool," Dahlia says, swept along on Rin's excitement. (It is also legitimately incredibly cool.) She remembers why she's *actually* here. "And so you do this"—Dahlia waves at the loom—"with modern computers now?"

"I sure do!" Rin tows her toward a different set of doors. "Come on, I'll show you my office."

Rin's office is full of fabric samples piled and draped on either side of her double monitors, the desk as chaotic and bright as she is. Dahlia doesn't understand most of what she talks about, but Rin's so excited to share that it's no chore to listen. Dahlia's just happy to bask in her glow.

Dahlia's been in the city three months when the first summer aetherstorm hits. She feels it coming all day, a prickle on her skin and a humid tartness on the back of her tongue. If she were on the farm, it would be time to check the crystals on the aether tunnels before going to the covered upstairs balcony to watch rainbow lightning flash across the plain. She's not on the farm, though, so instead she feels out of sorts.

"It's about to start bucketing out there, isn't it?" Rin slings himself into the streetcar seat next to her.

"It's going to be a real hair-raiser." Dahlia eyes the dark clouds rolling in over the buildings.

The rain starts behind them, sheeting down while their streetcar is still bathed in weird, watery sunlight, and they have to sprint for the apartment entrance in order to escape it. They tumble into the lobby with a foot to spare before the wall of rain washes over the sidewalk they just vacated, panting and laughing hand-in-hand.

"Holy sparks, it was like someone cast a spell," Rin wheezes, bent over to catch his breath. "*Summon rain* or something. We could have taken a *shower* in that."

"Back home, you could look out the front door and see that"—Dahlia tips her head at the pounding water—"and then look out the back door and see nothing but blue sky."

"That sounds amazing," Rin says, giving Dahlia's hand a squeeze. "It'd be cool to see it someday." He drags her toward the elevator. "Come on, if we hurry we might be able to beat it—"

The world flashes iridescent around them, leaving Dahlia blinking against the too-bright afterimages, and before she can start counting a bone-shaking *KRA-KOOOOM!* slams into her. Everything goes dark, and Dahlia shakes her head, trying to get her eyes to work.

"Yeah, nope." Rin sighs, trudging the last few feet to the elevator and punching an unlit button dejectedly. "The grid's knocked out." He turns to Dahlia, eyebrows raised. "Do you believe me now that the elevator hates me?"

"I don't think you can blame the elevator for this," Dahlia points out, sadly dropping Rin's hand to dig out her keys. There's almost *too* much aether in the air, and it takes only the gentlest tug to make her crystal keychain light up. "Looks like we're taking the stairs."

"How is that working?" Rin asks between floors two and three, glancing at the keychain with barely disguised wonder.

"It runs on aether." Dahlia doesn't understand the question.

"Okay, yeah, but so does everything else in the city, and everything else is—" He waves at the window, which looks out on a dark and rainy view.

"That's all on a grid," Dahlia says, pushing open the door and wincing against the sudden slap of wet wind that greets her. "This runs on the raw aether, so as long as I don't pull too much, it's still fine."

"That is really—sparks *alive*—" Rin splutters, having also met the weather whipping its way onto their walkway. Dahlia grabs his hand and pulls him along, skidding to a wet halt at her door, where they tumble inside after an inelegant interlude with her keys.

"It is raining *sideways* out there," Rin complains, shaking water out of his hair.

"It's a real humdinger," Dahlia agrees, picking across the dark room to the aether lantern on her end table. She presses her fingers to it and concentrates, creating the connection that allows it to sip the raw aether and burst into a gentle golden glow.

"Okay, what on earth are you doing, and how are you doing it?" Rin asks, looking astonished and damp in the lantern light. "Aether doesn't *work* during aetherstorms."

"It does?" Dahlia didn't mean that to be a question; she has an obviously working aether lantern in her living room right now. "You have to be careful about it because it's unpredictable, but if you do it right, it's fine."

"How do you do it right?" Rin asks, taking half a step closer. "How does work? You can just—you can just *use* raw aether?" He probably has more to say, but he shivers from head to toe so hard his teeth chatter.

"Go grab something from your place to change into," Dahlia orders, already heading for the kitchen. "I'll get some hot water going for tea, and I can explain once you're not freezing."

"You can *cook* with it?" Rin asks plaintively between shivers, but he ducks out the door into the storm without arguing.

Five minutes later, they're both in Dahlia's kitchen, drier and infinitely more comfortable. Rin watches from the table as Dahlia takes her kettle off her emergency aether burner, obviously vibrating with questions but managing to keep them tamped down until she sits down with mugs of herbal tea.

"Okay," Rin says, hands around the mug, eyes flicking between Dahlia and the aether lantern at the end of the table. "What are these? How do you run them on *raw* aether?"

"Well, the aether's there in the air, isn't it?" Dahlia gestures, feeling it tingle around her fingertips. "Everything starts from the raw aether."

"Yeah, but there are, like…procedures. To make it run things. If my *lights* ran on raw aether, we wouldn't be here." He blinks and adds, "Not that I'm mad about being here. I like it here."

Dahlia flushes and sips her tea. "Thanks." A pause. "I like having you here."

Rin ducks his head, rubbing a hand back over his still-damp hair. "Thanks." They drink in companionable, embarrassed silence. "That didn't answer my question, though."

"There are procedures." Dahlia touches the lantern and draws the aether out of it until it dims enough to show the carvings. "I have to prepare the crystals correctly and direct the right amount of aether into them. If I could use the raw aether, I wouldn't have to do all this first."

"Wait." Rin sets down his mug with a clack, goggling at Dahlia. "*You're* moving the aether? You're the one that—that puts it in the crystals to make them glow and stuff?"

Dahlia looks helplessly at the lantern, then at Rin. "Yes?"

Rin scrubs his hands over his face, smearing his eyebrows and mustache a little. "That is *so cool,*" he says with such sincerity that Dahlia wants to squirm. "I had no idea you could control the aether like that!"

"Everyone in my family can." Dahlia twists her mug around in her hands. "Most of us do, out in the country."

"Oh, damn, really?" When Dahlia nods, Rin flaps his hands against the table, bouncing in his seat. "Holy crap, okay, wow. I am *so* impressed."

This is unbearable. Dahlia wants to hide *so badly.* "It's not *that* impressive. I could do it when I was five."

"When you were *five?* How is that not impressive, Dahlia?"

Dahlia rubs her forehead, mostly for the face coverage. "It's just something we *do.* I mean—how am I impressive when I couldn't figure out how to turn on the *lights* when I first got here? I needed your help to turn on my stove."

"Well, apparently you would have been just fine without me, since you can use the *raw aether* to do your bidding." Rin lays his head on the table to peer up at her, cleverly evading her defenses. "I don't know why you have such a hard time believing that *controlling raw aether* is cool. You're the only person I know who can do that."

"Okay, but…" Dahlia picks up her mug and puts it back down. It can't save her from this. "I'm *not* cool, though. All my clothes are hand-me-downs and I wear the same five outfits all the time and I spend all my time carving crystals to make plants grow better! I'm not like *you.*"

Rin blinks. "Not like me how?"

"You know!" Dahlia waves a hand vaguely. "Fashionable, and

confident, and really attractive." The last slips out of her mouth before she realizes it, and she clacks her teeth shut. *Shit.*

Rin bites his lower lip, failing to hide his smile. "You think I'm really attractive?"

Well…fine. *Fine.* "Of course I do." Dahlia blusters through like a sheep determined to reach an off-limits garden. "Look at you. You have cool clothes and you know how to wear them and you're gorgeous as a woman and handsome as a man and that mustache makes you look great even when it's smudged." She crosses her arms and glares out the window. "I have functioning eyes."

"I do too." Rin leans his head on his hand. "That's how I know you look really good in your five outfits and you have a great smile and shoulders you could break me on and you move through the world like you expect it to give way before you—which is incredibly hot, by the way—and you're *so* smart and you listen when I talk." He gives her a very obvious once over. "I think you're really attractive, too."

"Oh." Dahlia's face is on fire. "That's… Thank you?"

"You're welcome." Rin slides along the table until he's in front of her again, grinning the whole time. "You like my mustache?"

Dahlia nods helplessly. "It really suits you," she says, and then figures she might as well go for broke. "I like everything about you."

Rin covers his face for a moment. "Okay, wow. I was about to tell you I like everything about you, too, but I needed to recover first."

Considering that Dahlia sort of wants to climb out the window, she can relate. "I've had a crush on you since I saw you in the elevator," she blurts, apparently determined to win this game of escalating confessions.

"Oh, damn, me too," Rin says sheepishly. "I thought I was being so obvious even though I was really trying to be cool."

"I was trying not to walk into poles when we went out together," Dahlia admits. They make eye contact, then both burst out laughing.

"We've been ridiculous," Rin wheezes, laying across the table.

"I can't believe we were doing the same thing," Dahlia agrees, wiping her face with a napkin. She catches her breath, considers the events of the last five minutes, and fixes Rin with a *Look*. "Come here."

Rin skids out of his seat and around the table at a nearly dangerous speed. Dahlia pushes her chair back and holds out a hand, drawing him down into her lap carefully. "Good?" she asks, even though Rin is staring straight at her mouth.

"The best," Rin says dreamily, and when she tilts her head back, he leans down and kisses her. His lips are soft, his hands are warm, he smells amazing, and Dahlia feels it shiver through her like an aether current.

"Do you want to stay the night?" she asks when they separate, foreheads pressed together in the glow of the lantern.

"Like a kids' sleepover?" Rin asks, playing with the hairs at the nape of her neck.

"If that's what you want," Dahlia allows, rubbing a slow circle on Rin's lower back. "But I was intending something with more making out."

"Oh, yeah, absolutely," Rin says immediately.

"Good," Dahlia says, leaning in for another kiss. It's a gentle exploration, and when they pause for breath she adds, "Though I really would have been fine with the sleepover if that's what you wanted—"

"I know," Rin cuts in, grinning widely, "but I don't want the kid's sleepover, so why don't you throw me over one of those farmer's shoulders and carry me to your bed?"

"If you insist," Dahlia says, and does just that while Rin squeals and giggles.

<hr />

There's more squealing and giggling later, with less clothing involved.

<hr />

It's the best aetherstorm experience Dahlia's ever had…

…until the next one, which she and Rin share by aetherlight in the apartment they live in.

Together.

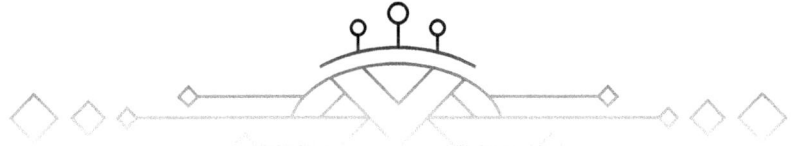

Ellen Faye

City of Light

bullying (past), childhood friends, london, modern with magic, non-binary, present
tense, reunion, student (college), third person limited point of view, united kingdom

*R*owan steps down into the lane, drawing their woolen coat
tight against the stiff breeze blowing up from the Thames. Had
it been this bitter at the Academy? Rowan supposes it must
have been—colder, even, but the Bavarians spent their winters inside,
for the most part.

The cobbled lane is barely visible as people stream past, heading for
the parade route on Fleet Street. Rowan can't help but smile as they take
in the crowd, young and old: from excited children holding tight to the
hands of their guardians to the older members of London's society moving more slowly.

Rowan checks their watch quickly—almost time for the parade to
start. Where in the heavens has Isaac got to? They step back through the
hotel door, casting a look around the foyer with narrowed eyes. He'd
been right behind them a moment ago.

There. Rowan spies their friend standing by the concierge desk, chatting with the dark-haired man behind it.

Catching Rowan's eye, Isaac says a hurried goodbye to the concierge
and joins Rowan by the door, grinning apologetically.

Rowan gives him a mock pout as he approaches. "If you could just
stop flirting with every person in a three-mile radius, we might actually

get to see some sights."

Scoffing, Isaac passes them and opens the door. "You have all day tomorrow to show me the city. Tonight, we need to know where the party happens." He pauses, looking back over his shoulder towards the hotel's reception desk. "And if my new friend happens to be there, all the better."

Rolling their eyes, Rowan follows him out into the bustling street. Isaac might be an incorrigible flirt, and his Bavarian accent gets him more attention here in England than is probably good for him, but Rowan's glad he was the one to win the second place on this trip. Had it been anyone else, the chance to see the festival lights and attend the city's gala dinner wouldn't be nearly as much fun. They both worked hard to win their respective academic prizes, and they've earned this break before their final year at the Aetherial Academy is over.

Rowan and Isaac join the progress towards Fleet Street, moving at a shuffling pace as many people wave long sticks with fluttering flags attached; stripes of aether-infused fabric glow in bright blues and greens, swirling gently in an invisible breeze above their heads. As they wave, they leave shimmering arcs in the air around them.

"Where do we get one of those?" Rowan wonders, then their jaw drops as Isaac unwraps a bundle he's just pulled from his shoulder bag: two flags, fabric still coiled around their handles.

He hands one over with a grin. "I found them earlier."

London hasn't changed much in the seven years Rowan has been away. The ancient, cobbled streets of the city are still the same, and the shining skyscrapers still soar into the skies, reinforced with aether-steel. Overhead, silver-and-black taxis carry their passengers between them. Tonight, for the first night of the festival, the glass faces of each build-ing are lit from within, a patchwork of colour pouring over the excited crowds.

They hurry along with the other festival-goers, jostled by the moving mass of humanity.

Once they reach the main parade route along Fleet Street, the crowd presses impossibly closer. So, when Rowan notices a space along the top of a brick fence, they grab Isaac's elbow and point upward. Thank-fully, the perch is high enough to get a mostly unobstructed view of the street, which is already full of dancers in brightly coloured costumes. The performers spin and twirl, their feet skating above the street on aether-lifted shoes. Some performers carry lit torches along, while others form marching bands creating music that Rowan can't help but tap their feet along to.

Rowan hasn't been to one of these festivals for years. Everyone always says it would be better to hold them more often than every four years, on the leap day, but traditions hold strong in the capital and the Festival of Light always encompasses the nights before and after February 29th. Rowan was just a kid the last time they were in a crowd like this, holding tight to their father's hand.

This year, they don't have a hand to hold—well, technically, they could hold Isaac's hand, but they haven't done that since that one awkward time in second year before they worked out they were better at being best friends than romantically involved. Rowan smiles, remembering how relieved they were to find out neither of them needed to break the other's heart.

A loud cheer rises from the crowd, and the first float comes into view: a dramatic arch and spiral of lanterns, rainbow-hued and bright with the glow of aether. Music blasts from speakers on board the float as it skims the ground, a thumping beat that Rowan can feel in their chest as it approaches. The people dancing on board the float are dressed in a similar aether-kissed fabric to the crowd's flags, shimmering with shifting colours as they move, smiling and waving to the crowd.

Rowan can remember staring up at the beautiful dancers last time, wishing they could dress up like a magical being and join the parade. They chuckle and shake their head. They'd become a magical being, all right, of a kind. Their mandatory Academy training had seen to that.

Before the float draws level with where Isaac and Rowan sit, something catches their eye across the street. A building, a balcony two stories up. A child, reaching a small hand out as their parent is distracted beside them.

The child overbalances.

Rowan shouts, reacting before they realise they are. They drop their flag, drawing aether to their aid and pushing forward off the wall and into the crowd. They lift their feet off the ground, trying to reach the barriers as people complain and mutter around them, but they are going to be too late—the child is already falling. Rowan reaches out, their hands bright with aether magic, and desperately tries to gather the air beneath the child as they fall, but it's not going to be enough.

The people in the crowd gasp as they realize what's about to happen, but then…the child's descent slows. Not much, but enough for them to land semi-gently on their butt on the awning of the shop beneath.

Rowan turns, confused. Isaac is right behind them, his hands raised with the glow of aether magic around them, but even with both of them, there's no way they're close enough to have such an effect on the aether across the street. At least not at short notice, without a focus crystal or a transponder to enrich the effects.

Suddenly, hands are clapping Isaac and Rowan on their shoulders, accompanied by cheers and congratulations from those who saw the child saved by magic. Rowan quickly scans the other side of the street. Could there have been another mage?

There. A person stands at the back of the crowd, barely visible, but their hands are raised and still bright with aether. The person quickly pulls their hands down and ducks behind the throng, but not before they lock eyes with Rowan in a startling moment of recognition.

It couldn't be…Priya? Rowan is almost certain the woman they've just seen cast aetherial magic is their friend from before they went to college.

Isaac grabs Rowan's arm, stealing their focus as he drags them back to their spot along the wall.

The man next to where they sit yells at them both over the noise, "Well done! You saved her!"

Rowan smiles, not sure if they should accept the praise.

Isaac leans in, his face flushed. "Mein gott…I can't believe we managed to catch him! What a rush though, right? I haven't had to summon aether like that at short notice…ever, I don't think!"

"I don't think it was just us," Rowan says, looking back across the road to where they had seen the other mage.

"You saw someone else?"

"Yeah."

"Someone we know? Come on, you look like you saw a ghost." Isaac laughs, waving his flag again so that it floats gently in the air above their heads.

"Maybe I did. Just looked like someone I knew from back home." Rowan shakes their head. "It couldn't have been, though. I must have been mistaken."

The floats of the parade pass by, bright lights and music, dancers and happy Londoners. All Rowan can think about, though, is the shock on Priya's face.

A knocking at their door wakes Rowan out of a dream—they were left with only a vague memory of what had been happening: Rowan being driven away from their childhood home in an aether-borne car while Priya stood at the door, left behind and in tears.

They blink a few times, getting their bearings before reaching up to rub tentatively at the ache behind their forehead. Seeing someone who looked like Priya must have messed them up more than they realised. Could it have been her?

A thin light makes its way between the pulled drapes. Last night had been a late one, in the end. Rowan isn't even sure how much they'd had to drink, but judging by the gritty eyes and the ashy mouth, more than a little.

Whoever is at the door knocks again insistently, and Rowan glances at the time, then closes their eyes again with a groan. How is it already after eleven?

They push themselves out of bed and stumble across the room to the door. It's barely open a crack before Isaac pushes it the rest of the way and comes in, his hands full of coffee cups and something that Rowan admits smells delicious.

"Come on, sleepy. I thought you wanted to show me the city? Here," he says, grabbing Rowan's hand and wrapping it forcefully around one of the paper coffee cups. When Rowan sits back down on their bed, inhaling the sweet coffee, he also hands over a paper bag with something warm inside.

Rowan opens the top of the bag to peer in. They look back up at Isaac, surprised but impressed. "You got us bacon sandwiches?"

Isaac plonks onto the other bed, nodding through the bite he's already taken. He speaks around his mouthful. "I asked Tony what was good around here the morning after." At Rowan's blank look, he adds, "The concierge? He said this." He gestured with his sandwich, grinning.

Tony had been right.

Bacon sandwiches on board, Rowan leads Isaac down to the river and onto one of the many bridges crossing the Thames.

The great Alchemical Museum stands on the southern side of the river in an imposing stone building. Isaac can barely contain his excitement as they pass under the arch of the entrance; he's been dying to come here for years, apparently. He flits from one section to the next, from the foundations laid by the ancient Greeks and the great discoveries made by Sir Isaac Newton himself, through the adoption of aether into more recent technology. As an engineering student, he's in his element, exclaiming in delight with each new exhibit he discovers.

Rowan has to smile as they watch him. Their own studies in senior year have been focused on the human element rather than the mechanical, but their thoughts are still too distracted by seeing Priya at the parade yesterday to focus on the ancient alchemists. They're lost in thought, following the way aether flows and collects in an early prototype of the aether-powered generators—the modern, more efficient versions of which power most homes nowadays—when Isaac nudges them with his shoulder, nearly making Rowan topple over sideways.

Isaac grabs them, holding them steady. "You okay? What's with you, anyway?" Isaac asks, his eyes staying on the generator in front of him. "You've been quiet. It's weird."

Rowan shrugs one shoulder, trying to shake off their worries. "Still tired, I guess." They watch as aether swirls around the generator, drawing it closer until it's captured by the gold rods on the top. Such a simple design, but one that has been used for centuries.

"You're still nervous about tonight, aren't you?" Isaac turns briefly to regard Rowan, then turns back to the display.

Rowan blinks at him in surprise. "I don't know," they reply. "No, I was nervous yesterday, but now we're here, I'm more..." They pause, trying to collect their thoughts. The nerves for tonight are still there, but they're not sure how to explain how much what happened at the parade last night has rattled them. "Okay, yeah. Still a little nervous."

"Hey, listen," Isaac begins, putting a hand on Rowan's shoulder. His voice is low, gentle. "We're here at this festival because we deserve to be, you got it? No one's going to have questions about that. And if they do, just point me at them and I'll tell 'em a thing or two about my friend Rowan. Yeah?" He frowns in a way that only makes Rowan choke on a laugh, and then grins briefly before turning towards the next hall of exhibits. "Come on, let's quickly see the vehicles and then get coffee, okay?"

Rowan shakes their head, smiling at their friend's words, but is glad when he lets it go.

It's not long before he brings it up again, though.

"It's not like we need to give a speech tonight or anything," he says, carefully setting his coffee down on the cafeteria table.

Rowan sips on the coffee, trying not to scald their tongue. "Heavens, no. I'm sure Dr. Morgan will introduce us to the people we need to know." Rowan has to admit, they're grateful the professor is joining them for this.

Isaac nods. "As much as I dislike the man," he says with a sour look, "it'll be nice to see a familiar face there."

"Hmm, yeah," Rowan replies. "Another one."

"Another what? Familiar face?" Isaac asks, one eyebrow high as he glances Rowan's way.

Rowan nods. "Yesterday, at the parade…I thought I saw someone I knew, remember?"

"Oh, you said that, yes. Don't worry, if they come near you, I'll—"

He raises a fist, but Rowan bats it away with a laugh. "No, no, nothing like that. If it even *was* her, she was a friend."

"Oh." Isaac sits back, taking in Rowan's face as they feel their cheeks rapidly warming. Isaac draws out his next word, with a smirk. "*Ohhhh.*"

"Stop it! It wasn't like that," Rowan replies, laughing again. "As much as I might have wished it."

"Really?" Isaac's smirk is there for the day, Rowan's sure of it.

They shake their head. "We lost touch after I was accepted into college. If I do see her again, she won't know me. I look pretty different these days."

Isaac looks them over. "Oh? Not so different, if she knows you."

"Maybe."

"Come on, we've still got time for the tower before we need to get back."

The observation level in the towering spire of the Alchemical

Museum stands high above the surrounding buildings, but it's no longer on a level with the steel towers of London City. The view is still incredible, though, and even in the years since the last time they were here, Rowan can see the changes in the skyline.

From so high up, the wintry light lies over the city's buildings and leafless trees with a golden glow as the natural aether is stirred in the atmosphere.

So many people living in this city, going about their lives, using their aether-powered devices without a thought for the forces that go into those objects' creation. They'll never know the joy in creating with aether, with designing a process and nurturing it to life.

Rowan used to feel unworthy of being singled out; after all, they were the only student from their entire year to be identified as aether-sensitive, and the first for several years from their school. It's been said that fewer and fewer students are being accepted to the Academy, that the ability to move and shape the fifth element without the use of tools is vanishing from the world. Two hundred years ago, there had been thousands of students at Academy campuses all over Europe. Now, there's barely six hundred at the sole Academy in Munich.

Sure, there are plenty of techs—with proper training, anyone can fix a machine that runs on aether. But without Aetherial Mages, creating and innovating with aether is nearly impossible. The world will recycle old tech rather than advance—not a catastrophic future, but a sad one, from an Aetherial Mage's point of view.

As they look out over the city, they can't help the way their thoughts return to Priya, about the dream that's still playing over in their head. It wasn't entirely a memory; they'd worked that out while walking through the museum. Aetherial Mages had come to their school and interviewed all the sixteen year olds, running little tests such as asking what colour a stone was and odd questions that had been far simpler than Rowan had expected. Couldn't everyone make aether flow along a tube between vessels?

Apparently they couldn't, though. Only a few days later, they'd left home in the company of Dr. Morgan, heading for Bavaria. It had felt like such an adventure, to get away from the kids at that school who'd made their time there so awful. What they'd told Isaac about the way they'd been treated, the comments about their appearance, about things they did that the other students labeled as "weird"…that was just the beginning.

They'd been happy to see the back of that place.

Priya had been inconsolable at losing them, though—enough to make Rowan wonder if they'd been wrong to keep their confusing feelings for Priya pushed down inside. They'd promised to write, but after a couple of emails back and forth, their conversation had trailed off.

Could she really be out there, somewhere in the city? Rowan's chances of ever finding her if they were to go looking are next to zero, but perhaps when they get home, their mum might know something.

"Hey, you with me?"

Isaac's voice breaks into Rowan's thoughts, and they turn to him with a start. "Sorry, what?"

Isaac beckons them back over towards where the elevator waits to return them to the ground level. "Come on! We've gotta go get ready for the party."

⊳⬦⬦⊲

Rowan steps out of the black cab. They thank the driver out of habit, even though the vehicle is driverless; automated hovercabs are planned for Munich but haven't yet arrived. In London, they drive along strictly cab-only lanes of the city's skyways, which means, to Rowan and Isaac's delight, that they are able to bypass the bulk of the city's traffic.

Isaac follows Rowan out of the cab, looking upward as he alights on the footpath. "Wow."

Rowan follows his gaze towards the city spires. From below, they seem to stretch into the sky, all soaring glass and steel.

Newton House was newly constructed in the last few years—this is the first time Rowan has seen the city's new cultural heart up close. They take a moment to admire the smooth façade, thankful they're here on a clear afternoon as the last light of the day strikes the tower and refracts into rainbow shimmers in the air on the eastern side. Later, the effect will be recreated with rainbow lights shining around the building. It had shown a similar display last night when Rowan had seen it from where they'd partied. This near, the scale of the building is overwhelming, as though it's looming overhead, poised to topple. Rowan hurries to the entrance with Isaac on their heels.

Dr. Morgan meets them just inside the foyer, his dark, official robes looking curiously outdated among the shining architecture. "There you are," the professor mutters, looking them both over. He nods, apparently satisfied. "You look presentable. Let's get inside. The council members are already here, and I want to introduce you both before dinner."

Rowan shares a look with Isaac. This is the part of the evening they'd been least looking forward to, and Rowan wishes all over again that they'd been allowed to wear something other than the Academy-regulation uniform so they could have been saved from self-consciousness. They adjust the collar of their blazer, wishing it would sit properly.

A grand stone staircase leads upward through the foyer of Newton House to a high-ceilinged reception area hung with several crystal chandeliers. The three of them are ushered through to the bank of elevators and then out through impressive double doors into an expansive ballroom. The large windows on the far side are bright with the last light of the day, but the view is barely visible past the crowd mingling in the room.

"Professor!" a voice says from one side, and Dr. Morgan smiles as he turns to greet a woman in a sparkling blue dress. This begins a whirlwind of introductions, as Dr. Morgan seems determined to present Isaac and Rowan to what feels like every person in the room. Everyone congratulates them for their academic success and wishes them well, and the names and positions begin to blur.

Rowan is finally able to get a moment to breathe sometime later, when Dr. Morgan begins a deep conversation with an official from the East London Alchemical Guild, and they, along with Isaac, are able to slip away towards the bar.

The two of them stand near the huge windows for a moment, looking out into the bright city. They're not many floors up, and the buildings reaching into the sky around them are lit with patterns of fire here, rainbows there. Others shine with arcs of floating lanterns strung between them. The aether in the air shimmers and buzzes—Rowan can feel it on their skin, like warm sunlight.

Isaac nudges Rowan in the shoulder, nodding to their left. "Incoming. I'll be over there."

He steps away before Rowan can stop him, and they curse him under their breath as they turn to see a tall, dour-faced woman approaching.

One of the councillors, they are almost certain—they try desperately to remember her name.

"Rowan, isn't it?" The woman says as she approaches. At Rowan's nod, she continues, "Ah yes. Morgan did introduce us, but I expect you're a little overwhelmed by all this. I'm Mathilde Baker, councillor for Wandsworth."

"Of course. Pleased to meet you again," Rowan says, grateful for the reminder.

"How are you enjoying the festival?"

Rowan repeats what they've told most people this evening in praise of the way the city lights up and makes pleasant small talk while internally cursing Isaac for abandoning them, but they find themself gradually relaxing. Councillor Baker seems genuinely interested in the study they've been doing for their anthropology major, and for the first time all evening, Rowan feels like perhaps they are meant to be here.

Councillor Baker begins explaining some of the community development work the council is doing, but she pauses, smiling at someone behind Rowan. "Rowan, may I introduce you to my personal assistant?" Councillor Baker gestures to Rowan's right and adds, "This is Priya."

Rowan nearly gasps in surprise but turns, heart in their throat, to take in the woman standing there. Yesterday at the parade, she had melted into the crowd, wearing something dark; it had been her magic that had drawn Rowan's eyes to her. This evening, though, she wears bright colours: blues and greens, a flowing dress showing off her curves. Rowan quickly lifts their eyes to see Priya smiling.

"Nice to meet you," she says pleasantly.

Rowan hesitates for a moment. Hearing her voice sends them right back to a simpler time, before expectations, before they'd been identified by the Academy and had to leave home. It was years ago now, but why does it feel like a lifetime has passed?

They steel their resolve and smile. "Actually, we already know each other," they say. "We were at school together in Dorset."

"Oh!" Councillor Baker's surprise startles Rowan out of their thoughts. "How lovely."

"Yes, ma'am," Rowan murmurs.

The blue aether-charged glass beads caught in Priya's dark hair sparkle, even in the low light of the room. She looks at Rowan in confusion for a few moments until recognition blossoms in her expression, and she murmurs, "Oh! Oh, yes."

Rowan's relief is such that they actually feel the flood of warmth to their cheeks. Maybe Isaac had been right, after all.

The councillor clears her throat slightly, and when Rowan glances at her, she smiles. "I'll leave you two to get reacquainted, then." She nods to Rowan and Priya, then moves away to speak to another group nearby.

"So... Rowan?" Priya is smiling when Rowan looks back to her.

Rowan nods, hoping their cheeks aren't too red. "That's who I am now."

They glance towards the dinner tables, wondering whether they could use food as a suitable escape route if things go sideways. Isaac is standing at the near end of the bar, talking to a tall person with long blonde hair.

Priya tilts her head to one side, considering Rowan's face. "The name suits you."

"Thanks." Relieved, Rowan smiles and glances back to Isaac in time to see him giving them an exaggerated wink and two finger guns, which makes Rowan choke out a short laugh they awkwardly try to turn into a cough.

Priya follows their gaze and looks back, one eyebrow raised. "A friend of yours?"

Isaac must have realised he's been seen because he heads over, glass in hand. Rowan is pretty sure this is a terrible idea.

Isaac smiles widely as he arrives. "Hey, Rowan! Did you try the Champagne? Delicious."

"Not yet." Rowan tries to convey a sense of *calm the fuck down* with only their eyes as they add. "Isaac, this is Priya. We knew each other back home, and now she's Councillor Baker's assistant."

"Oh." Isaac's eyes widen as something clicks into place, and he looks towards Rowan for confirmation. "Oh!" he adds, looking back to Priya with a grin.

"Nice to meet you," Priya says, bowing slightly.

Isaac bows in return, the charmer. "And you, Priya. I was just on my way to find the bathrooms, so I'll leave you to it, if you'll excuse me."

He downs the rest of the wine in his glass and then turns raised eyebrows to Rowan before he walks away. Rowan smiles at their friend's attempt at subtlety.

When Rowan turns back to Priya, she's eyeing Rowan's jacket, and they straighten their shoulders self-consciously.

"I'm glad the Academy sent you," she says. "Congratulations."

Rowan mumbles their thanks, wondering how in the heavens they can bring up the parade yesterday without sounding like a complete idiot if it turns out they're wrong. The longer they look at Priya, though, the more sure they are that it was her, holding up the aether to save that kid's life.

"So," Rowan says, opting for safer small talk, "assistant to the councillor, huh? Maybe I should congratulate you, instead."

Priya grins, nodding. "I lucked into that job, honestly—I did pretty well in my first couple of years of a planning degree. Someone suggested I apply for it, and here I am." She spreads her hands.

"Very lucky," Rowan agrees. "I hope I can do something similar by being here, in fact."

"Oh, well, I'm sure there are plenty of opportunities," Priya says.

A natural pause forms. Rowan wonders if they might simply pass out from the pressure of not asking outright about yesterday, but in the end they both speak at the same time to break the silence.

"So, did you attend the parade yesterday—" Rowan begins.

"So, how are you enjoying the festival?"

They glance at each other and laugh, and Priya says, looking down, "I did attend the parade, yes. The lanterns and flags are always my favourite."

Rowan continues carefully. "You weren't watching along Fleet Street, were you? I thought I saw you there."

"Oh no," Priya says, her smile faltering. "I was along near the cathedral—"

Rowan tilts their head. Was she trying to cover for herself? "The whole time? Because there was this child near us who fell, and someone caught them with aether. And I could have sworn…"

Priya's eyes are wide. "No, I—"

She might be denying it, but Rowan can feel her panic in the aether around them both. "It was you, wasn't it? You were holding aether… You saved that kid!"

Priya shakes her head, taking another step back. "Okay, I was there, but I didn't save anyone. That was you. You and your friend."

Rowan's heart feels like it's about to escape their chest. "No, we weren't close enough. I *knew* I saw you there."

"Keep your voice down," Priya says, glancing around. She puts one hand on Rowan's arm, drawing them closer to the window and the corner of the room. She sighs, her expression serious. "I had to do what I could to help."

"But this is brilliant," Rowan says, unable to contain their excitement. "You pulled aether to a precise location! Do you know how hard that is to do? One of our professors is here tonight. I'll introduce you, and you can come to learn at the Academy as well. I'm not sure what their policy on taking on students outside of the testing is, but—"

"Rowan," Priya says, interrupting, "please don't tell anyone about this. I'm not going to the Academy."

Rowan stares, taken aback. "But you...you have the gift. Why didn't you end up at the Academy with us?" They gesture towards Isaac, who is now deep in conversation with someone not far away.

"I... My ability wasn't very strong back then."

"But I keep reading that numbers are declining. People aren't able to work with aether the way they used to. You should learn to use your abilities, then you can—"

Priya keeps her voice low and light. "No. I didn't want to go. I couldn't."

Rowan pulls up short. "You couldn't?"

Priya turns away, looking out into the dark above the sparkling city below. She takes a breath in, then sighs it out again before continuing. "I couldn't leave Miah to look after Mum on her own. She was only fourteen at the time."

Rowan remembers Priya's little sister, Miah, and their mother—her smile and cheerful greetings had always brightened Rowan's days. Had their mum been unwell?

When Rowan doesn't say anything, Priya continues, still looking out the windows. "So, I purposely failed their tests and hid what I could do. Then, when you were chosen to go, I was...well, it felt like the world was falling apart." She shrugs, a half-smile on her lips.

Rowan shakes their head in wonder. "I've never heard of anyone who failed the tests on purpose."

Priya huffs out a short, humourless laugh. "I'm not alone. There are others, some who developed their abilities later, or who were missed by the Academy—people who use aether without even realising it. That guy who seems to have a knack for fixing any engine or generator. A girl who wonders why screens sometimes flicker when she walks past. That one was me," she adds, glancing Rowan's way. "For obvious reasons, we'd all prefer to stay out of the Academy's notice. Are you going to report me?"

"What?" Rowan says, "No, of course not."

They look out over the city again, the bright lights below barely registering in their mind as they try to grasp that everything they have learned about the aether-sensitive world might be completely wrong. More people are out there with the aetherial gift, some even unaware of it?

And Priya, denying her gift to look after her family? Rowan understands why she would do it, perhaps better than most of the other people crowding around them. Even though they could have had years together at the Academy, no one should be forced into a life against their wishes.

"Your secret is safe with me," they say, and Priya's answering smile makes the lights in the city outside the window seem dim by comparison.

"Come sit with me at dinner," Priya says. "I'd love to hear what you've been up to in Bavaria."

Rowan offers her an elbow, and they wander back towards the dinner tables together, hearts light.

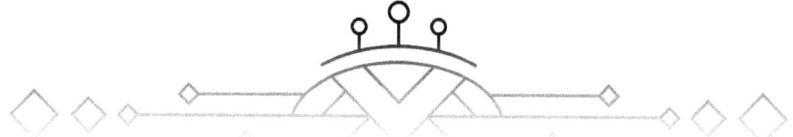

Terra P. Waters

Ancient Hearts Unearthed

academia, alternate history, cancer, f/f (background), f/nb, fat, first kiss, friends to lovers, getting together, hospital, illness (serious), mystery, non-binary, panic attacks, past tense, phobia (claustrophobia), pining, professor, science fiction with magic, scientist, third person limited point of view

*W*ork-roughened hands plucked a shard of pottery out of its foam-lined container and set it on the aetherwork console, taking an image and adding it to the auto-ledger of similar artifacts. "Let's see…" Associate Professor Sasha Edwards—who really needed to take on a graduate student to do this for them—sighed and pushed their red hair out of their eyes. They rummaged in their skirt before taking a pen from one of the many pockets of their dig vest and making a few notes for further reference.

As they double checked that the auto-ledger was correct, a perfunctory knock on the door preceded the arrival of Sasha's colleague, Victoria West. As was often the case, she wore her black hair in a braid that draped over her shoulder. Today, she'd laced an aether-imbued ribbon into the braid; it shimmered red and gold to match the embroidery on her loose-flowing shirt. Her dark-blue pants were fitted and tucked into her dusty brown boots. "Hey, Sasha! I have something for you."

"Let me guess," they said, turning away from the workbench and tilting their head to crack their neck and ease some of the stiffness. "You received a piece of mail that was meant for me." They sighed, holding out their hand. "Again."

"Got it in one!" Victoria skipped closer, placing a white envelope in their hand. "It says it's from the Sheriff of Adams County."

Sasha raised an eyebrow and turned the envelope over, finding it still sealed. "I'm surprised you haven't read it already."

With a roll of her eyes, Victoria sat on the stool next to Sasha's. "I did that *one* time, on accident."

Slipping their slender finger under the flap of the envelope, Sasha cracked open the seal and pulled out the letter.

> Dear Professor Edwards,
>
> You may have heard of the earthquake we experienced on September ninth. While its epicenter was considerably outside the city, it exposed a cave system that some teenagers explored and got trapped inside. We got them out shortly, thank God, but the rescue personnel found a number of old artifacts. We thought we should give you the opportunity to catalog the artifacts before we seal off the cave system again, in the interest of public safety. If you would like to set up access to the site, please contact my public affairs officer.
>
> Sincerely,
> Carl T. Knobbs
> Sheriff, Adams County

Sasha handed the letter to Victoria and waited for her to read and return it before asking, "Well? What do you think? Will Gardiner let us take some time for field work?"

"If we agree to show the pieces in the new wing of the museum he's opening next year, I bet he will."

With a sigh, Sasha took back the letter, looking it over again. "It's going to be months of work, lots of overtime hours to get everything cataloged so we can study it properly, even after it goes on display."

"I know, but think of what we could find!" Victoria's bright smile was infectious, and Sasha found themself smiling back at her. "A cave that's been cut off for who knows how long? You can't say you're not curious."

"Oh, I'm curious as hell," Sasha replied. They folded the letter and put it back in the envelope. "I suppose it couldn't hurt to go do an initial excavation, see if it's actually artifacts from the first Age of Aether, or whether it's something we should refer elsewhere in the department."

"You're making too much sense right now." Victoria rolled her eyes, which made Sasha laugh. "Let's do it!"

Sasha parked their auto-transport in the parking lot of the Green Canyon trailhead in rural Adams County. They turned to Victoria, admiring the scarf she wore over her hair, and said, "It's too early in the morning for this. Morning people have too much power."

Victoria laughed at the old complaint. "Come on! We're burning daylight."

Sasha groaned. "Only technically."

They followed Victoria, getting out of the auto and heading to the trunk in the back. The morning air felt damp and seeped through Sasha's cargo pants and jacket. They moved their caving gear out of the auto, loading it onto their backs and into their arms. As they passed the sheriff's sign and headed up the trail, Victoria gave Sasha an amused smile. "You know it's going to be a tight squeeze to get into the cave, right?"

"I know," they assured her, trying not to think about it. "This isn't going to be a Belgrade situation."

"No?" she asked with a teasing laugh. "Because I left extra time in our agenda today to talk you down from a panic attack."

"People are not meant to be buried in the ground. We're tree-slash-savanna creatures, and the fact that artifacts survive the elements longer when protected in caves is an unfortunate coincidence." They took a deep breath and let it out slowly. "I'll be fine."

"It's okay if you don't—"

"I'll be *fine*." Sasha overtook Victoria on the trail, hurrying around a bend.

A minute later, they got to the flag the sheriff had left, marking the new entrance to the cave. The undergrowth between the proper trail and the cave had been pushed aside, creating a de-facto trail Sasha hoped would survive the day's excavation. They weren't looking forward to finding their way back by aether lamplight in the absence of a well-distinguished trail.

"Do you think there will be any spiders in the cave?" Victoria asked them, laughing when Sasha shuddered. "What? Spiders are our friends!"

"Spiders are an unfortunate part of archaeology," they replied. "At least it's not a desert. No scorpions this time."

"Oh, but they glowed so prettily in the aether-light!"

"Here it is!" Sasha gestured to a bluff that jutted up out of the forest. A large crack split the rock face and several yards of the ground leading up to it. "Kids must have been getting in through here." Sasha gestured to the lower end of the crack, where the split between halves of the rock was widest. Sasha looked down at their soft belly and thick thighs, praying Victoria wouldn't let them get stuck.

Victoria raised an eyebrow and asked, "Well? Shall we?"

"Yeah." Sasha pulled their aetherwork torch out of their vest pocket. "Let's get this over with before I psych myself out."

Just when it seemed like the cave wasn't going to be as bad as they'd feared, the passage narrowed to a sliver. Victoria went first, claiming, "Come on! It's not that bad!"

Sasha squeezed themself through the narrowest part of the passage. Their heart raced, and they had to consciously control their breaths so they wouldn't hyperventilate. Sweat ran down the back of their neck and their palms were wet enough to make their hands slip readily across the rock. The cave walls pressed solidly against their back and loomed close against their chest. And then Victoria grabbed their hand and the air felt thinner. After a rush of it left their lungs, Sasha slipped through to the other side.

Victoria grinned and gestured to the cave, shining her torch around. "Look at this treasure trove!"

Sasha spotted pottery, a few bone tools, and even a few strands of some sort of fiber rope, all at the surface. Suddenly, they were glad they hadn't turned back at The Squeeze.

As Sasha brushed the dirt from an artifact, they tried to discern the material it was made of. Obsidian, maybe? Hand-carved for sure. As they leaned closer to inspect whether a fleck of brown was more dirt or an inclusion in the polished stone, the lantern hanging from a rock anchor above them flickered. Its light faded quickly; Sasha backed away from the dig so they wouldn't accidentally crush something when the light went out.

"Victoria?" they called to the other end of the cavern. "Please tell me you have another bulb for the lantern?"

"It's brand new." Victoria made her way over, then steadied herself with a hand on Sasha's arm and reached up to the lantern. "What the hell?"

Reaching toward her, Sasha lifted the ribbon she'd woven into her braid. "This isn't glowing either."

Frowning, Victoria abandoned the lantern and took her air monitor off her belt. The *click* of a switch flipping wasn't followed by the numbers on the face lighting up. "Huh." She looked around. "And the aetherwork sifter stopped working a few minutes ago, too."

"Aether shouldn't be depleted down here, should it?" Sasha took the lantern down, smacking their palm against the side. "If anything, there should be *more* aether available this far from the city."

Victoria gave a thoughtful hum. "I do have one of those novelty…" She rummaged around in the pockets of her vest, then took out a jangling set of keys. On a thin chain dangling from the rest of the bundle hung a small oval with a clear tip. Victoria grasped the oval with her thumb and forefinger, and a red light appeared. "It runs off that electricity thing I was telling you about."

"Talk about niche." Sasha held up the still-dim lantern, casting the last of its light toward the cavern entrance. "Maybe we should figure this out somewhere other than a hundred feet underground."

"Yeah, maybe," Victoria said, giving Sasha a look—pursed lips and one eyebrow raised.

Sasha gave a nervous laugh. "It's not going to be that hard to get back in here."

"You're already sweating."

Wiping their brow, Sasha scoffed and led the way to The Squeeze. "Remind me to go on a liquid diet until we're done with this excavation."

"Sasha, you're not that tight a fit. You just have to avoid panicking."

"Mind over matter," they said with a deep sigh. "We can do this."

Except now they were at the entrance to The Squeeze and…Sasha frowned and asked Victoria, "Did my eyes adjust, or did the lantern get bright again?"

"It's not just you." Victoria cocked her hip and put a hand on it as she stared at the lantern. "What the hell is going on?"

"I feel like we should approach this scientifically."

"You would."

Ignoring the joke, Sasha moved away from The Squeeze and back to the excavation site. With every step, the lantern dimmed. Four steps past the dig site, it went out, and Sasha was trapped in the pitch black. Forcing themself to focus on the science and not their fear, they said, "Aether is supposed to permeate all of space relatively equally. That's the theory."

"The theory all of modern society is based on, yeah." Victoria's voice echoed around the cavern, and Sasha couldn't tell how far away she was.

"Being this deep in a cave shouldn't affect the concentration of aether. The entire metro subway line runs on aether, and most of that is carved even deeper under the city streets."

"There are some spots," Victoria said, turning her red light back on, which allowed Sasha to pinpoint the direction of her voice, "where aether gets depleted. In the city, like you said. But it comes right back as soon as the power-hungry device is switched off."

Goosebumps ran up Sasha's arms. "That suggests there's something in *this* cave depleting the local aether."

"But these artifacts are several thousand years old." Victoria stepped closer, putting her hand on Sasha's wrist. Had their heartbeat always sounded so loud in their ears? "Aether wasn't even discovered until a thousand years ago."

"How would an artifact from before aether's discovery draw this much power?" Sasha shook their head and pulled their wrist from Victoria's grip. "It's got to be something modern. Someone hiding some stupidly engineered invention down here."

"But the cave opening was blocked until the earthquake. How would anyone get an aetherwork that big through The Squeeze?"

"Maybe there's a larger entrance." Sasha felt a grin pull at the edges of their lips. "Maybe The Squeeze isn't the only way to get here!"

Victoria gave a dark laugh and said, "That sounds like wishful thinking." Then, she pointed her light past Sasha, deeper into the cavern. "It's coming from that way, isn't it?"

"That's the way I was headed when the lantern went out." Sasha stumbled along behind Victoria, following the vague shadow of her body between them and the light. "All I can think is that we're probably trampling priceless artifacts because we don't have enough light to avoid them."

"Oh!"

"What?" Sasha almost ran into Victoria, stopping short. Over her shoulder, they saw the cavern wall. It was a dead end, but the appearance of the rock was unusual enough to draw Sasha's attention. "Those markings are too regular to be natural." They stepped around Victoria and reached out to run their fingers over the rock, feeling the way shapes had been carved into it. "They're pictographs. Or runes, perhaps?" They turned to Victoria. "What does the ancient rune expert have to say about them?"

"I'm…" She took a long, silent moment to look at the wall, moving her light around and tracing the shapes with her fingers. "I can't see them well enough. We need the supplies to make rubbings. And more light."

"Where can we get anything other than aetherwork light sources?"

"Candles, I suppose." Victoria looked down at her hand, pressing the red light on and off. "Or some sort of electricity lamp." She snickered. "Whale oil?" Then Victoria turned and ran a hand over the runes again. "What bothers me is that these are early Age of Aether markings. You see the way they're using archaic forms of our letters?"

Sasha leaned closer. "I'll be damned. This doesn't match the bronze-era artifacts in the rest of the cave, either." They made a tiny humming noise. "Who else would have this much knowledge of ancient runes?"

As Victoria leaned as close as she could to the wall, she asked distractedly, "What do you mean?"

"Obviously, it's a fake," they said, mulling over the problem in their head. "Sanderson has wanted my place on the admissions committee since he joined the department."

"What if it's not a fake?" Victoria made a tiny, excited noise. "What if this is early Aether Age work? What if this is a secret that's been buried for almost a thousand years?"

Sasha's heart swooped at the thought. "We have to find out what that inscription says."

The next morning, after Sasha had endured The Squeeze twice more—much to their displeasure—they and Victoria returned to the cave with an oil lamp hastily constructed from items Sasha had found around their kitchen. As they ignited it with a small aetherwork lighter, Sasha told Victoria, "I don't know how long this much oil will last."

"We'll keep an eye on it," Victoria said, using the aetherwork lamp to guide their way back to the inscribed wall. It dimmed and sputtered out before they got there, leaving them with only the light from the small oil flame to see by.

Sasha approached the wall, holding the oil lamp close to the etchings as Victoria rummaged around in her bags. Crouching down, they followed the inscriptions and noticed when they changed. "Hey. This is in Latin, isn't it?"

"Really?" Victoria leaned close, and Sasha noticed the floral scent of her hair. "Nordic runes, Latin. I think this one here is a version of Greek. Someone really wanted to make sure their message was understood." Victoria placed her hand against the wall, and her face looked softer than usual in the dim light from the lamp Sasha held. She mumbled to herself, then said, "'Precious sleepers lie beyond.'"

"That doesn't seem right," Sasha said, leaning close to the text Victoria was pointing at.

Then she moved her finger to the line below. "'Enter with caution.'"

Sasha frowned, squinting at the old Latin alphabet. "Enter? Enter where? The cave ends here."

"Does it?" Victoria turned to them, the white teeth of her smile glinting in the lamplight. "Come over here. I think I feel a seam."

"A seam in the rock? Like a deposit of metal?" Sasha brought the lamp closer to where Victoria's fingers caressed the stone of the wall.

"No, like a fault," she said, her finger tracing a crack that ran from floor to ceiling.

Their heart thumping with excitement in their chest, Sasha took one of the chisels from their tool belt and tapped it against the rock. Rather than the clanging of the chisel and a dull thud in the rock, the rock crumbled in with a hollow sound. "Victoria, I don't think this wall is made out of rock."

"What is it made of?" she asked, her voice an excited whisper as her fingers trailed over the wall to the divot Sasha's chisel made. "Oh! It's plaster! It's been painted to look like rock. Quick, see if you can cut through to check how thick it is."

Sasha handed Victoria the lamp, then put the edge of their chisel against the seam. They took a hammer from their belt and set it against the back of the chisel. As they drew back the hammer, they paused. "As excited as I am to see what's behind this wall, I can't in good conscience do anything more to it until we at least do some rubbings to preserve the writing," they said.

"Spoilsport." Victoria stuck her tongue out at them. "Then let's do the rubbings."

After the documentation was complete, Sasha set their chisel against the plaster wall and began chipping through it. Normally, they worked slowly and carefully. Archeology was about discovering and preserving the past. They had spent their career up to this point learning how to be gentle, how to use the aetherwork lights to make sure they weren't cutting into anything important. Here, in the half-dark, the acrid smell of the burning lamp oil suffusing their nose and sinuses, sweat dripping down their back, Sasha broke through the plaster wall with abandon. They had preserved all they could, and there was *something important* behind this wall.

Suddenly, their chisel broke through and slid almost all the way into the hole it had made. Swearing softly to themself, Sasha used their fingernails to pry back the head of the chisel, eventually getting their fingertips around it and pulling it back out of the plaster. A puff of colder air followed its removal, cooling the sweat on Sasha's cheek. They pushed a finger into the hole, pulling at the plaster before lifting the nearby oil lamp to it. "I think it's about ten centimeters thick," they called back to Victoria, who was hunched over her rubbings, an oil lamp in one hand and a pencil in the other.

Scratching a quick note in her notebook, she looked up at Sasha and replied, "They wanted it to last, didn't they?"

"Yeah." Sasha wiped the sweat from their brow. "Any luck figuring out what that says?"

"Well, I don't have all of my books here, but it definitely talks about multiple people lying on the other side of the wall."

"A burial? I can't think of any early Aether Age cultures who interred their dead in hidden caves."

"Me neither," Victoria said; the flickering oil light made the shadows of her face dance. "And the grammar is weird. It doesn't mention anything about the afterlife, or any deities. Just to be cautious. And a plea only to disturb them with noble intentions."

"Not the usual sort of warning for grave robbers, I agree." Sasha wiped their sweaty hands on their pants and rolled their shoulders back. "We have noble intentions, don't we?"

"Of course!" Victoria stood and hurried closer, putting a warm hand on Sasha's arm. "What could be nobler than learning? Discovery? The intent to deeply understand another, long-gone culture?"

With a laugh, Sasha said, "You don't have to convince me to like archeology. I'm about 15 years into a career that would be pretty awkward if I didn't."

Victoria blinked at them for a second before the joke landed, and her face opened up with surprised delight. Her laugh had a musical lilt that made Sasha's heart flip in their chest. They chuckled along with her, cheeks suddenly hot. Wiping the sweat from their brow again, Sasha returned to the task of chipping through the plaster wall a few centimeters at a time.

After a few more minutes, they realized, "This would go much faster with a sledgehammer."

Victoria gave a hum of acknowledgment. "We only have the aetherwork jackhammer."

"We're too dependent on aether," Sasha said with a grumble, though they weren't quite sure they believed it. They were just hot and sweaty and overcome with terrible curiosity.

Suddenly fed up, Sasha dropped their chisel and hit the plaster with their hammer. A chunk fell away, and the hammer went through the wall, twisting in Sasha's grip. When they pulled it back, the claw end caught on more plaster and it pulled loose, the hammer jerking toward Sasha and making them stumble back half a step. Setting their feet, they deliberately pried off another chunk, then another.

It took another half hour of sweaty, back-breaking work, but eventually they made a hole big enough to slip through. They took up the oil lamp and called back to Victoria, "I've got it! Come on!"

The air beyond the plaster wall was stale and tasted oddly metallic. Sasha's footsteps echoed off the chamber walls, and when they held up the oil lamp, they couldn't see the ceiling. "This place is huge!"

"Huge, yes," Victoria agreed, slipping into the chamber behind them. "But why does it sound so empty? It can't be empty." She scuffed her toe against the sandy floor, the sound echoing back and forth.

"Someone's idea of a prank, maybe." Sasha sighed, wiping their brow before slowly moving forward into the dark. "Put up a puzzle and a plaster wall, confuse future archaeologists for a laugh."

"That sounds like something only a philosophy major would find funny." Victoria's voice came from farther away than Sasha expected, and they turned to see her lamp bobbing at least a dozen yards ahead. Wait, was it moving downward?

"Are you crouching?"

"No," Victoria called back. "There's a decline over here. Watch your step!"

Sasha started in that direction until a glint of *something* caught their eye. At first, they thought it was gold, but as they moved closer, they realized it was a plaque of some kind. Brass, they would guess. Barely a patina, as if it'd just been polished yesterday. They moved closer, and the dim light from their lamp glinted off another material. Glass. Perfectly smooth glass stood upright above the plaque.

What was a window doing in a cave?

Sasha put their hand against the glass and had to shut their eyes against a sudden, brilliant white-blue light. "Ahh!" they cried out in surprise, their eyes watering.

"What's making that light?" Victoria called, panic in her voice as her footsteps hurried closer.

Blinking as their eyes adjusted, Sasha told her, "I think I found the thing that's sucking up all the aether."

"No kidding."

The window was actually a rectangular case, twice as long as it was wide and high. The longer Sasha stared at the case, the more clearly they could see. "There's something in there." They circled it, fingers brushing the glass as they stared into it and tried to understand what they were seeing. "It's a body. No, two bodies. It's a coffin."

"Like Snow White," Victoria said, sitting on the floor in front of the brass plaque. "It's written in the same three languages as the wall."

The bodies had been laid to rest shoulder-to-shoulder, and they were both approximately the same size. One had a darker complexion than the other, with black hair cropped much shorter than the blond waves arranged around the lighter one. Their faces were just like any other Sasha would see on the street or around the university. "There doesn't seem to be any decay," Sasha realized. "The aether must be preserving the bodies."

"For a thousand years?" Victoria stood, joining Sasha at the side of the case. "They look like they're sleeping."

"Yeah," Sasha agreed, putting their palm against the glass. "I don't think *anyone* has reported funerary practices like this before."

"We'll be famous!" Victoria gave a short giggle, then took Sasha's hand, pulling them toward the plaque at the foot of the coffin. "Look. This sentence says, 'We are…', but I can't remember this word."

"You're the translation expert," Sasha said, but crouched down to take a closer look at the plaque. They studied the first line of each of the languages, a slight memory tugging at the edge of their mind. "This word—" They pointed to the matching text for each. "An older version is found in a lot of the late Bronze Age mentions of the afterlife. I always thought it meant something like 'second life.' Like 'in the hereafter,' you know?"

"But that means this"—Victoria used her finger to underline one of the Italian lines—"says, 'We are second life.' "

"The bodies are preserved. Perhaps they thought by doing so, they would remain alive in the underworld?"

"That could explain putting the coffin in a cave. It's closer to the under—" She stopped short. "It doesn't mean second life. It means *alive*."

" 'We are alive'?" Sasha's eyes widened, and they scrambled to the head of the coffin to examine the bodies again. "They're still alive in there?"

"How?" Victoria's gaze flew back and forth as she read the plaque. "It says something like, 'the case stops hours.' "

"Stops time, perhaps?" Sasha's heart thumped vigorously with excitement. "Someone in the early Aether Age figured out how to use it to stop time itself? That's impossible!"

"So were all the other things we use aether for today, once." Victoria went quiet, focused on the plaque.

Sasha gave the figures one last glance, noting they both had soft, delicate features except for the lighter one's angular nose. They had never found a burial this well-preserved.

If the plaque was true, this wasn't a burial at all: it was a time capsule. "I wonder what they were running from."

Victoria gave a thoughtful hum, then asked, "Why do you think they were running from something?"

"Why else preserve yourself out of time?" They looked again at the two figures. "Why invent something that no one else in the past thousand years has managed to invent? They must have been desperate."

"Wait!" Victoria's eyes lit up. "This says there was an illness."

"Something contagious?" Sasha took a step back. "They were trying to outrun it?"

"No, something…" Victoria looked into the case, placing her hand against the glass. "It says the fair one is dying of a wasting disease. That's how the early Age of Aether people talked about diseases like cancer and heart disease." She took a sharp breath, removing her hand from the case and tracing the last line of the inscription. "This is a plea to whoever finds them. To *us*."

"What does it say?"

"It's a rough translation, but I think it says, 'Only disturb us if you know a cure.'"

As the enormity of the responsibility set on their shoulders by this last line settled in, Sasha's gut twisted. They had always imagined what the people of the past had been like, how they had used the items Sasha discovered buried under centuries of earth. Those people had always belonged to, and remained, in the past. The only responsibility Sasha had toward them was to make hypotheses about what their lives had been like.

People from the past had never had faces before.

"Oh! Professor Edwards! A moment of your time?"

Sasha grimaced as they closed the trunk of their auto. Sasha put on their most neutral face and turned to meet the chair of their department. "Yes, Professor Gardiner? How can I help you?"

"I got a call this morning from the dean of the School of Medicine. They said an unusual number of their faculty had canceled classes this week, and that it might be due to a project you've been running. Would you like to fill me in?"

Holding back a grimace, because they'd known Victoria's plan to just bypass University bureaucracy was going to bite them in the ass, Sasha kept their voice polite as they said, "I'd love to discuss that with you. Please walk with me." They took a moment to collect their thoughts as they walked down the now-familiar trail. "I am working on a written report, so you and the department will have all the information, but Professor West and I discovered something in that cave of Bronze Age artifacts."

"Well, I should hope so," he replied, readjusting his aether-bright tie, which shimmered blue and green. "But is it really something that warrants disrupting the entire medical school?"

"We discovered probably the oldest functional aetherwork device outside the Belgian Sun, and it's technology we don't have today. The secret of how to build it was lost to the ravages of time."

"Since the Belgian Sun?" Professed Gardiner frowned down at his tie. "So, early Aether Age, then?"

Sasha nodded.

"Some sort of pseudo-wind device? Most of the early aether devices replaced ones that had already been engineered to run like windmills." He put a hand to his chin and looked like he was about to start in on his favorite (and oft-heard at faculty meetings) lecture from his 300-level class.

Sasha quickly jumped to say, "Engineering is more your forte than mine, but this device is too large to move from the cave without specialized equipment. That's why we're bringing the experts to it, rather than the other way around."

He bristled for a moment. "It's just, you're spending *so much* of your budget on this project. How are you going to get another grant if you don't finish the aims of your last one?"

He didn't understand; Sasha was going to have to let more information slip. "You and the museum director wanted a flashy new exhibit to lure in new donors, didn't you?"

"Well, *yes*, but—"

"The device we discovered has preserved two bodies for almost a thousand years."

"A thousand—"

"Actually, they might still be alive." Sasha led Chair Gardiner into the cave, picking up one of the oil lamps and lighting it before leading the way. The trek was silent, all the way up to and through The Squeeze (which they'd widened with the jackhammer to fit some of the larger equipment through, much to Sasha's relief).

When they reached the chamber, Victoria was already there with Dr. Bingham—a leading surgeon in her field—both of them holding an aetherwork device over the glass case.

"Have you been able to get that to work?"

"Yes, we figured it out," Victoria said with a bright grin, putting down the device. "Dr. Bingham remembered when our capture of aether used to be worse, and people used antennas to gather enough of it for their big machines." She pointed to a cable on the ground. "We've got it bringing aetherpower from outside the cave."

"What did you find?" Chair Gardiner directed the question at Dr. Bingham.

"We were able to get a transverse image." Dr. Bingham's gray hair was tied back, and she wore green scrubs under her jacket. The wrinkles at the edges of her eyes deepened as she smiled. "Subject A has a mass on the descending colon. With modern technology, it's operable. Long-term survivability will depend on further tests and biopsies."

The sleepers had put a burden on the people who discovered them. *Do not wake us unless you know a cure.* Sasha had to ask Dr. Bingham, "What are the odds of survival?"

She smiled. "Of course it varies, but with the treatments we have now, five-year survivability for a tumor this size is over 50 percent."

"Is that high enough?" Sasha looked at Victoria, needing her input, too. "Is it worth waking them up?"

"You have to think," Victoria replied, stepping closer to Sasha and wrapping her hand around their wrist, "they stopped time because they wanted more of it together. If the treatments we have now can extend her life, even by six months, that's six months they wouldn't have had a thousand years ago."

"I didn't see any satellite tumors," Dr. Bingham said. "That doesn't mean there aren't cancerous cells in other sites around the body, but it does increase the odds that our medicine will be successful."

Gardiner cleared his throat, finally joining the discussion. "We have to wake them up. This technology could revolutionize not just archeology, but the world. We can't only think of the two people in that case. We have to think about the billions who live today."

Dr. Bingham added, "If we could use it to stabilize people who have been wounded and get them to the operating room before they die of blood loss, we could start saving lives tomorrow."

Sasha gently pulled their wrist out of Victoria's hold and went to the case, looking through the glass at the people inside. They scratched a hand through the hair on their face and sighed. If there was a good chance they could spend more time with the person they loved… They turned to Victoria and said, "Let's wake them up."

She smiled broadly. "All right! I've translated the writing on the outside of the case, and this section here"—she joined Sasha next to the case and indicated a brass plate—"lays out the steps for waking them up. Shall I follow them?"

Dr. Bingham cleared her throat. "If I may? I'd like to have a few medics here, and an auto-ambulance, so we can get them to the university hospital as quickly as possible."

"That's a good idea," Sasha agreed. Then they gestured to the plate. "Let's triple check that translation together."

After a few hours, a plan had been made and everything was in place. Dr. Bingham turned to Sasha and said, "Well, Dr. Edwards? Would you like to do the honors?"

Sasha reached for the case, then paused with their hand halfway to the panel. Turning to Victoria, they asked, "Are you sure you don't want to do this?"

Smiling, with her arms wrapped around herself, she shook her head. "This is all you, Sasha. You're the one who found it. You're the one who decided we should wake them up." She stepped closer and whispered an encouraging, "You can do it. Everything's going to be fine."

Distracted by the floral scent of Victoria's perfume, Sasha nodded absently, needing an extra moment to process the words. Turning, they met Victoria's eyes, and their heart swooped in their chest. Right. They had a plan. Everything was going to be great.

Sasha set their hand against the brass panel and said the phrase indicated by the markings on the case.

Nothing happened.

"Oh!" Victoria pulled her notes out of her pocket. "Try more of an 'ooh' on the vowel in the first word. Pronunciation will have shifted, of course."

"Of course." Sasha tried again, trying to force their tongue to take on a more ancient accent.

The case hissed and went dark, plunging the cavern into the dim, flickering light of the solitary oil lamp in the corner. A hand clutched around Sasha's arm, and they recognized it was Victoria's. As the a etherwork lamps in the corners of the room began to illuminate—the aether wasn't being drained any longer, so they could work now—Sasha watched the case slide open, revealing the two sleeping figures to the group of breathless academics.

Although the figures were wearing clothes emblematic of their age, the people looked like anyone they might meet anywhere in the modern world. The dark-haired figure had a small wooden carving of a bird on the leather tie around her neck, and Sasha couldn't help but think that someone who loved her must have made it for her.

How many times had Sasha ever *made* something for a loved one? A few times as a child, perhaps? With the way aether had facilitated the mechanization of fabrication, things were easier to buy than ever. Of course, there were vibrant communities of artists everywhere, but Sasha had always been focused on what they could find from bygone eras. Looking at the way Victoria's fingers were wrapped around their arm, Sasha suddenly regretted never attempting to make something. For a *friend*, of course. They could give Victoria a gift, as a friend, couldn't they?

Everyone in the room startled when the dark-haired figure took a sharp gasp. Dr. Bingham was the first to jump into action, talking low and soothingly as she approached the people in the open case.

The fair-haired one wasn't moving yet.

The dark-haired one opened her eyes and looked around, and Sasha began to fear that they were too late. She grasped her companion's hand, murmuring something, before turning to the room and holding up a hand. She said something to Sasha and the others, but it was unintelligible. Sasha stood there, unsure what to do, but Victoria let go of their arm and stepped forward.

The sounds that came out of Victoria's mouth didn't make sense, either, but the woman's eyes went wide, and she nodded.

Sasha took their comm unit out of its pocket on their dig vest. Turning it to the translation function, Sasha held it out as Victoria and the woman spoke haltingly to each other. To their surprise, it actually began to work.

"What's your name?" Victoria asked.

Her eyes still on where Dr. Bingham was attending to her companion, the dark-haired one said, *"My name is Fae."* Turning to face her companion, whose eyes had opened, Fae said, *"Her name is Asha. Please, help us."*

"Our doctor,"—Victoria gestured to Dr. Bingham, who approached them carefully—*"has a plan she thinks will work. Will you let us take you to our..."* Victoria paused, then said in modern speech, "hospital?"

The auto-comm translated Victoria's word, which made Fae start. *"It speaks?"*

"It translates," Sasha said, trying not to be too distracted by the fact that they were speaking to a living example of thousand-year-old history. "It uses aether, like your machine."

Fae turned back, putting her hand on the bed of the case. *"I wasn't sure it would work."*

"It worked beautifully."

This made Fae smile and nod, half her attention on where Dr. Bingham and the medics were helping Asha into the narrow wheelchair they'd brought to help get her to the auto-ambulance outside the cave. *"How long were we asleep?"*

"It's 2046," Sasha told her.

Fae gasped, and Sasha couldn't help but chuckle. *"The translation must be wrong. My machine worked for over a thousand years?"*

"Yes!" Sasha moved closer to Fae. "What you've built here, we've never seen before. The technology must have been lost during those thousand years."

Fae looked away. *"Must have been."*

Sasha arrived at the hospital with a bouquet of flowers, several of them aether-modified for better shine and lifespan. Victoria was at their side, clutching a plush dog to her chest with one hand and using the other to knock on the hospital room door.

"Yes?" called a voice in a thick accent. The next two words were unintelligible, so Sasha pulled their comm unit out again.

"It's Sasha and Victoria," they said, pausing to let the comm translate as they stepped into the room. "How are you?"

Fae appeared from behind a curtain, and Sasha was surprised to see her wearing an outfit that was only a few years out of date. Of course, it made sense that Dr. Bingham would've had someone at the hospital help provide Fae and Asha with new clothes and toiletries and things. Sasha felt bad for not thinking of it until now.

Fae gave them a tired smile and said, *"Everything is going well."* She gestured to the space behind the curtain. *"Asha is already feeling somewhat better. The doctor says she might have to take a medicine that will make her sick for a while."*

"That's pretty common," Sasha said, remembering the summer their grandfather had to wrestle with a similar illness. "Our scientists have managed to enhance chemicals with aetherwork to make the medicine more effective."

"It's wonderful," Fae said with a bright grin. *"I can't tell you how grateful I am. We both are."*

She pulled back the curtain, showing Asha lying in bed, looking through a magazine. Her eyes were drawn to the group, and she lifted a hand in greeting. *"It's you!"*

"It is us!" Victoria gave a wide grin and hopped forward, holding the plush out to Asha, who took it with delight. She fingered the aetherwork ribbon around the little dog's neck.

"How pretty!"

Sasha handed the flowers to Fae, who took them to the windowsill.

"We're glad to see you're feeling better." They stuffed their hands in their vest pockets. "I was afraid we might have woken you up too early."

Fae shared a look with Asha, then said, *"A thousand years was long enough."*

"We also come with an offer from the University." Victoria took a packet of papers out of her bag. "I've translated these as best I can, but maybe we'll have the comm take a pass on them as well."

Taking hold of the packet, Fae paged through it, then asked, *"What is it?"*

"It's a job offer! Sasha knows more of the details."

When Fae looked at them, they said, "Yeah, it's… We have a museum. It brings a lot of money to the University, and…we could use someone with your expertise."

"And!" Victoria added, "You can work with our aether-engineering department to publish the details of your device, so everyone can understand how to build a case like yours."

"On smaller scales, for the most part," Sasha added, outlining a bread-sized box with their hands. "It would make our world better."

"Better? This world is already a thousand times better than the one we came from." Fae sat on the edge of Asha's bed, giving her a smile and taking her hand. *"I would be honored to help in any way."*

"The University is giving you a place to live as well." Sasha gestured to the stack of documents. "I made sure they rented an apartment close to the hospital, in case Asha's treatment takes longer than a few weeks."

Fae held Asha's hand close to her heart and nodded, tears welling up in her eyes. *"It's more than we could ever ask for. Thank you."*

After a bit more chitchat, Sasha noticed that Asha looked tired, so they and Victoria said their goodbyes and left the couple to rest. As they walked down the hallway to the aetherwork lift, Victoria asked, "Would you leave behind everything you ever knew for a chance to save your partner? Sleep for a thousand years. Wake up to a whole new world? It has to be overwhelming."

"It does," Sasha said, taking a deep breath. They let it out slowly, then grasped Victoria's hand gently in theirs. "I would if that someone was you."

Victoria stopped and turned toward Sasha, searching their face like she thought they were making a joke. Sasha did their best to show sincerity, holding back a nervous laugh. If they were wrong about this—

Surging toward them, Victoria went up on her toes and pressed a kiss to Sasha's mouth. As she dropped back down onto her heels, she smirked and said, "I thought you were never going to notice."

Sasha's heart soared, and they finally let out that laugh, wrapping their arms around Victoria and hugging her close. "It's not every day I follow someone through The Squeeze. No one else would've been able to convince me."

Victoria gave a delighted laugh and kissed Sasha again. "Thank the aether that I did."

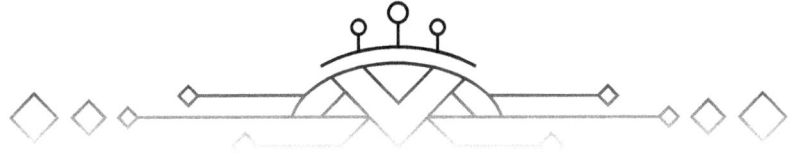

Mikki Madison

Mixed Dough

alternate history, bakery, bed and breakfast, character injury (graphic descriptions), character injury (permanent), cults, death of a sibling (past), emotional hurt/comfort, food (graphic descriptions), gender exploration, gender non-conforming, getting together, hurt/comfort, m/nb, non-binary, past tense, plane crash, tattoos, third person limited point of view

A distant noise like a swarm of angry insects—buzzing incessantly and getting louder with each passing second— drew Jules's attention away from the weeds in his garden and to the clear blue sky above.

Seconds later, a plane came screaming overhead, a trail of black smoke and burning residue in its wake, and plunged toward the pond. Jules watched, heart in his throat, unable to believe his eyes. A gas-powered plane? *Here?* What the—?

He shook himself out of his shock and ran for the bike. Someone was in danger, and while he *knew* it was unlikely anyone would survive that, if there was even a chance, he had to try.

He zipped out of the garden and over the field toward the pond, calling emergency services on the way. They'd need a fire truck for sure, and maybe—hopefully—an ambulance.

He *prayed* they would need an ambulance.

Jules pulled to a stop not far from the wreck and left the bike humming quietly next to a copse of trees. The plane had crashed near enough to the pond that the water had taken care of the flames, and now steam rose in addition to smoke.

He re-tied his hair into a bun on top of his head and hurried to the wreck. He hadn't seen a gas model in twenty years, at least. The cleanup was going to be brutal.

Only one person was inside the cockpit, with dark hair and pale skin and a few days of stubble on their cheeks, a trickle of blood running down their forehead and over their face.

Jules banged on the glass. "Hello? Can you hear me? Can you move?"

The pilot's eyelids fluttered, but that was the only indication they might still be alive.

Good enough.

Jules wrenched the cockpit open and dragged the pilot free of the smoldering wreckage. It was probably not the best decision—the pilot could easily have had injuries that movement would make worse—but leaving them in the wreckage when Jules could smell gasoline mingling with the smoke and he had no idea if the fire was out entirely seemed an even worse idea.

He pulled the pilot as far away as he dared. Sirens blared in the distance. Help was on the way. Jules glanced back at the plane, trying to gauge if the danger had passed.

The pilot groaned, and Jules whirled back around to lean over them. Their eyes were open now, dazedly focused on Jules.

They had the bluest eyes he'd ever seen.

He gave what he hoped was a comforting smile. "I'm Jules. Can you tell me your name?"

The pilot said nothing.

"Your plane crashed," Jules explained. "You're badly injured. Help is on the way. I'll—"

The pilot's eyes grew wide, and they struggled to speak. Jules leaned in closer, putting his ear as close to the pilot's mouth as he dared.

"Where...?"

It was the only word Jules could make out. "You're in New Blanchard. Or, well, just outside of it."

The pilot's eyes closed and their whole body sagged. "Thank fuck."

They were still breathing, albeit barely, so Jules didn't panic. He glanced back toward the bed-and-breakfast and the road; the ambulance lights were pulling into the driveway. "The ambulance is here. I'll…"

His eyes fell on a tattoo peeking over the collar of the pilot's shirt. In and of itself, that wasn't a cause for concern, but given the shape and that the pilot had been in a gas-powered plane…

Jules pulled the shirt down to reveal a tattoo of three interlocking rings, about the size of a half-dollar.

Well. Shit.

"It's a damn miracle they're not dead," Dr. Mac said when she came out of the surgery to meet Jules in the waiting room.

Jules tightened his grip on the ceramic mug of tea he'd been pretending to drink for the past hour. "Will they be all right?"

Dr. Mac dropped into the chair across from him. "Yes, thankfully. Two or three weeks and they should be mostly healed up. No significant damage to their internal organs, which is shocking. I'm told the plane was pretty messed up."

Yes, and Jules's friend and coworker Martha was overseeing the operation to get the damaged plane out of the pond and to somewhere it could be disposed of safely. "I'm surprised the pilot managed it as well as they did."

Dr. Mac hummed in agreement. "They also have a tattoo at their collarbone."

Jules's own collarbone itched, and he threaded his fingers around the mug to keep from rubbing it. "I noticed that, too."

"Will that be a problem?"

Jules arched an eyebrow. "Was I?"

"You know that isn't what I mean." Dr. Mac leaned forward, resting her elbows on her knees. "Crashing a plane into a pond isn't a great first impression."

A memory of huddling in the back of a truck, praying he wouldn't be discovered, surfaced in Jules's mind. "It may have been their only way out."

"Maybe." Dr. Mac looked to him. "They'll need someplace to stay."

"I have spare rooms," Jules said without hesitation. "Tourist season doesn't start until closer to October."

Dr. Mac smiled slightly. "I figured you'd say that. Still, be careful,

Jules."

Jules returned the smile. "I always am."

New Blanchard was one of the first communities in the United States to have converted completely to aether-run infrastructure and technology after aether was discovered nearly fifty years ago. Along with Harbor Village and Berrytown, they made an aether-powered enclave that had proved to the country that they no longer required fossil fuels to function. Aether was an endless supply of clean energy.

Not everybody had been happy about that. Multiple groups had sprung out of the country's woodwork, swearing up and down that aether use heralded the end times, trying desperately to cram that genie back into its bottle. They bawled about what it would mean for the oil and gas industries, about the expense of converting the outdated grid to run on aetheric energy and the cost to convert cars. They screamed and railed when gasoline vehicles were banned, even though aetheric vehicles were as fast and far less expensive to maintain.

However, the march of progress couldn't be denied, and they ended up pushed to the fringes, deliberately cutting their communities off from the aether and priding themselves on being tough and self-sufficient.

The Three Rings was one such group, one of the first to—very publicly—break away from society at large, when a group of a hundred people stood up and marched out of a town hall meeting in South Carolina when the council voted to transition to aether energy.

Originally, they'd had communities all up and down the East Coast, but by the time Jules had left nearly two decades ago, that number had dwindled to just a dozen, with probably fewer than a thousand people between them. Although he no longer kept up with the news as he once had, he knew that number had continued to shrink, especially as younger members grew tired of an unnecessarily hard life and sought something different, as he had.

And as had, presumably, the pilot standing in the bed-and-breakfast's living room.

Jules still hadn't gotten their name. They'd said nothing for the two weeks they'd been in the hospital, nothing in the truck on the ride here, and nothing since they'd stepped inside.

Well, that was all right. Jules would *like* to have a name at some point, but he could do without one until the pilot was ready to share it.

"Let me show you to your room." Jules gestured to the stairs. "We're not very busy at the moment, so you should have most of the place to yourself. Tourists may show up on the weekends occasionally, but we won't see a major influx until the harvest festival at the end of October. You can stay as long as you'd like."

He opened the door to their coziest room, a simple one with a bed piled high with fluffy blankets, a plush chair, and a fireplace. One wall was nothing but bookshelves, and the south-facing window overlooked the garden.

Jules opened a door across from the bed. "This is the bathroom. It's private, so even with guests here, you won't have to share."

The pilot's eyes widened briefly, and a flash of longing swept across their face before it receded into the same fierce scowl they'd had since waking up.

Mm-hmm. They weren't fooling anyone.

"Dinner's at six," Jules said. "Breakfast is at eight, although we'll leave some in the fridge if you'd prefer to sleep in. Martha will bring up some clothes."

"What kind of clothes?"

Jules blinked, startled; he hadn't actually expected the pilot to respond to that. "Jeans and a T-shirt, probably. Although we'll need to get you something warmer if you stay for more than a few weeks. Fall comes early around here."

The pilot looked somewhat relieved. "So...normal clothes."

Jules arched an eyebrow. "Yes? All we have are normal clothes. But if you'd prefer something more exotic, like a chainmail bikini, I'm sure we could find it. Might take us a few days, though."

The pilot's jaw worked, and their eyes darted away from Jules. "Sorry. I just meant I didn't want a skirt."

Jules looked down at himself and the brightly patterned ankle-length skirt he was wearing. "Ah."

He shouldn't have been surprised—the Three Rings had been very rigid in terms of what was acceptable clothing for a man to wear—but it still threw him for a moment. "Well. You won't be asked to wear clothes you aren't comfortable in. Just be aware that other people may take offense to the implication that their clothing isn't normal."

The pilot had the decency to look abashed. "I'm sorry. That was a bonehead comment."

"Consider it forgotten." Jules folded his arms and leaned against the doorframe. "So, do you have any questions about the place?"

The pilot shook their head. "And it's…Jules, was it?"

"Mm-hmm."

"And…you're a guy?"

"Last I checked," Jules said dryly.

"No, that's…" The pilot shook their head again. "I just wanted to be right when I said thank you, Mr. Jules. You don't have to do this, and I appreciate that you are."

"It's not a problem," Jules said. "Besides, I like company. And I didn't catch your name."

"Uh." The pilot glanced away. "What did they call me in the hospital?"

"Jay Doe is what they had on the chart."

The pilot shrugged. "Doe's fine, then."

"And do you prefer 'mister,' or something else?"

The pilot—Doe—looked themselves over. "Isn't it obvious?"

"How you like to present and what you like to be called don't necessarily have to sync up." Jules swept a hand over his skirt. "Exhibit A."

There was a flash of surprise across their face—as if Doe had genuinely never considered that. "Yeah. Mister. That's fine."

"Then, Mr. Doe, I'll let you get settled." Jules pushed himself off the door. "And we'll see you at six for dinner."

Doe was quiet throughout dinner, although not rude—he picked up his plate when he'd finished, helped to clear the table, and thanked Jules and Martha for the meal. He disappeared back upstairs after that, and Jules let him be. He was still recovering, after all.

In fact, Jules saw him rarely the first few days—only at meals, or when he stopped by the room to check on him. Doe was usually asleep when he did, face pinched in pain, and Jules wondered if it was because his body was still healing or because of his dreams.

Jules remembered his first week of freedom vividly, even after twenty years. The first few days, he'd been terrified he'd be found out. Then, when he realized no one was coming after him, he'd collapsed as years of fear slid off him at once, and he'd done nothing but sleep for the next several days, like he was trying to recover the rest he'd been deprived of all at once. It had taken him weeks to realize that it was safe to leave his room, safe to explore the town, safe to find something new in his life that wasn't rigid adherence to the path the Three Rings had determined for him.

So it was a surprise when Doe came out to the garden on his fifth day at the bed-and-breakfast and said, "What do you need me to do?"

Jules looked up from where he'd been pulling weeds to see Doe towering over him, wearing a faded shirt advertising a brewery in Berrytown and a fierce look. "What do you mean?"

"This place." Doe gestured around, encompassing the bed-and-breakfast and the garden. "What do you need help with?"

Jules wiped the sweat from his forehead with the collar of his shirt. "Nothing, at the moment. You're not even three weeks out from a plane crash. You could stand to rest a little longer."

Doe grumbled and eased himself into a lawn chair nearby. "I'm bored. And I don't like doing nothing while you're working to take care of me. Doesn't feel right."

"I'm taking care of my business right now." Jules gestured to the rows of cabbages and carrots behind him. "I'd still be out here even if you weren't here."

Doe scowled deeper. "So? I can still help. I don't like feeling useless."

"You aren't," Jules snapped. "You're recovering from being injured. Badly. You aren't *supposed* to be doing things right now. Your community is supposed to help take care of you until you heal."

Doe blinked at him, taken aback. "That sounded…personal."

Jules blew a strand of hair out of his face; it had escaped containment from his bandana. "Sorry. Maybe it was." He sighed. "If you really want something to do, you can help weed the garden. But take it easy. If you start to hurt—"

Doe launched himself out of the chair, winced and swore, and knelt at the nearest garden patch much more cautiously. "If it hurts too much, I swear I'll stop. I just gotta do something before I lose my *mind*."

Jules held up his hand. "Wait."

Doe looked like he was about to snap something in half. "I swear—"
"I thought of a better idea." Jules stood and swiped his dirty hands over his jeans. "How would you like to go into town instead?"

The light of excitement in Doe's blue eyes was all the answer Jules needed.

New Blanchard's picturesque downtown was only a ten-minute drive from the bed-and-breakfast. During the tourist season, a shuttle came by hourly to take the tourists into town, where they could walk, shop, and eat to their heart's content. The town square also had the town hall, and beside it, the aetheric history museum. The actual aetheric collection station was closer to Berrytown, but lots of people took the shuttles over there for a tour.

Doe looked around the square. "It looks...normal."

Jules raised an eyebrow. "It is."

Doe shook his head. "I mean..." He rubbed his collarbone, roughly over his tattoo. "They always told us it wasn't. That it's unnatural. But it doesn't look like that." He paused. "Well, maybe a little unnatural."

Jules followed his gaze to two people standing outside the bakery, one with a neon-pink bob and the other with a shaved head decorated with rainbows. He laughed. "Well, if you decide you want to try it, you should see Tammy at the South Street Salon. She's a genius with color."

Doe flushed all the way to his ears. "I don't... That's not..."

"I'm joking," Jules said. "Well, mostly. You don't have to do anything you don't want to, but if you want to experiment, nobody will bat an eye. Hell, most of them will have advice."

"Is that what you did?" Doe asked.

"Yup." Jules nodded toward the bakery. "Come on, let's get some muffins."

He led Doe across the square and didn't miss how he kept studying the people around them out of the corner of his eye. Not in a concerning way, but a thoughtful one.

Jules pushed open the the bakery door and called out, "Hey, Myron!"

"Jules!" Myron popped up from behind the counter, gold hoop earrings swaying with the movement. Their mustache and goatee were blue today. "How've you been?"

"Good as can be," Jules said. "This is Doe. He's staying at the bed-and-breakfast."

Myron waggled their eyebrows, which were steel gray, a sharp contract to their facial hair. "Well, hey there, handsome."

Doe might have looked less surprised if someone had hit him with a two-by-four. "Uh."

Jules covered a smile.

"Did I break him?" Myron asked.

"Maybe a little. He's new in town." Jules moved in front of the pastry case. "What have you got that's good?"

"All of it, of course." Myron swanned over to the display. "Although if you wait about ten minutes, I've got some croissants that'll be coming out of the oven."

"Yes." Jules immediately revised his muffin plans. "We'll take those."

"Great!" Myron set a couple of muffins on a plate and pushed it across the counter. "Those are from yesterday. Have a snack while you wait."

Myron returned to a counter near the oven and started kneading the dough there, and Jules delivered the muffins to Doe, who was still standing, mouth agape, like the two-by-four had smacked him again.

Jules popped a bite of muffin into his mouth and considered that look. "Everything all right?"

Doe jerked at the question as though he'd forgotten Jules was there. "Er. Yeah. Everything's fine. Just not what I expected."

"Myron or the bakery?"

"Both?" Doe rubbed the back of his neck and watched Myron kneading the dough. "What's he doing?"

"They," Jules corrected. "And they're making bread."

"They?" Doe looked confused.

"Myron's nonbinary and only uses they/them pronouns," Jules explained. "They decided a long time ago that they didn't care for the gender binary."

"Hm," Doe said in a way that sounded like he was putting that aside to consider later. "So…bread? Like sandwich bread?"

"Among other kinds." Jules gestured to a glass case nearby, layered with the various baked goods that came out of the oven.

Doe's eyes went wide.

Jules frowned. "Have you never baked before?"

Doe shook his head. "No. They said cooking and kitchen stuff was woman's work, so…"

Jules didn't have to ask who *they* were. "Perhaps you should try it while you're here, then."

Doe looked at him, surprised. "Do you know how to bake?"

"Not as well as Myron, but I've got a few things I can do pretty well. I've got some banana-blueberry muffins that I like to keep on hand whenever we have guests." Jules slid a look at Doe, who was still watching Myron with interest. "Why don't you help me make some when we get back?"

Doe's attention snapped fully back to Jules. "What?"

"Would you like to make muffins when we get back to the B-and-B?" Jules asked.

The play of reactions over Doe's face was something to behold: the initial anger, a puffed-up protection of his masculinity, followed by hesitation, followed by the way he sank in on himself, as if he realized the only good answer was to say what he actually wanted to do.

"Sure," Doe said quietly. "Why not try something new?"

Jules smiled and popped another piece of muffin into his mouth. "Why not, indeed."

⌁⟩◁⟨⌁

Back at the bed-and-breakfast, Jules gathered what they would need to make muffins and, on an impulse, cinnamon-sugar scones. Neither was too difficult, and unless he missed his guess, Doe would enjoy both.

Jules walked him through the muffins first—mashing the bananas, adding the wet ingredients and then the dry, folding in the blueberries, then scooping the batter into the muffin tins. Doe followed the instructions with a face so serious it was like he was defusing a bomb.

"You know, you can relax," Jules said once the muffins were in the oven and he was showing Doe how to cut butter into flour for the scones. "They're just scones. It doesn't matter if we mess them up."

"A waste of good food," Doe said grimly, and then he snapped his mouth shut.

Ah. It had been too long; Jules had forgotten how tight-fisted the Three Rings had been when it came to resources. "A valid point," he said smoothly, "but even if they don't turn out perfectly, they'll still be edible.

That's all I meant."

Doe nodded once, more of a downward jerk of his head, and kept his lips clamped firmly together. He dug the pastry blender into the flour and butter with renewed vigor.

Jules sighed inwardly. He supposed he couldn't blame Doe for being so cagey, but it felt like as soon as they were making progress, he clammed up again.

They finished putting the scones together just as the muffins came out of the oven, and Jules swapped the muffin tin for the baking sheet and set the tin to cool on the counter.

"How come you don't use the magic to make food?" Doe asked.

The question didn't make any sense. "We do." Jules tapped the side of the oven. "It's aether-powered like everything else. Much safer than gas or electric, unless someone badly messed up building the oven in the first place."

"No, I mean…" Doe flexed his hands and studied his flour-covered fingers. "The aether's magic, right? Couldn't you have a machine that pops up whatever kind of food you want? Like in that old sci-fi show?"

"A replicator?" At Doe's nod, Jules continued. "Yes, we have those. And lots of people use them. It's very easy when you've had a long day. But there's something to be said for making the food yourself." Jules leaned over the muffins and inhaled the smell of warm bananas and cinnamon, one of his favorites. "You get to partake in creating something, and it is delicious."

Doe laughed. "Where'd you hear that?"

"Rosalie. She took me in when I first came to Berrytown. I stayed with her until I was able to buy this place a few years ago. She taught me how to bake, among other things."

"Oh *really*?" Doe waggled his eyebrows.

Jules rolled his eyes. "Not like that. She's forty years older than me and happily married to Kevin and Wanda."

"So, you aren't from here?" Doe asked.

"No." Jules pulled down the collar of his shirt. "I'm not."

His tattoo had been covered years ago, but one who knew what to look for could see the three interlocking rings hidden among the red roses nestled along his collarbone. It had been his present to himself exactly one year after he'd escaped.

Doe's eyes went wide, and for a split second, Jules was positive he was going to run.

Instead, Doe clenched his fists and took three measured breaths. "You got out."

Jules nodded. "When I was sixteen."

"How?"

"Stole a bike, drove it until I ran out of gas, and then hid in the bed of a truck coming here, back when they were still using trucks to transport goods. Rosalie found me sleeping in her garden shed."

Even now, with the benefit of time and distance, Jules spoke as quickly and dispassionately as he could, as if that might somehow keep him from tripping into the painful hole that still lurked in his memories. But if anybody deserved to hear how someone else had made it out, it was Doe.

"What made you run?" Doe asked quietly.

"A lot of things." Jules grabbed a warm muffin off the cooling rack and peeled off the liner, giving himself something else to focus on. "But the tipping point came when I was injured in an accident, and they had me working again within days because I wasn't useful if I wasn't working. I had no time to heal, and it fucked up my leg beyond repair."

"I'm sorry." Doe's sharp blue eyes dropped to his legs. "Did they fix it here?"

"In a manner of speaking." Jules pulled up his skirt to show off the shiny prosthesis that made up the lower half of his left leg. "By the time I got here, the leg hadn't just healed badly, it had gotten infected. They had to amputate it to save my life."

Doe cringed. "I'm sorry."

Jules picked at the muffin. "It's all right. It was a long time ago."

Doe's eyes snapped with fire. "It may have been a long time ago, but that doesn't make it all right."

"You're right. It doesn't," Jules agreed, and went for his own more personal questions. "What about you? What made you run?"

Doe hesitated, studying the oven, his stubbled jaw working. "My sister," he finally said, voice rough.

Jules waited for further explanation, but there was none forthcoming. "What do you—?"

"So can we eat the muffins yet?" Doe asked.

Subject closed, then. Jules sighed inwardly and tossed another muffin to Doe. "Eat up. See how your first muffin tastes."

Doe looked it over and then took a giant bite out of the top. His eyes rolled back, and he let out a pornographic moan.

Jules cleared his throat. "So, I take it they're good?"

"They're amazing," Doe said between shoving bites into his mouth. "I can't believe we made this."

"You made it, really." Jules finally tried the muffin himself; it *was* rather good. "I just gave instructions."

"Mmm." Doe had a gobsmacked look on his face, as if he'd just had a religious experience, and his gaze fell on the muffins again. "So. Uh. Are you saving them for anything in particular, or…"

Jules waved at the cooling rack. "Knock yourself out. Just save some room for the scones."

Doe grabbed a second muffin, digging in with gusto. Jules stepped aside and covered his smile with his own muffin; he didn't want Doe to think he was laughing at him.

The scones came out of the oven shortly thereafter, and Doe made noises over them that were equally pornographic. And, Jules noted, there was a distinct spark of pride there.

"You know," he said conversationally, "Myron teaches baking classes twice a week."

Doe looked up from his scone, eyes wide and hopeful. "Really?"

He was quite handsome when he forgot to be guarded. "Yes. Maybe you should check out the next one. It would give you something to do."

Doe's eyes went back down to his scone. "Yeah. Maybe."

Jules left a schedule of Myron's classes on Doe's door, along with a list of local events leading up to the harvest festival. It couldn't hurt him to look for things that might interest him; Jules never would have discovered gardening if Rosalie hadn't urged him to go to a couple of classes at one of the nurseries. You never knew what you might like until you tried it, and it was unlikely Doe had had a chance to try much outside of what would have been considered "right" for a man like him.

A few days later, about an hour before the first class, Doe shuffled downstairs with the schedule clutched in one hand.

Jules did *not* do a victory dance there in the kitchen, but it was close. Doe thrust the paper at him. "Can you go with me?"

"Go with you?" Jules repeated.

"Yeah, I just..." Doe rubbed the back of his neck with his free hand. "I need a ride, and I don't want to go alone."

Jules immediately revised his schedule for the night. "Sure. I can go. Why don't we head on into town and grab a bite to eat first?"

Doe's shoulders dropped, and he smiled, just barely. "Sounds good."

Dinner was fish and chips at the shack on the bay, where all they sold was fried fish, fried potatoes, and clam chowder. It was a nice evening for eating on the waterfront, and with fall rapidly approaching, these nice evenings would soon be in short supply.

They didn't talk—Doe wasn't much of a conversationalist in general and especially not when he was eating—so Jules sat back and enjoyed the smell of salt on the breeze and the spectacular colors of the sunset. People strolled by on their way to the bay or the square, most of them studying Jules and Doe not-so-subtly as they did.

He hoped Doe was too focused on his dinner to notice. But given the way his shoulders hunched whenever people passed by, Jules suspected he did.

It was to be expected. Like the good doctor had said, crashing a plane outside town wasn't a great first impression, and everybody knew what the three-ringed tattoo meant. Jules had been fortunate to be in a situation where he could hide his until people got to know him. Doe was not so lucky.

Perhaps it was a good thing Jules was going with him to the class.

Twilight had fully settled on the town by the time they walked across the square to the bakery, the colors of the street muted except for the lighted shop windows. A handful of people were already inside, and to his great relief, Jules spotted Lydia and Bethany among the group.

He ushered Doe over to them. "Hello, ladies."

"Jules!" Lydia exclaimed and hugged him around the neck. "I had no idea you'd be here."

"I came with a friend." Jules pulled Doe—who was trying to *hide* behind him, honestly—forward. "This is Doe. He's new in town, and he's staying at the B-and-B. Doe, this is Lydia and Bethany. They're sisters who own the greenhouse between New Blanchard and Berrytown, and Lydia taught me everything I know about gardening."

Lydia shoved his shoulder, her dark eyes sparkling. "Oh, *hush*, you've picked up a lot more since then."

Doe nodded first at Bethany, then at Lydia. "It's nice to meet you."

Concern flitted across Lydia's face before she pasted on a bright smile. "Well, hey there, handsome. Have you ever been to one of Myron's classes before?"

Doe shook his head. "I just learned to make muffins a week ago. Jules thinks I'll like this."

Lydia arched an eyebrow at Jules. "Well, one of the things you'll learn if you stick around is that he's often annoyingly right about things like that."

Jules scoffed. "Hardly."

"Do you like it here?" Bethany asked.

Doe nodded. "Yeah. Y'all have a nice town."

His shoulders dropped microscopically away from his ears, and the tension in Jules's back eased in response.

Myron bustled out from the back room and clapped. "Evening, everybody! Looks like we've got a great crowd. Come on over here and we'll get started." They beamed, blue mustache twitching. "Hope y'all like cookies, because we're baking tons of them."

Jules glanced at Doe, who was very definitely watching Myron while trying to look like he *wasn't* watching Myron.

Well. Maybe this had been a good idea for more than just the baking.

"Did you enjoy it?" Jules asked as they drove back to the bed-and-breakfast.

Doe had a box of cookies on his lap, hands wrapped protectively around the sides. "Yeah."

"Good."

"They don't…"

Jules glanced sideways; Doe was frowning at the dashboard. He waited rather than prodding for more.

"Bethany and Lydia were okay," he said after a long pause. "But other people don't like me."

"They don't know you," Jules said gently. "All they know is you crashed a plane and you have a tattoo that marks you as someone dangerous. They'll come around. Baking cookies with Bethany and Lydia will go a long way toward helping with that."

"You never asked why."

"Why what?"

"Why I crashed the plane."

"Would you have told me?" Jules huffed a laugh at Doe's scowl. "I didn't think so. I thought you might talk about it when you're ready."

The box crinkled under Doe's fingers. "You've also never been scared of me."

"No," Jules agreed. "I haven't."

"Why aren't you scared?"

"I know you," Jules said quietly. "And perhaps more importantly, I know what it's like to try to find a new way that goes against everything you've been taught. It's worthwhile, but…it's not easy."

"Is that…?" Doe cleared his throat. "Is that why you started wearing dresses?"

"Something like that," Jules said. "I suppose it's more that… When I got here, and when it sank in that I could stay, I started trying everything I'd never been allowed to do or that I'd been punished for. Dresses, makeup, shaving my legs, baking and sewing and gardening. I even went by Julia for about three hours before I realized I liked being male. I just didn't like being masculine." He shrugged. "This feels like me."

Doe was quiet for a long time, and the only sounds were the soft whirring of the engine and the swish of the grass as they passed over it.

"So you can just try stuff out and nobody thinks it's weird?" Doe asked as the truck pulled into the driveway.

"Exactly." Jules turned off the engine. "In fact, most of them will not only encourage it, they'll give you advice."

Now that he wasn't driving, he could see how serious Doe was, the way he studied the top of the cookie box like he might divine the meaning of life from it.

Doe nodded once, like he'd made a decision. "Okay."

"Okay?"

"I'll try things. Like baking and other stuff. Just…start figuring myself out, I guess."

"That's good." Jules smiled. "And if I can help, let me know."

"Yeah. I will." Doe looked him full in the face now. "You know, you're the prettiest man I've ever met."

Jules blinked at the unexpected compliment. "I… Thank you."

"You're welcome." Doe got out of the car. "I'll see you in the morning."

"Good night," Jules said, even though Doe was already out of earshot.

Over the next two weeks, Doe went to every baking class Myron taught. Jules dropped him off and used the two-hour block to do his own in-town errands or to attend festival committee meetings, which grew more frequent the closer it got to October. Sometimes he was late to pick Doe up, but he didn't seem to mind; more than once, Jules found him and Myron working companionably at bread dough when he finally made it to the bakery.

Doe also started helping around the bed-and-breakfast with basic repairs. He was damn handy with tools, which Jules had never been, so he was more than happy to have Doe make some minor updates and repairs he'd been putting off before the bulk of the tourists arrived for the festival. A handful of guests had already come for brief getaways in advance of the season: an older couple for a few weekdays, a family over the weekend. Even though Jules and Martha could handle running the bed-and-breakfast just fine, it was nice to have Doe on hand for additional help.

"Why are you giving me money?" Doe asked one Saturday morning when Jules handed him an envelope over breakfast.

"You've been working for me," Jules said. "So, you get paid."

"You're letting me stay here for free," Doe pointed out. "I can't take it."

"Consider it an investment toward getting your own place."

Doe's face fell. "You kicking me out?"

"Of course not! But if you like your solitude, a bed-and-breakfast isn't a great place to live." As if on cue, the twin toddlers whose family had checked in the day before started screaming, and Jules winced.

"We'll have more tourists soon, and I'd understand if you wanted to live somewhere quieter."

"Hm." Doe seemed to be considering. Then he shoved the money back. "I'll look around town for work if you'll let me borrow the bike. It don't—doesn't—feel right, taking your money when you've done so much to help me."

Tentatively, Jules took back the envelope. "You don't have to find a job if you're not ready."

"Nah, I'm mostly healed up." Doe lifted his arms as if to show off his range of motion. "It'd be nice to feel more useful. Hey, maybe I can help out at the bakery."

Ah. Jules hid his smile behind a coffee cup. "I think that's an excellent idea."

Myron was, indeed, looking for part-time help, and that meant three mornings a week, Doe took the bike into town to start baking well before dawn. Jules missed him at breakfast, but he was back by lunch. And he seemed much happier when he returned, so Jules counted it as a win.

And it was a good thing Doe had found a space for himself, because now that the weather was getting cooler and the leaves were turning, the number of guests had turned from a trickle into a deluge. Between that and festival preparations a few evenings every week, Jules was so busy he scarcely had time to think.

That didn't mean he didn't notice Doe, though, who handled the influx of people better than Jules had expected. He was as quiet and polite as ever, and asking their guests the same kind of questions that he'd asked Jules: *how did you find out who you wanted to be?*

Jules wasn't sure if Doe had found his answer yet, but he *was* looking.

And for Jules's part, it was fun to see the experimentation. Watching Doe trim his scruff—well, beard now, really—into a new shape, or letting a teenage guest paint his nails, or listening to him pick out music on the piano in the den. Jules even saw him wear a skirt for all of ten minutes before he made a face and changed back into jeans, which he and Martha had found *extremely* amusing. It had earned them a scowl from Doe and a flat refusal to fix anything *not* requested by a guest for the rest of the day.

It was a different routine, but it was still a routine, and Jules found himself enjoying it very much.

Late one night, just a week or so before the festival, Jules went out to the back garden to enjoy a cup of hot chocolate before bed and was surprised to find Doe sitting in one of the Adirondack chairs, looking up at the sky.

Jules took the chair next to him. "Everything okay?"

Doe started as if he hadn't realized Jules had come out. "Oh, yeah. Everything's fine. Just wanted some space to think."

"Ah." Jules readjusted his shawl around his shoulders and started to stand again. "I'll leave you to it, then."

"Nah, it's okay. You can stay." Doe looked down at his hands. "Might help to talk out loud a bit, if you don't mind."

"Of course not." Jules settled back in the chair and cupped his hands around his mug; the October night was chilly. "What's up?"

Doe frowned. "Is it supposed to be this hard? Figuring things out?"

"What do you mean?"

"I dunno." Doe dragged his hands through his dark, messy hair. "It's like… When I realized I liked baking, I thought 'hey, this is it, I've got it. I can figure everything else out. What's me and what was them.' And I thought it all would be that easy. But I just feel…I dunno, like what if I'm trying to fix a problem that ain't a problem?" He paused, and then asked softly, "What if I'm wrong?"

Jules considered it for a long time. "One of the first things Rosalie told me, when I debated whether to grow my hair out, was that it wasn't set in stone. Even if I liked it long then, I didn't have to keep it long if I changed my mind." He gestured to the garden. "Growth is a process. Sometimes it's quick and easy. Sometimes it's slow and hard. Sometimes you start over. But as long as you're alive, it doesn't really end. If you've found something that's true for you now, even if it's not true for you forever, then I don't think you're wrong." He closed his eyes, recalling a similar conversation he'd had so many years ago. "I don't think we're meant to be set in stone, and I don't think we're meant to let fear keep us from growing."

"Huh." Doe sounded thoughtful. "You know, that makes a lot of sense."

"I'm glad you think so. I mostly stole it from Rosalie."

Doe laughed and turned to Jules. "Can I say something weird?"

Jules sipped his hot chocolate. "Of course."

"I'm grateful I ended up crashing into your pond."

It wasn't *really* funny, but Jules chuckled anyway. "Me, too."

The day of the festival arrived in a blur of preparation, and Jules and Doe were the last two in the bed-and-breakfast once it was time to leave, the guests having already boarded the shuttle into town.

"Doe! Are you ready?" Jules called up the stairs.

"Yeah, one sec!"

A moment later, Doe came down the steps, dressed all in black, with his hair short and his dark beard full.

"You look very handsome," Jules said.

"Heh. Thanks." Doe rubbed the back of his neck, and Jules might have said he looked bashful. "Before we go, I got…well, I got something to show you, something to tell you, and something to ask you."

Jules raised his eyebrows. "Oh? What order do you want to go in?"

"I guess I'll show you first." Doe undid the first couple of buttons on his shirt and pulled his collar aside.

It took Jules a second to register what he was seeing. When he did, he put a hand to his mouth to cover his smile. "Did you cover your tattoo with a blueberry muffin?"

"Blueberry-banana, and yeah." Doe buttoned his shirt back up. "It was the first thing I baked, and it helped me realize I *liked* baking. Which leads me to what I want to tell you."

"I love the tattoo. Please continue."

Doe took a deep breath. "I told you I left because of my sister. Same thing happened to her that it did you. She got sick, and nobody would let her rest. I tried to help her, but there was only so much I could do. And it wasn't enough."

"I'm sorry."

"It's why I stole the plane. Why should I help those bastards anymore when they let her die? I wanted to leave everything behind. A real fresh start. It's why I never told you my name. I didn't want it anymore."

Jules took his hands and squeezed them.

Doe cleared his throat. "Anyway. I did what you suggested. Been trying to figure things out. I never liked who they made me be, but I couldn't figure out why. 'Til we saw Myron and you told me about 'em. How they weren't a guy or a girl. I didn't know you didn't have to be one or the other."

Jules stared. "Wait, does that mean—?"

"You like being a guy, but you don't like being masculine. I like being masculine, but I don't like being a guy." Doe shook his—their—head. "Myron told me there are a lot of different types of…of…of not being either, and I don't know which one I am, but I know I'm one of 'em. So I'm not Mr. Doe. It's Mx. Doe. I figure that works out pretty well, since I want to be a baker."

Jules absolutely *lost it* laughing. "Oh my God. Mixed dough. What a terrible pun. It's perfect."

"Isn't it?" Doe grinned.

"So, you've shown me what you wanted to show me, told me what you wanted to tell me. Now, what did you want to ask me?"

Doe took a deep breath. "Will you go to the festival with me?"

Jules frowned. "But I am going to the festival with you."

"No, I mean…*with me.*"

"Oh." Jules blinked. "But I thought… You mean you aren't interested in Myron?"

"Nah. I like 'em, but not like that. Lydia called it 'gender envy' at one of the classes."

Suddenly it all made sense, and Jules recognized that he'd *badly* misread the situation. "You wanted to be *like* them, not be with them."

"Yeah, exactly. That's exactly it."

"Oh. Well, in that case, yes, Mx. Doe, I would love you to be my escort."

Doe held out their arm. "Well, all right then, Mr. Jules. Shall we?"

Jules took their arm, and together they walked out into the cool autumn night.

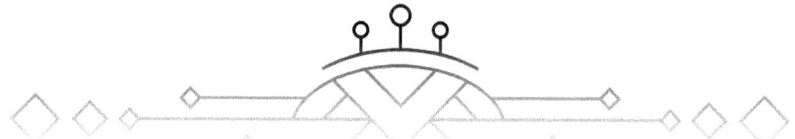

Sebastian Marie

Un Charco, Un Lago

bigender, bipoc, fat, food (graphic descriptions), friends, latinx, non-binary, present tense, repairperson, scientist, third person limited point of view

*T*he office phone rings just as Victorie is about to leave. "Lenape Valley Aether Repair, how can I help you?"

"We're still meeting at the library tonight, yeah?"

"Antonia." Victorie's customer service voice disappears. "Stop calling me at work. I'll see you later."

"We made a deal."

"You'll see the draft when you see the draft. Which is not while I'm working."

"But the application is due in less than two months!"

"Again, a problem for when I'm off work."

"Fine. But you better be there!"

"I will be there, but only if you hang up right—"

The call disconnects immediately. Victorie snorts. Antonia is not a patient person, and he can't even call xem back because the solar aether-battery is running too low. Instead, he grabs a piece of aether from one of the pockets of her work vest. It's brown, translucent, and the size of a peppermint. She licks it, then says quickly, "Message to Antonia Temprano." The aether-crystal hums. "Third floor, six-thirty. And the library on Welton this time! I got one more job today, but I'll see you soon."

After five seconds without a continuation of the message, the crystal hums again and takes on a gentle yellow glow. She slaps it onto the phone and positions the phone in a place where it can pick up sunlight. Once the batteries charge enough, the message will be sent automatically. Then he hears a whistle from down the street and rushes to lock the office door so she can make the shuttle to her last job of the day.

The person who answers the door to the townhouse is short, brown, and wearing a tired expression and paint-splattered overalls. Victorie sees this look often in her line of work; plumbing disasters take a lot out of people. He adjusts the strap of his work bag on his shoulder and begins his spiel.

"Hello, hola. English or Español?"

"Ingles," the person responds, then yawn. "But either is good."

"All right. I'm Technician Victorie, public works wizard at your service." Victorie points to her name tag that helpfully states "he/him" and "she/her" under his name. "And you must be Lago Cabrera?" Victorie checks his paper. "Elle/le or they/them?"

"Yes."

"Do I have your permission to inspect the problem, a…" Victorie consults the paper again.

"My sink is fucked up," Lago says bluntly, and Victorie almost laughs. "Come in, please."

They turn quickly; Victorie hurries to follow and is immediately distracted by the bright paintings and murals that cover the walls from floor to ceiling. The artwork is fantastic—all bright swirls and folklore creatures with impossible biologies and improbable numbers of wings. Without meaning to, Victorie says very loudly, "How can I get this in my life?"

"If you want some, I sell it." Lago smiles, clearly proud of their work, "but can you look at my sink first?"

They lead Victorie down the hall into a small kitchen, where the sink's faucet head is leaking into an already full sink. Lago has set up a small funnel to catch the water in a bucket on the floor.

"The faucet is off, but the water keeps coming. I don't know how plumbing works."

"That's why I'm here!" Victorie loves his job. He immediately begins unpacking his kit and putting on his gloves.

Suddenly, there's a loud crash from behind a closed door to Victorie's left, followed by a high-pitched whining.

Lago quickly says, "That's my Chimichanga. He's not good with people who aren't me, so I'm keeping him in the bedroom until you leave."

"I love dogs! How old is he? What breed is he? Does he like gravy?"

Lago laughs, the tension disappearing from their face. "He's three months old and he'll eat anything he can stick his face in."

"What breed is he?" Victorie asks again.

"Uh." Lago pauses, their face doing something funny. "He's a hybrid," they say, moving closer to the sink. "So, do you think this'll be an easy fix?"

Already getting under the sink, Victorie says, "Let me take a look!" He's expecting a simple problem, but one can hope for weird problems to make the day more interesting.

⌖⌖⌖

Ten minutes in, Victorie can tell this is a weird problem.

He's examining the physical aether compound placement charms beneath the sink with her special goggles that allow her to see the electromagnetic signatures, and what he's seeing doesn't make sense.

"¿Señore?" Victorie calls out for Lago without removing her head from under the sink.

"¿Sí?" Lago pokes their head back into the kitchen, having been sitting on a chair in the hallway, drawing in a sketchbook. Not quite comfortable enough to leave Victorie alone, but not so nervous as to sit at the kitchen table.

"Did you manipulate your physical aether compound placement charms to try and fix the problem on your own?"

Lago looks incredibly confused. "My…my physical what?"

"Okay, let's go with charms. The little disks that got attached to your sink when this place got retrofitted for aether, they're called charms. Did you touch them at all?"

"No. I couldn't tell you how any of this works—this is my first place that's completely aether-powered, and I've only lived here six months. My mamis were late holdouts to the stuff; I got raised old-school. You want a drain unclogged, or a generator serviced, I'm your friend. But magic plumbing? Sorry, not my specialty."

"Huh." Victorie comes out from under the sink and stands up. "I can sort this out in a few more minutes, no problem, but would you mind if I did some poking around the rest of your plumbing? This is a really weird problem to have if you weren't trying to fix it yourself."

Lago looks anxious as they answer. "I would mind, actually. If you can get it fixed, I'll be fine. Do you send an invoice, or do I pay in cash?"

"The company will send you an invoice in the next couple days, but I don't say no to a tip. I'm not supposed to say that, but a dude's gotta eat."

"I have majarete," Lago offers, and Victorie hasn't had good Caribbean food since the last time she went to visit her moms. Fresh corn pudding with cinnamon is not something he can turn down.

"That works too. Now," Victorie says with great gravitas as he sets about adjusting the electromagnetic signatures, "tell me about that painting of a ciguapa in the hallway. Why did you give her a chicken's head?"

Lago lights up faster than an aether charm. "I was inspired recently, and the inspiration said to paint green versions of my chickens!" they say cheerfully as they retrieve a mug to put the majarete in. They point out the back window, to a chicken coop in the small backyard.

"*Please* tell me more," Victorie begs. Weird plumbing problems are one of his favorite things, and discussing weird art while dealing with said weird plumbing is even better.

The state of the aether charms keeps scratching at Victorie's brain as she rides the shuttle to the library, snacking on a third helping of majarete ("For the road," Lago had insisted). He's never been good at letting things go. Especially when they are not only unusual and a good distraction from thinking about the frustration of an uncompleted thesis proposal, but also aether-related.

Victorie's whole life is aether. It's given her her academic career, her day job, and all her hobbies.

It's transformed the whole world, making the impossible possible.

About thirty years back, some grad students from Rutgers created the first aether sample. They'd been working on a biofuel sustained by microorganisms, and after hitting a wall in the research, they'd just started throwing compounds together. Different bacterias, different chemical compounds, until one trial yielded a green, translucent, semi-adhesive substance that altered the laws of physics around it. Gravity, light, electrical conductivity, material properties, you name it. Everything behaved strangely around the compound that one of the students named "aether" after the mythological fifth element.

One of the grad students happened to be an anarchist. She went public with the aether recipe and production methods, handing it off to friends, and friends of friends, and friends of friends of friends, making it impossible for anyone to patent it or make a profit on it.

Within a couple of months, aether, in all its myriad forms, spread globally. It was ridiculously easy to produce. All you had to do was grow a couple kinds of mold, maybe cut up a bug or something for the microorganisms living in it, and throw it in with some basic household compounds without poisoning yourself.

People got weird and brilliant with it. A team from the University of Da Nang in Vietnam discovered the compound variation that reversed gravity fields in a localized area, making plumbing easier to deal with. Two teenagers from Belarus mixed a variation into building cement to strengthen the foundations of their house, revolutionizing the construction industry. A women's safety group in Morocco developed fluorescent compounds, giving people a way to carry lights around without any need for batteries.

Governments tried to ban aether and failed, and then they tried to regulate aether development and failed.

And then it was discovered that treating particular variants of the semi-adhesive substance with seawater caused it to crystallize, and the resulting crystals could store energy better than the most efficient solar batteries available.

It took a few years, but when people can make clean energy in their kitchens, energy markets crash. There were years of confusion and worry. But people adjusted, the world kept turning, and the age of aether (and sustainable living, closed-loop economies, and more equitable markets) marched forward.

Victorie had been born into a world that was rapidly changing.

Victorie had been born into a world in which helping her fellow people in real, tangible ways was infinitely more possible.

When it became apparent that serious research on aether was needed, a lot of money was funneled into public education. Victorie was pursuing a graduate degree for free. Well, free with teaching and research deliverables, *and* if she finished in under two years.

This meant Victorie had a responsibility.

Her responsibility, as accorded to him by the resources he had at her disposal, was to find a way to help people. To create something with aether, whether that be a new compound, or an application, or field of study, that truly made a difference for people.

Therein lay the problem.

There were a hundred, a thousand, a million directions someone could go in if they wanted to work with aether.

Victorie helped on a small scale every day; he already had her dream job working as an aether repair technician—people fondly known as public works wizards who were on the city's payroll to help fix the problems that arose when literally everyone was using a very new technology for everything from plumbing to electricity to internet.

But Victorie wanted to change the world.

Antonia, Victorie's insane, beloved roommate and best friend, didn't help. Xey had known what xey wanted to do with xer life since xey were eight, and that was developing variations of wax-consistency aether in transit applications. Specifically, cross-country trains, because Antonia really liked trains. Xey believed in picking one thing to care about and caring about it very deeply, because that was how you got things done. And Antonia only worked on xer project during normal human hours, instead of thinking about it twenty-four/seven like Victorie did, so xey were completely uncomprehending of Victorie's plight.

⟶⟩◇⟨⟵

"Vicky!" Antonia shouts as Victorie enters the room. In their usual third-floor study room, Antonia has taken over an entire table, with an aether-powered laptop set up in the center of a sprawl of papers and diagrams. Antonia is short and fat, with dark, tanned skin and a shaved head. In xer quest to give Victorie a nickname, xey stand up on top of a chair in an attempt to lend xem height and authority.

"No." Victorie closes the door behind her, swinging her bag to the ground. The two of them come here often enough that the place is practically theirs.

"Tori!" Antonia stares down at Victorie from atop the chair, xer new height conferring absolutely zero authority.

"No." Victorie stares back, undaunted.

"Victorie?" Xey slumps back into the chair, defeated—only temporarily, in all likelihood.

Victorie smiles pleasantly. "How can I help you?"

"Hand me your draft and check my math."

Victorie leans against Antonia's seat, sitting on the floor because he doesn't like the way the chairs feel. "Let me get my calculator out—"

"Draft." Antonia pulls gently on Victorie's short curls.

"Did the supply chain stuff trip you up again this time?"

Antonia pulls harder. "Draft."

"'Cause I was thinking about it, and if you make the aether on the train, there's no need to stop at depots—especially because you could make a lot of relevant variations by mixing the right cyanobacteria with some of the engine lube and non-potable water, so instead of finding reliable lime and potassium suppliers, all you have to do is find a steady supply of agar, which is a higher up-front cost, but compared with what you'll save from having an in-house aether lab—"

"Where's your draft?"

"I'll show you, but anyway, agar suppliers are more common these days—"

"I've already considered that option," Antonia says, "which you would know if you read my work. But I want to read your draft. Where is it?"

Victorie pulls out five stapled bundles of paper from his bag. "None of them are done, but—"

Antonia grabs the papers and starts going through them, then gives up and drops xer face into xer hands. "This is exactly what you said you weren't gonna do! More importantly, it's what I told you not to do!"

"I know, I know," Victorie starts excitedly, "but I was thinking about how the gravitational applications of the fungal bacteria strains affect both air and ground travel, and when you break it down and breed those pretreated bacteria with those ones that eat PFAs, it means a lot for mitigating old industrial waste, and on that topic..." Victorie pulls an academic journal out of his backpack. "There's been some really promising work going into reforming aether once it's been hardened, so it can be reused on a much faster timescale than plastic—"

"Victorie." Antonia cuts him off with a stern expression. "You need one idea. One! Just one! Why are you making this harder on yourself? The application deadline for the graduate program is in two months!"

"But what if I write a discipline-spanning thesis that revolutionizes the field of aether studies as a whole?" Victorie grins, trying to win Antonia over.

"You have a higher chance of doing that if you concentrate on one area. Flying around from discipline to discipline"—Antonia shakes two handfuls of proposals at him—"because you have the next great idea about how to save the world means you're not actually doing any work."

Victorie tries really hard not to whine. "We have the potential to really help people!"

"You'd get a lot more done by *focusing*. Right now, focus on checking my calculations. Later, focus on *one* topic for a proposal."

Victorie knows she's not gonna win this argument. So she pouts. "Put on music, it helps me focus."

"Heavy metal?"

"Heavy metal," Victorie confirms.

Antonia fiddles with xer speaker. It's an older model, probably older than xem, and has been restructured to accept an aether-battery. Most of Antonia and Victorie's tech is like this: old machines that, under different circumstances, would have been dumped in a landfill, but with the help of aether and a bit of DIY, now have a much-extended lifespan.

Antonia vigorously shakes the aether-capsule that powers the speaker—which is not necessary, but xey enjoy it—and places it in the small machine. The music starts, and Victorie settles into work while Antonia reviews Victorie's drafts.

"So," Antonia begins in xer politest tone of voice, which xey usually save for after xey have annoyed Victorie. "How was work?"

"There was a leaking sink on the last job," Victorie says, "and they had a dog. I didn't get to see him, but they said he was a hybrid. I wonder if he was a labradoodle. Those are cute."

Antonia's face lights up. "That reminds me!" Xey launch xemself toward xer bag in the corner and come back with a packet of papers xey toss into Victorie's lap. Xey pat Victorie's head.

"What's this?"

"You mentioned you were reading up on aether-hybrid breeding a few weeks ago. I saw that the other day in the library and thought you might like to read it."

Victorie's eyes go wide. "You know, there's been some interesting stuff going on in local labs. Do you think they'd let me into their facilities to take notes on gestation periods?"

Antonia appears to realize xer mistake. "No! This is for pleasure reading, not another thesis idea!"

"But—"

"Nope, never mind, I'm keeping it." Antonia snatches the packet away. "Go back to work."

Victorie pouts again.

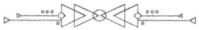

Over the next couple of hours, Antonia thoroughly marks up every uncompleted proposal Victorie's brought.

Antonia flips through one of them. "Victorie, what even *is* this? It's not even half-finished—" Xey pause. "Is this written on the back of another proposal?"

"Oh, is that the construction one? I was thinking that if we look at—"

"Victorie." Antonia looks up from the pile of paper. "Do you care about this?"

"Absolutely! The ability to reconstitute wreckage would drive industrial waste production down by at least forty percent—"

"Do you care about this?" Antonia asks again, clearly annoyed that Victorie is not getting the point. "Do you have a passion for this thing in particular? Has it made you hurt? Are you going to be able to stick with this for two years and actually do something with it?"

Victorie is struck silent. After a moment, she manages, "I just want to do something that matters to people."

"Then you have to find something you can put care behind. I really care about my trains, you know?"

"Yeah, I know."

"And that's why I'm going to help make them more efficient. I'm doing my part. If you cast your net too wide, you won't catch anything that's waiting in the depths."

"But I need to catch something now! You're the one who keeps saying that the deadline is getting closer."

"It's not worth getting something in on time if it's something that won't matter to you. If you don't care about it, it's not going to be the world-changing thing you want it to be. Now," xey say dramatically, "you've been staring at my logistics calculations for ages. How bad did I do?"

Antonia is brilliant at many things, just not at math.

"You're only off by around seven percent," Victorie reports. "You forgot to take the self-weight of the compounds into account again."

Antonia groans. "Why am I, a theorist, being forced to do hard math?"

"Because you care about it."

"I do," Antonia moans. "I really, really do!"

And Victorie laughs. It's getting late, so he proposes they pack up and get chili cheese dogs, and Antonia happily agrees.

The next day after Victorie finishes his classes, his work schedule sends him back to Lago's house. As he knocks on the door, he tries very hard not to appear too excited to find out what the problem was. She's very good at her job, and it's not often she has repeat clients.

"¡Hola! ¿Ingles?" Victorie bounces inside as soon as Lago opens the door. Victorie shuts it behind her as Lago walks toward the kitchen.

"Whatever works for you." Lago looks even more tired than they did yesterday. There are some scratches on their hands, and they have at least three new colors of paint on their overalls. One hand is entirely purple up to the wrist. There's a banging on the door that Lago has once again kept Chimichanga behind.

"Oh, poor perrito. Can't you let him out?"

Lago sighs. "He's been really worked up since last night, so believe me when I say keeping him behind closed doors is best for everyone." There's a faint growl and a noise that almost sounds like a squeak.

"Is he playing with one of your chickens?"

Lago freezes. "I don't want to be rude, but can you look at the sink? Are you sure you fixed it right?"

"I'm very sure, but let me at it."

Victorie settles himself under the sink and pokes around. "YO!" he shouts. "It's the same thing!"

"Explain." Lago is holding a plate of chicharrones in their unpainted hand. Victorie really hopes the chicharrones are her tip for today.

"The physical aether putty is still in place," Victorie says from under the sink, "but the electro-signatures are nowhere near where they need to be. It's like they got all scrambled up. Is this something you could have done by accident? Or"—Victorie giggles—"you got any enemies who wanna sabotage your plumbing?"

"I'm more likable than that," Lago retorts. "I didn't touch the charms!" They throw their purple hand up in despair. "I don't go under the sink much, and I definitely didn't touch the putty—"

"It's not just the putty, it's the energy fields around it—"

"The *what* now?"

"The—OW!" Victorie hits his head on the underside of the counter. He does not let this deter her, because she now has the opportunity to explain aether science to someone who isn't a colleague, undergrad student, or her moms. Victorie rubs his forehead as she stands up. "Aether puts out this field around it, with different types of electromagnetic and bioelectric wavelengths. Technicians and researchers wear goggles like these"—Victorie holds up her goggles—"and gloves with aether worked into them so that we can see and manipulate those electrical fields."

Victorie pulls out some glow-aether mix from his work bag. He rolls the putty in her hand and pulls her goggles over her eyes, revealing the spiky-smooth waves of latent energy emanating from the putty. It's reminiscent of a thermal imaging scan. With her other gloved hand, she gently grabs one of the wavelengths and twists it slightly. The putty floats out of Victorie's palm and starts glowing with a warm yellow light. She sends the putty flying with a gesture, making it dance around the room before it settles in her hand again.

"How did you do that?" Lago breathes.

Victorie smiles, pleased and excited. "We're called wizards for a reason. It's just like magic." He twists the wavelength back to its original position, and the glow dies down. "I use these as flashlights. Basically everyone can manipulate the wavelengths if they're holding a smaller piece of the same aether compound or they dip their fingers in a couple different chemical mixtures, but the goggles and gloves make it easier if you're doing it for a living."

"And those are the charms?"

"Yeah. If you want, I can show you how to make this specific mix and work with the charms so if this problem comes up again, you can deal with it."

Lago gets a funny look on their face. "I appreciate that, really, but no thank you. The last time I tried mixing aether to set up my phone, it didn't go so well."

"Oh, did you mess up the phenoxyethanol-to-sodium-chloride ratio and burn yourself? I did that once—took my eyebrow a month to grow back, and I got a funny scar." Victorie pushes up his goggles to show off the crescent-shaped mark in his left eyebrow. "Some kinds of aether are more homebrew-friendly than others."

"You burned your eyebrow off," Lago says tonelessly.

"To make aether? Yeah. I was working on mods for my cousin's electric scooter, but I messed up the ratio 'cause I confused it with the recipe for the engine combustion mix."

"Must be nice to have a public works wizard in the family," Lago muses.

"I was nine at the time. I burned both my eyebrows off last year 'cause I was experimenting with an anti-grav mix that would float on its own with no manipulations needed. But that wasn't so much a problem with the aether mix as me tripping into the containers holding my chemicals. Big boom," Victorie says fondly. "Anyway, if you change your mind on wanting a crash course in aether chemistry, let me know. Aether chemistry is one of my favorite things—it's like everything fantasy books promised witchcraft would be."

"I didn't know it was this complicated. Thought you were just gonna be a...a... ¿Que es la palabra por fontanero?"

"Plumber."

"Thanks. Did you have to go to school for this?" Lago sits on their counter, looking genuinely interested.

"Nah, the guilds and unions train you really well when you apply, as long as you prove you're not an idiot and you can keep up with the speed the tech changes at. But I'm in school anyway 'cause it's a good way to make connections, and my research portfolio got me scholarship money."

"You mean the research that set your eyebrows on fire?" Lago raises their eyebrows.

Victorie grins. "Exactly. Innovation at its finest."

"I take it back," Lago laughs. "You're to be admired. And I thought permanently staining your fingers green was the most dedicated you could be to a craft." They wiggle their fingers, which actually are faintly green, and Victorie laughs. "Do you mind showing me what you did to fix the sink?"

"You want to learn?" Victorie asks, gleeful.

Lago laughs long and hard. "No. I want you to do the light spell thing again after I grab my sketchbook. The way you work the lights is worthy of a painting. Maybe a series," they say thoughtfully.

"Gimme chicharrones."

"Deal."

Victorie leaves Lago's home three hours later with a new contact saved to his phone. He calls Lago as soon as she gets home, and they continue their conversation about aether theory. Lago throws question after question at Victorie, especially on biomedical applications, and Victorie responds with the full force of her seven years of professional aether experience.

Victorie is very pleased to have made a friend, especially when the same issue pops up in Lago's kitchen the following afternoon, and she can spend another four hours hanging out while discussing the finer details of plumbing charms and the combined Chilean-Dominican influences on Lago's art style.

⟿⟫▷◁⟪⟞

"VICTORIE!" Antonia screams from the dorm living room.

"¿QUE?"

"There's a call for you on the hall phone. Did you forget to charge your phone again?"

"Look, sometimes I forget to stick the crystal in the sun! I'm SORRY." Victorie is very tired. She's spent the last few days taking extra shifts to make up for the afternoons spent with Lago, and tonight is the first night this week he might go to bed at a reasonable time. He's wary of things that might keep him awake longer.

"Go pick up the phone." Antonia immediately turns xer attention back to the radio show xey'd been listening to. It's a program about trains, so Antonia will not be responding to external stimuli for at least the next hour. Victorie goes into the hallway to pick up the phone and is immediately met with Lago yelling.

"Victorie! The sink's exploding again—in the kitchen but now in the bathroom, too—and the lights keep turning on and off and I think the heater angered God because it's hot like Satan's dick in here!" Lago sounds like they have been having a very rough day.

"How?" is all Victorie can get out in his own weary state.

"I don't know! I followed the instructions you gave me, and you saw the scan I sent you—it looked fine! And why would the kitchen sink mess up the bathroom and the heat and lights? ¿Por qué hay charcos?" Now Lago sounds on the verge of tears.

"I don't know why puddles keep coming up, okay? But we'll figure this out."

Victorie tells Lago to turn off the main water valve and promises to be over as soon as possible before hanging up.

Victorie then immediately begins to worry a little.

A little worry turns into a lot of worry.

This is how Victorie ends up sitting on the hallway floor for a few minutes until Antonia calls out for her.

"Vicky!"

"No."

"Tori!"

"No."

"Victorie?"

"How can I help you?" Victorie says weakly. "I thought you were listening to a train program."

"Yeah, but then I started wondering where you went." Antonia comes to sit beside Victorie. "How's the floor?"

"If I can't fix this problem, how am I supposed to fix the big ones?"

"What problem? Is the plumbing still awful at Lago's?"

"They're depending on me, but I can't solve anything! I can't figure out my thesis proposal, I can't come up with interesting research, and I don't know how I'm gonna help the world when I graduate!"

"This is a lot smaller than the world. A lot more doable. It's what you do best. Get up."

"I want to keep sitting here, thank you."

"No, come on, you're getting up." And Antonia grabs Victorie by the wrist, wrestles him into his shoes, and has her out the door and heading toward the station before Victorie can formulate an argument as to why he's an idiot, actually.

And then Victorie's on the train, reminding herself that Lago is depending on her. So she is going to be there for them.

When Lago leads Victorie into the house, there are huge puddles in the hallway and kitchen. Lago's put towels under doors to keep the flooding as contained as possible, and canvases that had previously been resting on the floor are piled precariously on top of every available piece of furniture. The lights are flickering like it's a horror movie, and it is indeed hot as Satan's dick in here.

"Is Chimichanga okay?" Victorie asks.

"I wrapped him in blankets to keep the lights and noise from bothering him too much. I read somewhere that it's good for dogs, so I thought it might work."

Victorie nods. "Okay, that's good."

Lago sits on the kitchen counter to keep their feet dry, staring at Victorie in exhausted awe. Their pajamas are covered in charcoal and pastels. As Victorie pulls on her gloves and goggles, she wonders if this is their natural state, or if the plumbing emergency has interrupted nighttime artwork.

Victorie goes to work, squinting and pulling and whispering and tugging at the charms, drawing designs in the air and muttering to himself. The lights dim and go to full brightness and then return to an ordinary level. Victorie gets the heat turned off and opens the window with a wave of his hand.

With those issues out of the way, he sets up a charm that will siphon the water from the floor into a container, then settles himself under the sink for the fourth time this week. Lago tries to stick their head under there with her, but there's not enough room, so Victorie narrates everything she's doing.

Ten minutes pass as both of them take turns asking questions and cursing out whoever invented modern plumbing.

"Okay, so!" Victorie narrowly avoids banging her head on the counter as she jumps to his feet. "The good news is, I patched it! I put up some wards and keyed it to me, so no one should be able to mess with it."

"What's the bad news?"

"I don't know what's causing the problem, and you shouldn't turn the water back on until we get that figured out."

"So no water and we don't know what the problem is. That's...that's just great. Why can't you figure out what the problem is? Can't you use the aether to tell you things?"

"Aether is not..." Victorie pauses, looking for a way to explain. "Aether's not an intelligent force. I can tell it to look for common problems—things I've seen before. I did that and got no results. If the problem is caused by something I've never seen before, then I can't tell it to look for it."

Lago makes an attempt to not look frustrated and fails.

Victorie sighs. "Listen, I'll forward a message to my office and you'll hear back in the morning. They'll get a specialist out to you in a day or two to figure everything out. This isn't just a plumbing issue anymore—you need someone who's got experience with building-wide issues."

Lago tenses before breathing out. "The specialist has to see the whole house?"

"Most times, yeah—"

Lago shakes their head. "Chimichanga is too territorial. I can't have more people in the house." As if on cue, there's a scratching noise and a whine from the other room. They sigh. "What am I gonna do?"

The fact that Victorie can't solve the problem is eating at her. But where technical expertise fails, he can fall back on courtesy.

"Well, do you think he'd be okay if he weren't at home? Maybe you guys could stay with us while everything's getting sorted. I'd have to ask my roommate, but xey'd probably be fine with it. I'd really like to help."

"Are you kidding? You taught me how to fix my shit for free and just offered to let me move in with you!"

"It's what I do." Victorie shrugs. "Also, you're like, the only person I know who hasn't heard me ramble about aether a million times. And you're cool about art. And you feed me."

"All I did was give you majarete and chicharrones! And we've only known each other for a week!"

"What does that matter? There'll always be a point when you've known your friends for just a week. Doesn't mean you're not gonna be friends."

"Huh."

"The offer stands."

Lago tenses again, then seemingly forces themself to relax. "Let me think about it—I need to figure out what's best for Chimichanga. But thank you." They smile.

"I'm sorry I can't help more." Victorie really is. "If you need anything, send me a message. We'll get you a specialist, but I'm gonna do some research on your problem on my own."

"You don't have to."

"No, I'm gonna. I wanna know, and it's like, on-the-job training. Plus, you need your water working, m'dude. Do you like being called 'dude'?" Victorie asks. Lago shrugs with an expression that reminds Victorie of the icky feelings she gets when anyone calls her a lady. "Buddy it is, then!" Victorie says. "I'll message you when I have news."

"Victorie?"

"Yeah?"

"Thank you. Really."

"Hey, I love problems, love aether, and like you." Victorie smiles and winks. "This is a win-win-win for me."

⊱────≼◆≽────⊰

The next day, Victorie drops off supplies to Lago. They insist she doesn't have to, but Victorie's mamas raised him to be polite, and also to bring people Jarritos soda when they are suffering.

Unfortunately for everyone, the public works specialists are in the middle of a much higher-priority job working on the city sewers and won't be free for at least a week. Victorie despairs; Lago's problem cannot be solved with Jarritos alone.

Victorie is not good at dealing with being unable to help. She lies on the floor of his bedroom, feeling useless. Just as he's on the verge of exploding from frustration, Antonia walks in and nudges him with xer foot.

"If you promise—and I mean if you *promise*—not to make another thesis proposal out of this, I have something to make you feel better. For relaxation purposes only, understand?"

Victorie grunts his agreement. Antonia holds out a sheaf of papers.

Victorie reaches for it, but Antonia immediately snatches it back.

"You promise?"

"I promise, I promise! Let me read!" Victorie slumps onto the floor. Antonia drops the papers onto his face and leaves him to read. It's an interesting-looking study detailing a Canadian team's research on the biologies of aether-hybrid animals.

Two minutes later, Victorie bolts upright and scrambles for his phone.

"LAGO!" Victorie screams into the phone. "WHAT KIND OF ANIMAL IS CHIMICHANGA?"

"*¿Por qué es importante?*"

"Because if Chimichanga is at least fifty percent draconic, he might be the cause of your plumbing problems."

Lago says nothing.

"Lago," Victorie says slowly and carefully, "is Chimichanga a dragon?"

After a long moment, Lago asks, "So you know how to fix my plumbing?"

"I want to meet him! I have so many questions!"

Lago exhales heavily. "Come over tonight—we can talk then." Lago abruptly hangs up.

Victorie just smiles.

"I dropped outta school when the art career took off last year," Lago begins, once Victorie has been pacified with the promise of a plate of tostones, fried rice, and ropa vieja after the serious conversations are out of the way. Chimichanga is in Lago's lap.

He is a delightfully improbable creature who looks as if a snake ate a chicken and a lizard simultaneously but then threw up halfway. His body is feathery, and he has four scaly, muscular legs and seriously large claws, along with two reptilian wings that look too delicate to get him off the ground. He's purring and flicking a forked tongue out into the air periodically. Victorie cannot stop looking at him.

"What were you studying?"

"Biology, but I was friends with a bunch of people in the aether-studies lab, and we did some collaborative research." Victorie opens his mouth, and Lago holds up their hand. "I will answer questions later. If you start trying to get into details now, we will be here all night."

Victorie pouts.

Lago continues, "When I left, no one cared if I took some stuff out of the rejects pile. It wasn't classified as a biohazard—you know how all over the place the aether regulations are—and I wanted a souvenir. I took a couple capsules I thought were inert and brought them home. They were egg-shaped and stayed warm for hours if I put them in sunlight for a while, so they were great for when my chickens got broody." They shrug like they're embarrassed, but this makes perfect sense to Victorie. "I let my mamacita Chanclasita sit on one of them."

"Chanclasita?"

"She is sturdy and smelly. Like a chancla. She makes a good weapon in a pinch, also like a chancla."

"Okay." Victorie is barely stifling a smile.

"So I let Chanclasita sit on a capsule, and three months later, Chimichanga popped out." Lago pauses, then blurts out, "I think he's technically a cockatrice." Another pause, and then by way of explanation, Lago adds, "I liked fantasy shit when I was a kid."

"That is the coolest thing I have heard in my life."

"But he acts like a toddler! He breaks things and screams a lot, and I started getting worried because I figure taking lab materials and hatching a dragon has to be some kind of illegal, right? I refuse to go to jail for a dragon I named after my dinner who hatched from a chicken named after a shoe! But I can't be mad at him because it's my fault. I don't know what stimuli he's reacting to half the time, and I can't do anything to help him. I brought him into this world and now he's suffering." Lago hugs Chimichanga to their chest so tightly that he squeaks; it sounds like a kitten's meow.

In that moment, Victorie has something approaching an out-of-body experience. He watches himself staring at Lago and Chimichanga, and a plan that's more than half-baked starts formulating in her mind. Suddenly, the path before him is incredibly clear.

This is how he's going to help someone.

And not just anyone, but her friend.

He shakes himself, gets back in his body. "I can fix this."

"You can help?"

"Better! I can research! I can get resources on this! I can get you money to properly take care of Chimichanga!"

"How?"

"I'm going to write my thesis on you!" Victorie is flush with victory before remembering to be polite and also have research ethics. "With your permission."

"And that helps fix my plumbing, how?" Lago raises their eyebrows.

"What?"

"On the phone earlier—you made it sound like you knew what was going on."

"Oh, right! Dragons can control aether with their minds."

Lago's eyes go wide. They very deliberately place Chimichanga on the floor. Chimichanga runs off, claws clicking on the kitchen tile. There's a *thud* as he runs into a wall for the third time since Victorie arrived. Victorie wonders if the cause of this is specific to chicken-hatched cockatrices, or if it's just Chimichanga.

"Please explain," Lago says.

"Okay—last year, some researchers in Toronto published a paper on draconic aether-breeds, proving that those creatures can see the energy fields that aether gives off—"

"Like the ones you can see with your special glasses?"

Chimichanga runs through the kitchen again.

"Yeah! They can see the electromagnetic wavelengths and manipulate them with their own bioelectricity! To an extent. They can't do much to big networks like the ones that cover phone lines or a whole building's electricity, but I guess the plumbing aether is low power enough that Chimichanga can mess with it."

"Why would he start now? He's lived with me for months and I haven't had problems. Do you think it's on purpose?"

There is a series of loud Chimichanga-running-into-things noises as he does another lap through the kitchen.

"We won't know without research, but making an educated guess, yes. I think it's scaring him, and he's worried it's going to hurt him and you. Notice how he's doing laps? My working theory that I came up with about two minutes ago is that he's checking for threats, and thinks the aether's electromagnetic signature is a threat, but he only recently matured enough to do anything about it."

"So he thinks the sink is a threat."

"Yeah."

Lago pulls on the hem of their shirt. "Of course I hatch a dragon and the problem isn't fire-breathing or government hunters, it's plumbing."

"It's always the little things," Victorie says sympathetically.

"So what can we do about it?"

"That's where my thesis proposal comes in! I can study how Chimichanga's genetics let him interact with aether! You were a bio student, yeah? You know the protocols around testing with live animals are amazingly strict. If I can get a proposal accepted, and I will, 'cause the birth of a non-lab-controlled aether-experiment breed is unprecedented, Chimichanga would be protected as a research subject!"

Lago makes a face as they consider this.

"And," Victorie adds, "it would be cheaper for my program to give you money directly instead of having to keep Chimichanga housed and fed under the current research standards. It's cheaper to give you stuff than it is for them to have to pay for access to other people's equipment and research if you went to another institution, or—god forbid—a private company." Victorie is suddenly gripped by panic. "Please don't go to a private biotech company with him—there'll be all kinds of proprietary messes and also lawyers terrify me; my cousin is one and I don't understand him."

"Slow down. Why would I ever go to a company with him? He's my little friend. I just wanna be able to make things good for him."

Chimichanga comes running back into the room.

Lago scoops him up before he can hit his head on the table again. "You're gonna help me make things good for him, right?"

"It's what I do," Victorie replies, smiling. Lago smiles back. Chimichanga purrs.

Victorie ends up writing many papers on the subject of Chimichanga. The first, his thesis, is about Chimichanga's genetics. The half dozen following it are about everything from researching how Chimichanga can see and manipulate aether to cultivating the intelligence of draconic creatures so they can be equal partners in aether exploration. It isn't long before Victorie is considered *the* expert in draconic aether-breeds.

Whenever a journal asks for an author photo, he always sends the one from Victorie's and Antonia's graduation, taken the moment

Chimichanga figured out how to escape his leash. Lago is visible in the foreground reaching for him, Antonia's face is frozen in joyful shock, and Victorie is laughing her ass off.

It may not be a professional picture, but it's his favorite.

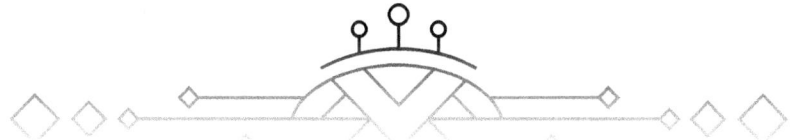

Zel Howland

Flower and Rot

bipoc, body horror, break-up (past), california, character injury (graphic descriptions), death of a parent (past), first person point of view, found family, jewish, los angeles, magic use, modern with magic, mystery, natural disaster, non-binary, past tense, private investigator, second chances, self-esteem issues, suicide (mentions of), systemic inequality, telepathic communication, trans male, undeath, united states of america

Aether buzzed through my body in electrifying pulses. The copper coil implanted in my temple drew the ambient Aether toward me, and my focus attracted even more of it for the Aethercoil to collect. At a certain point, the channel became self-amplifying as Aether cycled through my body and back into the Aethercoil, with only the coil's dampener preventing an overchannel.

As usual, I had the dampener switched off.

A warm thrum tickled the back of my mind: my bond with Jamal, resonating with the increased flow of Aether. I resisted the temptation to open my mind to it, turning back to the job at hand.

Even in the early morning dark, I could see the overgrown canopy shifting toward me, attracted by the surge in Aether. It was a bizarre sight, if I stopped to think about it instead of trying to keep my over-channel from frying my nervous system—a riot of incongruous plants from every biome in existence, mixed together with feathers and fur and antlers and horns and skin.

I knelt down before a mound that could have been mistaken for earth save for a small coil of copper half buried in moss and leaves. A multitude of trees and other plants burst from the mound, partially obscuring the shape, but with my mind surfing on waves of Aether, I could clearly see the outline of a woman curled in peaceful rest.

"Marisol Jiménez?"

A pair of warm brown eyes appeared as the Transcendent who had once been a Salvadoran woman in her thirties peeled open eyelids that had barely stirred in eight years. What was visible of her blissful expression under the moss didn't change, but her gaze did shift toward me.

I pulled a card from my pocket and held it sideways so she could read it.

> *Mx. Rook Waldvogel (they/them)*
> *Crenshaw Investigations*
> *(CA BSIS License #23258)*

"I was hired by Elaine McIntyre to find her stepson Calvin McIntyre," I said. "Cal is your son, right?"

The yew tree sprouting from her ribcage shivered as she took a deep breath she no longer needed. Old habits died hard, I supposed.

The grove around us rumbled with her response, the impossibility of trees and grasses and moss trying to speak. Thanks to the Aether flowing through me, I heard her true voice echoing laboriously through my mind, layered with the voices of the other Transcendents who'd bonded with her.

Is…Cal…in trouble?

"I don't know," I told her honestly. "He didn't come home after school on Friday, and nobody has heard from him except for a text telling one of his friends he was leaving."

…leaving?

Tendrils of green wrapped my knee in a worried vice. I winced but didn't give in to the temptation to push my overchannel into the spot to dull the pain. Despite what comic books said, buffing with Aether was usually counterproductive. The hangover as soon as I stopped overchanneling would dwarf any relief I felt in the moment. Not worth it.

"Mrs. McIntyre is worried that he hasn't been channeling long enough for his body to transform any injuries," I said. "Do you know when he got his Aethercoil implanted?"

The expression on Marisol's face remained frozen, but her voice was thick with fear. *When he was...five...I think... Is that enough?... He's only...fourteen...*

"I know," I said, putting a hand on her bark-covered arm. There was no guarantee that she could feel it, but the tendrils gripping my leg loosened. "I'll find him and make sure he's safe, Ms. Jiménez."

He came here...

"What? When?"

Yesterday... He talked with me... I couldn't answer... We don't have... communers for the grove...

"Yeah, I noticed," I muttered. Most groves had a communer on retainer if not on site, but this grove was publicly funded for low-income Transcendents. I was probably the only private investigator in the country with enough communer experience to even have this conversation with Marisol. Lucky me. "What did he say to you?"

He just said...he was sorry...

"Sorry about what?"

Sorry he couldn't...be here with me...when his time came... I don't know what he meant... Then he left...

"Which direction—?"

The vision in my left eye blurred and warped. The skin and muscle around it tingled with electricity, pulsing in time with the Aether I was channeling. And—fuck. There was something *growing* deep inside my eye. I *felt* it bursting from the retina, creeping through the vitreous humor at an unnatural rate.

I clapped my hand over the eye. The skin felt mushy and swollen under my palm.

Are you...all right? Marisol asked.

The rest of the grove focused on me with matching concern and curiosity. None of them seemed to have seen anything—yet.

"I'm fine, just—migraine." I climbed to my feet, hunching under the branches leaning attentively over me. "I have to go, I'll let you know when I find Cal, thanks for your help—"

Four dozen minds linked by Aether watched me through thousands of leaves and roots and flowers as I hurried away. Their attention bored into my back right up to the moment I switched off the Aethercoil and the flow of Aether abruptly stopped. The grove became just an unusually lush garden. I was alone once more.

The thing growing inside my eye stopped too, but I couldn't afford to hope that it had shriveled away without Aether to feed it. My vision was still cloudy in that eye, and the whole area was delicate and tender.

Spitting rain formed halos around the streetlights as I reached the drugstore parking lot. I·clumsily fished for my keys with my left hand, keeping the right firmly covering my eye. My shitty sedan was the only car in the lot, but I checked every line of sight around me before stepping into the driver's seat. I was pretty sure I was alone.

I couldn't take the chance that I was wrong.

I already knew what I would see, but I had to know how fucked I was. I pulled down the visor and flipped open the mirror.

Rot.

The skin around my eye was black and crusted with pus. As I pulled my hand away to get a better look, a chunk of skin stuck to my palm and painlessly peeled away, leaving the bone of my socket exposed. More pus, mixed with blood and something viscous and black, oozed from the gangrenous sore. The cornea had turned a sickly yellow laced with red, and the iris was deformed and milky. Peering closer at the pupil, I could just catch what was growing deep within my eye: something white and spiked. More fungi.

Fuck. *Fuck.*

It had been too much to hope that my next change would be like the circle of black feathers on my back, my only faunal transformation. My only *palatable* transformation. But if it *had* to be another grotesque transformation, couldn't it just be *mushrooms*, like the ones on my scalp that I shaved as part of my undercut? The fungal spikes along my collarbone, painful as they were, could at least be hidden under my hoodie. The rotted lengths of my forearms—and the strange, webbing-like vines of muscle and sinew that grew from the festering mess to twine up my biceps—were disgusting and they smelled like bad meat, but at least the hoodie could hide some of that as well.

This was *rot* on my fucking *face.*

I shouldn't have communed. I knew at least a half dozen old coworkers who could've stopped by, no questions asked. People who could channel Aether with only the joy of Transcendence awaiting them, who would leapfrog death and decay to land directly in the bliss of becoming one with the universe.

Instead, I'd channeled a year's worth of Aether through my body over the course of five minutes. Me, a grot, doomed to the putrefaction that the rest of the world could ignore.

"Motherfucking *idiot*," I snarled at myself. I pawed through the junk in the glove compartment to grab the obnoxiously big sunglasses I'd bought a decade ago when I was on a more feminine kick. I shoved them on my face with no attempt to be gentle, then checked the mirror again.

Thank fuck. The darkened lenses and ridiculously rhinestone-studded rims were big enough to hide the rot. I grabbed a tissue from my pocket and wiped away the extra…liquid.

There. Like nothing had happened. Everything was okay. Nobody would know as long as I wore the sunglasses.

Forever.

I shook my head. A problem for another day. Right now, I had a missing teenager to track down. I lifted my hand to my Aethercoil so that I could start the car—then froze.

The Aethercoil. If I turned it back on, it would automatically start channeling Aether. It might have taken a burst of Aether to get the transformation started, but now that it had begun, channeling *any* amount would spur it on. It was barely hidden behind the sunglasses as it was. If it grew any further, I wouldn't be able to hide it at all.

And when people saw…

Whatever people's personal (disgusted, hateful, horrified) opinions of grot transformations, the law was clear, even in liberal California. No matter our history or the Aetherbond between us, Jamal would be forced to boot me from Crenshaw Investigations, and any job available on the other side would be…undignified.

My hand shook as I lowered it from the Aethercoil, but I was oddly detached from the panic creeping over my body.

It was fine. It was all fine.

My phone was dead. That was fine. I could always find a crowded spot and bum some Aether from the communal cloud.

The car was…all right. The backup battery had enough to jumpstart the car and get me back to the office. Maybe farther. Not a problem.

I could do this. I could keep living my life. I could find this missing kid, and I could do it without channeling any Aether whatsoever. Everything was fine.

"—just need to *talk* to them."

I opened my eyes blearily and barely avoided knocking my cold coffee off the desk as I stirred from sleep. Damn it. What was the point of staying up all night tracking down Marisol Jiménez's grove if I couldn't stay awake long enough to act on her information?

"Do you really think they'll talk to *me?*" Jamal's voice carried from the shitty break room—less of a room and more a corner of the cramped office separated by a faux-wood screen. "They never even told me—"

"Told you what?" That was Beatriz. Great, both my investigative partners talking about me behind my back. Not a great sign.

"Nothing. Never mind," Jamal said.

Beatriz sighed. "I'm just worried. When was the last time they even went home to sleep?"

"I really wouldn't know."

"C'mon, Jamal. Even after everything, you're still closer with them than I am. You have a fucking Aetherbond. They'll listen to you."

"They've had that Aetherbond closed off for *months*, Beatriz. I'd have more luck talking to a transphobic Republican than I would talking to Rook."

That was enough. I stood, stretched, and yawned loud enough to stop the conversation in its tracks. I grabbed my coffee cup, checked that my sunglasses were still on, and meandered past the desks to join them.

Jamal and Beatriz made an admirable attempt to look busy as I dumped my old coffee and poured myself a new cup.

"What time is it?" I asked.

Beatriz shot me an unimpressed look, which as usual only affected half her face—the rest was frozen in a wry grin by the redwood bark covering most of the left side. "Don't you have a phone you can check?"

"Left it at your mom's place," I said, smiling blithely.

"Really, Rook? That was weak, even for you."

"It's a quarter past eight," Jamal cut in before I could escalate my conversation-derailing plans with an even more disappointing joke.

Better to retreat. "Thanks," I muttered. I headed back to my desk while chugging the too-hot coffee to avoid seeing the look shared between my coworkers.

It was harder to avoid Jamal when he followed me. Even leaning casually against the desk, he towered over me with his soft bulk and carefully constructed concerned expression. "Rook," he said quietly. "What's going on?"

I kept my eyes firmly on the notes scattered across my desk, pretending to be absorbed by them. "I'm looking for a runaway teen," I answered, shuffling the papers into something resembling a pile. "You know, his stepmom seems like a piece of work; I'm worried there's something more going on than just teenage rebellion. Do you still have the number for that social worker—what was her name, Anita?"

"Rook."

A shower of pale-blue flower petals drifted through the air to land softly on my hands and desk. No doubt from Jamal scratching his head in a nervous habit.

The clusters of forget-me-nots and cornflowers growing amid his dreads like delicate jewels were always my favorite of his transformations. Even more than the intricate, almost lace-like patterns of white birch bark that grew out of his top surgery scars and contrasted beautifully with his dark skin. I'd always loved finding petals mixed with my things for days after he'd spent the night.

I swallowed and forced myself not to fidget with my sunglasses; it would only draw attention to them. Even with my hands at my sides, though, I smelled the faint odor of spoiled meat rising from my arms. Maybe the musty carpet and the yeasty aroma from the bakery next door would be enough to hide it. Maybe.

"Your phone's been off," Jamal said.

I did my best to imitate the smile I'd given Beatriz. Less successful this time around. "Yeah, I, uh. I turned my Aethercoil off. For... Shabbat."

"It's Monday. Also, you haven't been to Temple since you were a kid."

"I'm trying to get back into it. For my sister."

"Sarah lives in Boston."

"She's visiting."

"No she's not. Why is your Aethercoil off?"

"Maybe I'm enjoying disconnecting for a while."

"And the sunglasses?"

"We live in LA? You know, the city of perpetual sunshine?"

"It's raining, and we're inside."

I lost my grip on the lighthearted rhythm. "Well maybe I just *want to wear* them, Jamal," I snapped. "What do you want me to say? You're not my boyfriend anymore, so *back off.*"

His expression turned hard. He glared at me, a muscle twitching in his cheek where a sweet smile ought to live. "Fine," he said stiffly. "I guess I'll leave you to it." He turned to busy himself at his own desk, his sloping shoulders climbing up to his ears.

I bit my cheek to avoid calling him back. I *couldn't* explain. The end result would still be him walking away, except for good. It was always going to hurt.

I felt Beatriz's sharp gaze on my back, the radiating aura of Jamal's hurt in front of me—but most of all the hot, mushy feeling of my eye slowly dissolving out of my socket. Hurriedly, I scooped up my notes—everything I knew about Cal McIntyre's history—and retreated to the safety of my car.

The battery was almost out, but I had enough to get the fuck away from here.

The last dregs of rain spattered on my sunglasses as I surveyed the building before me. The oil refinery looked…rickety, to put it generously. My cursory research said it hadn't been in use since the '80s, back when cars stopped running on gasoline, and the property had been sitting in legal limbo ever since. Even from a distance I noted rust on every metal surface and no doubt unstable structures throughout the huge facility.

Even the chain-link fence surrounding it was neglected. There were at least three separate spots where I could slip in without resorting to the bolt cutters I kept in my car for emergencies.

In short, it was the perfect spot for teens to hang out and get themselves into trouble. The only question was whether *Cal* had come here.

His friends had only mentioned the refinery in passing after a long list of other, more popular spots. But my gut said that Cal wouldn't have gone someplace where he might run into people he knew. He was a smart kid, and something about the text he'd sent his friend and the visit to his mother evoked desperation and loneliness.

Just like this place.

I climbed through a gap in the fence and started toward the main body of the enormous refinery. It was going to take me hours to search it well enough to be sure there wasn't a scared teenager hiding in an out-of-the-way corner. Maybe I should have brought Jamal, even with... everything.

I hesitated beside the defunct security shed. There *was* something I could do to speed the process, but...well. The sunglasses barely covered the rot on my eye as it was. Channeling Aether to try and trace any other Aether usage in the area would be excessive. I could find him without resorting to that.

The huge lattice of pipes and metal platforms looked the most promising. Empty beer bottles, discarded blunts, and graffiti confirmed my hunch as I approached. Popular with teenagers, then.

I had searched the entire first level and was just starting on the second when movement caught my eye. Across a big gap in the metal flooring, someone was climbing down to ground level.

"Shit," I muttered, whirling around to slide down the ladder I'd just left. My knees creaked in protest as my feet hit the uneven concrete flooring. "*Shit.* Ow." I raised my voice as I limped toward the figure. "Cal? Are you Cal McIntyre?"

He paused near a rusted vat, deep in the shadows under the rusted structure. He was tall and skinny the way kids get after a major growth spurt. His bad posture meant that his dark-brown hair hung dramatically over his face, but not enough to hide the nervous way he looked at me.

"Who wants to know?" he said. He didn't really sell the attitude, not while shivering in a too-thin jacket and damp jeans.

I took a few slow steps forward so he could see me more clearly. "My name's Rook," I told him. "I just wanted to check if you're okay, and to talk a bit."

"What about?"

"I know you ran away from home—"

"Elaine sent you, didn't she," Cal interrupted. He scoffed at the ground, hunching even farther. "I told her I'm not going back."

"You're having issues with your stepmom?" I stepped closer still. Cal didn't try to run again, which was a good sign—or maybe it was just that I effectively had him cornered.

"You a social worker? Shrink?"

I opened my mouth to reassure him, but sudden movement in the ground shocked the breath from my lungs. Metal groaned above as the earth convulsed below, nearly knocking us both off our feet. Instinct overtook me. I crouched down and clung to the nearest pipe, my other arm shielding my head.

The earthquake only lasted a few seconds. I looked up as the shaking subsided to see Cal, a California native unlike my East Coast ass, standing unconcerned.

"Huh," Cal said. "I'm gonna guess…4.5, 4.6."

"Are you—?"

The ground gave out beneath us.

It seemed to happen very, very slowly. Adrenaline doing its thing, probably. The concrete beneath me tilted, then disappeared. Like a magic trick, a tablecloth ripped out from under the cutlery, leaving me hanging in the air like Wile E. fucking Coyote. In the cartoons, he only fell once he looked down—but, well, it's not like I *wasn't* going to watch the earth swallow me.

I caught up to the concrete slab within half a second; it didn't so much break my fall as it redirected it into a roll down a sixty-degree slope. My joints seemed to catch every crack in the concrete, every bit of rebar jutting out at odd angles, every bump that could possibly add to the cacophony of pain screaming through me until eventually the concrete disappeared again. I slammed into the mud.

I lay there for a long time, breathing in the rust and dirt. Stillness was a novelty after falling for such an eternity.

Eventually I pushed myself onto my back, groaning as the movement righted my twisted left arm. Twisted, but by some miracle not dislocated or broken. No broken bones that I could feel or see—though maybe the bruising pain covering my whole body was masking the pain of a fracture. Even more miraculously, my head felt fine, even if my neck was stiff and sore. Overall, I couldn't have been luckier in avoiding injury after falling…however far I'd fallen.

Then I looked around and my optimism drained away. The sinkhole was nearly twenty feet across and just as deep. The walls were soft and muddy, and the concrete I'd rolled down was broken in enough places to make for a difficult climb to the surface.

A whimper drew my attention away from the walls.

Cal.

Shit.

I whipped around, ignoring the answering twinge in my neck. There. He was lying not far away, covered in less dirt than I was, but unlike me, he had his eyes screwed shut in pain.

"Cal!"

I dragged myself to my feet and hobbled stiffly over to him. He shifted when he heard me approach, trying to sit up and hissing at the effort.

"Hey, easy," I said, kneeling next to him. He had several bruises, including one on his forehead that worried me. "Don't try to move, all right?"

A few tears leaked out from his eyelids as he ignored me to prop himself up on his elbows. "It's—it's just my ankle," he said tightly. "Think I landed on it—"

"Don't worry, I'm gonna get you to a doctor," I said. Cal's Aethercoil was powered on, which meant I could use it to power my phone without worrying. I pulled it from my back pocket—then sagged. It was cracked almost entirely in half. The screen gave a half-hearted sputter when I pressed the power button, then remained stubbornly black.

I glanced up and met Cal's eyes. He gave me a bleak smile. "I dumped mine," he said. "I didn't want anyone tracking it."

"Shit."

Cal finished pushing himself into a sitting position. "Guess it didn't matter anyway," he said. "Who are you, again?"

"Rook Waldvogel. I'm a private investigator."

He laughed humorlessly. "Congrats on finding me."

"Yeah, yeah. Nice digs you've got here."

I looked around us with a more discerning eye. Maybe it wasn't as bad as I'd thought. The broken concrete slab stopped about four feet from the bottom of the sinkhole, but otherwise the slope looked…manageable. Maybe. I stood up and tested some of my weight on it. The slab held rock steady. Maybe it was being propped up from underneath. If I was quick about it, I could make it back to the surface.

Cal cursed behind me. I turned to see him scooting backward, dragging his broken leg as he went, to lean against the earthen wall.

I *winced.* I could make it back to the surface, if I left Cal behind. No way he was climbing out when he could barely sit up, and I wasn't strong enough to carry him.

Well. *Technically* I wasn't strong enough—unless I overchanneled Aether. I could make myself beefier than a bodybuilder if I switched on my Aethercoil and called on my bond with Jamal. I could carry Cal through an entire obstacle course and half a marathon before the crash would hit me.

I'd also come out of it looking as if Frankenstein's monster had been moldering in a mushroom farm for a few weeks in hot weather.

I shook the thought out of my head. There was another solution. There had to be.

"Hey, stop moving around," I told Cal. "You're going to make it worse."

"It's fine," he said, clearly in more pain than he'd ever been in his whole life.

"Oh yeah?" I sighed. "Let me take a look at it."

Cal flinched away so violently that his head smacked into the dirt behind him. "NO!" he shouted. He threw his hands up to warn me back, then snatched them away just as quickly, a wild look in his eyes.

Too late. I froze, the pieces finally clicking into place. Why Cal had run away without a word to his stepmother. Why he'd visited his mother's grove like it was a final goodbye. Why he had come here, where he wouldn't be bothered by anybody—or rather, wouldn't be a bother *to* anybody. Where nobody would see the little white mushrooms growing out of the blackened scrapes on his palms.

He cradled his hands to his chest and stared at them. This time, I didn't think the tears in his eyes were from pain.

"Just go," he said dully. "Leave me behind. I'm already dead and rotting anyway."

I closed my eyes. In some ways, this was worse than if he'd run from an abusive household or been involved in a gang. With anything else, there were systems in place, roads he could take that would lead him out of despair. But this...I knew intimately how deep this pit went, how impassable the walls were. Anything I said to the contrary would be a bald-faced lie.

There was only one thing I *could* say. "I'm not leaving you behind," I told him, opening my eyes again.

He hunched in on himself. "You already did the job you were hired for," he said. "You can tell Elaine she won't have to worry about anyone else finding out. I'll stay here until I Transcend, and nobody'll ever find me."

"That's not going to happen."

Cal snorted. "Well, I don't see how you expect to drag me out against my will. I don't think you could get me out even if I wanted to leave."

"Is it really so bad at home that you'd rather stay here?" I asked, already guessing the answer. Being a teenager with an overbearing parent was bad enough. Being a *grot* teenager, with nothing to look forward to but abandonment and disgust… Yeah, the sinkhole wasn't too bad. The dirt was almost soft, and the refinery above kept out the rain.

"Why should you care?" Cal snapped. "You don't know me. *Elaine* doesn't care, and she's the one paying your bills."

I sighed. "I *care* because you're a person having a shit time, and I'm not a monster," I told him. "And also because…" I hesitated, but there was really no point in hiding it. I hobbled over to sit next to him. "Look."

Somehow, my sunglasses were still on my face, and more-or-less intact. I took them off slowly and tilted my head so that he could see the entire grotesque effect.

"What the *fuck*—" he shouted, recoiling as if it was some kind of infectious disease rather than just my face.

"Yup."

He stared with horrified fascination, as though he'd never seen a grot transformation before. Maybe he hadn't, aside from his own little mushrooms that were honestly more cute than disgusting.

"I have more," I said after a moment of silent gaping. "My arms are much grosser than this."

"Really?" he said, looking queasy. "Can I see?"

I laughed a little. Of course a teenager would be eager to see more rotting flesh. I pulled off my mud-soaked hoodie, revealing the spikes of fungi on my collarbone, the muscle and sinew wrapped around my decomposing arms in a bizarre lattice of vines.

"Gross, you can see the *bone!*" Cal said, grabbing my wrist to pull the grot right up to his face. I saw the instant the smell hit him, though to his credit he didn't gag or drop my arm. "Can you feel stuff through these things?" For emphasis, he covered his hand in his sleeve and poked at the vines.

"Ow—*yes* I can feel that," I said, snatching my arm back.

"Sorry," he said, unrepentant. "But—how the hell are you working as an investigator? I thought grots could only work as like, garbage collectors."

"Hazardous waste disposal," I said. "Long-haul trucking. Jobs that keep you from interacting with the public."

"Doesn't sound like private investigator fits."

"Nope," I said, popping the "p."

"So…you're hiding it. The grot stuff."

"Why else would I wear sunglasses on a cloudy day?"

"What're you gonna do when it gets worse?"

I tilted my head back to rest against the earthen walls. The bulk of the refinery loomed over us, keeping out the spitting rain but threatening a more ominous fate. We were lucky the whole structure hadn't collapsed on us.

I closed my eyes. "I don't know," I said honestly. "Lose everything, I suppose."

We sat in silence for a while. I was going to have to figure some way out of our predicament eventually, but I just kept my eyes shut, mind empty.

"You seem cool, I guess," Cal said. "You could come back here, and we could make a grove. A really gross one, but still."

I huffed a laugh. "The smell would really be something."

"Do you think there are grot groves? Out in the desert or in the ocean or wherever they get carted off to?"

"No idea. Maybe."

Cal hummed. "I think there are. Being alone sucks." He paused. "Being a grot sucks," he added, so quietly I had to strain to hear him.

I peeked open my eye to look at him. He was looking at his palms again, scowling at the tiny fruiting bodies. Enoki? Something you'd find in a grocery store, anyway. "You're pretty young to have any transformations," I said.

Cal shrugged. "Elaine is really into that Transcendentology crap," he said. "She thinks every different leaf or their, like, arrangement says something about your soul, or whatever. Once my dad passed, she had me channeling Aether all the time so I'd get some transformations for her to put on her stupid charts."

I thought back to when I'd met Elaine McIntyre two days ago. She'd been wearing a specially tailored dress that showed off the iridescent green scales on her hand and the carefully maintained bouquet of lilies on her shoulder. She'd given me the once over and treated me far more brusquely in person than she had over the phone. At the time I'd ignored it, but now I guessed it was because I'd been swallowed in a shapeless hoodie with no transformations visible at all.

"Yeah, that tracks," I said.

"When my first transformation was poison ivy, she was so mad," Cal said quietly. "She tried to rip the leaves off. Gave her a giant rash all over her hands though. That was kinda funny."

I bit my tongue to keep silent. She'd tried to *rip it off?*

"But it was still flora, you know?" Cal continued. "Bad flora, but still. When the mushrooms showed up, she looked at me like...like..."

"Like you're a walking corpse?" I suggested.

He hunched farther into himself. "Yeah..."

I sighed. "I know the look." The doctor claiming to be grot-friendly, the stranger in a public restroom who'd caught sight of my arm when I washed my hands... At least I'd managed to hide it from my family and friends, so I hadn't had to deal with that look from *them*.

"What about your mom and dad?" I asked to avoid thinking about that particular inevitability. "Do they know?"

Cal looked at me like I was fully crazy. "They're dead," he said. "They're Transcended."

He shrugged. "Same difference. Not like my dad would give a shit about me anyway. And my mom..."

"You saw her yesterday, didn't you?"

"I saw her—her *shell* yesterday," Cal corrected bitterly. "She wasn't really there. It's nice she's living her perfect sublime life or whatever, but it doesn't change the fact that she's *gone* and she left me behind."

"Hey," I said sharply, catching his gaze. "Stop. Your mom's not gone. I spoke to her this morning. She was *worried* about you."

It took a moment for my words to sink in. When they finally did, Cal gaped at me in utter confusion.

"You did? She was?" he said. "How?"

"I used to be a communer," I told him. "It's still useful from time to time." Cal continued to give me a bewildered stare. I chuckled. "Why do you think I'm so far along in my transformations?"

"I don't know," Cal said, coming back down to earth. "Because you're old?"

Oof. That stung. "I'm thirty-six. That's not old."

"Okay, boomer."

"I'm a millennial!"

Cal laughed, but it died out quickly. He looked down at his broken ankle, where no doubt Aether was already working to heal the injury—at the cost of a happy life.

I glanced at my own bruises. I'd been lucky in the fall. Bruises didn't usually heal with Aether, meaning I wouldn't spontaneously burst into fungi all over my body. Lucky me.

"What's it like?" Cal asked suddenly.

"Hm?"

"Communing," he clarified. "What's it like talking to Transcendents?"

"Oh," I said. "It's…a lot. Just the overchannel is—well, overwhelming. It takes a while to get used to that. And when you temporarily bond with the grove, it's…" I stopped, struggling to find words. There weren't any—that was kind of the point. "You can feel a lot of what the Transcendents are feeling. All the Aether bonds that make up the grove, the—the love and connection between them all. And the feeling of…the feeling of being one with the world? I guess that's how everyone talks about it. You get all that thrown at you at once, and then you have to try and bring sense into it. It's pretty intense."

"And that's what we'll never get, isn't it," Cal muttered.

I squeezed my eyes shut. Sometimes I wished I'd never learned to commune, never felt the joy of being part of a grove. "Maybe not," I said. "But…maybe you were right. Grots are all sent to the same place when they get too far in their transformations, so who knows. Maybe they've made their own groves in the desert, and you and I will get to have every bit of that feeling. Just not…"

"Just not with the people we love," Cal said.

"…right."

"You're doing a shit job motivating me to go back, just so you know," he commented. He shifted, then hissed when the movement jostled his ankle. "If I even could go back on this leg."

I hummed. "All right, how about this: do you want to learn to commune with your mom?"

Cal whipped his head around to look at me, still wincing in pain but now utterly focused. "What?"

"I could teach you how. It's not actually all that hard."

He stared at me. "Don't you gotta go to a fancy school for that?"

I shrugged. "I did, but honestly it's not necessary. It just takes practice. Well, practice and some balls. The overchannel is intimidating if you're not used to it."

Excitement eclipsed the pain—physical and otherwise—on Cal's face. It had clearly never occurred to him that he could learn to speak with his mom again or do anything involving overchanneling. It wasn't exactly a broadly accessible skill.

"That would be—" Cal began, then stopped. Despair sank down on his shoulders. "But…wouldn't that just…make it all worse?" He looked at the mushrooms on his palms, the hope disappearing as quickly as it had come.

I looked at his transformation, then at my own bared arms. They really were disgusting, much more so than the innocent fungi on Cal's hands.

But then, why was it any more disgusting than if it was ivy growing from my wrists?

That was what I had expected, when the transformation had first begun. I'd been taking a road trip with Jamal, cruising up the coast with the windows down and my exposed arm getting a slight burn from the summer sun. I'd spotted some discoloration on my forearm, just a little patch of dark green on the skin, and idly wondered if I would grow a climbing vine like an arm-sleeve tattoo.

Inside our sinkhole, the light shifted. I squinted at the brightness after a day of gloomy skies and gloomier sunglasses. The new light revealed the deep, complex reds and purples and blues of the fleshy lattice on my arms. If it had been a tattoo, it would have been fucking sick. If it had been a tattoo, I could say it was in honor of that week I'd spent with Jamal, of all the people I'd helped by overchanneling.

In a way, it was.

I glanced at Cal, who was still scowling at his enokis. I'd spent enough time delaying, sitting in a mud-pit with the moody teenager I was supposed to be helping. I couldn't leave him behind, and that was that.

"Overchanneling Aether does speed up the transformations," I said, hoisting myself to my feet. "But it does a whole lot more than that."

I reached up and switched on my Aethercoil.

Aether buzzed through my body and mind. I pushed it through my mental channels quickly, reaching the threshold for overchanneling in less than a second.

A warm thrum. I closed my eyes and gave in to temptation. The mental block I'd built so carefully came crashing down, letting me feel for the first time in months what scientists said was merely a resonant energy signature, but which I knew in my heart was Jamal's soul.

I sent a zap of energy through the Aether bond, just enough to let Jamal know where I was and that I needed help. Then I refocused, directing the now nearly screaming energy back into my own body. A kind of transformation that I controlled. Muscle and sinew and bone changing not into verdant plant life or animal appearances or decaying death, but into something I chose. A body capable, however briefly, of lifting hundreds of pounds, of navigating the most treacherous obstacle, of reacting lightning-quick to the slightest stimulus.

"Ho-ly shit," Cal said. I opened my eyes to find him gaping at my newly buff form. "What the actual fuck—"

I grinned. "I told you. Overchanneling can do a whole lot." I bent down and offered my hand. "Want a lift out of here?"

I maneuvered Cal onto my back, with only one incident of him hissing in pain from his ankle changing positions. Once settled, I turned toward the concrete slab that had given me so many bruises on the way down.

Ha. Piece of cake.

Despite being a full head taller than me, Cal seemingly weighed nothing as I climbed. The buzz of Aether and the new strength in my limbs was a heady, heady thing; I grinned maniacally as we crested the top of the sinkhole and took off through the oil refinery at a jog.

The Aether bond with Jamal vibrated—Jamal was on his way and bringing help. I felt a barrage of questions waiting to be asked, but thankfully he didn't send them through the bond. Most of his questions would be answered when he got here anyway.

The skin around my eye was rapidly changing texture and

composition, but it almost blended with the euphoric feeling of the overchannel. Transcendence was a joyful thing, after all.

I carefully set Cal on the ground beside my car, then dropped down next to him. Only once I was firmly seated did I let go of the overchannel and let my body return to normal.

The exhaustion hit me like ten freight trains colliding at top speed. I slumped against the car, only barely remaining upright.

"Holy shit," Cal said again. I could barely think through the fatigue, but I laughed anyway.

My eyes tried to close, but I refused, stubbornly keeping them open even if I wasn't really seeing what was in front of me. I'd promised I wouldn't leave Cal behind, and I sure as hell wasn't going to fall asleep on him.

It might have been minutes or hours later when sirens dragged me from my stupor. I blinked as a swarm of paramedics hopped out of the ambulance and began assessing us with professional detachment.

"—on Earth were you thinking, Cal?" a vaguely familiar voice was saying from some distance away. I squinted against the bright sunlight reflecting off the clouds to find Elaine McIntyre scolding her stepson from fifteen feet away while a paramedic kept her from storming closer.

"Sorry, Elaine," Cal muttered, possibly too quietly for her to hear at that distance.

I leaned toward him as the paramedics grabbed a stretcher. "Hey," I said, fumbling in my pocket and pulling out a now crumpled and somewhat muddy card. "The offer stands. Come by the office whenever, and I can teach you."

Cal snorted. "Yeah, whatever boomer," he said.

I smiled. "Not a boomer. Think about it, okay? At least talk to someone who isn't your stepmom about…all this stuff."

Cal's expression softened, and he tucked the card into his pocket, hopefully where he would find it again before his jeans were washed. "Okay, yeah," he said. "…thanks."

I finally let my eyes close as the paramedics took Cal away. One EMT came toward me with a look of concern, but I waved him away as best I could. I was fine, and even if I wasn't, I didn't need to see the poorly disguised look of disgust at my newly rotting face or hear the awkward lecture about the dangers of overchanneling.

Thankfully, the paramedic seemed to believe me—or he just didn't want to get any closer to me. Either way, it was a relief to be left alone with the sun warming my face and arms. My eyelids drooped, then closed completely. Getting up and back home was a problem for future Rook.

"Jesus fucking Christ, Rook, you scared me half to death."

"Sorry," I mumbled, then opened my eyes again to find Jamal kneeling in front of me.

Too late, I realized that my jacket and sunglasses were still in the pit. I was exhausted, muddy, and now fully exposed as the grot I was. *Shit.* The bolt of fear that passed through me was enough to jar me from the fog, but all I could do was watch Jamal as he realized what he was looking at.

Multiple expressions passed over Jamal's face, too quick to read, but belatedly I realized I could still feel the emotions behind them through the Aether bond. I must have left it open when I stopped overchanneling. It wasn't like I was going to let go of it now.

Realization. Frustration. Understanding. Unease. Fondness. And… relief?

I swallowed. "Jamal…"

His eyes darted over my face, taking in the transformation that even I hadn't seen fully yet. Hesitantly, he reached out to cradle it in his hand, his fingers so gentle I could barely feel them. "Does this hurt?" he asked quietly.

I shook my head and reached up to press his palm more firmly into my cheek. "Jamal, I—"

"We'll talk later," he said. "When you're not wilting." He lurched forward then, like he couldn't help himself, and wrapped me in a crushing hug. "God, you're such an idiot," he whispered into my hair.

"Hah, that's been well established," I mumbled. After that overchannel, it felt like his arms around me were the only thing keeping my body from physically falling apart.

"No, I mean you're an *idiot*. Did you think I wouldn't figure it out? You wore long sleeves all last summer."

"Plausible deniability?" I hedged.

Jamal sighed in exasperation. He tilted his head down until his forehead rested on my shoulder. I couldn't imagine the position was comfortable, but he made no attempt to move away. When he spoke again, his voice was small. "Did you really think I would care?"

I felt tears gathering at the corner of one eye and dripping from the stalk of the fungus now bursting from the other. "I—I don't know," I said. "Most people would."

He finally shifted to look me in the face, his expression fierce. "Rook," he said. That was all he said, but I felt it. Surging up through the bond, so powerful that it was pointless to deny it.

"Oh," I said. What could I say? Words weren't enough. They never were enough, that was the point.

He buried his face in my shoulder again. All around me was the scent of forget-me-nots and cornflowers, the warmth of the sun emerging from the storm, and the Aether bond we shared.

"Even so," I said quietly. "The world cares."

"We'll figure it out," Jamal said. "I promise."

I swallowed and didn't say anything. I just rested my head against his, breathed in the smell of flowers, and let myself be warmed.

Index

Backers

Our Top-Tier Patreon Backers

Anonymous
A Taylor
Sam Brown
Tina Houck
Aria L
Karen Welborn

Our Premium Kickstarter Supporters

Anonymous
Serena Wolf Denham
Alex Gruendl
Craig Hackl
Lowes and Sebastians
Ben Milman
The Perry-Scidmore Family
Ash Stone
A Taylor
Samantha Thompson
Nic Wicks
Rachael L. Young

About the Authors

Ellen Faye

Ellen has been a dreamer and designer of worlds all her life. She has been involved in many fandom environments over the years but most recently jumped with two feet into Supernatural and never surfaced. She has shared many stories online (as Ellenofoz), but she's grateful to be able to take the leap into published works with the *Aether Beyond the Binary* anthology.

Ellen lives in Brisbane, Australia, and spends her days writing code. By night, she reads and writes stories, watches shows, and plays games involving magic, science, historical adventures, or romance—sometimes all at the same time. She co-hosts a podcast about Supernatural fanfiction, and can also be found enjoying Star Wars, Marvel, Doctor Who and other assorted fandoms.

Scarlett Gale

Scarlett Gale is the author of *His Secret Illuminations* and *His Sacred Incantations*. Long ago, under another name, she was the co-author of *Needles and Artifice* (Cooperative Press; 2012), featuring a rollicking romantic steampunk adventure novella and associated knitting patterns, of which she also designed several. She writes and produces fringe theatre plays based on B-movies, such as "Bodacious Barbarian Babes vs. The Indigo Empress" and "Showgirls of Beast Island." She is a co-producer of the Alison-Bechdel-approved Bechdel Test Burlesque, which in 2017 was included in the Women and Gender Studies curriculum at the University of Oregon. She lives in Seattle with her wife where she gardens, knits, reads, and drinks warm beverages. Unsurprisingly, she also has cats.

Catherine E. Green

Catherine E. Green (pronouns: xe/xem/xyr or they/them/their) is an agender person, one who's had an on-again, off-again love affair with writing. Xe began writing when xe was a wee thing, when xyr other major pastimes were playing xyr mother's NES and roughhousing with the boys next door. It's only in the past few years that they have begun writing consistently and publishing their writing, fanfiction and original writing alike, leading to their first published short story titled "Of Loops and Weaves."

Outside of writing, xe is a collector of books and sleep debt and an avid admirer of the cosmos. Playing video games, reading a variety of fiction genres (primarily fantasy, queer romance, and manga and graphic novels of all kinds), and working on wrangling their own personal data-archiving projects occupy most of their free time. Xe is also proud to announce xyr graduation from crocheting a single scarf to crocheting several scarves and other projects.

Elior Haley

Elior has spent much of the past few years primarily writing for fanfic exchanges. Currently, he's in the process of slowly working his way through university. When not writing or studying, he can be found binding books, drawing, ice skating, and—very occasionally—playing the violin. His story in *Aether Beyond the Binary* is his first published work.

Zel Howland

Zel (they/she) is a writer and artist currently living in Los Angeles with their partner. When not writing, they spend their time painting, embroidering, analyzing literature and tv shows, and playing Dungeons & Dragons. They are the author of many a fanfiction, as well as the novel *The Shadow of Ophelia Walker*.

ilgaksu

Full-time fandom cryptid, Furby enthusiast, and the human embodiment of that one gif of Elmo on fire, ilgaksu was born and raised in an undisclosed location, lived in several others, and now currently residing in [REDACTED]. Their interests include collecting haunted toys, using their artistic practice as an excuse to forget to do their laundry, and playing with fictional men like Bratz dolls. They have not unclenched their jaw yet today, but they do remember to drink lots of water.

Bettina Juszak

Originally from Germany, Bettina has (so far) spent time in the US, the UK, and Canada. She is particularly interested in exploring questions of music and language in imaginary worlds, aided by degrees in linguistics and literature. When not writing, she loses herself in hobbies such as archery, cross-stitch, attempting to learn yet another language, and complaining about the amount of space her book and notebook collection takes up. Her first published work appeared in the *Upon a Twice Time* anthology published by Air and Nothingness Press, and she is working on a second original novel—despite the first one not having seen the light of day yet.

Nicola Kapron

Nicola Kapron has previously been published by Neo-opsis Science Fiction Magazine, Rebel Mountain Press, Soteira Press, All Worlds Wayfarer, Mannison Press, and more. Nicola lives in British Columbia with a hoard of books—mostly fantasy and horror—and an extremely fluffy cat.

Kelas Lloyd

Kelas is a disabled, trans, bi author and artist currently (unfortunately) living in Texas. They graduated from the University of Central Florida with an English degree and love cats, tea, and all things speculative fiction. A lot of their writing features magic or disability or both, and they're often found in Star Trek, Mass Effect, Babylon 5, and Untamed spaces. You can also find them in a lot of bead and resin spaces, because they love making sparkly jewelry of all sorts.

Previously published pieces include an article on disability in *The Last Of Us*, short stories in two publications by Shacklebound Books, a pair of poems about being trans, an essay on disabled life, and a whole bunch of pieces about San Diego Comic-con. They're single, an Ernie looking for their Bert, but they have a found family that stretches around the globe and some of their birth family accepts them for who they are.

Lyonel Loy

Lifelong maladaptive daydreamer, finally working up the courage to write those daydreams down. Spends time cosplaying as a Responsible Adult With A Job.

Mikki Madison

Mikki Madison has been writing stories since she was seven years old. While she is most prolific in fanfiction and has works scattered among more than a dozen fandoms, she has been making strides into original fiction. Her favorite genres to read are romance, fantasy, and cozy mysteries. When she isn't reading, writing, or falling headfirst into a new fandom, she can be found baking, doing puzzles, walking her foster dog, doting on her niblings, or playing Pokemon Go. She has also written under the name M. K. Mads.

Sebastian Marie

Sebastian Marie (he/him) is an engineering student with a lot of opinions about dragons, pirates, and sword fighting. Track him down on Ao3 or Tumblr and he'll share these opinions gladly, just be prepared for music and some excited shouting. His original works often combine fantasy and dystopia into what he calls "queer fantasy hopepunk," something that will be explored in his future novels. He loves to write conflicting traditional and non-traditional family dynamics, especially where they intersect with queer relationships. And if he can throw werewolves and brujas into the mix? So much the better. When not writing, frantically studying, or reading, he can be found singing loudly, sewing impractical coats, and going on long rambling walks while plotting stories (and occasionally falling into rivers).

Also, he's the guitarist and one of the lyricists of folk punk band Here Be Dragons.

This is his third time writing for Duck Prints Press, having previously contributed to *Aim For The Heart* and *She Wears the Midnight Crown*. This brings his grand total of published works up to three! He's looking forward to more, as soon as he gets some sleep.

Alec J. Marsh

Alec lives in the Pacific Northwest, where they write romantic adult fantasy and self-indulgent fanfiction. They make candles inspired by their favorite characters.

Flore Picard

I'm a linguist and translator who lives in France, and I have been itching to write since I learned how to. I started writing (fan)fiction more regularly when I was procrastinating on my PhD dissertation, and I haven't looked back since. I'm also an artist who loves drawing both fanart and original art, and I have a passion for patterns and systems, for the beauty at the edge of chaos and the complexity of being human. I tend to write about queer and disabled characters finding themselves and each other and learning to take up space in the world.

S. J. Ralston

S. J. grew up in a distinctly weird, distinctly southern hometown, then hied out West for grad school before landing in Texas, where they currently work as a planetary scientist. They've been writing original works and fanfiction since they could hold a pencil semi-correctly, and continue to write both whenever possible (as well as still holding a pencil only semi-correctly). In their clearly copious spare time, S. J. enjoys hiking, tabletop RPGs, jigsaw puzzles, and enthusiastically crappy sci-fi.

Em Rowntree

Em Rowntree's first foray into the world of writing was with a story called "The Magic Land" that featured a unicorn and a flying carpet the size of a country, and they've been chasing that high ever since. They've been sharing their writing online for almost nine years, and have had poems and short stories published in anthologies. They live in the UK.

Terra P. Waters

Terra is a scientist by day who lives in the Pacific Northwest with her family. She has been writing fiction as long as she can remember, and has always told her partner of 17 years that if she wasn't a scientist, she would be an author. During grad school, she discovered fanfiction and immediately began writing her own. After many years and several fandoms (including Teen Wolf, Hawaii Five-0, and Stranger Things), she returned to writing original fiction. To date, she has self-published two novellas in a '90s-nostalgia polyamory comedy series and has drafted two YA/NA sci-fi novels. When not doing science or writing, you can find Terra indulging her yarn addiction and knitting.

About Duck Prints Press LLC

Duck Prints Press LLC is an independent publisher based in New York State. Our founding vision is to help fanfiction authors navigate the complex process of bringing their original works from first draft to print, culminating in publishing their work under our imprint. We are particularly dedicated to working with queer authors and publishing stories featuring characters from across the LGBTQIA+ spectrum.

Back us on Patreon to get a bonus *Aether Beyond the Binary* story!

Find us online at our website, **duckprintspress.com**, or on social media:
Bluesky: duckprintspress
Dreamwidth: duckprintspress.dreamwidth.org
Facebook: duckprintspress
Instagram: duckprintspress
Mastodon: @dppunforth
Patreon: duckprintspress
Pillowfort: duckprintspress
Pinterest: duckprintspress
TikTok: @duckprintspress
Tumblr: duckprintspress

Goodreads: https://www.goodreads.com/user/show/129902473-duck-prints-press-llc
Storygraph: https://app.thestorygraph.com/profile/unforth